# The Marionette in the Clockwork Circus

## THE CLOCKWORK CHRONICLES: BOOK 4

LOU WILHAM

*To Mom & Dad
who nurtured the story teller, the artist,
and the dream inside of me.*

# THE MARIONETTE IN THE CLOCKWORK CIRCUS

## A STEAMPUNK PINOCCHIO RETELLING

LOU WILHAM

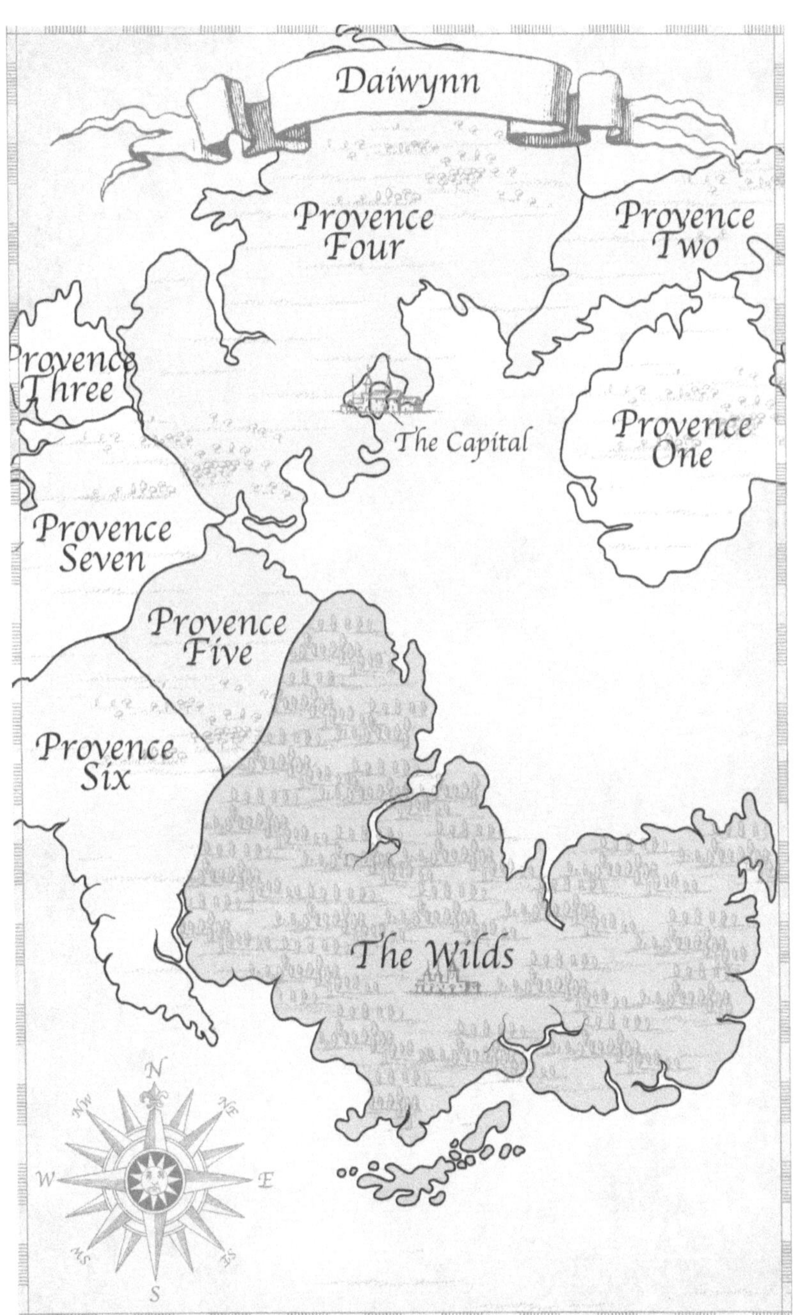

Daiwynn
Provence Four
Provence Two
Provence Three
The Capital
Provence One
Provence Seven
Provence Five
Provence Six
The Wilds
N
NW
NE
W
E
SW
SE
S

# ONE
## CHIRP

They were missing data again. They didn't know *how* they knew , seeing as how it was missing, but Chirp *knew* they were missing it. Knew there was a space in their circuits and memory stores where once something had been and now it was not. A past they could reach for but could only just brush their metaphorical fingers against. Just out of reach. Maybe it held a clue to who they had been before, to where they had come from.

Except . . . there shouldn't have *been* a before.

Not with the way there were so many parts of them on the table. Not with the way there were schematics taped to the wall. Chirp should not have even had a name—they were a wholly new creation, it seemed—but they did. They had a name, and they had a past. If only they could remember it.

The man who had been building Chirp, up until a few moments ago, smiled down at them toothily. He was missing one of his eye teeth, leaving a gaping blackness that Chirp thought they might fall into if he leaned in any closer. They would probably never be able to escape if they fell in. It would be bottomless. An oubliette.

Oubliette. What a strange word for a robot to know.

"It's awake," he said, breath hot against the right panel of their face, making the sensors there light up with activity.

Not *feeling* so much as *knowing* what the temperature was—98.3 °F. Chirp was sure that if they had sensors with the ability to smell, they would find that the man's breath was foul. They were grateful to whatever gods looked out for robots that their maker hadn't seen fit to outfit them with such a thing.

"And the upgrades?" a familiar voice asked from somewhere off in the dark recesses of the room. Chirp didn't need to see his face, because the moment he spoke, his tone oily with greed, their software supplied his name—title, rather: the Ringmaster. The word alone sent warning signals across all of Chirp's internals. Alarms only they could hear blared in their central processing unit. Lights only they could see flashed behind their visual sensors. They didn't remember their past, didn't know what the Ringmaster had done to them, but the trauma was circuit deep. There would be no erasing the fear response brought on by that man, no matter how many times Chirp's memory banks were wiped.

"The upgrades went well, sir," the mechanic chuckled, his eyes alight with some kind of manic mischief that Chirp decided instantly was not good news for them. *Upgrades.* They hadn't built Chirp from scratch, then. That made sense. That explained the feeling of a before. The space where a previous life should have been. But it didn't explain the emptiness of it. It didn't explain why they would have tried to erase that past from Chirp's memory banks. Unless they thought doing so would make Chirp more subservient, easier to control.

*Joke's on them.* Chirp let out a soft huff of steam, a snort more than anything else. There had been someone once upon a time who would have seen the action for what it was—they knew that much—but the Ringmaster and the mechanic just jerked back at the sound as if stricken.

"What is it? What's wrong with it?" The Ringmaster's

voice was panicked as he strode forward into the light, his face contorted with fear but no less beautiful for it. That was the thing about the Ringmaster: for all the poison that seeped out of him like stink from a bog, he was still achingly lovely. A fine aristocratic nose. A sharp jaw. Even the speckling of gray amid his long dark hair had done nothing to change it.

Analogies. Were those things robots were able to use and understand? Longing. Was that a thing a robot felt? Chirp didn't know. If they had known another robot before, those memories had been erased. Even if they had asked another robot—for research—that data was gone. They supposed they would have to conduct their own research as a means to better understand themselves.

"I don't know." The mechanic leaned in closer, that gap in his smile looming, waiting to swallow Chirp whole. Chirp tried to shift away, to slide from the cold, hard table beneath them and escape, but nothing would move. No part of their outer shell even twitched at the command from their hard drive. "It seems to be in working order. It's ticking right along and looks to be processing visual stimuli fine according to the schematics."

"Is it overheating?" The Ringmaster pressed closer, his head blocking out the light above the table Chirp was on. Table? Workbench? They couldn't tell, and it wasn't like it mattered. Whatever they had done to Chirp was done now, and there was no escaping it.

With a grunt of disagreement, the mechanic shook his head. "No. Its levels are fine."

"Then what *was* that? You better fix it, Levi. I can't have my best marionette out of commission when we get to the palace." The Ringmaster bent closer, his handsome face taking up Chirp's field of view as they did everything in their power to wriggle away, to escape. There *was* no escape, though. They were a prisoner in their own body. A marionette without a puppeteer. And the Ringmaster was going to delight in watching them dance. The very thought turned something in a part of Chirp's body that they could only identify as their stomach.

Strange; they thought robots didn't have stomachs. A dissatisfied whistle left Chirp's "mouth" as they focused their attention on a single part, just one finger. All they needed to do was lift it. Maybe not even lift it. Maybe just twitch it. Prove to themselves that they could.

"Don't strain yourself," the Ringmaster said, his voice soft and falsely kind. He was looking down at their hand now, as if he had seen something that Chirp hadn't felt. Maybe they had managed to twitch the digit? Maybe they simply hadn't noticed with the panic pounding through their wires. Or maybe it was the way their visual circuits were fluttering. There was really no way to tell with him, or with how heavy their body was starting to feel. Weighed down onto the table, like they needed to be wound again. Had the mechanic even given Chirp a full turn before turning them on? Probably not.

Another dissatisfied hiss left Chirp, making the Ringmaster chuckle darkly.

"I can't figure out what's wrong with it, sir." Levi sounded near panicked now, his words and breath staccato. Chirp could hear his heart pounding against his ribs, and there was a bead of sweat sliding down the side of his face from his hairline. Poor man. He seemed to know exactly what the Ringmaster was capable of, even if Chirp didn't. Not that it mattered that they didn't. They could feel the fear without knowing. Knowing wouldn't change anything. Still, it was nice, validating, to see that this man *did* know and he, too, was afraid. At least Chirp wasn't the only one.

"Nothing," the Ringmaster rumbled through another

laugh that had started low in his chest. There was a gleam in his eyes when he said his next words. "Nothing at all."

Chirp didn't like that look. They didn't know what it meant, but they didn't like it. It couldn't mean anything good. There was a grinding of gears, the sound of something made of clockwork fighting against itself to do something, and Chirp only realized after it had stopped that it had been them as they fought against the heaviness weighing down their own limbs.

"Isn't that right, my dear?" Sharp teeth shone in the overhead light of the workroom, and Chirp wanted nothing more than to go back into hibernate mode. For their last wind to run out so they didn't have to look at that smile any longer. "Or is it *Chirp* now? I suppose that's what they were calling you in that place, weren't they?"

"Wh—Wha—What—" Chirp choked on the words, unfamiliar with forming them after so long without a voice box. When had they been given one? "What place?"

The Ringmaster hummed, delighted, his eyes going wide, bright, and shiny with greed. That's all Chirp was to him: a product. Something he could use for his own gain. Chirp didn't know how they knew, or how they knew that information wasn't a surprise to them. But they did. "That doesn't matter now, does it, Chirp? You're back where you belong."

His hand brushed too roughly against the plate on top of their head. The one the mechanic had screwed closed but a few minutes ago, before flicking Chirp on. Chirp felt their spine cringe away from the touch, even as the Ringmaster played at being gentle. Caring and sweet where he was neither.

"I want to go home," Chirp said without thought. They didn't even know where home was, or what it meant, but they knew that with the Ringmaster was most certainly *not* where they belonged.

"I thought you wiped its memories?" the Ringmaster snarled, whirling on the mechanic with a jagged sneer that made Chirp wish the table would open up and swallow them whole.

"I did, sir! I swear I did! This must just be—"

"Must just be *what?*" Chirp could no longer see the Ringmaster's face—he had turned his whole body around to back the mechanic toward the edges of the room again.

Their attention drawn away, Chirp realized now was their chance to escape. They sent down the message from their central cortex to move, run, *flee*. But nothing happened. Not even a twitch. They remained firmly rooted to the table at the center of the workroom. Worse yet, every insistence dropped their power reserves lower. Until finally, the room grew dark, and Chirp went into hibernate mode again.

WHEN NEXT THEY WOKE, the room was empty and dark. The Ringmaster and the mechanic off seeing to other things. Chirp took a moment to focus their attention on their body again, to feel the upgrades that had been made while they were asleep. They were taller now, lankier. More akin to a human adult than an android. Strange. Why would the Ringmaster bother—

Chirp's visual sensors focused on a polished bit of metal against the wall, and they gasped, choking again on a voice box that was still too new. Scraping their lower half against the table, they pushed to their feet, wobbling a little from the new height, to get a better look at themselves in the reflective surface.

The Ringmaster had used the word "marionette" before, but Chirp hadn't thought too much of it. Their empty memory banks told them that he always used words like that, throwing them around like flower petals at a parade. They lost their meaning after a time. But what Chirp saw when they looked in the mirror was a marionette of the highest quality, the Ringmaster's pride and joy. Beautiful, gilded, and graceful.

Reaching for their reflection, Chirp scraped the hard tips of their fingers over the metal, making a screeching sound that ached in their auditory sensors. Gods, they were so sensitive all over now, although they didn't know what they were comparing this to. They supposed whatever they had been before their upgrades was very different. Shorter, less appendages, less . . . *everything*.

The stunned marvel of finding themselves in a body that was so foreign and so familiar all at once didn't last nearly as long as it might have in someone who wasn't afraid for their very existence. Because Chirp knew, to the very depths of their circuitry, that if they didn't escape or do what the Ringmaster wanted, he would make sure they ceased to exist. Panic gripped Chirp's wiring, and they stumbled to the door of the workroom, feet skidding against the worn floorboards.

Their fingers scrambled against the knob, leaving scratch marks on the wood of the door as Chirp tried in vain to escape. To run. To flee. But no. The knob wouldn't turn.

The knob wouldn't *turn*.

And even if they *did* escape, where would they go? They were marked now. The Ringmaster would find them. Just like he did before. Just like he always would.

Prince Brend was bored. So very *bored*. And it seemed like he had been his entire life. Spending his days on the outside looking in. Watching as *other people* did exciting things. *Other people* ruled the kingdom. *Other people* got to travel. *Other people* went on adventures.

While Brend stayed locked up in the castle at the heart of Daiwynn, protected, given everything he could ever want except the one thing he wanted the most: freedom. He knew it was because he was the heir to the kingdom. He knew it was because he was the prince, and his mother was relying on him to take the crown when the time came. He also knew that it was partly due to his own weakness of body. The cane he had to use since his teen years and the potion he took in the morning made sure to remind him of that every single day. But that didn't make him any less bitter about it. That didn't make him any less a prisoner in his own home, his own life, his own body.

"And that is why you cannot leave the castle," his mother said, concluding this week's lecture—which had taken place in Brend's own drawing room of all places—about how dangerous the Enchanted were to their people in general, and to him in particular. He had heard this exact same lecture so many times that he could practically recite it in his sleep. Sometimes she updated it—that was always fun—to include the most recent atrocities the Enchanted had committed against humans. Like about six months ago, when they had blown up one of the labor camps.

"But mother," Brend started, his tone distinctly whiney, even to himself. He should probably *not* whine; it didn't do him any favors. But he'd already started now, so it was likely too late. Leaning farther back in the thickly cushioned chaise he had flopped himself into when this lecture began, he could practically hear his mother's teeth grinding. "I really think—"

"Oh, darling, don't do that." His mother clicked her tongue, stepping forward, around the ornate table at the center of the sitting room, so she could pat his cheek before lifting her hand to ruffle his already hopelessly mussed curly hair. "You're much too pretty to think."

The words should have stung. Maybe they would have if Brend hadn't heard them so many times. His mother didn't mean anything by it, he knew that. She wasn't trying to be cruel or condescending. It was simply her way of speaking, the way she saw him. And maybe that was worse. Maybe it was worse that she didn't think he had anything in his head, nothing behind his eyes. How could she ever trust him to rule Daiwynn if that's what she thought of him? He supposed that's where the advisors would come in. He would be as much a figurehead then as he was now.

"Mother," he grumbled through cheeks that were smooshed together by his mother's soft hands. She pinched the left one, pulling the skin out a little as if forcing him into a half smile. He had ceased to enjoy this type of affection years ago, but he hadn't been able to tell *her* that yet. One battle at a time. "I really just want to—"

"I said *no*, Brend." Queen Eloise pulled back, her gray eyes narrowed in something close to a threat as she lifted her chin to look down on him with an expression he could only equate to a queen giving a decree. Brend wasn't sure what she'd do if he kept pushing it; he'd never tried it before. She was always almost too kind, too caring. Hovering over him to ensure that he was happy and healthy. Or rather, happy *enough*, given that the one thing he'd always wanted she seemed unwilling or unable to give him. He liked to think that it was unable. He liked to think his mother would never do something to intentionally make him unhappy. She was just protective, that was all. She just didn't want to see him get hurt. That was all.

Brend huffed, puffing out his cheeks petulantly. He wanted to push further. He wanted to see how long it would take before his mother yelled at him. She never had before, and he was beginning to wonder if she was capable of it. If she even cared enough to bother. Would it change anything? Likely not. It certainly wouldn't get him what he wanted, but then, neither had being a docile, good son. So why not try something new?

The words crawled up his throat, clawing at it like a living thing, but the moment he looked into his mother's eyes again, they curdled on his tongue. No. Today was not the day he stood up to her. Maybe he would try again tomorrow.

"Have I made myself clear?" Queen Eloise asked, her brows raised high up into where her auburn hair had fallen across her eyes. It was a challenge, an invitation to fight back, but instead of rising to it as he likely should have, Brend swallowed the words like a too-big bite of food and dipped his head in submission.

"Yes, Mother." He didn't bother lifting his head to see the beatific smile she graced him with—he knew what it would look like. Just like he knew that this time, it would have a slight edge to it, a sharpness that might not have been there years ago. A knife he could cut himself on but that Brend didn't really understand.

"Be sure to take your medicine, darling," she murmured, giving his face another condescending pat, then turned. The door shut behind her with a soft *thud*, an air of finality that Brend knew meant she thought the argument was settled. She always seemed to think that. And yet, this discussion was repeated over and over again. Brend had lost count of how many times now, but he supposed it didn't matter because it always ended the same. What was that old human saying about trying something over and over and expecting a different result? He couldn't remember. But he was fairly sure it wasn't a good sign.

"You shouldn't push her like that, Your Highness," a soft voice said from the shadows as Clancy emerged from where he'd been watching the entire exchange. He swept a hand through his dark curls, so much like Brend's but a deep almost chestnut-red instead of the more orange shade Brend boasted, pushing them out of his eyes so he could narrow cool gray irises on his prince in quiet admonishment.

Clancy was every bit Brend's opposite, his shadow, with smooth freckle-less dark skin where Brend's was pale and littered in blemishes. A broader, sturdier build where Brend was slight and weak from years of illness. And those rugged good looks where Brend often felt his own face was too sharp, too pointed, more rodent-like.

"How many times do I have to ask you not to call me that?" Brend groaned, scrubbing his long, thin fingers over the ache that had settled between his eyebrows. It did nothing to ease the tension and no doubt left a red blotch behind where he irritated the skin, but he didn't care. "I've known you all my life, I think it's fine if you call me by my first name."

Clancy didn't scoff, but the twitch of his lips said that he wanted to. That he had swallowed it down like every other vaguely negative emotion or word that ever appeared on his tongue. Brend wished he'd stop doing *that* too. They were friends, of a kind, and Brend hated to see Clancy trying to stifle or be less of himself just so he wouldn't offend Brend. As if Brend had the capacity to be offended. Especially by Clancy, of all people.

"I hardly think it appropriate, *Your Highness*, that your whipping boy call you by your given name." The title was said with a lilting air that might have almost been mocking if Brend didn't know better. Brend did know better. Clancy had never mocked him and likely never would. Which was a real shame; it might put them on more equal footing if he would.

"Oh please, Clancy, you aren't my whipping boy. When have you ever been whipped?" Brend laughed, leaning his head so he could look at the other man over the back of the chaise. It strained his neck, but that didn't seem to matter at all as Clancy stepped in closer and brushed his fingers through Brend's hair, pushing it away from his eyes, his stomach pressing into the top of Brend's head. An intimate gesture that Brend was sure if his mother saw, she would have Clancy *actually* whipped for. There had been some hesitation when they had started this little—well, Brend hesitated to call it a "tryst," but that's what it was between them. But after a year or so, that had faded, and now there was a comfortability, an intimacy, that Brend didn't get from anyone else in his life, least of all his mother.

Clancy hummed, giving Brend's hair a gentle tug before he stepped back out of arm's reach, much to Brend's dismay, and around to sit on the chair opposite, his legs splayed to take up far more space than Brend had ever been comfortable doing himself. "I still wish you wouldn't push her."

"Why not?" Brend flopped his head forward again, his

hair falling limply into his eyes. This was another well-trod conversation, but nothing Clancy said was able to change Brend's mind. He blinked wide brown eyes at Clancy, curious, doing his best to ignore the way his skin still tingled from the soft brush of Clancy's calloused fingers.

Clancy blew out a frustrated breath, lifting his hands to scrub at his face, mumbling expletives into them. When he pulled his hands away, he fixed Brend with an expression that said his next words were going to be obvious. "Because she's the queen."

"I don't see why I can't go into the city and see what's out there. I know the Enchanted are dangerous, but I hardly think they're going to recognize me. Besides—" Brend leaned forward to brace himself on his knees, ignoring the subtle twinge the movement sent up his right leg into his hip from sitting for too long. A slow smile curled up the corners of his lips, making his cheeks dimple in a way he knew Clancy struggled to say no to. "You'll be there to protect me if anything were to happen. Won't you?"

Dropping his hands into his lap, Clancy tilted his head to one side, a brow raised incredulously. "Really?"

"What? Are you not going to be?" Poking out his bottom lip, Brend widened his eyes further.

"That's what you're going with?" Clancy continued, undeterred by Brend's pouting.

If it weren't for the playful lilt to Clancy's tone, Brend might have thought he'd already lost. Instead, he just pouted harder, making himself look as pathetic as possible. It had worked before with other things. Although he'd never once convinced Clancy to go outside the castle with him. This seemed to be a sticking point between them. A sticking point that Brend was fairly sure he was wearing Clancy down on. Just a little more wheedling, and he'd give in, Brend could tell.

"What do you mean?"

"I mean," Clancy said, taking another deep breath, just like he did when gearing himself up for a duel with a particularly difficult opponent, "your plan is to go out into the city with *just* me for protection? That doesn't sound terribly wise."

"When have I ever claimed to be wise?" Brend shot back, without a second thought. He knew he wasn't wise, or clever, or sharp. Not like Clancy was. That's why Clancy had been assigned to him when they were children. But Brend also didn't ever *claim* to be something he wasn't. He knew his own limitations.

Choking back a laugh, Clancy bowed his head and shut his eyes, no doubt to hide the fact that he had just rolled them in wry amusement. He took a moment, and Brend watched his shoulders rise and fall as he sucked in slow breaths, swallowing around whatever he really wanted to say in favor of something more "appropriate."

"I suppose you never did," Clancy said when he finally had control of his tongue again. "I still don't think it's a good idea."

"But you're going to come with me anyway?" Brend brightened at the resignation in Clancy's tone. He'd won. *Finally.*

"You're planning to leave without me even if I don't agree, aren't you?" Clancy's shoulders sagged, making him look tired suddenly, which almost made Brend feel bad. Almost.

"Probably."

"Fine." Clancy sighed, slumping deeper into the cushions of the chair. An involuntary twitch made Brend's hand jerk a little, his body instinctively trying to reach out to Clancy, to soothe him the way he had so many times before. But they were in a place too easily walked in on. So, he forced himself to stay where he was, grabbing his trouser leg in a tightened fist to stay put. "But we're *planning* it all out. I'm not taking any chances with your safety, Your Highness."

With a delighted laugh, Brend pressed himself to his feet and grabbed his cane. "I've got to get started on my disguise!"

Clancy mumbled, "Yes, because *that* is the most important part," from where he'd ducked his head into his hands again, but Brend wouldn't be deterred.

This was going to be *fun*.

It was a small miracle that there wasn't a path worn into the floorboards of the captain's quarters with how long Persinette had been pacing. Her nerves buzzed beneath her skin as she tried to think over all the information they'd gotten in the last couple of weeks.

"Tell me again," Agnes said, his tone softer than it had been hours ago. He, too, seemed tired of the constant talking and planning. Which was a little amusing considering that out of all of them, he seemed to be the best planner. He had lain in wait in MOTHER's headquarters for decades, a sleeper agent just watching for the signal from the Uprising and Eddi. If Sully hadn't pulled him out, he likely would have waited decades more, languishing while Eddi went off and did whatever they wanted to, ruining any chances the Enchanted had for peace entirely.

"How many times do we have to go over this?" Manu groaned, throwing his head back so it hung over the back of his chair. Persinette was surprised he hadn't dug into his liquor stores yet, but that likely had more to do with the fact that Benard refused to pour for him than the fact that Manu didn't want to be inebriated while they planned. Not that she could judge him any. She was reaching her wit's end as well. How much more time could they waste just talking about everything before they missed their window of opportunity to stop Eddi and Queen Eloise from tearing their world apart over some *petty sibling squabble?*

"Until it makes sense." Agnes rubbed at the bridge of his nose, his gaze narrowing on Roy again, who looked like he might want to shrink in on himself beneath the penetrating stare. Poor Roy. He was such a proficient information gatherer, good at infiltration even for all that he lacked magic, but he also didn't seem to have the courage to stand up to Agnes.

"Don't growl at the poor kid." Sully nudged Agnes, tsking his tongue in a reprimand. "He's doing his best."

Agnes's blue eyes narrowed on Sully, nose curling up as if he wanted to bite back at the comment and tell them all that he thought Roy's best wasn't good enough. But he seemed to think better of it, likely realizing that it would only end in another fight. So, Agnes sunk farther down into his chair, turning the wedding ring on his finger around and around petulantly as he gave Roy a nod to continue.

Roy inhaled deeply, his chest puffing up with the action, and smoothed his fingers over his clothing as if to press out the wrinkles. It would do him no good. They were all hopelessly mussed. Dirty and wrinkled from weeks on a ship, hopping from place to place to avoid MOTHER and the Uprising. Persinette didn't know how long they had before the two organizations caught up to them again, but she would wager it wasn't long at all. They needed a plan before that happened. Their supplies were running low, and they were all getting tired. They'd slip up if this didn't come to an end soon.

"Eddi means to infiltrate the palace somehow," Roy repeated the words he had said hours ago when he first returned to the *Duchess,* letting the glamour Penny created for him with her magic slip away into nothing. Penny slumped at his side, her wings fluttering tiredly. Persinette felt bad that they'd been sent in to spy, but everyone knew the rest of them. They were infamous. Wanted posters had been slapped on every free surface all through Daiwynn. Even if they hadn't been actively introduced to any of the other Uprising agents, people would know who they were. There was no escaping that.

"*Somehow.*" The word left Rose like a curse, her tongue rolling around it in disgust. She'd removed her spectacles an hour ago and rubbed at the bridge of her nose until the spots where the nose pads normally cut into it were red and raw looking. Kindle shifted at her side, watching Rose out of the corner of her eye. "What does that even mean?"

"I don't know." Roy slumped farther into his own chair, the cushions threatening to swallow him whole, and Penny reached out to give his shoulder a comforting squeeze.

"Then we need to divide our efforts," Persinette said, her throat dry from not having spoken this entire time. She'd been trying to absorb all of Roy's words, all of the theories, everything they knew about Eloise and Eddi thus far. There was a surprising amount of knowledge between the lot of them. Eddi probably should have thought of that before they double crossed each and every one of them.

"Divide them how? We don't even know what we're up against." Penny's tone was tired and hopeless, dragging down the pit of Persinette's stomach. Penny hadn't signed on for this. She hadn't wanted to be one of them. She'd been brought into it because she couldn't let Roy face everything alone. That's what love did to a person, Persinette supposed.

Persinette sucked in a breath, pushing her fingers through her short lavender locks, and straightened her spine. They were all looking to her as a leader. Someone to guide them through this. And there she was, wanting nothing more than to hide away from the world. The Great Library had offered no solutions for Manu's curse. The Uprising and MOTHER were closing in. This was not what Persinette meant when she'd said she wanted adventure all those months ago.

"We're going to have to wing it, to some extent." She hated to say it, probably more than anything else. The words were as hollow and hopeless as Penny's. But she didn't know what other options there were.

"Pers," Manu said, a warning in his tone. He wasn't trying to tell her what to do, she knew that. They were a team, after all. But he did have more experience out in the world than she did, and she valued his advice and his counsel as much as she did any of the others', maybe more so because of her feelings for him.

Still, that didn't change the facts. And the facts were these:

"We don't have *time, Manu.* MOTHER and the Uprising are closing in on us. Soon enough, they'll figure out how the portals work and be waiting for us on the other side of one. Or they'll build up the resources to go over the wall and go after those we left behind in the Wilds. The longer we wait, the more likely it is that we'll lose the element of surprise. We can't chance it." The words left her all in a single breath, a rush to make her point and steady her own nerves all in one. Persinette's hands were still shaking when she was done, so she stuffed them into the pockets of her trousers before anyone noticed. Sweat gathered in the lines of her palms, and she wiped it on the insides of her pockets.

"So, what do you propose we do?" Sully lifted his brows, his dark face open, whereas Agnes's flattened into something more closed off. He was giving her a chance, and she was grateful for it. It wasn't much, but she would take it. Especially as she knew how stupid her next words were going to sound. She hated having to say them at all.

"Well, first off . . ." Persinette swallowed, the paper in her pocket crinkling against her trembling fingers. "Alys and Stella will need to be contacted. I want them in charge of finding the Uprising base. Rose, you'll work with them. If anyone can weasel out where Eddi has hidden themselves, it's you. Find them, find a way in. When we go after Eddi and Eloise, I want it to be at the same time, a two-pronged attack."

"I don't think we have enough people for that." Agnes's dark brows pinched in the middle, his lips twitching into a scowl that was so reminiscent of the old Agnes that Persinette almost flinched. Biting down on the inside of her cheek, Persinette managed to restrain the urge. Things were different now, she reminded herself. They were on the same side.

"We *also* don't have enough people for this to turn into a full-out war," Benard pointed out. He, too, had been silent for most of this conversation, his glowing green eyes flitting from person to person as he took in everything, clever mind working over the problem. Persinette was grateful to have him, and all the others, really, on her side in this. She couldn't have done this alone, any of it. Without them, she'd have withered and died in MOTHER custody. Now she had a family. A cobbled-together one, but a family nonetheless.

"He's right. We aren't soldiers," Sully murmured, his own brow creased in thought, fingers tapping at his jaw. "And we don't have armies to command like they do. We have to use our resources more wisely. Make sure we don't spread ourselves too thin."

"So where will the rest of us be going?" Rose asked. She hadn't taken her eyes off of Persinette, the intensity of her gaze crawling over Persinette's skin like a brand. Persinette's next swallow was rough and dry, scraping all the way down, until it burned in her stomach. This wasn't her best plan, maybe, but Persinette didn't see another.

"We're going to join the circus," Persinette said, pulling the paper from her pocket and carefully unfolding it. She smoothed her fingers over the deep ridges from where it had been pressed into a square and handed it to Rose.

"The circus?" Kindle leaned over Rose's shoulder, her chin perched on it, and scowled down at the wrinkled event poster.

"Tell me what I'm looking at." Agnes ripped the paper from Rose's hands, earning a kick to his shins for his troubles, which only resulted in a grunt. It looked even more hopelessly wrinkled in his hands when compared to Agnes's\ neatly manicured fingers and his carefully pressed clothes. Of the lot of them, he was the most put together. Persinette wasn't sure how he managed it, exactly, other than sheer stubbornness.

"Felicity brought this back after her trip to the scrap yard the other day." Persinette stuffed her hands back into her pockets to keep Agnes from seeing them twitch. "It seems this circus will perform for the queen in a couple of weeks. If we can place people among the acts, then we'll have direct access to the castle and the royal family."

"And how do you expect us to place people?" Kindle still hadn't taken her chin away from where it rested on Rose's shoulder, and now they were both looking at Persinette with twin expressions of mild annoyance. Maybe not every couple was a study in opposites after all.

"I assume we'll have to audition?" Persinette wasn't really sure how circuses worked. She'd only ever read about them in books. But joining one had always sounded like a lot of fun. The kind of escape she'd longed for, that Manu had provided.

Rose's eyes narrowed for a moment, then she let out a breath, dislodging Kindle from where she was perched. "It does seem like the cleanest route inside. So we'll have to find this circus before it reaches the castle and join up as quickly as possible. That way, the guards have less reason to scrutinize us."

"Exactly." A nod made Persinette wobble on her feet, so grateful was she that Rose seemed to be on board with this plan.

"Then we have a week to refine our acts," Sully declared, a bright smile lighting his face that seemed to be almost excited at the concept of joining the circus. Which was good, because Persinette would hate to be the only one.

"Our acts," Agnes grumbled, his shoulders hunching a little. "I'm not joining the circus. You can count me out."

"Aww, you're no fun, Aggy," Sully simpered, then laughed when Agnes gave him a hard shove that almost toppled him to the floor.

And just like that, the tension was broken. Persinette could breathe again. They could do this. They could do *all* of this. Join the circus. Infiltrate the Uprising and the castle. Destroy Eddi and Eloise. Bring Daiwynn into a new day.

It all seemed within reach.

# FOUR
## CHIRP

Something strange had happened to Chirp's hardware overnight. It was not an upgrade, nor a transfer of their software into another shell. It was not like when they had woken up on the table in the workshop, Levi the engineer hovering over them while the Ringmaster snarled instructions. No, this was different. This wasn't scientific or logical at all, in fact.

This was . . . Well, they hesitated to call it magic because they knew what the implications of that word in their world would mean. But that's what it was. That's all it *could* be.

Magic.

It sounded silly—ridiculous—even inside Chirp's own head. But as they looked down at the way the moon caught on the soft skin of their arm, they did not have any other explanation. Robots didn't just *become* human—or humanoid, anyway. They stayed robots. Remained circuits and wires and hard exoskeletons made of metal.

Not that Chirp had never thought about it, they realized, watching the way the hair on their arm stood on end in the nighttime chill.

A chill. What a strange sensation. They had known temperature before, but only insomuch as they needed to avoid melting or locking up. It was never something that was comfortable or uncomfortable. The cool air through the window of their room was decidedly uncomfortable. It left them cold, the fine hairs on their skin rising with gooseflesh, and had Chirp reaching for a blanket that was not there because the Ringmaster had no need to provide such things for a robot.

But they were not a robot anymore.

Slipping away from the window, deeper into their empty cell of a room, Chirp took stock of everything with new eyes. There was no bed, no soft furnishings of any kind. There was not even a mirror or a wardrobe full of costumes as they assumed some other performers might have had. All the Ringmaster left them was a single chair, propped up near the window so that Chirp could look out on the night and the land of Daiwynn drifting along beneath them, blurring slightly, like an oil painting, as the Ringmaster's flying circus bobbed along. That and a thin shift that hung from their form like a shroud.

Another glance out the window told Chirp that the moon was full and bright. The sky a cloudless wonder of twinkling stars. It was beautiful. Perhaps more beautiful than anything they had ever seen in their entire life, if they could've remembered anything before waking up on that table some hours ago.

*Days*, their internal software told them. It had been three *days* since they had woken up on that table, and obviously Levi had done something wrong when upgrading their hardware. Maybe he had loaded a cursed cog into their body and not known it. Or he was experimenting with things he didn't understand behind the Ringmaster's back. Maybe Chirp should tell on him, get in the Ringmaster's good graces. But then the Ringmaster would undo whatever it was, and Chirp would lose the first brush with humanity they'd had in—

"Psst," someone whispered from somewhere in the room.

Chirp stopped, their visual cir—eyes. Their *eyes* swiveled around to find the source of the strange voice, but there was no obvious sign of another person in the tiny room. Where would they have even hidden if there were? Out the narrow slitted window, hardly even big enough for a pixie to shimmy their way through? Doubtful.

"Psst," the voice came again, and Chirp crouched to look under the chair set against the wall. There was nothing there, of course. Not that they had thought there would be. It was a simple wooden chair, no cushions or upholstery to speak of. No place to hide, really. But Chirp was running out of options, and they were rapidly beginning to think this was all a bad dream. Their wiring—veins, their *veins* thumped hard against the inside of their skin with a pulse that was racing in equal parts fear and excitement.

"Not over there," the voice said, and it sounded like whoever it was had scoffed at the sheer ridiculousness of Chirp bending down to inspect the chair as if it would provide them with answers. They supposed it was likely an amusing sight, if one was on the outside, watching it happen. But Chirp did not find it amusing. In fact, they found it very annoying. Why couldn't the voice just tell them—"By the door."

*Ah, that answers that.* Chirp squinted. Their eyes were not as useful as the visual sensors that had previously been installed into their hardware—those would have been helpful in the low lighting—but Chirp would make do nonetheless. They always did. So, they took a slow step toward the door, peering at the wall that surrounded it for a moment as if it might give them some obvious clues as to where the voice had come from. Then they saw it: a little crack off to the right side, tiny and hardly noticeable, but when they looked closer, light was coming through from the other side. Whoever was over there had a lamp or something. Their shadow moved in front of the light, and it was lost. Chirp thought they saw an eye peer at them through the little space.

"Ah, there you are," the voice rasped, so quiet and breathy, it was hard to tell if it came from an adult or a child, a man or a woman. "Hello."

"Hello," Chirp repeated, their own voice sounding strained in their ears. Bending down, they fell onto their backside on the floor, the shift someone had clothed them in pulling tight over their knees as they folded them in front of themselves. It was an awkward position, and they couldn't really see the person on the other side of the wall at all, but it was better than leaning over to peer through the crack, or at least they thought so. The hardware of this body was far more sensitive. The muscles ached from holding one position too long. Chirp found that peculiar. How did people survive like this? Were they just in pain? All the time? That seemed to be a design flaw.

"Don't sit down!" the voice hissed, scolding and condescending all at once.

"Why not?" Chirp blinked—they had to remember to do that, their eyes would dry out otherwise. Another strange concept. How inefficient a humanoid body was.

"Because you need to get out of here while you still can." There was shifting on the other side of the wall, like someone moving around and their clothes making noise. Or what Chirp imagined that would sound like, anyway. Whoever it was must have been settling in closer, trying to get a better look at Chirp.

"I can't get out." Chirp hadn't tried the knob on the door, but they knew that would be the truth of it. They hadn't been able to escape the workshop. Why should now be any different? And even if they did leave their cell, where would they go? The Ringmaster's ship lazed through the skies of Daiwynn, high enough from the ground that a leap from it would most assuredly kill this fragile humanoid body. If they were still an android, things would have been different, but without their hard exoskeleton, there was no chance of survival.

"You could take one of the escape pods," the voice said, seeming to understand their hesitation better than even they had. Chirp wondered for a moment if they had muttered what they were thinking out loud. Humanoid creatures did that sometimes, talked to themselves to make sense of the world around them. Not that Chirp understood why, but it seemed mostly involuntary, so why wouldn't Chirp fall into the same problem?

"They'll be locked." That didn't mean they shouldn't *try*, Chirp knew that. They knew that escape was necessary if they wanted to survive. They also knew that they had done it before, although they couldn't remember how or when. The Ringmaster would have taken precautions to avoid that happening again. He was evil, not stupid.

"So you're just not going to *try*?" The voice was goading, irritated. Like the person couldn't believe that Chirp would just shrug off their choices that way.

The tone made Chirp want to curl in on themselves, their narrow shoulders hunching forward to hide their torso from an incoming blow that would never come. Is this what fear and trauma did to a humanoid body? No wonder so many of them walked around slouching as if they would disappear at a moment's notice to avoid the ire of the world. This was all so enlightening. Chirp wished they had a journal to write down their experiences.

"I don't see where I have any other options." It was a defeatist way to look at things, but Chirp hadn't been free in many, many years. Again, they couldn't remember how they knew that, but they did. They knew that this new body, this new chance, was the most freedom they had ever known.

And still, they were trapped. No longer by their own hardware but by the lock on the door.

It wouldn't hurt to try, they supposed. To turn the knob and see what would happen.

"No, it wouldn't," the voice agreed.

Chirp pushed to their feet, their knees crackling slightly at the motion. What did a humanoid person do when their knees made those noises? An android would oil their joints, making the motion more smooth, but humanoid beings had no such ability. Perhaps there was a food they could eat that would do the same thing? Or a drink? They would have to ask the next humanoid person they came across. They would have asked the voice on the other side of the wall, but they had no way of knowing if that person was humanoid or another android turned such, just like them. Which would not be conducive to real answers.

The voice made a soft hum, like Chirp had said as much aloud and it was considering their words. Chirp would deal with that later. They reached for the knob on the door and were surprised to find that it turned in their soft palm. With a little push, the door gave, and Chirp could see a warmly lit corridor on the other side through the space.

Shutting the door quietly, they bent back to peer through the crack in the wall again, hoping the person on the other side hadn't abandoned them entirely yet. "It's open."

"Good. You should get going." The shadow had moved away from the crack again, letting the light from the person's room fall through, a single bright star in the darkness of Chirp's cell.

"Should I come and let you out?" It seemed wrong that Chirp should escape and not help their new friend do so as well. That's what people did in situations like these, didn't they?

"No. I don't think that's possible," the voice mumbled, the

sound muffled by something, like maybe they were rubbing their face. Or moving away from the wall. Or hiding behind something. Chirp could not tell.

"Then . . ." Chirp licked their lips and cleared their throat, their mouth suddenly dry around the possibility of what was to come. "Then, what's your name?"

"Amara," the voice said, a lilt to their tone now, like they were smiling. Chirp didn't know what they had said that amused Amara so, but they hoped that it made Amara's imprisonment better, more bearable.

"Amara," Chirp repeated, letting the name sit on their tongue for a moment. It felt familiar. Like it belonged in their mouth. Like it belonged to them. They shook their head, pushing long, dark hair back from their face. "I'll come back for you, Amara."

"Don't bother. Just get out of here." Amara huffed a laugh, and Chirp pushed the door open again. The corridor on the other side was empty of all life, likely due to the late hour. Chirp inhaled deeply, the air filling soft and fleshy lungs, before they slipped through the crack between the door and its frame and shut it behind them.

"I need a new cloak," Brend said, his tongue between his teeth as he examined his reflection in the long mirror of his dressing room. The lighting in this room always made him look sicker than he did anywhere else; it was too bright, making him squint in the glare. But the tailor insisted she needed the room to be as well lit as possible for her craft, and who was Brend to tell her otherwise?

Charlotte—or Charlie to the people she'd taken a liking to—looked up and muttered through a mouth full of pins, "A new cloak? I just made you a new cloak last winter."

"That one is . . ." Licking at his teeth, he tried to think of a way to say what he was thinking without tipping Charlie off to what he was up to or offending her—he didn't need an irate tailor on his hands. "Perhaps a little much."

All movement stilled, and Charlie narrowed her amber-colored eyes at him in the mirror. She was one of the few people in the castle who seemed quite happy to look the prince in the eye. Well, her, Clancy, and that devil woman who worked in the garden. What was her name? Harriet? Something like that. He didn't know if it was because her clever fingers had made every stitch of clothing he'd worn since the day he was born, thus making her more grandmother than servant, or if there was another reason. But either way, he was grateful for it. Grateful to be treated like a human being. Even if it was only for short stints of time, and only when his mother wasn't looking.

"A little much?"

"Yes. A little much."

Charlie hummed and said nothing else on the matter, but in the morning when he rose, there was a long dark cloak made from a more practical fabric across the trunk at the foot of his bed.

IT WAS a task and a half to keep the cloak up around his face and balance his weight on his cane. Especially with the streets as uneven as they were and the wind blowing from one side. But Brend was making do, because what other choice did he have? Clancy wouldn't let him leave the castle without the cloak, even as it caught around his legs, making it a struggle sometimes to shuffle along. And he wasn't going to abandon his plans just because of a minor inconvenience. Maybe that's what Clancy had hoped would happen when he suggested Charlie make it. Maybe he thought that the annoyance would make a prince who had spent his life having all of his needs catered to, his life made easy, would just give up. He was sorely mistaken.

"You're more stubborn than I thought." Clancy chuckled fondly, confirming Brend's suspicions. Brend cut him a narrow-eyed glare from the corner of his eye but thanked God that at least Clancy hadn't called him "Your Highness." Although that might have been more for safety than anything else.

"Does that mean you're going to stop trying to annoy me

into staying behind?" Unlikely, Brend acknowledged, but he hoped that maybe this would be the end of Clancy's efforts. Besides, one never got what they wanted without asking for it.

Clancy poked his head around the corner of the alley they'd taken away from the castle. His hand rested almost casually on the pistol hidden in his pocket. Like he needed to feel the cool metal against his skin to reassure himself that it was there. To know that he could keep Brend safe. It would have been sweet if it weren't so irritating. Brend wasn't completely helpless. He had taken plenty of self-defense courses at his mother's behest. He may not be as capable as someone like Clancy, whose entire life was learning to protect another person and who had spent a fair amount of time down at the boxing rings in the lower city. But he wasn't completely incapable, damn it.

"This way." Clancy motioned when he decided the coast was clear, and Brend followed him out through the mouth of the alley onto another narrow street that was barren of any people. Strange that the capital could be so empty in the early evening like this. Brend was no expert, but he would have thought the capital would be full of life. It always seemed to be so when he looked from the windows of the castle. Loud and thriving. That's what he'd been hoping to see when he made the plan to leave the safety of his home behind in favor of excitement and exploration.

"Do you even know where we're going?" Brend asked, stepping carefully behind Clancy to avoid a rut in the road. Rain had gathered in it, and he had little doubt that it would have soaked his pant leg. He also had little doubt that Clancy would have found that amusing.

"You wanted to go to the marketplace, didn't you?" A crooked grin curled up one side of Clancy's face that, had they been in the privacy of Brend's quarters, he would have wanted to kiss away. It continually astounded Brend how one person could make him feel so many things all at the same time. Annoyance. Frustration. Petulance. Desire.

"Are you going to buy me a souvenir from our adventure?" Brend shot back instead of answering the question. A smile ticked up the side of his mouth that he was glad Clancy couldn't see for the shadow of his hood. He didn't need to encourage such behavior. Not that he could really *discourage* it; Clancy was set in his ways by now.

Clancy fell into step beside him, his hand swinging where it brushed lightly against Brend's, a comfortable warmth emanating from it that made Brend feel safe. Nothing could touch him so long as Clancy was there. Nothing could hurt him. That is what he had learned over the years. The world could be a harsh, cruel place. It could be small and limiting to someone like him. But Clancy would always be there. Clancy would always protect him.

"What kind of bodyguard would I be if I didn't get my charge a souvenir?" Clancy teased, his voice light, but Brend could see how his eyes didn't stay still for long. How his head tilted a little to listen to the sounds of the city around them. Looking for any sign that there could be danger. His diligence and preparedness meant Brend could relax, take in the sights, enjoy. Well. . . once there *were* sights to take in. So far there hadn't been much of anything.

"So, what do you want, Your Highness?" Clancy continued, doing a little skip in his own excitement for what was to come, and Brend smiled wider. Giddiness settled low in his belly that had nothing at all to do with their adventure and everything to do with what Clancy's happiness could mean for them both later. "Some fancy bauble? A sweet treat?"

"No. No." Brend laughed and reached to slip his fingers through Clancy's for a moment, giving them a firm squeeze before they reached the end of this particular alley. The hum of life waited for them beyond. People buzzing. Going about their day. Brend couldn't see them yet, but he could feel their energy. Their steps were heavy enough to make the very cobblestones vibrate. "Nothing like that."

"Then what?" Clancy gave Brend's hand a returning squeeze, then dropped the hold so he could check the traffic of the street on the other side of the alley.

The darkness of their hiding spot made the rest of the street too bright by comparison, and although Brend could see people moving about, they mostly appeared as shapes and shadows. An ache was settling in behind his eyes, making Brend want to shy further away from the light.

He lifted one hand to press the heel of his palm into his right eye, hoping to mitigate some of the ache, but it did little to help. Was the pain from not taking his potion? He and Clancy decided that he should hold off on taking it until they got back, as it usually made him tired, and Brend couldn't afford to be sleepy while they were outside of the castle walls. It wouldn't be safe.

"Brend?" Clancy's tone was quiet, worried, as he turned to grip Brend's shoulders lightly. There were lines around his mouth, concern shining in his eyes, and it made Brend's stomach lurch. "Should we head back? Maybe that's enough for today."

"No. I'm fine." Letting his hand fall away from his face, he sucked in a steadying breath. It helped. A little. Then, forcing a smile, he said, "Really, I'm all right."

Clancy didn't look terribly convinced, but he nodded anyway, resignation drawing his shoulders down that Brend almost felt guilty for. "If you say so."

"I do." Brend lifted his chin, adjusting his tone to something more sure and proud than he felt. "As for the souvenir," he said, hoping the change of subject would keep Clancy from seeing how uncertain he really was. It didn't seem to.

Clancy's gaze was still heavy on his features, making heat crawl along his skin like a brand. He cleared his throat to dislodge the discomfort knotted there but only succeeded in moving it up instead of down, so that his next words came out slightly strangled. "I think you'll know it when you see it."

"I suppose I will." A smile cut across Clancy's face, showing too many teeth and not crinkling his eyes in the way that Brend had always found so charming. But at least he allowed them to move past Brend's limitations, and Brend would take that little victory. "Are you ready to get moving again?"

*Not really.* His right hip was starting to lock up from walking for too long on ground with no kind of padding under it. Sitting too long made it ache. Walking for too long made it lock up. There was simply no winning. But Brend wasn't going to let it stop him, just as he hadn't let it stop him in so many other ways. "Definitely."

Narrowing his gray eyes, Clancy gave Brend another once-over before letting out a short breath and ordering Brend to "stick close." As if Brend would do otherwise. Then he stepped from the alleyway and into the push and pull of traffic with Brend close behind.

There were too many people, Brend decided almost immediately. The street was not so packed that other people jostled him, brushing shoulders against his, but the warmth from all of the other bodies made Brend uncomfortably hot under his hood. Like he was suffocating in the fabric. Sweat trickled down his neck. Still, he wasn't going to let *that* stop him *either*. He pushed through, only about a half step behind Clancy as he cut a path for them through the crowd. It took an unbearably long time to reach the market. The seconds stretched into what felt like hours but couldn't have been more than a couple of minutes. Then Clancy stopped at the mouth of another small alley, where the crowd seemed to be flowing in and out like two separate streams.

"This is it," Clancy murmured, his broad shoulders blocking Brend's view of what was on the other side.

Holding his breath, Brend moved onto his tiptoes, leaning heavily on his cane to look over Clancy's shoulder. What lay before him was a colorful wash of fabrics and people. Everyone seemed to be dressed in their finest. The overhangs above the stalls, while worn and dirtied from use, were all still bright and vibrant. And it was all so loud. So *alive*. This was what he'd been imagining when he decided to come out into the city. This was what he'd wanted to see in the capital.

"It's beautiful," Brend breathed, his fingers digging into the fabric of Clancy's shirt, likely making the seams creak. Not that he could hear it above the subtle roar of the crowd.

"Isn't it?" Clancy murmured, looking at Brend over his shoulder with a soft smile. They stood like that for a moment, Brend soaking it all up. Until someone bumped him lightly in the back, jerking him out of his reverie. "Come on, let's go get a closer look."

"Okay." Stumbling along, Brend let Clancy drag him into the marketplace proper. A laugh left him, the sound swallowed by the noise around them, but he didn't care. He couldn't possibly. Because there was so much to see. So much to do. And Clancy was going to show him all of it.

What followed was a whirlwind. Too much to see, taste, and smell for Brend to even properly focus on any of it. He'd never been so overstimulated in his life, but he found he didn't mind. Soon enough, the ache behind his eyes was forgotten, he was so distracted by everything else.

Pressed shoulder to shoulder with Clancy, they browsed tables of pastries and flowers, books and antiques, handmade jewelry and scarves. So much that Brend found himself increasingly overwhelmed by everything on offer.

They still hadn't found that perfect souvenir by the time they reached the table with the knitted caps. Or at least Brend didn't think they had. But Clancy leaned in and murmured, "Don't move. I'm going back to grab something," before he slipped away into the crowd, leaving Brend alone.

Which should have been fine—at five and twenty, he was an adult. He could take care of himself for a few minutes until his bodyguard came back. There was no reason that—

A flash of something bright flitted past the corner of his eye, drawing Brend's attention away from the expertly crafted knitted hats. Before he realized what was happening, his feet were shuffling along the cobbles, following the tiny wisp of green light away from the market.

# SIX
## CHIRP

The corridor seemed to stretch on forever, but Chirp wasn't sure if that was an illusion, a spell, or the truth of it. The Ringmaster's ship couldn't possibly be that large. It did have to house the entire circus, but considering how little care he gave to those in his employ, Chirp would have been surprised to find that any of the others were given much more than them. Even the ones who were humanoid and needed a place to sleep at night had probably only been given a single bed, if that.

Still, the hallway with the softly flickering sconces and the doors every few feet seemed to have no end at all. Stretching on into eternity. *This must be a deterrent to keep people from trying to escape.* A way for the Ringmaster to give his employees the illusion of freedom without actually having to worry about them leaving.

*We're all prisoners.* Chirp's balance shifted, the heaviness of that surety making their equilibrium completely useless. They wanted to stop and let everyone else out of their rooms. Tell them that the Ringmaster couldn't stop them all. That if they worked together, they could escape. But Chirp didn't.

They couldn't identify the reason why they didn't. Maybe it was fear—if that's what the racing of their heart and the burning of their palms was, then it must be fear. Fear of what, Chirp wasn't sure.

A deep inhale expanded their chest, they hoped it would calm the *thump-thump-thumping* against their ribcage. It didn't. But it did unstick their feet from the floor, at least enough to allow them to begin shuffling across the rough boards. The lights flickered again, dimming, so that the end of the corridor seemed to disappear entirely. A black hole sucking Chirp in.

Which way? Were they even going in the right direction? Chirp looked over their shoulder, trying to tell if they had chosen the correct path, and shook their head. There was no way to be certain. Chirp could only hope that they had made the right choice, sending up a silent query to whatever deity looked out for wayward robots.

Hope. What a strange thing. Chirp didn't think robots *could* hope, but then, they supposed they weren't a robot any longer. They were . . . whatever they were now. Something *else*.

The floor seemed like it was sloping downward, making Chirp stumble along toward the blackness at the end. Or maybe it was just because they weren't used to walking, their legs wobbly and unsteady beneath them with every step they took. They stopped, bracing themselves against the wall, and looked back to get their bearings, to see how far they had come. But there was no way to tell. All the doors looked the same. Chirp could have been walking for miles for all they knew, or maybe it hadn't been more than a couple of feet. They wished Amara had decided to come with them, her steadying voice a beacon to guide them. It was too quiet out there in the hall all alone.

But they pushed forward. One step. Then another. Each one aching through Chirp's bones like nothing they had ever known before. There was a prickling feeling in their feet, like screwdrivers poking at the skin, testing motor function to see if everything worked the way it was supposed to. Chirp had been through enough of those diagnostics to know what it felt like. But the familiarity of it didn't make it any easier to deal with.

A humming started, a quiet, broken, off-tune melody. Like the person making it didn't really know what humming was supposed to sound like. Or didn't know how to make their voice box do the thing it was supposed to do. Or maybe they just couldn't carry a tune. But it was a nice sound, Chirp decided. Comforting, in its way.

After another couple of feet, Chirp realized that the humming was coming from them. That the tune was something they remembered vaguely, like out of a dream. Which made no sense because robots didn't dream. And as far as they knew, they hadn't had any human dreams since whatever magic changed them into this form had been cast. Still. There was something like . . . *home* about this melody.

It softened the loneliness of the hall. Made the journey less cumbersome. It couldn't do anything about the ache and the pricking of their limbs, but it was more than Chirp could have hoped for when setting out on this journey alone.

Eventually, the corridor turned. What Chirp had thought of as a black hole at the end was really just a place where the lights had gone out, hiding the corner from where they had been in the middle of the hall. They pressed their back to the wall, squeezing their eyes shut and willing them to adjust more quickly. Visual sensors definitely would have made this easier. They adjusted automatically without having to be told to do so by the brain, whereas the organic, soft, and fleshy bit of this body worked so much more slowly, taking time to adjust and understand the stimulus around it.

With their eyes closed, they were able to focus more on the sounds of the Ringmaster's ship moving through

Daiwynn. The subtle whistling of the wind. The creaking of wood shifting with the currents. The gentle snores of someone in one of the rooms Chirp had no doubt passed but not noticed. And the voices. Hushed and muffled by a door, or a wall maybe. But they were voices all the same. A whispered and hurried conversation that someone was having in the dead of night. And in spite of Chirp knowing it was a bad idea, in spite of all logic dictating that they should head *away* from the voices instead of toward them, Chirp's curiosity got the better of them.

Rounding the corner, Chirp found another corridor, this one no less long, but the doors were more widely spaced along the left wall, and on the right, there were windows. Slitted, like the openings of a medieval tower. Enough to let in light, but not enough to really give someone a good view of the outside.

About midway down the hall, there was a door left ajar, the light from inside cutting across the dark hallway.

Fear gripped Chirp again. Holding onto the wall, Chirp tried to steady themselves, their fingernails digging into the wood, creating little splinters that fell silently to the floor. They needed to move. One way or the other. Either go toward the voice and find out who was behind that door, or head back and cower in their cell. They knew that if they went back, they wouldn't continue past their cell to see what was on the other side. They would lose their nerve.

Chirp's next swallow burned all the way down, like bile in their throat and belly, and gulped too loudly in the echoing quiet that surrounded them. But they made up their mind. They knew what they needed to do.

The skin on the bottoms of their feet was so very soft, it didn't make sense. The rough floor scraped against it, threatening splinters. They pushed forward. Because they needed to know who was on the other side of that door. Needed to hear what was being said.

One peek through the crack of the open door revealed the Ringmaster, hunched over a long table at the center of the room. There was a big screen on one wall with an image projected onto it from somewhere across the room. The Ringmaster was facing it, his shoulders rigid beneath his wrinkled dress shirt.

"I heard you the first time, Eddi," the Ringmaster said with a snort, pushing himself up from the table so that he could walk around it and lean against the other side, his arms crossed. "But I'm unclear on what you want from me."

Eddi's face hid behind a pair of goggles that magnified their eyes to the size of bottle caps. Chirp hoped they couldn't see them, that the shadow would hide them. But there was no way to tell.

"You have a royal appointment." Eddi raised a brow, their nose wrinkling.

"I wouldn't call it an appointment." The ringmaster shrugged, his posture going lazy and almost insolent as he slouched against the table.

"Rowan," Eddi huffed, exasperated. "You're making this needlessly difficult."

"I am not." The Ringmaster—Rowan—sounded like he was smiling, the words crawling up at the end. "If you want me to do something, Eddi, you need to tell me exactly what you want. And," the Ringmaster hummed, leaning forward more, his head tilting to one side, "what you're willing to *pay* for it."

Eddi's eyes narrowed, a hiss twisting their lips into a scowl. "Pay?"

"Yes, you know I don't do anything for free." Bracing himself on his hands, the Ringmaster tilted his head back to look up at the ceiling, a little chuckle leaving him. "So, what exactly do you want from me, and what are you willing to pay for it?"

"I want you to kill the royal family," Eddi murmured, the words curling like dread and ice up Chirp's spine.

Someone gasped, the sound too loud in the silence that followed such a declaration. The Ringmaster whipped around, his eyes narrowed as he looked through the crack into the hall. "Who's there?"

Panic gripped Chirp again, leaving their feet glued to the floor. They wobbled, trying to escape, even as they couldn't move their feet. Their arms pinwheeled, but it didn't help Chirp to regain their balance. Their bottom hit the ground with a hard *thud*, jarring their spine and making their ears ring so loudly that Chirp didn't even hear what Eddi said to the Ringmaster before he flung the door open and found Chirp there on the floor of the hall.

"Well, well, well," the Ringmaster murmured, his voice low and dangerous. "Look who it is. A little cub out all on their own."

Chirp struggled backward on their hands and feet, an awkward crab walk that didn't really get them away from the Ringmaster as quickly as they wanted it to but was better than nothing. Still, it didn't stop Rowan from reaching down, grabbing Chirp by the hair, and yanking them to their feet. He didn't stop there, though. He dragged them down the hall, Chirp scrambling to keep up, until at some point, the world went black.

CHIRP DIDN'T KNOW how much time had passed before they woke, but they were *wrong* again. Joints too stiff, and they could no longer feel the roughness of their shift against their skin. The ache inside their head had gone, and when they lifted a hand to rub at their eyes, the skin wasn't . . . *skin* at all. It was the hard exoskeleton of a robot.

Choking on a gasp, Chirp sat up quickly enough that in a human body, it would have made their head spin, but as a robot, it just made their joints creak with the need for oil. Their visual sensors widened as they looked about the tiny cell again—no, not again, this was a different cell, there was a bed now—finding the Ringmaster sitting by their bedside looking relaxed.

"You're causing me quite a lot of trouble, Chirp," Rowan said, examining his nails.

"What happened—" Their voice came out stilted and robotic. Cleaning their throat, they tried again. "What happened to me? I was—I was *human*."

"Not quite human, but close. Enchanted." The Ringmaster crossed one leg over the other, getting more comfortable in the hard, straight-backed chair. "And you were, once upon a time."

"What does that mean?"

The Ringmaster smiled a little, teeth sharp. "It means, if you want to go back to being Enchanted, to know the freedom that body provides you, you're going to have to do something for me."

"You want to strike up a deal." Chirp scrubbed at their face, scooting so they could lean against the wall behind the bed. They were cold all over, uncomfortable now that they had known what it was to have skin instead of an exoskeleton, eyes instead of visual sensors. Being Enchanted had been overwhelming, but going back to *this* was suffocating. Like being stuffed in a box with only a tiny hole cut in the side to see out.

"That's what I do, isn't it? Strike up deals." Rowan laughed, leaning farther back in his chair, his hands moving to fold behind his head, completely relaxed. "That's how you got here, isn't it?"

"I don't remember. You erased my data stores." And oh, how they hated him for that. If they could only remember who they'd been, where they'd come from, they knew things would be different. *They'd* be different.

"So I did. Hmm." Head tilted to one side, he braced his feet on the edge of the bed and pushed his chair up onto two legs. Then he shrugged. "Either way, let's make a *new* deal."

Chirp didn't think they liked this idea. It felt too much like signing their life away. But what choice were they being given? None. "What kind of deal?"

Rowan's smile crawled further up his lips but still didn't reach his eyes. He dropped the legs of the chair down to the ground with a hard *thud*. "You help me kill the prince of Daiwynn, and I'll release you from all contractual obligations you have to me."

"What contractual obligations . . . exactly?"

Holding up one hand, a scroll appeared on Rowan's spread palm. He pulled it open, humming as he perused whatever was on the paper, then nodded to himself. "The deal was, you give up your autonomy for a place to belong. We never specified what that meant, but as I run a *clockwork* circus, well, you can guess. Thus, upon signing this contract, you were turned into one of my clockwork creations. Now—"

"But I wasn't clockwork last night."

"A loophole." Rowan rolled up the paper, and it disappeared again. "A very convenient one considering what I need you to do. Either way, if you would like to regain your autonomy, and your 'humanity,' as it were, you need to get close to the prince. Close enough to kill him."

"And if I refuse this new deal?" Chirp didn't think they

wanted to know the answer to that question, but they knew they needed to.

"Then we default to your base contract, which had an end date of . . ." The scroll reappeared, floating in front of Rowan so that he could peruse it at his leisure, a wicked grin playing at the corners of his lips. "Oh, yes. Here it is. Never."

"Never?"

"Never."

Chirp wasn't sure why they would have agreed to such a thing. Been so desperate for a home that they would sign away their entire life. But the knowledge sat like a shackle around their neck, weighing them down. They needed to get out of it. No matter what that meant. They couldn't go back to living in this cold box, their data stores erased whenever the Ringmaster saw fit until they lost every shred of themselves. They needed to escape.

"I don't . . . I don't know." They clutched at the thin blanket beneath them, trying to find an answer, but none came. They *needed* to escape, but could they sacrifice another life to do that?

Maybe.

The world narrowed down to a single point. The brightly glowing light, bobbing and weaving through the darkness. Brend wasn't even sure how long he had been following it, but it always stayed just out of reach. Every time his hand lifted, trying to feel its warmth, it would zip away, drawing him deeper into the darkness, until he forgot what he'd been doing beforehand. Where he was. *Who* he was.

One step. Two. Five. Then the world tilted strangely, his stomach falling out through his feet, and someone had ahold of his collar.

Brend squeezed his eyes shut and opened them again until they focused on the strained face of Clancy above him. His arm was outstretched to hold Brend by the collar of his shirt, keeping him from falling into the abyss below.

"What the hell were you *doing*?!" Clancy shouted, his face reddening from the effort it took to hold Brend up. He looked furious and terrified all at once, two emotions Brend didn't think he'd ever seen on his guard's face before.

Brend opened his mouth to answer, but Clancy shook his head and started pulling. The seams on Brend's shirt gave a threatening creak, and he squeaked, arms flailing about to grab onto Clancy's wrist at the sudden realization that the abyss below him was at least a five-story drop. A roof. He'd been on a *roof*. How had he gotten up here?

"Are you going to *help*? Or are you just going to hang there gaping like a fish?" Clancy asked through clenched teeth, tightening his fist in the fabric.

"Right." Brend scrambled against the side of the building, looking for some kind of foothold where there was none, just the smooth, shiny glass of a pre-Daiwynn era building. The soles of his shoes, slippery and not at all designed to help one scale the side of a building, did nothing to help.

A ripping sound followed Brend's struggling, and Clancy's eyes went impossibly wide, the pupils eating up the gray of his irises as fear became the predominant emotion. "That's not good."

"You think?!" With a hard tug, Clancy managed to get Brend *almost* back up to the edge of the rooftop, his fingers *almost* able to curl over it to help pull himself up. But just as his fingertips touched the cold metal, the ripping came again, and the bit of fabric that Clancy was holding onto came away from the rest of the shirt.

Brend fell, his arms windmilling around him, reaching for something to hang on to, but there was nothing. He was going to die. Oh God, *he was going to die*. Out there in the middle of the capital. His mother was right. She was *so* right. It was too dangerous for him out there. He was too immature, too *weak*. She'd been right. She'd always been right. He was—

He was floating? He was floating!

The rush of wind stopped whistling past him. And while the abyss still loomed below, it was no longer rising up to meet him. Brend chanced a look down and found a good three stories still between himself and the ground. The people below went about their business, unaware of the prince hovering above them. He swallowed hard to keep from throwing up what little breakfast he'd been able to eat in his excitement, then looked up to Clancy again.

Clancy had leaned half his body over the edge of the rooftop, looking dangerously like he meant to follow Brend over. Not that that would have done anything except get them both killed. But it was a sweet notion. His gray eyes were wide with some other emotion, the color having drained from his face.

"Get your ass back up here," Clancy hissed, reaching down for him again.

Brend opened his mouth to tell him that he didn't know *how* to do that. That he had no control over whatever it was that had kept him from plummeting to his death. But then something shifted along his back, and he was pushed upward by a current of air. His arms lifted above his head, and Clancy grabbed on as soon as he was within reach, hauling him over the side of the building and onto the rooftop.

Crushed into Clancy's chest, Brend could hardly breathe through the thick fabric of Clancy's jacket. But Brend's arms wound around him, holding him close as he tried to get his breathing back to something that might be considered normal. The thing at his back that had pushed him up to the rooftop had disappeared, leaving no explanation behind. Not that it mattered. None of it mattered. Because Brend had almost died. He'd almost been led off the edge of the roof by a—

"What *was* that?" Brend asked when he was sure that he could do so without his voice shaking.

"A will-o-wisp, you fool." Clancy held on tighter, his grip almost painful and suffocating, but Brend didn't care. Because it was nice to have someone touch him like this. To have someone hold onto him like their very life might depend upon it. Even if that was mostly because, if his mother found out Clancy had accompanied him out of the castle and Brend had died on the journey, Clancy would be beheaded for his part in things.

"A will-o-wisp," Brend repeated, trying to line up what he'd seen with his lessons over the years. His mother tried to keep him from learning too much about the Enchanted. Her main points had always been that they were dangerous and they killed indiscriminately. That they didn't care about life, especially human life, and that was why they needed to be collected and locked away. For the safety of their kingdom and their people. Brend had never really understood it. "Why did it do that?"

Clancy huffed, pushing Brend away by the shoulders so that he could look into his eyes. "What do you mean, *why?*"

"I mean, why did it try to hurt me? I didn't do anything to it. I wasn't hurting it. There was no reason for that." Brend had never believed that Enchanted were evil. Maybe they weren't *good.* Maybe they should have been kept away from the mortals of their world. But he didn't think they were *evil.* He didn't think they'd maliciously hurt someone without any reason. He'd always just thought maybe they were a little more easily angered, maybe their magics made them a little more volatile. That made sense. And it lent credence to what his mother was trying to do by separating them from the humans of their kingdom. But this act, it had been . . . unwarranted, malicious, vindictive, *evil.*

"Does it need a reason?" Clancy pulled himself away entirely and began to tug his jacket from his shoulders. His bare arms were littered with gooseflesh. "Put this on. I can't take you back like this."

Brend looked down at himself, seeing his torn shirt and that the cloak he'd been wearing was lost, probably somewhere along the way up to the roof, or maybe when he was hanging over the edge. He wasn't sure. Clancy was right, he couldn't go back like this. Even if someone from the castle didn't see them sneaking back in, they would cause a stir in the street with him dressed this way. They didn't need that kind of attention. So, he let Clancy force his arms into the sleeves, the cuffs coming down over his fingertips, the seams hanging oddly off his own shoulders. He tugged the collar up tighter around his neck, warding off the chill threatening to settle into his bones.

"Come on, let's get you home," Clancy murmured, helping Brend to his feet. He wobbled a little on the unsteadiness of his legs, his hip pulsing sharply with a pain he hadn't noticed until he put weight on the joint.

"Where's my cane?" Brend scanned the rooftop, looking for the shiny lacquered cane his mother had gifted him just last year. It wasn't the only one he had, but it was certainly the nicest and a personal favorite. He probably shouldn't have brought it out with him; that was just asking for trouble. But it was his favorite for a reason, and not just because it looked the nicest. It was also the perfect height to relieve the pressure on his joints. It was hard to get that, and the loss of it would make life more difficult than he could ever express.

"I'm afraid it's gone, Your Highness." Guilt pinched Clancy's brow as he sidled closer, offering himself for Brend to balance on. But Brend didn't want to do that. He hated doing that. He had pain, yes, but he didn't need someone to do for him. He wasn't *helpless*. "By the time I caught up to you, you didn't have it."

"Oh. Well." Brend cleared his throat, forcing a smile onto his face even as his heart plummeted. "Someone will find it and make good use of it, I'm sure."

"I'm sure." But Clancy sounded doubtful. He jammed his finger against the button to the elevator once they'd gotten back inside the building, shifting nervously on his heels as he waited. The day's events had unsettled him in a way Brend hadn't expected them to.

"I won't tell anyone what happened," Brend promised, his words soft, meant to be reassuring.

They didn't seem to help, because Clancy just grew even more rigid, his shoulders hunching forward like he could protect himself from whatever blow came next. "That thing wanted to kill you, Your Highness."

"It did." That hadn't settled in yet, but as they loaded onto the elevator, it sunk into his bones. That Enchanted had wanted to kill him for no other reason than that it was able. It had lured him in, drawn him away. Had it taken him up the stairs or on the elevator? How long had he been following it? Had no one bothered to try to help him until Clancy realized what was happening? They walked out into the darkened streets, and with the adrenaline worn away, the cold settled more deeply into Brend's skin. The slight breeze seemed to cut him down to the bone.

It took a long minute for him to focus on the street around them, and when he did, he frowned. "I don't recognize this part of the city."

There was a steep hill all the buildings seemed to be built into. The street itself looked like it hadn't been touched in over a decade, crumbling away little by little. The part of the city where the marketplace resided had been packed with people out for an early evening stroll, their clothes put together and clean. This place looked nothing like that. What figures littered their path were shrouded in long black cloaks that hid their faces and any recognizable shape. Like they could disappear into the shadows at any given moment.

Clancy ducked his head closer, his eyes wide and flitting about them as if he could take in the entire street at once, all while helping Brend carefully up the hill. "This is the neighborhood where the Enchanted live. Stay close."

"I'm not going anywhere," Brend promised, and he meant it this time. He'd had enough adventure for one evening, possibly his entire life. And these . . . these *creatures*. Who knew what they'd do to him if he didn't have someone to protect him. Suddenly, the heaviness of Clancy's pistol in his pocket felt more a comforting weight than an over-precaution. Maybe his mother had a point in using MOTHER to round the Enchanted up after all.

# EIGHT
## MANU &
## CREW

T he fake mustache, which Sully had insisted Manu needed right before the group disembarked from the docked *Duchess,* was itchy. Normally, he would have been game for a fake mustache—it did seem very much his style. But without his sight, Manu constantly felt like he was one bad sensation away from sensory overload.

Benard said this was completely normal. He said it was nothing at all to worry about. That eventually, Manu would grow accustomed to the loss of his sight, and things would even out for him. But they hadn't yet, and it had been months. And not having Persi there was really just making a bad situation worse.

Hiccup must have noticed it, because he sidled in closer, pressing his hard shoulder into Manu's thigh and letting out a soft whistle.

"Remind me whose idea it was to meet the Ringmaster of this gods' forsaken circus on his home turf?" Rose asked out of what sounded like the corner of her mouth.

She had a habit of doing that when she was uncomfortable, Manu had learned. He had learned a lot about his companions and how to tell what they were feeling without being able to see their faces. He'd also learned that tone couldn't lie. Words could, but tone couldn't. Even when someone was trying to use it to lie. There was always an underlying current. A soft edge to a lie.

That helped with all of . . . *this*. The *this* being his continued blindness and need for Hiccup's assistance. The *this* being the fact that his curse would likely never be lifted, even for all Persi's positive pep talks. She tried. She was a sweet woman, and she loved him, and she tried. But Manu was a realist. He understood that sometimes curses were permanent.

The *this* being that even when he shifted into a tiger, using the Cindaku magic he'd inherited from his ancestors, he was still unable to see!

Sometimes there was no going back.

"Yours, I believe," Agnes murmured back, his own tone cutting and cold but with an undercurrent of softness Manu didn't think he'd ever understand. Although, perhaps he should have, since he and Benard's relationship was not too dissimilar to Agnes and Rose's.

"No one asked you." Rose huffed, her boots squeaking a little as she shifted from foot to foot on the rough-hewn deck of the Ringmaster's ship. They'd been told to wait here for him. That he'd be up shortly, once he finished some other business. But Manu felt maybe that was just a lie, so the man could inspect them without having to face them. So he could look for chinks in their armor, in their disguises.

"Would you both stop bickering for five minutes?" Manu stuffed his hands more firmly into his pockets, wiping the sweat from his palms onto the lining there. The disguise magic Agnes was holding up for them shifted over his skin like an ill-fitting waistcoat, suffocating and too tight, making him itch in places that Manu didn't think he could scratch in polite company. Under the skin, particularly. But at least Persi didn't have to see him like this. He was sure he was hideous, if Agnes had anything to say about what his disguise looked like.

"No," Agnes and Rose said at the exact same time, making a twittering whistle leave Hiccup that was most definitely a giggle. Ridiculous, the lot of them.

"Tell me why we couldn't have brought Benard and Owen instead?" Felicity asked. She and Drea had been quiet up till that point, lingering behind the small group like bodyguards or minders. Which was amusing, as they were the youngest of the group, veritable babies compared to the rest of them. They were also the least well-known, and the least likely to get their asses captured. Maybe they should have come alone—that would probably have been safer—but Manu wasn't exactly going to poke holes in Persi's plan. That's not what co-captains did.

"Because they needed to stay behind to help Persi with the ship." Manu ran his thumb over the rough edge of the mirror in his pocket. It had been a rush job, and probably wouldn't work once they were behind the wards of the castle, but it brought him comfort to know that Persi and the rest of his crew were a mere mirror call away. It wouldn't save them in a pinch, but at least it was something.

"Here he comes," Drea murmured, her voice a low rasp. Manu felt her shift behind him, stepping closer to Felicity if he were to guess.

It was amazing how close they had all grown over the last few months, but not as amazing as how mature the two young women he'd saved from the cells of MOTHER along with Persi were now. They had been young adults, teenagers really, and Manu hadn't been able to see what good they would do. Just two more people he'd have to protect and take care of. But they'd come into their own. Felicity was quick and clever, able to keep up with Rose when she went off on a mechanical tangent the likes of which made Manu's head spin. And Drea was a fighter that rivaled even Owen, light on her feet and too cunning by half. It was a relief to have them at his back in all this.

Heavy boot treads followed Drea's words. Manu liked to tell people that he could tell a lot about a person based on their footsteps, and to some degree, he could. The Ringmaster's feet didn't scuff or shuffle as he made his way across the deck, indicating no lack of confidence. And there was a certain amount of height to him, based on how far apart they were spaced—either that or he just took hysterically long strides. Which, Manu conceded, was entirely possible. But Drea wasn't snickering, so he thought he could count that out.

"You all want to join my circus?" the Ringmaster asked, his words slow and lazy, turning up a little at the edges, like he was smirking. That, more than anything, gave Manu a pretty clear picture of the man before them. Cocky. Arrogant. And likely to try to con them into signing something that they'd never be able to get out of. Manu liked this plan even less than he had when Persi had originally come up with it.

"We do," Agnes said, stepping forward to be their spokesperson. Manu didn't remember agreeing to let Agnes speak for them, but it would be just like the unicorn to take it upon himself to do such a thing. That was the trouble in all of this *teamwork* business: there were far too many cooks in the kitchen for Manu's taste. He was used to being the one in charge, and now he had to share that control with not just Persi but Agnes, Sully, Kindle, Roy, Alys, and even—he shuddered to think—*Stella*.

"Care to tell me why?"

Someone's boots creaked, and Manu could imagine the Ringmaster rocking back on his heels, making himself long and relaxed. Nonchalant. It was all an act, Manu knew that for sure because the heaviness of the Ringmaster's gaze slammed against his disguise like a battering ram. Trying to push through it to see what lay underneath. Manu wondered if it would hold up against the poking and prodding of another magic user, but Agnes hadn't said the panic word yet, so Manu supposed they were still fine.

"Do we need a reason?" Drea piped up, then grumbled something under her breath when Felicity nudged her.

"No, I suppose you don't," the Ringmaster agreed, but it sounded too sly. Oily and slick, like a used ship salesman. Manu didn't trust him, but then, he wasn't supposed to. They were meant to be on their toes at all times while they were on the Ringmaster's ship. Stick together, stay alert, call if you need help—those had been Persi's instructions. She left the rest in their very capable hands.

"If you don't need extra hands, we can always find work elsewhere." Manu stuffed his hands deeper into his pockets, forcing his shoulders to slouch a little like he didn't care. Like he didn't need this job to fulfill his mission. Like the whole of Daiwynn didn't stand on a knife's edge, waiting for Manu to fail or succeed. Sweat trickled down the back of his neck, no doubt staining his collar. He hoped it didn't show through the glamour, but he was sure that it did. Agnes would never be kind enough to hide something like that. Good thing it was hot out today. The heat from the machines and too many people trapped by the thick layer of steam that blotted out the sun.

"Now, now, let's not be hasty." The Ringmaster's clothes rustled, his measured steps bringing him right in front of Manu, and he felt the heaviness of the Ringmaster's gaze latch onto him and stay there. Had he been looking at Manu this whole time? Inspecting him? Trying to push through his glamour? Or were the others in danger of being found out as well?

"We're not being hasty, we just don't want to stand around here waiting. Wasting daylight." Manu forced himself to stay standing the way he was. To not straighten his spine and lift his chin the way he wanted to. Not tighten his jaw in a defiant slant, challenging the Ringmaster to find fault in him as he might normally. It would draw too much attention, and they wanted the Ringmaster to think they'd be easy to take advantage of. So, Manu slouched in further on himself instead.

The Ringmaster hummed, his breath warm and too close for comfort, and murmured something to himself before he pulled back to clap his hands too loudly in the space in front of Manu's face.

Manu nearly jumped at the sudden sound, and Hiccup let out a dissatisfied whistle, a warning that he'd scorch the skin off the Ringmaster's face with his steam if he didn't stop startling his captain. It was sweet but ultimately unnecessary. Part of a protective nature Manu was sure Persi had programmed into the little bot herself, because that seemed like something she'd do. Gods, he loved her so.

"Well?" Manu asked when the moment stretched on for far too long. "Do you have jobs for us or not?"

"You, definitely," The Ringmaster said, and Manu could hear the oily smile in his tone. "Yes. Yes. I've always wanted a matched set," he murmured to himself, which made absolutely no sense to Manu, but he wasn't about to argue over it so long as it meant he got the job. "I don't know that I have positions for your friends."

"We're a package deal." Agnes stepped closer, and Manu wondered if this was a rare show of Agnes actually caring for someone outside of himself and Sully, or if it was just that he was that desperate to see this mission succeed. It didn't matter one way or the other. He was right. Manu wasn't staying here by himself, and he had always been a gambling man. So why not gamble his own worth to the Ringmaster? See what it got him?

"Oh, all right." The Ringmaster's laugh was boisterous and grating all at once. It made Manu's eardrums recoil from the sound, and his hands tightened in the lining of his pockets again. But he'd stopped sweating. They'd won this particular hand—maybe not the game, but this hand, and Manu was going to count that as a victory. "We will be needing extra acts once we reach the castle anyway, and I can never have enough stagehands. I'll just need you to sign some contracts."

"Of course you will," Drea muttered bitterly.

"What kind of contracts?" Rose hedged, caution lining her tone. Good, at least one of them was as nervous about this as Manu was. He didn't like the idea of signing a contract with someone like the Ringmaster. Someone whose magic had a distinctly tangy scent to it. That usually didn't mean anything good.

"Oh, nothing important. Standard terms will apply, of course." The Ringmaster flapped his hand, something on his wrist jangling. "If you'll follow me, we'll get you all signed up and settled."

His boots were heavy when they walked away, and Manu could hear the rustle of his friends' clothes as they all looked at each other, trying to sort out what to do next.

"We don't have much other choice," Manu reminded them before nudging Hiccup to lead the way and following closely behind. Still, he made a mental note to have Rose and Agnes read the contracts carefully before anyone signed. There was no sense in taking chances.

"I 'll give you some time to think about it," was what the Ringmaster had departed with. He'd patted Chirp's knee, like they were old friends, like he understood that this was a hard decision to make, then left them to their cell and their solitude.

Chirp knew what choice the Ringmaster would make were their circumstances reversed. It was the choice that most might have in their position. What was someone else's life when compared to their own? They didn't even know the prince of Daiwynn. And what had the prince of Daiwynn done for them anyway? Nothing.

But there was a feeling of wrongness about it that settled into Chirp's circuits. A reminder that *they* had gotten themselves into this mess and they shouldn't use another person's life to get out of it. It wasn't right or fair.

"But what is right and fair, anyhow?" Chirp wondered aloud, their metal fingertips scraping at the wall beside their bed. The Ringmaster had moved them to one of the cells that offered a cot, or something resembling one anyway, and though robots couldn't sleep, Chirp had taken to laying down every night just as a person might. Slipping into hibernate mode for a few short hours, only to be woken up by dreams too vivid and too real for any robot to be having.

"But that's the thing," a voice whispered from the wall beside the door, "you aren't a robot, are you?"

"Amara?" Chirp blinked into the darkness of their cell. It wasn't nightfall yet, but the clouds and smoke from the capital of Daiwynn had blotted out the sun, casting the tiny room in a night-like dreariness that made something in Chirp want to curl up and go into hibernate mode again. Likely the human lurking in their depths, waiting for the moon to brush their exoskeleton to escape the hardened shell the Ringmaster had trapped them in. Chirp still wasn't sure how to feel about that whole thing. They knew the Ring-master did advanced magic and there was something he had used to tie all of his people here. But they had never really thought too hard about it.

"Yep," Amara chirped, a brightness to her voice Chirp thought was vastly unwarranted for the current circumstances.

If Chirp's face could do such a thing—which it couldn't because they were a robot—they would be frowning in confusion. A whistling whirr sounded from somewhere inside of them, a puff of steam shooting out their right ear as they tried to comprehend how Amara could be here but also have been just on the other side of the wall of their old cell. Had the Ringmaster moved her as well? That didn't make sense. Why would he bother? And for that matter, Amara's voice had come from a crack in a wall that had the hall on the other—

"Don't think about it too hard. You'll only hurt yourself," Amara teased, a laugh in her voice that drew Chirp completely out of their own head. "Tell me what's going on in that head of yours."

"I'm thinking that I don't have a choice in this." Chirp let their body slump back against the wall behind their bed with a loud thump. How many days had it been since their little journey through the ship? Since the last time they'd felt the softness of Enchanted skin instead of an exoskeleton?

The landscape below had changed. Chirp wasn't sure how they could tell, but they knew they were in the capital. The air was humid with steam and thick with smoke from too many people crammed into too small a space, all of them using clockwork and coal to power anything and everything they might need. Blotting out the sky.

"Of course you have a choice." Amara's tone seemed affronted by the mere insinuation, and Chirp supposed that was fair. If she knew Chirp was something other than a robot and there was a choice to be made, then she probably knew that Chirp had sold away whatever hope they had of freedom long ago. If Amara were to judge them for that, Chirp couldn't exactly blame her. If Chirp were in her position, they would likely be judging themselves too. What kind of fool signed their life away like that? A young one, probably.

Chirp shifted uncomfortably on the bed, something crawling through their circuitry that was distinctly itchy. Like they didn't fit their hardware. Only, that didn't make sense because robots always fit their hardware—they were *primarily* their hardware. Another useless humanoid emotion that they couldn't adequately identify. How many of those would there be now that they'd been humanoid?

"It's your life or his," Amara said, simplifying Chirp's dilemma to five little words in a tone so straightforward and cutting that Chirp was sure they'd felt them like a knife on their skin. If they had been unclear about Amara's opinions on this choice before, they were sure about them now.

"Yes, that is the choice." The words scraped against a voice box that sounded distinctly rusty. Could one oil such a thing? Perhaps they could ask Levi the Engineer if they were ever to see him again. If the Ringmaster hadn't done away with him like Chirp thought. "But it's not as simple as that."

"Isn't it?" Chirp imagined Amara tilting her head. Even if they didn't know for sure what Amara looked like, they had a picture in their mind of a young woman with long dark hair and bottomless dark eyes set into a face of smooth, light brown skin. Beautiful and untamed in a way that Chirp would never and could never be. Because they were all cogs and bolts, a bucket of rusty pieces tied together with magic. Except, of course, when they weren't.

"No, it isn't." Chirp's hands tightened into fists in the thin coverlet of their bedding. If anything, it was worse than that because it was the measuring of one life against another's. Of a prince's life versus the life of . . . whatever Chirp was. They didn't know exactly *what* they were. A commoner, of course, but what kind? And how valuable could a person's life be after they willingly signed it away to a man vindictive enough to trap their soul in the body of a robot? Probably not very valuable at all.

"It's pure selfishness if you think your life is worth more than his." A scoff left Amara, her tone gone derisive and condescending. And as much as Chirp hated to admit it, she was right. Chirp's life wasn't worth more, or even as much, as the life of the prince of Daiwynn. They had ensured that by auctioning it off to the highest bidder like one might a painting or a prized calf. "You're not selfish, are you?"

The question rang like an echo in Chirp's head, bouncing off the internals of their hardware and drawing something out of their empty memory banks.

*An older woman, her face wrinkled with age, crouched in front of Chirp. Hunched over and clutching at her knees to keep her upright, a little smile ticking one corner of her lips. She looked remarkably like how Chirp imagined Amara—maybe this could have been Amara's grandmother.*

And even for all Chirp knew they had not seen this woman since waking up in the workroom days ago, this memory felt familiar. Well-worn and soft around the edges.

*"It's mine," a little voice said, and it took Chirp a moment to realize the little voice had come from themselves. Their little fingers tightened on the ball in their hands, digging in as they refused to let go. "I don't want to share."*

*The woman huffed, standing up straight again and bracing her hands on her hips. "You're not selfish, are you?"*

"No, I'm not," Chirp said, answering both the woman and Amara at the same time. Although they didn't know how they knew that they weren't selfish. They really had nothing to base this assurance on, they just knew it down to their wiring. They were not selfish. And thus they could not trade someone else's life for their own.

"Then might I suggest you find another way?" Amara asked, but there was no triumph in her voice even though she had won the argument. "Try escaping."

"I did try. Remember? And the Ringmaster caught me and brought me back." Chirp wasn't even sure how. Well, not how he had caught them, *that* they remembered. But how he had gotten them back to their cell. He must have had help.

"Try again. Don't stop trying!" Amara hissed, her voice closer now than it had been. Like a whisper in Chirp's ear. A reminder of who they were and who they should be. "You can't just—" A noisy inhale, almost wet with tears, choked off Amara's words. "You can't just let yourself sink to his level."

"All right. All right." Pushing to their feet, Chirp ignored the subtle squeak of their knees as they stood to their full height, which still felt abnormally tall when they were used to hardware that was much shorter. That thought brought another memory swimming to the surface: a heart-shaped face with brilliant red hair and red wings spread out behind it. A friend, they thought, or hoped, rather. But they didn't know the name of the person or where they knew them from. Still, it made something pang in their chest.

"Go. Before he comes back. *Go.*"

Chirp nodded, swinging the door open perhaps a little too hard. Then they were struggling down the hall, their steps loud against the floorboards as their metal limbs made them unwieldy, coltish. Everything about their hardware was foreign now that they knew what humanoid limbs were like and the familiarity of that body.

They went the other way this time, hoping this would lead them out of the ship, not deeper into it as it seemed they had gone last time. Not that there was any way to tell where they had started before; all of the doors looked the same, all the halls so eerily similar. But Amara was right, they needed to try.

Just like before, the corridor was empty. There were some murmuring signs of life from the other rooms but no one wandering around. A hunted feeling settled over Chirp's shoulders, making them tight with a tension Chirp could not quite explain.

This time, the hallway ended in a small flight of stairs with a door at the top that light emanated around. From the other side, Chirp could hear footsteps as they pressed their auditory sensor to the hardwood panel.

Footsteps and voices. The Ringmaster's voice, in particular. They took a moment to consider their options. Return to their cell. Go back and tell Amara that they had failed again. *Or* push through and see if there was a way out on the other side of the door.

Ultimately, there was no choice at all. The door opened with the soft creak of hinges in need of oiling, and Chirp was able to peek out onto the deck of the ship, where the Ringmaster was meeting with a small cluster of people. His many-ringed fingers twisted and turned in the light as he spoke, emphasizing words like "matched set" and "contract." All words Chirp was sure he had used to get them to sign their life away.

But Chirp couldn't focus on any of that. Not even a little bit. Because across the deck, amongst the small collection of people who the Ringmaster was trying to con into being his prisoners, was a man that nearly matched the image of Amara in Chirp's mind. The color of his eyes was different, but the shape was the same. And his nose almost perfectly mirrored Amara's. Which was strange because Amara's face was just something Chirp had made up, right? Unless it wasn't. Unless it was something Chirp had gathered from a memory. A memory of this man, perhaps.

The Ringmaster turned, his face in profile, and Chirp realized that if they could see his face, then he could see them. So they dipped farther into the shadows, pulling the door closed, and rushed back down the corridor toward their room. They would try again come nightfall.

# TEN
## BREND

One would think fear would make for a deterrent, something to keep Brend from trying again, but it turned out to be quite the opposite. In fact, it turned out to be a motivator. The adrenaline rush had been the kind of kick to the gut he couldn't ignore, and once he had a taste of freedom—and all that it entailed—the walls of his mother's castle felt stifling by comparison. The rules she'd put in place to "protect" him were restrictive and controlling. Every day in the interim, it felt like his world was closing in around him, little by little. There would be nothing left of it before long. Every inch of his time would be strictly regimented by his mother, and when that was done, how much of *Brend* would be left? Would he even be his own person anymore?

"You almost died," Clancy felt the need to remind him whenever he saw Brend's leg jittering just so. Which was more and more frequent as the days wore on.

Discontent sat abuzz under Brend's skin. Always just below the surface. Fear, but not fear of what had almost happened—fear of the sameness of his days, of the regularity he was forced to abide by, of the mundanity, shimmered across his skin. Making it too tight. A noose that would one day cut off his air supply entirely. Surely that was a worse death than falling off a building.

"No," Brend corrected, his voice a little strangled from the way he was forcing it to remain even. He didn't want to let on just how excited he was by the prospect of what had almost happened. Didn't want Clancy to see that he'd created a monster. Not that Clancy didn't already know. He wasn't an idiot. He could see the way Brend was fidgety, high-strung, the days endlessly boring and making him jump at every possible sound. Plus, they'd talked about it a couple of times already. Because Brend and Clancy talked about every-thing. After a long moment of trying to control his rabbiting heart, Brend whispered, "I almost *lived*."

Clancy's sigh was so loud, it sounded like a howling wind, battering against the outside of the castle, threatening cold air and colder toes. He lifted one hand to rub at the space between his brows, his eyes squeezing shut. "I'm not taking you back out there."

"Then I'll just go by myself." Brend shrugged, taking a too-big bite from his breakfast and cringing at how the porridge burned the roof of his mouth. "I don't need your permission to go places, I'm the prince."

"No. But you do nee—"

"If you say my mother's, I'm going to dump this entire bowl on your head. And I'll warn you, it is very hot, Clancy." Brend pointed his spoon at his personal guard and was grati-fied when Clancy held up his hands in surrender. "Besides," he continued, taking another big bite of too-hot porridge that scalded his gums—it was better than having to actually taste the stuff, "if I'm to be king, shouldn't I know my kingdom?"

Clancy frowned, his face going pinched and thoughtful.

Brend considered this progress and kept pushing. "What

kind of king doesn't know his kingdom or his people? How can I make laws for my people without—"

"All right. All right. I get the point you're trying to make." Clancy groaned, scrubbing at his face with both hands now. Brend had clearly given him a headache, but he didn't exactly have much sympathy for the other man. After all, Clancy could come and go as he pleased. His whole life had not been the same set of walls seen day in and day out. And one day, Brend was sure of it, Clancy would fall in love with someone else and he would leave these walls forever. Brend would be alone then, with nothing and no one on his side. And he needed to take advantage of the one friend he had before—

His inner ramblings were cut short by the press of a finger to the skin between his eyebrows. Brend blinked at Clancy, who was looking at him with an expression that could only be described as understanding. It sent Brend's innards wriggling in a way he decided he'd best not think about, lest he be tempted to pull Clancy down into his lap.

"No more scheming. You already got what you wanted."

"I'm not scheming." Brend huffed, swatting Clancy's hand away, much to Clancy's obvious delight, as a moment later he was chuckling softly. A sound so warm and lovely that Brend couldn't find it within himself to be angry about being laughed at. "Just thinking."

"Well, stop it. It's distracting," Clancy teased, leaning in to press a kiss to Brend's still furrowed brow before pushing to his feet. "I'm going to go get things ready. You finish your breakfast, and don't forget to take your medicine."

"Yes, yes. I remember." Waving him away, Brend eyed the softly glowing liquid that his mother foisted upon him every day. It was in a small juice glass, set just beside the orange juice that had been served with his breakfast. And if it weren't for the glowing, it might have just looked like milk.

But Brend knew better. The door shut softly behind Clancy, and Brend rose, taking the glass with him to pour it into a plant in the corner of his sitting room. He couldn't afford to be sleepy if they were going out into the city again.

"NO WANDERING OFF THIS TIME," Clancy said, a distinctly worried note to his voice. He was nervous. His hand over-warm where it rested in Brend's, his fingers trembling just so. Not enough for Brend to call it quits on this whole thing, but enough for Brend to notice. Maybe he should have taken pity on the poor man. He *was* putting Clancy in a distinctly uncomfortable spot. But then that meant Brend would be locked up again. And the need for air that was not filtered and homogenized by the castle had made it feel like Brend was living under water for the last few days. He couldn't pass up this chance, not if he wanted to survive.

"Wasn't it *you* who wandered off last time?" Brend asked before he could think about whether it was a good idea or not. Based on the narrowing of Clancy's eyes and the pursing of his lips, it hadn't been a good idea. *So, sarcasm is out for the remainder of this trip, noted.* "Sorry. Sorry."

Clancy nodded, his hand tightening around Brend's, leading him down through the servant passages to the kitchen at the back of the castle. People slipped past them, hardly giving the prince and his personal guard a second glance. Brend supposed it helped that they had spent a fair amount of time playing hide and seek in these very passages growing up. The servants were used to seeing them. In fact, there had been a time when other children had accompanied them on those games. When Brend had enough friends to have a whole game of tag in the tunnels, the tight space echoing with life. It didn't do that anymore. Now the only echoes were silence and footsteps.

"Where are you taking me this time?" Brend murmured as the door to the stables came into view. Looking over his shoulder, Brend checked to make sure they hadn't drawn any attention to themselves as Clancy pushed the door open. But no one had so much as blinked at their escape out into the open air of the courtyard beyond. Sucking in a breath of air so humid it burned his lungs and left him lightheaded, Brend let Clancy set the pace as they made their way across the courtyard to the back gate reserved for deliveries.

"It's a surprise," was Clancy's only answer, the words rushed and almost breathy with something that might have been excitement or fear. Brend wasn't sure which, and he didn't have time to examine it, as a moment later, Clancy pulled him out into the dirty alley that ran behind the castle and beyond, into the capital city, where all words were eaten up by the echoing of their hurried footsteps bouncing off the surrounding buildings, then by the sounds of a city full of people once they had reached the more inhabited parts.

What felt like forever later, Clancy pulled Brend from the shadows of an alley into the rush of a wide-open space that could only be described as a town square. But Brend knew it couldn't be one, as they hadn't left the city. The surrounding buildings were smaller, newer, likely built within the last few decades. And as the sun faded over the horizon, light glowed from lanterns on the awnings, casting the whole area in a golden hue that made it feel distinctly magical.

Music floated from somewhere amongst the crowd of people in the square, the notes rising above the soft buzz of conversation. And at the very center, a small group had taken to dancing in a circle to the tune, their steps lively, their faces bright.

Brend didn't realize he'd stopped entirely in the way of

foot traffic until Clancy gave his hand another little tug, and he stumbled forward. Clancy caught him before he could go sprawling and pulled them both off to one side so the people behind them could get past, but Brend's eyes never left the dancers. He'd been to balls, of course—that was part of his job as a prince, to attend balls and make his mother look good by being just as handsome and untouchable as everyone always said he was. But this was entirely different. The people who danced at balls always seemed stiff and almost still, even for all that they were moving through the steps. Like they were made of stone instead of flesh and bone. The people dancing in the square were so very *alive*. It made Brend ache all over to be a part of it.

"Would you care to dance?" Brend asked, turning his head up to smile brilliantly at Clancy. He took a step back, pulling his hand away from Clancy's to hold it out to him in the way that would be proper for someone asking for a dance, his form bowing a little.

Gray eyes flicked from the extended hand to Brend's cane, then up to his face. Clancy's expression did something complicated, like when he calculated the risk of a maneuver in training. Then he made up his mind, a shy little smile pulling up one corner of his lips, and took Brend's hand. "Only if you let me lead."

"Pffft. I don't think so." Brend snorted, dragging him in close by his hand until their chests pressed together, then swept him out into the crowd beyond, moving too quickly for anyone to get a good look at Brend's face once his hood fell away. The cobbles were uneven, but Clancy was used to providing support for Brend when he needed it, and between the two of them, Brend would wager they made quite the sight. Honestly, he didn't care. He didn't care what anyone thought. If he stumbled and looked silly. Or didn't really know the steps. The warm, humid air burned his lungs, and his hip ached with the activity, but there was freedom in this dance, *so much* freedom. It hummed through his veins, brushed along his skin, raised the hairs on the back of his neck. Brend felt alive, maybe for the first time in his entire life, and he couldn't imagine sharing this moment with anyone else.

He tilted his head back, red hair falling away from his face, to smile brilliantly up at Clancy. Who was looking back with that steady but sure smile of his. The one Brend found himself daydreaming idly over whenever his lessons grew too boring. Brend's heart did a threatening little stutter in his chest, and his foot trod on Clancy's toe, but the other man just laughed, shaking his head. Clancy's gray eyes sparkled with mirth, and Brend forgot how to breathe. He'd known, for some time now, that he loved Clancy, perhaps more than Clancy could ever love him. But that fact had never sat so close to the skin before as it did now. Threatening to rub Brend raw. Still, he couldn't take his eyes off of Clancy as they spun round and round at the center of the square. Couldn't help the smile that split his face.

But dances, like all good things, had to come to an end, and eventually, the song wound down. The dancers slowed to a stop and clapped for the band as the people of the square gradually started to disperse. An expression crossed Clancy's face that Brend couldn't hope to understand, for he'd never seen it there before.

"We should get back," Clancy said, his breath a little short, but one hand was firm around Brend's fingers while the other reached to tug Brend's hood back into place.

"Yes, I suppose we should." Brend took one last look around the square, hoping to burn it into his memory for the days to come when he would remain trapped in the castle.

The feeling of freedom lingering on his skin even as he let Clancy guide him back the way they'd come.

The servant passages were oddly devoid of servants upon their return, but Brend had a hard time caring as he tried to swallow past the smile that had overtaken his face and not let go. He didn't know that it ever would. His cheeks would be aching for weeks after as the memory slowly became worn and faded with his pulling it from its place amongst the small pile of happy ones he had. Creased and dulled with age, but no less beautiful.

"When do you think we'll be able to go again?" Hushed and hopeful, Brend's tone was fragile, timid. Because he thought he already knew the answer. Even for all that there had been no incidents this time. That he had proven to Clancy that he could go out without getting into trouble. Clancy couldn't continue to take the risk. "Maybe next time—"

"There will be no next time," an all too familiar voice said from the darkness of Brend's sitting room. The light flickered on to reveal his mother sitting on the chaise, her lips pursed in displeasure.

Brend's gaze flicked from his mother to Clancy, whose eyes had lowered, head bowed, dark curls falling into his face, guilt lining every single feature. "Clancy? Did you—Did you tell her?"

The way Clancy dropped Brend's hand like it burned him was answer enough. He had been betrayed by the only person he'd thought truly cared for him in this prison he called home. An ache started up beneath his breastbone, sharp and throbbing, and Brend wondered for an idle moment if that's what heartbreak felt like, and if it would ever go away. It took everything he had to not rub at the spot where the pain resided, to not let it show on his face. He'd have time to cry about Clancy's betrayal later. For now, he had to defuse this situation. He had to convince his mother that she didn't need to do anything drastic.

"Mother," Brend murmured, turning his pleading gaze to her and stepping forward. "Please, nothing happened. I was safe. And—"

Queen Eloise rose from her seat, her chin held high and her eyes hard. "You are bound to the castle from now on, Brend."

"Wha—what?" He didn't understand what that meant, but a heaviness spread across his skin, weighing down his bones, sticking his feet to the castle floor. *Magic.* His mother had used *magic* against him. "Mother . . . What—what have you *done*? How could you?"

"I have done what I needed to, son." She stepped forward, putting her hand on his shoulder as he hunched inward, trying to alleviate the weight of the spell. He wondered what creature she'd ordered to cast it and if they had done so willingly. Probably. An Enchanted would love knowing they had been able to use magic against the prince of Daiwynn, wouldn't they? "Get some rest. You've had a long night."

She was gone again before Brend could sort out the words jumbled together in his head. Brend fell to his knees and released the most inhuman whimper he thought he'd ever heard with his own ears. His eyes burned with tears that he did everything in his power to suck back as the walls closed in on him again.

Clancy stepped forward, his hand outstretched. Brend could see him out of the corner of his eye, moving slowly so as not to spook him. "Brend, I—"

"Enough, Clancy," Brend growled, refusing to lift his head and look at the man he had thought of as friend—a lover. His next word left him like a broken thing, ragged around the edges. "*Enough.*"

Drawing in a breath, Clancy dropped his hand to his side

and murmured a quiet, "Good night, Your Highness" before leaving Brend to grieve the freedom he had not even quite tasted.

# ELEVEN
## CHIRP

T he circus was a breathtaking flurry of activity. Every door on the ship was flung open wide, the performers mingling and gossiping so loudly that Chirp could hardly think through the noise of it, their auditory sensors on overload. There had not been a time in recent memory when they had been so surrounded by life and noise. It was overwhelming, too much, almost to the point of being painful, but also so very *beautiful*. So many bright colors. So many twittering voices. How could Chirp ever hope to focus on a single thing?

"Is that what you're wearing?" a young woman with bright blue hair asked. Over her shoulder, Chirp could see into the small room that had obviously been designated for the girl and her companion, a tall, dark young woman who was eying Chirp with enough suspicion to make Chirp want to cower. Their hands, still hard metal, twitched to cover ears that were nonexistent, to duck away from the pair.

"I feel like the right answer is probably no?" Chirp asked instead, looking down at themselves to study the shift again. It was the only thing the Ringmaster had given them, even though he planned for them to perform in the circus for the queen to garner the prince's attention. But then, they supposed he had been quite busy the last couple of days with his new toys. The young women before Chirp were two such toys. "This is all I have."

"That's all you have." The dark-haired girl curled her lip, her brown eyes flicking past Chirp to something over their shoulder, maybe the door across the hall. Two men, an android, and another woman—the rest of the blue-haired girl's group, presumably—had all crammed themselves into the room opposite. Chirp wasn't sure why, but seeing the mess that had become the young women's room, they thought they might understand. "That's all they have, Felly."

Felly wrinkled her nose, a short lock of blue hair falling into her eyes as she looked Chirp over again before nodding to herself. "Well that just won't do, will it? Come in, come in. We'll get you fixed up."

Felly reached for Chirp's wrist, and Chirp recoiled, backing up half a step to get out of her reach. "No. I'm all right. Really."

"Nonsense. Let me and Drea fix you up. It'll be quick, we promise." Felly reached again, and Chirp retracted themselves farther, evading her searching fingers.

Their heel caught on something, then they were stumbling, balance upended by a rug or a bit of uneven floor, arms pinwheeling. Felly lunged, trying to catch them, but there would be no saving Chirp. They could see it as the ceiling tilted, the floor coming up to meet them too fast and too hard. It would dent them. Damage their hardware and probably shake something loose. They would need repairs. And that would set them back. Make them unable to perform in the show for the queen. Then what?

"Woah," a voice called, and a set of big hands were on Chirp's shoulders, righting them again. They looked back to see that one of the men from across the hall had caught them, his blank eyes blinking forward, unseeing. But the small android was at his side, its arms held up as if to help catch Chirp. "Felicity, what did Rose tell you about bothering the locals?"

"Not to," Felly—Felicity—mumbled, shrinking in on herself, making her seem all the slighter for it.

"They weren't bothering me," Chirp defended, stepping away from the man and turning so they could see him better instead of having to look at him over their shoulder. He looked so very familiar. Like someone Chirp had seen in a dream once. Someone from a memory that had grown so faded and worn, the face was blurred. But also . . . different. Which made absolutely no sense. They shook themselves. "They were just trying to help."

"Right. Of course they were," he said, but his tone was disbelieving, his eyes narrowed even though they didn't focus on the two young women, who had stepped back into their room as if they might hide away from his stare. One dark brow raised in question, and Drea let out a little grumble.

"Come on, Felly, let's stop bothering the nice droid. We've got work to do getting ready." Drea pulled Felicity into their room again and shut the door behind them in Chirp's face.

The sound of the door closing felt like the slamming and locking of a gate. It reverberated through Chirp's auditory sensors, bouncing off the inside of their head. Reminding them that, for all they could pretend to be like the others, they never *would* be. They were alone. Alone and trapped. And they would continue to be alone and trapped until they had done what the Ringmaster wanted them to do. That was all there was to it.

"Sorry about them," the man offered, taking a step back into his own room and scrubbing at the back of his neck. "They're young and excitable."

"They really weren't bothering me." But even as Chirp said it, they could tell this man didn't care what Drea and Felicity were trying to do. And he wasn't listening to what Chirp had to say about the matter. He was distracted, his mind elsewhere. Probably wherever he and his people planned to go when they left the circus. Because they, hopefully, had been wise enough to not sign their entire lives away to the Ringmaster. Chirp thought to ask—they thought to stand in the hall and see just how many of the Ringmaster's performers he'd taken full advantage of. But they knew the answer. They knew that it was only the truly lonely and lost—the desolate—and this man and his people weren't there, not yet. They just needed temporary work.

Before anything else could be said, before Chirp could make any more of a fool of themselves in front of this oddly familiar man, they shook their head and took a step back toward the quieter part of the ship, the permanent quarters, their prison. "I should get back to my room and finish getting ready for the show."

Then they fled, their feet too loud against the floorboards and echoing in the emptiness of the Ringmaster's permanent collection. These, Chirp had discovered, were the rooms where others like themselves lived. Where the Ringmaster kept his experiments, out of sight and out of mind from his more . . . *fleshy* employees. Probably for the best, they reflected; they didn't need people gawking at them or feeling bad for them the way Felicity and Drea seemed to. No. It was better if they escaped to the underbelly of the ship and hid away. Better if they didn't say anything outside of performances and pretended that all of this was somehow normal.

It wasn't. And it never would be, they realized, not if they did what Amara told them to. Not if they didn't give the Ringmaster what he wanted. Because there was no escape, there was no way out. And ultimately, Chirp realized, their circuits buzzing like their pulse might if they were human, they *were* selfish. Like most people.

They burst into the Ringmaster's office a moment later and found him sitting behind his desk, his head dipped over the papers he was working on—plans for the queen's show, no doubt. Without lifting his head, he grumbled, "This had better be important."

"I'd like to take you up on your offer," Chirp said, the words rushed and breathy, which was strange because they had no need of air like a person might. But it seemed some things could not be logic-ed out of them, and they had always been more humanoid than android, even before, when they had lived . . . somewhere else. Somewhere full of books? Somewhere that had a friend? The memory was murky, and it made a grinding sound come from Chirp's inner hardware. The gears had a hard time keeping up with the power it took to remember that place.

They thought to push harder, to latch on to the memory and keep it forever, but the Ringmaster was looking at them expectantly, his brows raised in question. He must have said something.

"Huh?" *Elegant, as ever Chirp.*

"I said, what offer?" the Ringmaster repeated, his tone hedging on impatience. Chirp was treading on thin ice. There would be time to delve deeper into their memories later, after they had signed over their soul and vowed to do something they didn't even know if they actually could. Chirp had never killed anyone before, not that they remembered, but if it was some stranger or their own freedom? Well. They *were* selfish.

"I'll assassinate the prince if you give me my humanity and my freedom." A rawness settled into Chirp's throat that made absolutely no sense. It was not soft and fleshy, it could not possibly be raw. But it was like their software didn't remember that. Like their software hadn't caught up with the fact that they had gone back to being a robot at some point. Maybe it never would. Maybe it wouldn't have to. Not if the Ringmaster was going to give them back their humanity. Not if they killed the prince.

"'Humanity' is such a strange word, isn't it?" The Ringmaster pushed back from his desk, the wheels of his chair screeching with effort as he rose to make his way to the filing cabinet in the corner. It was such a strangely mundane movement that Chirp found themselves completely enraptured by it. Normally, he would just snap whatever he needed to himself, magic expended to prove how powerful he was. But they supposed he didn't need that here. He held all the cards, and he knew it. "You aren't really *human*, you know that, right? None of us in my circus are."

Chirp let out a soft whistle of annoyance, and if they had eyes, they probably would have rolled them. "Whatever I am, then, return me to it. Give me my freedom and return me to it, and I'll do whatever you ask."

A soft chuckle left the Ringmaster, and he shook his head as he dug through the filing cabinet. "You shouldn't say things like that. It's dangerous to promise a magical being anything they want in exchange for something so small."

"It's not small to me." Chirp was breathless with desperation, their fingers digging into the hard exoskeleton on their arms as they tried to hold themselves together, to keep from reaching for the Ringmaster and shaking him until his teeth rattled. There was a feeling in their gut, a twisting, turning of betrayal, when they thought about what they'd tell Amara upon returning to their rooms. But it made no difference. Because they would be free. They had to be. What other choice did they have? Die? Like this? No. That was not an option.

"No, I suppose it's not." The Ringmaster tsked softly and returned to his desk, a folder smacking loudly on the surface as he gestured Chirp forward. "But then, what would you know about the vastness of our world?" he murmured to himself, grabbing a pen from the cup on his desk. "Sign here."

"Sign what?" Chirp leaned over the desk to look down at the contract. It was a blank sheet of paper with two lines at the bottom. Unease crawled through them, making the joints of their fingers stiff, in need of oiling. "Chirp isn't my real name."

"No. But I already have your true name. I don't need it right now. I just need your intent." The Ringmaster wiggled the pen in front of Chirp's face, a sing-song quality to his voice. Like he was luring in a child. Maybe he was. Chirp had no idea how old they were—only the Ringmaster would know that. Only the Ringmaster would know anything.

"Will I get my memories back?" Chirp asked, the pen held too tightly between metal fingers, where it hovered above the paper, ink threatening to drip off the tip of it down onto the sea of blankness.

"What do you need those old things for?" With a tilt of his head, the Ringmaster's smile looked that much more twisted. Broken and unnatural. "They'll only make you sad."

"Is that the trade?" It wasn't really going to stop them from signing, because their freedom felt imperative now. Like they wouldn't survive without it. What were a few memories in service of that? What was someone else's life in service of that? Nothing, in Chirp's mind.

*You're not selfish, are you?* They remembered the old woman asking again, but even those words didn't still their hand as it lowered to rest against the paper, preparing to sign. "My memories for this deal? Nothing's free with you."

The smile ticked up higher on the Ringmaster's face, eating up so much of it that Chirp swore if it grew any larger, it would swallow him whole. Would there be anything left of him after that happened? Chirp didn't think they wanted to find out. "You have grown clever in the time you were away, haven't you, Chirp?"

"I wouldn't know. I don't remember."

A bark of a laugh left the Ringmaster, his eyes bright with some strange sharpness that Chirp didn't *want* to understand. Cruelty lined every inch of this man, and they didn't think staying under his thumb one moment longer was wise. What would he do to them if they didn't fulfill their end of the deal? What had he done to them already that he had erased from their memory stores? A chill ran up their circuits, making them shudder. "Just sign the papers, Chirp. I have things to do. You're either in or you're out."

*In*, Chirp decided, then dropped the point of the pen to the paper, signing a name they didn't recognize across the line and didn't have time to read before the Ringmaster scooped it up, and it disappeared entirely, replaced by a heavy-looking golden key.

"Excellent. This is the key to your dressing room. I'd suggest you go get acquainted with your things. We have a show to put on in a couple of days." He shoved the key across the desk but didn't wait for Chirp to take it before he returned to whatever work he'd been dealing with beforehand.

The key scraped against the desk, too loud, as Chirp scooped it up and, without thinking about the movement, stumbled out into the corridor. The Ringmaster's office door clicked decisively closed, leaving Chirp in the darkened hall with naught but a key for direction and a weight in their midsection that they didn't think they'd ever experienced before.

They looked down at the key, turning it this way and that, blinked hard, and frowned.

Fingers. Hands. Skin.

They were humanoid again. Maybe forever this time. And that was enough to bury the anxiety of what they'd have to do, at least for the moment.

# TWELVE

## BREND

Brend didn't think he'd ever be over the betrayal and the indignity of his most trusted friend, his closest confidant, someone who he'd thought *loved* him, telling his mother that they had been out of the castle visiting with the commonfolk.

"You can't be angry with me forever," Clancy said. He was lying on the chaise across from where Brend had curled into one of the big wing-backed armchairs to read.

There was something languid and beautiful about the way Clancy splayed himself that could only be intentional. Which just made the pose even more annoying to Brend because he knew Clancy was trying to draw him back in. Trying to return them to how they had been not but a week ago. But the truth of it was, Brend didn't think he could ever go back. He couldn't forgive what Clancy had done. Something between them was intrinsically broken the moment he'd realized Clancy had been the one to tell his mother.

Instead of answering, Brend pointedly turned the page of his book and didn't look up from it. Clancy was just looking for attention, as he did sometimes when he was feeling bad about himself. But if he wanted that, then maybe he shouldn't have tattled on Brend like a five-year-old who'd broken his mother's favorite vase. Except worse, because in doing so, he had broken Brend's trust. A fragile thing that Brend learned long ago not to bestow upon many.

"Come on, Brend. You know I just did it to keep you—"

"Your Highness," Brend corrected, his tone stiff, bitter. "You will refer to me as *Your Highness*. And as my personal guard, I don't think it appropriate for you to be quite literally lying down on the job."

Clancy stared at him a moment longer, his gaze heavy on Brend's skin in a way it never had been before. Something assessing and calculating there that Brend didn't care for, had never before associated with Clancy. Maybe that had been his mistake. Maybe seeing Clancy as something other than a tactician, whose every word was calculated and contrived to have the most effect, had been Brend's miscalculation. He'd genuinely thought Clancy *liked* him, maybe even loved him, although perhaps that bit had been wishful thinking. He'd thought that their relationship was something untouched by Clancy's desire to climb the ranks within the castle. He'd been a fool, and that hurt impossibly more. An ache in his belly, making it hard to eat or sleep.

Forcibly turning another page in the book on his lap, Brend tried not to shift under Clancy's searching gaze. He stared down at the pages under his nose, not really seeing the words but knowing that if he looked at Clancy, he'd cave. Brend didn't want to cave. He wanted to stay mad at Clancy until the end of time. Until the pain of what he had done had scarred and left behind a wound that ached when it rained. Until there was nothing left of the pain except the memory of where it had been. Maybe then he'd be able to forgive Clancy, but likely not even then. Because Brend had learned his lesson.

"Very well," Clancy said with a sigh, pushing to his feet, "if that's how you want it, Your Highness."

"It is." Brend hoped that would be the last time he had to

talk to Clancy about this. That those words would be the end of this whole discussion. But he knew better than that. Clancy could be persistent when he was of a mind to be, and Brend wished he didn't like that so very much about him. Wished that there were *many* things he didn't like so very much about Clancy. This would be a lot easier if there were.

Narrowing his gray eyes, Clancy took another long look at Brend, his mind working over something, jaw grinding as he seemed to chew on the words he wanted to say.

Brend held his breath, preparing himself to react badly to whatever next came from Clancy's beautiful mouth, no matter how kind and sweet it might be. He couldn't afford to back down now. He couldn't afford to accept an apology, forgive and forget. Because he couldn't forget. *Ever.*

Whatever Clancy had been about to say, he swallowed, letting out a long breath through his nose, and Brend saw him nod out of the corner of his eye. His hands fidgeted as he straightened his clothes, then Clancy stepped forward, past Brend, and disappeared from view. A moment later, Brend heard the door to his chambers close softly.

The anger and self-righteousness that had been keeping Brend upright left him in a rush. He slumped forward, pressing his forehead to his book, and tried to breathe around the broken shards in his chest. How long, he wondered, would he have to live with those ragged pieces of himself? How long before they healed over and calloused? Not soon enough.

Brend went to bed early that evening, with nothing better to do and no one to speak to. His book lay forgotten on the armchair as Brend pulled the blankets up over his head, wishing not for the first time in his life that he simply didn't exist. That he'd never been born. Wouldn't everyone be better for it?

THE FOLLOWING morning was much the same. Loneliness clung to the walls of Brend's chest, making it hard to force himself to sit up, even as a servant brought breakfast and set it up on the little table in his sitting room. Brend watched them through the door, flitting about, murmuring softly. He thought to ask if he could eat in bed but knew better than that. Clancy, Mother, they wouldn't allow it; they never had before.

So he dragged himself from his bed, the covers still draped across his shoulders so that he looked more like a walking pile of blankets than a prince, his tangled red hair falling into his face. Through the curtain of it, he could just see a shining piece of paper on the table next to his breakfast tray, the early morning sun bouncing off the clean white material, washing the chaise beside the table in its pale light. Scrubbing at his face, Brend flopped down onto the chaise and took a long drag from the glass of juice sitting on the tray before he finally allowed his stiff fingers to reach for the paper.

It nearly slipped through his grasp when his eyes finally focused on the swirling letters printed on the crisp white page.

"Clancy!" With trembling fingers, Brend pushed his long red curls from his face and looked to the door. It creaked open, and Clancy stepped through, a little smile playing at the corner of his lips. He knew what he was about, which didn't make the excitement buzzing under Brend's skin lessen, although he wished it did. Wished that this was not enough to numb the pain in his chest. But even as he choked out the words "A circus?" he knew that it was.

"A circus," Clancy confirmed, that twitch of his lips ticking, threatening to turn into a real smile.

It was a distraction, Brend knew, he wasn't a fool. But he couldn't seem to ignore it, and besides, would it be so bad if he forgave Clancy? Would it be so bad if he let the excitement and the joy humming through his veins numb the heartbreak? He could forgive Clancy this, couldn't he? It wasn't like Clancy had done it to hurt him. He'd done it to protect Brend. That was forgivable.

"I'd suggest you eat your breakfast. We've much to do before the first show this evening."

"Is this your idea of an apology?" The words slipped from Brend's mouth, only half considered, but he had to know. It was working, *of course* it was working. Because even as the walls of the castle pressed in around him, a distraction provided a way out of his own head, if just for the moment. A way to escape himself, if just for a few hours.

"Is it working?" With his head tilted, Clancy looked so young, his dark hair falling into his eyes. Young and deceptively sweet. The ragged pieces in Brend's chest, the remnants of his heart, gave a pulsing ache, a reminder. But his fingers twitched to reach for Clancy, and he supposed that was answer enough.

"I suppose it is." Brend dropped the invitation back onto the table, and returned to his breakfast, tearing his gaze away from Clancy. He couldn't look at Clancy as his shoulders sunk in relief and that half smile took over his face. It hurt too much, like staring at the sun.

"Don't forget to take your medication, Your Highness," Clancy murmured gently and settled into a chair across from Brend to keep him company while he ate. A welcome presence, even for all that Brend had hated the very sight of him the day before.

MEALS EATEN, lessons done, wardrobe decided, Brend joined his mother, Clancy, and a selection of visiting nobles in the main hall for the show. It had been transformed into a circus tent, the gilded walls hidden by lush red curtains that went all the way up to the vaulted ceiling but didn't hide the skylights. The moon waned above them, bright, the stars shimmering like gems, casting the entire place in a light that made the evening seem that much more magical.

Along one wall, someone had set a short row of his mother's most comfortable chairs. The cushioned ones that always made Brend feel like he was sinking into a cloud. He settled against the deep blue velvet, letting it hug him and relieve the pressure on his hip. Clancy sat behind him, a comforting presence at his back. A reminder that Brend was protected.

The lights dimmed and brightened, a subtle sign that the show was about to start, and Brend shifted in his chair, getting more comfortable as the hum of gossip faded around him. Then the music started, low at first, like a rumble of thunder in the distance, only felt through his bones instead of being heard. But it grew steadily with each tick of the clock, and the lights flicked off entirely, casting the room in the silvery light of the moon.

"What's going on?" one of the nobles whispered, but Brend couldn't tell which one in the dark. Another shushed them, and they fell silent once more as the music rose above the sound of Brend's pulse racing in his ears.

Nothing happened for what felt like a small eternity, only cut by a quiet gasp and the upturn of every head in the room. He followed the eyes of those around him and saw the acrobat descending from the ceiling, their body twisted up in ribbons but little else. The ribbons reached up so high that there was no way to tell where they began, making it look like they were floating in mid-air. Brend's breath caught in his throat, his eyes burning from the beauty of the sight before him.

The music hit a crescendo, and nothing else existed as the body wrapped in ribbons tumbled down from the ceiling. Another startled gasp left the crowd before the figure came to a halt, hanging lazily for a moment, spinning until Brend could see the serene look on their round face, their eyes shining in the low light.

"Heavens," Brend rasped, leaning forward in his chair to get a better look at them.

"Beautiful, aren't they?" someone murmured, and Brend would have turned to see who it was, but he couldn't tear his eyes away as the figure twisted and turned, climbing back up seemingly without trying. If he could have, he would have seen the man in the top hat, the Ringmaster, taking a step closer to him, heedless of those around them who had been lost to the spell of the acrobat.

"They are." It was the truth, perhaps truer than anything else Brend had said in his entire life. His next words didn't even feel like his own, but they were said in his voice, so he knew they must be. "I'd love to meet them."

"That can be arranged."

# THIRTEEN
## CHIRP



You have an admirer," the Ringmaster said from the door to Chirp's dressing room. It was a tiny space, smaller even than their cell had been. Hardly big enough for the tiny vanity shoved into the corner and the little stool which Chirp had pulled from beneath it. But it was a space of their own, and it had their name on the door, making it more theirs than anything had ever been before. The vanity was littered with cosmetics they couldn't hope to understand but that one of the other performers had helped them apply. The Ringmaster's patience with their silence stretched thin, and he asked, "Did you hear me?"

"I did." An admirer didn't matter at all to them. They didn't want one. If they could simply go about performing and draw no attention to themselves, that would be best. That's why they had agreed to go first in tonight's act, hoping that by the end of it, they would be forgotten completely. Things would be better that way, they decided. Then they could slip through the castle unobserved and do the thing they'd come to do. All of this would be over, finally, and they would be free. What they would do with that freedom, they had not yet decided.

"Do you want to meet them?" the Ringmaster pressed, his posture forced into relaxation where he leaned against the doorframe when Chirp caught a glimpse of him in the mirror. But for all that, his gaze was sharp, cutting. This wasn't a question or a choice; this was an order. If Chirp ever wanted to be free, they would have to play by the Ringmaster's rules, do as he asked. At least until their task was complete.

"Who are they?" Chirp set down the wet cloth they had been readying to clean their face, straightened their posture, and turned around to look at the Ringmaster in the doorway. He stood up, the smile cutting across his face sharp enough to slice themselves on. Chirp hated that smile, almost more than they hated the man himself. Because they knew what it meant. Knew the crawl of it. A warning shuddered up their spine.

"Come see," was the Ringmaster's only answer as he stepped back into the darkened corridor. Another order with no option but to rise from their stool and follow him over the threshold into the low light of the hall.

The warmth of sconces shone golden on the red hair of a young man leaning heavily against a cane outside of Chirp's dressing room, and suddenly they felt vastly out of their depth. It was hard to see his freckles in the dimness, but Chirp knew them well enough, had seen them while they were performing. The prince.

"Your Highness," Chirp said, half in disbelief. Were they supposed to curtsy? Bow? Kowtow? They didn't know. All they seemed able to do was stare. He looked impossibly young up close, his eyes so dark, Chirp couldn't even tell their color in this light.

"You two should go." The Ringmaster shooed them toward the door at the other end of the corridor. The one that Chirp knew led out to the courtyard. They weren't sure why he was nudging them that way, and they didn't think they trusted it, but the prince nodded and started walking, clearly expecting Chirp to follow. So, Chirp took one last longing look at the tiny dressing room, and the hope of getting the thick layer of gunk off their face then followed. What else could they do?

Just before they reached the door, Rowan murmured something, his magic sweeping over it, glittering. The prince didn't seem to notice. Maybe his eyes were weak, or maybe it was a typical human reaction, ignoring what he could not explain. Chirp didn't care one way or the other. The sooner they completed their task, the sooner they could escape this horrible place, breathe again outside these suffocating castle walls. The prince reached the door first, stumbling out of it into an alley Chirp was fairly sure was nowhere near the castle at all. They followed behind him and turned just in time to come face to face with the Ringmaster, his expression more serious than they thought they'd ever seen it.

"When you wish to return, use this key in any door." He pressed a key into Chirp's hand, the metal heavy, hot from his magic. Chirp nodded, tucking the key into their pocket, and watched as the door swung closed of its own accord and then disappeared altogether. But not before there was one more whispered command, meant only for Chirp they were sure: "Not yet."

"Well, that was . . ." The prince laughed, breathy and short, making his chest rise and fall at a pace that could not possibly be normal for a human.

Maybe Chirp ought to be worried for his health. But why would they, when they were meant to kill him? *Not yet*, the Ringmaster had said, but soon, they were sure.

"That was something." He laughed again.

"Yes, it was," Chirp agreed and turned toward the alley to gauge where they had been dropped. Not that it would matter; they didn't know anything of this city or, indeed, this kingdom at all. But their feet turned in a direction they thought they knew, familiarity settling into their bones. "This way."

"Where are we going?" the prince asked, stumbling along beside them. Chirp slowed their steps, allowing him to get his footing and keep pace as they headed for the mouth of the alley, but they didn't answer. Because the truth was *they* didn't know where they were going. An answer they didn't think would make the prince feel very safe with them at all.

They reached the mouth of the alley, and Chirp stopped, their eyes narrowing to look this way and that, checking to see if it were safe for them to enter the road on the other side.

After a moment, they decided to go right, following the familiarity in their bones toward . . . what? They just knew that *something* was this way. Something they *knew*. Something they cared for. Home? Maybe. Not that Chirp had ever known one before. But some magic seemed to guide them.

"I'm Brend, by the by," the prince said, still a little breathless with what Chirp hoped was excitement and not fear.

"Huh?" Chirp stopped, their head tilted to one side, eyes going wide with confusion as they tried to process the words the prince had said, but they couldn't. Because surely he wasn't introducing himself, was he?

"Brend, that's my name." The prince smiled, brushing a long strand of curling red hair back behind his ear before he held out a hand. Here, in the brightness of the streetlamps, Chirp could see a constellation of freckles across his cheeks. He was . . . not beautiful, not in the way that Chirp thought a prince ought to be. He did *have* high cheekbones and a strong jaw. He was also rather pale, as it stood, and small—a full head or better shorter than Chirp—only made smaller by how he drew his shoulders in, hunching a little.

"I see." Chirp was unsure what knowing Brend's name had to do with anything. Brend's red brows drew together, causing a wrinkle to form, and an awkwardness settled between them that Chirp decided abruptly they did not like. Instead of addressing it, they spun on their heel and started walking again, expecting Brend to follow.

"It is customary," Brend said around a chuckle, "when someone introduces themselves that you introduce yourself in return."

"Is it?" Chirp was only half paying attention as they looked at the street signs that surrounded them. They didn't recognize any of them, but then, why would they? They did not know anything outside of the circus ship and the few hazy memories they somehow managed to dredge up of rooms full of books. A library maybe. Why should they know this city?

"You're very strange." Brend walked along beside Chirp because, although they decided to ignore his attempts at cordiality, they had not hastened their steps, making it possible for him to keep up. There was no need to be outright mean. "Did you know that?"

"I did not." Biting the inside of their cheek, Chirp took a turn down another street. It was somewhere in this direction. What *it* was, they didn't know, but they knew it was this way. Like their very bones knew the way when nothing else did. "Or, rather, I have never been told before."

"No? Are all your friends like you, then?" Brend tilted his head, his long hair falling into his face.

Chirp wondered if that was annoying to him. They had tied their own long dark hair back in a tight bun to be kept out of their line of vision while they performed. When it *was* free, they hated having it in their face. They had thought this normal. But the prince seemed to spend half of his time brushing it from his eyes like some kind of . . . rogue.

*Rogue.* Where had that word come from? *A book,* Chirp's mind told them, but they could not remember which book, nor could they remember having read it. All they knew was the word "rogue" and the general idea of what it meant.

"I don't have friends," Chirp said, the words springing from their tongue, a truth that didn't sting nearly as much as it likely should have.

Brend stopped in his tracks, and when Chirp looked back to check on him, he was looking at them with eyes so wide, Chirp was sure they could swallow the whole of Daiwynn. His thin mouth had twisted into something that could only be said to be remorse—not that Chirp much understood the emotion, they just knew how to identify it on another's face.

"What?"

"I want to be your friend," Brend said, as if it were that simple. Maybe to him, it was. A prince could be friends with whomever they liked. But Chirp knew better. Because a prince should not be friends with the person who had been hired to kill them.

"I don't think that wise." Chirp turned back to the path, their feet continuing on until they stopped in front of a building half crumbled away, the glass cracked and splintered, likely from the merging of the two realms during the war. No lights were on inside, and Chirp knew without even entering that it was abandoned. Which—Which *hurt*. Their knees trembled beneath them, then gave out entirely, and they sank to the hard cobbles of the street. "They're gone."

"Who's gone?" Brend was at their side, his voice soft. He had come up to stand next to them, not touching, but close enough that Chirp could feel the heat of his side against their own. A comfort that Chirp didn't deserve.

His question registered a moment later, and Chirp tried to put to words the amorphous thing residing in their chest. The misshapen wound had healed over but never closed up. They tried to understand what it was and how to explain it to someone who may have never felt something like it before. And after staying silent for what might have been too long, they found a word for it in their software, a word that encompassed all of what they were feeling.

*Grief.*

Not just for the loss of something but also for the loss of not knowing what it was they had lost. Because Chirp didn't know what they were missing, they just knew the pain it left behind. "I don't know."

Chirp waited a long time for Brend to ask them to explain, for him to poke and prod at the strangely shaped hole inside of them, trying to understand it in a way only an outsider might. But he didn't. Instead, he stood there next to them, his side pressed to theirs, and waited until the moisture had dried from Chirp's face and their knees had begun to ache. He waited in the cold, leaning on his cane, until Chirp rose and met his eyes.

"I don't know the name I was given at birth, not anymore," Chirp said around something that felt wet and wad-like in their throat. Still, they held out their hand, trying to force their face into an expression that might be considered friendly. "But these days, people call me Chirp."

"It's nice to meet you, Chirp." Brend smiled, taking their hand to shake, and Chirp found the misshapen hole inside of their chest shrinking just a little.

# FOURTEEN
## BREND

What happened to them? Brend wanted to ask, to better understand the first person to show him real vulnerability. Even Clancy hadn't ever allowed himself to show weakness before Brend. But he knew that he couldn't ask, couldn't force answers from perhaps the first real friend he'd ever had in his life.

Chirp had given him so much of themselves more than anyone else, showing a courage that Brend knew he'd never have by sharing with a relative stranger. Still, he sucked in a breath, straightened his shoulders, and vowed to do the same once he'd thought of something that was of equal value.

"We should get back," Chirp said, scrubbing at their eyes as if they could hide the tears that had already fallen. Brend had the decency to not mention it. He didn't even reach for his handkerchief as he might have if he came across someone else crying. Tilting back their chin, Chirp ran a hand over their dark hair as if brushing flyaways back into place, but there were none, just the tight pull of a bun wound at the back of their head. "Before the palace guard is raised because I kidnapped the prince."

"You didn't kidnap me." But he helped Chirp to their feet, a little smile tugging at the corner of his lips. He didn't think he'd mind being kidnapped by Chirp. They seemed the type to get up to plenty of trouble—the good kind. "I went willingly."

"That's not how it'll look to them." Starting back the way they came, Chirp looked back at him to offer a flat smile over their shoulder. He wondered if they didn't know how to really smile, or if they only pulled it out for special occasions. Amusing that spending time with the prince of Daiwynn wasn't a special occasion. How much would it take to truly impress someone like Chirp? Maybe he'd endeavor to find out.

They walked in silence for a while, the stillness of the streets a heavy weight that was impossible for him to balance on his shoulders. It hadn't been quiet like this where Clancy had taken him. Those streets had been full of chatter, traffic, *life*. Clancy had shown Brend a world made better for the queen and her rule. A world that was happy and whole. That was not what Chirp was offering. The buildings that surrounded them now were in disrepair, falling down around them, unlivable. Much like the ones near where the wil-o-wisp had lured him.

"Where are all the people?" It was mostly an errant thought. Brend didn't expect Chirp to answer.

Chirp tilted their head, listening to something it seemed, their light brown skin crinkling around their nose as they scrunched it, dark eyes squinting. The pale light of the moon above glinted off an ear full of piercings, more metal than skin and slightly pointed, as they hummed in thought. After some time, they straightened, although they still didn't meet Brend's eyes. "I suppose they're all tucked away in the relative safety of their homes."

"*Relative* safety?"

"Well," Chirp said, licking their lips as if nervous, "how

safe can they really be when MOTHER could barge in at any moment?"

"What?" Stopping in the middle of the uneven street likely wasn't for the best as the dark crawled around them, but those words didn't make sense to Brend. What he'd always known of MOTHER was that they kept people safe. They protected and defended. They didn't– They didn't rip innocent people from their beds. *Did* they? "MOTHER protects people."

Chirp turned to blink at him, a look of something like pity crossing their face, then they shook their head and kept walking, not waiting for Brend. "They protect people like you," they shot over their shoulder.

"What does *that* mean?" Brend sped up, heedless of the ache that settled into his hip from dealing with the uneven pavement of the streets and standing too long, while Chirp had their moment. The shoes he'd been wearing for the performance did absolutely nothing to cushion and support like his boots usually did. The cane was more decoration than function. All in all, not ideal.

"It means"—Chirp squared their shoulders, lifting their chin, like they were readying for a battle that Brend didn't think he'd ever understand or win—"that MOTHER was created to make the Enchanted afraid."

"To keep them in line. To keep them from hurting the mortals," Brend argued back, no heat in his voice. He was willing to have this debate. He didn't think it needed to end in a fight. But there was something combative about Chirp's posture. Something that said they would not be letting Brend simply walk away from this discussion.

Maybe coming out into the city with someone Brend didn't know wasn't his best idea. Maybe they meant to hurt him. He'd been foolish, arrogant to think he was above such things. To think he was untouchable. His hand slipped on his cane, palm made sweaty by fear. Could he even defend himself from Chirp if they tried to attack him? They were taller, more muscular from training as an acrobat, and he had no weapons. He definitely should have thought this through.

"To keep them from hurting the mortals." Chirp snorted, tilting their head back to stare up at the foggy night sky. "You're such a child."

"I am not a child!" But he was, wasn't he? What did Brend know of the world? What did he know of life outside the castle walls? This little jaunt with Chirp was only the third time he'd ever left the safety of his home and the hovering of his mother. He didn't really know what it was like outside of his own life. He didn't know what people were dealing with. How could he?

They had stopped at some point, though Brend hadn't noticed, and Chirp turned to face him. Their dark eyes widened, then narrowed in something that looked like annoyance. Whatever vulnerability they'd shown him before, whatever friendship they might have begun to conjure, it was gone now. Chirp was– Chirp was an Enchanted faced with someone who thought they were dangerous. Brend's breath caught in his chest, threatening to turn into a hiccup.

"You understand very little of your world." Chirp's tone had gone soft, deadly with sympathy. They shook their head, dipping it forward to look at their shoes, now scuffed and dusty from the street. "And I remember very little of my own."

"What does that mean?" How could they not remember their world when they had led him directly to the place that they used to call home? Or so he assumed based on their reaction to the place. It made no sense. For that matter, how could someone know where home was but not know their own name? There was some horrible magic going on here. Something that Brend needed to better understand, to figure out. A mystery.

"Any doorway. Any doorway," Chirp muttered to themselves, their attention already turned from Brend to search their surroundings. They had produced a key from somewhere, the moonlight glinting off it as they fidgeted with it, fingernails tapping against the metal, a soft *tink*ing sound in the otherwise unbroken quiet.

"Ah, here we are." They rushed across the street to a shadowed door, hidden mostly by the crumbling awning above it.

"What are you doing?"

"I'm taking you back, Your Highness," Chirp said, tone gone cold and detached. "This was a mistake." They didn't wait for an argument. They stuffed the key into a lock that looked far too small for it but somehow expanded to fit.

*Magic*. It was *all* magic. The Ringmaster must have been an Enchanted too. How many of the performers were? Did his mother know that? Did Clancy? Did MOTHER? What would they do if they knew? Would they arrest the entire circus? Would they imprison them for infiltrating the castle without letting anyone know? Would they—

"This wasn't a mistake," Brend tried to say, but the words came out more akin to a croak, and Chirp didn't stop to decipher them. They ripped the door open, revealing the corridor Brend had followed them through not but an hour ago. Chirp grabbed him by the wrist and tugged him inside, careful to not let him stumble onto his aching hip, their hand too hot against his night-cooled skin like a burning brand. They dropped it as soon as the door slammed behind them, then fell into a deep bow that felt like a dismissal.

"I'd like to say it has been a pleasure, Your Highness." They were shaking, whether from anger or fear, Brend wasn't sure. Did they know what he was thinking about the circus all being Enchanted? Did they realize the danger Brend posed to them? And what did it mean that even in his own mind, he realized his thoughts *were* dangerous to the person he had hoped to call friend not ten minutes ago? That he realized the knowledge he had could hurt Chirp and the others? Did he *want* to make Chirp afraid? Did he want the Enchanted in his midst to fear him? He didn't . . . he didn't *know*. He'd spent so much of his own life cut off from what lay outside the walls of his home, there was power in knowing he could make someone else feel fear, if just for a moment.

"We both know you'd be lying," Brend tried to joke, but it came out far too stiff, accusatory, and Chirp jerked like they'd been smacked. Their shoulders sank inward, like they were trying to make themselves smaller. Brend had never been hit before, but he recognized the posture from seeing some of the staff in the castle, some of the people who had been punished by his mother over the years.

"We do," Chirp agreed readily, not lifting out of their bow, and the lack of eye contact, the lack of showing Brend if they were serious or teasing, hurt more than anything else possibly could have in that exact moment.

Brend lifted a hand to hide his wince and didn't force any of the words he wanted to say past the tightness in his throat as Chirp turned and retreated to their dressing room. He stood there, holding his mouth shut, until the door closed behind Chirp, leaving him alone in the corridor again, where silence reigned.

Taking a deep breath in through his mouth and exhaling out through his lips, he forced himself to follow the trek he'd taken to get there in the first place, back to the ballroom and then out into the castle at large. Clancy was waiting for him there, a knowing look in his gray eyes, disapproval lining his lips.

"You left again, didn't you? After your mother bound you to the castle." Clancy crossed his arms over his chest, looking down on Brend from his taller height. Brend hated every one of those handful of inches Clancy had on him, more than he hated the ones Chirp had. Because where Clancy used them to his advantage, taking every chance he got to make Brend feel small, Chirp had seemed to shrink in on themselves, trying to make them both the same size. Like they felt gangly, unsure in their body.

There was a story behind that, and although Chirp might hate Brend now, he knew he had to hear it. He had to know all of it. Not because Chirp was beautiful or alluring, or any of that—even if they were—but because Brend had never encountered an actual mystery before. Mysteries didn't happen in real life. Except now, it seemed.

"Clearly it didn't work." Although he wasn't sure why . . . Brend tilted his head back, meeting Clancy's narrowed gaze, defiant. All the while, his stomach turned, his toes curling in his shoes, readying to . . . what? Run? That wouldn't stop Clancy from telling Brend's mother what he'd been up to. That wouldn't stop the inevitable punishment that would follow. No. He supposed there was no way out of this.

"Clearly." Clancy's lips twisted up into a snarl, his gaze going colder than Brend thought he'd ever seen it before. Like Brend finding a loophole was a personal affront.

"Maybe we could just . . . not tell her about this?" Brend asked, hunching forward, his hand tightening on his cane as he peeked up at Clancy through his hair, a hopeful smile playing across his lips. The same smile he'd used on Clancy plenty of other times to get him to agree to something. It would work. It *always* worked before. Why wouldn't it work now?

Clancy let out a long sigh, his face smoothing as he slouched back against the wall. "Oh, all right. But next time, you aren't going alone."

"Deal." Brend grinned, holding a hand out to Clancy. The smile only grew wider when Clancy took it, the heat of his palm warming Brend's clammy fingers and crawling up along his skin. And like that, the air between them cleared.

"It's impossible," Penny said, flopping back against her chair. She looked so tired; they all did.

Persinette had exhaustion sinking into her very bones. It had been a long few days, and they didn't know how many more they had. How long before Eddi made their move and this was all over? How long before the war began and there was no stopping the destruction of their kingdom?

Daiwynn balanced on a knife's edge, the siblings had kept it that way for centuries now, but the limited peace they had found was coming to an end. That was clear in how MOTHER had become more aggressive, how more than one of the smaller towns under Queen Eloise's rule had been razed to the ground.

"It's not impossible," Persinette argued, because what else could she say? She couldn't admit defeat, not yet, not when she was their commander. Not when Manu left her in charge of their ship and their people. "We just haven't found the way in yet."

"The way in," Roy repeated, his own tone flat, lifeless, lost. It landed like a blow to Persinette's chest. She'd thought Roy would be the one who would stay with her the longest on this. Not that anyone was leaving, but their motivation was

127

dwindling along with what hope there was left. Daiwynn *would* fall if she couldn't do something to get them back on track.

"Yes, a way in." Persinette leaned forward, bracing her elbows on her knees as she'd seen Manu do so many times before. She didn't know what the pose was meant to instill in his crew, but she'd seen it work, and she wasn't above trying it now.

"It's not just *a way in* we're looking for, though." Sully hunched over the table in the corner, maps strewn in front of him haphazardly. He'd been staring at those maps for what felt like hours, but he'd yet to offer anything useful.

She wasn't sure how he didn't know where Eddi hid themselves. She'd thought he was one of Eddi's nearest and dearest, their best warrior. Apparently not.

"I was too close to Aggy," Sully said, as if he'd read her mind. Maybe he had—she still wasn't quite clear what powers a kelpie possessed. Sully seemed keen to keep them to himself. "Eddi didn't trust me enough to tell me where their headquarters was."

"Then who *did* they trust with that information?" Kindle scrubbed at her face. She was worn and brittle around the edges, and Persinette could understand why. Rose and Kindle hadn't exactly signed up for this, they'd been dragged into it, enlisted, like Penny.

Everyone else agreed to help the war effort; those two had just wanted to disappear after their trials at the library, to live a peaceful life. But Kindle didn't feel she could when it was her own siblings tearing apart the world they lived in. The responsibility of it all weighed heavily on her, making her shoulders sag a little more every day.

Persinette hoped, for her sake, that this was all done soon.

"What about Warner?" Benard asked, his shrewd eyes glowing just a little brighter as his lips curled back in a snarl.

Fury lit Persinette's veins, making her feel too hot all over at the mere mention of Ivy Warner. But it was a reasonable proposition. Ivy had been one of Eddi's special operatives, given the mission to stop Manu and Persinette any way that she could. Which was the whole root of Persinette's problem with the other witch. "Would it matter if she did have that information? We can't get to her. She joined MOTHER, remember?"

"While I was imbedded in the Uprising I heard she went rogue after the attack on the library," Roy volunteered. He sat up a little, some hope filtering back into his eyes, and as much as Persinette hated this idea, she could see where it might be their only option. Ivy Warner was a vicious, manipulative snake who had teamed up with their enemies the moment it was convenient for her. She would not hesitate to betray them to either or both sides if it got her something she wanted. But she might very well be the only person they knew who had actually been to Eddi's base. "She disappeared during the attack, and MOTHER lost track of her."

"How?" Penny frowned, her wings fluttering behind her in discontent. "I thought they were putting trackers on all of their operatives now."

"The library." Kindle lifted her head from where she'd buried it in her hands to eye all of them. "She used what magic resided in the library."

"There couldn't have been that much left." Sully moved from where he was hunched over the table to lean against the back of Persinette's chair, his words echoing over top of her head, a note of cautious hope in his voice. Persinette hated that. Hated that the hope for their cause rested on someone who had cursed her co-captain, someone who had hurt the one person in the world who had looked at her and seen something more than just a weak, freckled Enchanted.

"There wouldn't have had to be. Not if she was as experienced as you all make her sound. Isn't that right, pixie?" Kindle leaned back on the couch, her arms spreading wide over the back of it so that her fingertips could give Penny's wings a gentle tug, which only made Penny growl and jerk away from her.

"How should I know?" Penny grumbled, curling closer to Roy. Persinette didn't understand Kindle's need to poke and prod and tease now that Rose wasn't around. Maybe it was just how she dealt with stress, or maybe she just wasn't a very nice person, there was no way to tell. And without Agnes, Persinette supposed they needed an instigator in the group. Things had become a little too peaceful, even for her.

"All right then," Persinette said, calling them back to order. "How do we find Ivy Warner?"

"Well that's the easy bit." Sully chuckled, coming around the chair so that Persinette could look at him while he shot her a wide smile full of arrogance.

"And what's the hard bit?" Penny asked.

"Getting into that witch's house." Sully shrugged and turned back to the table of maps.

"Ivy's?" Curiosity curled around the edges of Persinette's tone. It felt like it had been so long since she'd gone on a real adventure, one that didn't have the weight of the world dragging it down. She only wished Manu could have been there with them. It wasn't right to go on adventures without her co-captain. He would be upset that he had missed this.

"No. Old Lady Warner." Sully laughed, like he was in on a particularly good joke. Persinette's gaze flicked around, and she frowned a little. No one else seemed to get it, but Sully didn't seem to care; he was still chuckling to himself, grabbing a map and a bit of parchment. "Can you get me that tracking spell we used to hunt down the circus?"

"Yeah, sure." Kindle rose from her seat, still looking skeptical, and headed off to retrieve the spell book that would help them hunt down Ivy Warner.

A WHILE later found the group sitting cross-legged around a circle Sully had sketched onto the floorboards of the rec room with charcoal. A map sat at the center of the circle, the edges curled with moisture from some unknown source. Sully lit a match, the flame flickering and gleaming in the reflection of his eyes.

"All right, Persi, do your thing." He grinned at her, the flame glowing brighter, or so it seemed.

Pride licked at Persinette's tensed jaw, making her lift her chin a little more. She was the only witch amongst them, the only one able to do spells, and she had grown. Her magic, which had once been an ember, stunted and almost smothered by the restrictions of MOTHER and the belief that she wasn't worth the very space she took up, now burned brighter. Manu had made sure Persinette *knew* her worth, once and for all. Always murmuring words of encouragement and faith. He had said more than once over the last few months that he felt *he* was the real victor in this war, even if they lost Daiwynn in the process. But Persinette knew differently. It was she who had truly won.

"Persi," Benard murmured, nudging her with his elbow, and she nodded curtly.

Murmuring the spell that Kindle had shown her, Persinette let the magic flow through her veins out into her fingertips, where she held a thin strip of paper with Old Lady Warner's name on it. Maeve Warner. A glittering lavender flame caught the edge of the paper, charring it from corner to corner, and Sully leaned forward to touch his match to the map at the center of their circle, trusting Persinette's magic to do the rest.

It caught on the dry paper, going up like a bonfire, so hot, it made Persinette feel like her skin was likely to peel off. When it died away, there was only a tiny scrap left behind, a charred dot burned into it to show them the location.

Benard leaned forward to scoop it up, hissing when the paper scalded his skin. "That's hot."

"Obviously," Owen mumbled, a laugh crawling at the edges of his voice that only became more tangible as Benard shot him a bland look. "It was on fire not but a second ago."

"Are you done?" Benard glared at his husband, clutching the paper close to himself so no one could see it without him first revealing its contents.

Owen hummed, looking like perhaps he wanted to continue his teasing, but he nodded anyway, keeping Benard from devolving into a full-on tantrum. For which the rest of the crew was grateful.

"Good. Then it looks like we have a heading, cap'n." Benard smiled at Persinette, the words slipping from him like he'd been waiting to say them for quite some time. Maybe he had. It seemed like forever since they'd last had a heading, even with having chased down the circus. Persinette could see how that might have left Benard feeling aimless. He was a first mate, after all. And what was a first mate without a heading?

"Where to?" Persinette leaned back on her hands, tilting her chin back in question. She wished she had the hat Manu had picked out for her for when she officiated Agnes and Sully's wedding, but it had disappeared. Probably taken away by bilge rats. Or maybe abducted by Stella—she seemed the type. Either way, it was gone, so she'd have to make do without.

"Hugo, " Benard said.

The paper fluttered down onto Persinette's knee, showing her the charred spot at the edge of Hugo. "We're going to need more detailed directions once we get there."

"I'll have to scrounge up another map." Sully stood, stretching his arms above his head. "Let me know when we get to Hugo. I've got to make a call."

"Agnes?"

"Agnes." Sully's eyes looked bright at the thought, as if just the mere mention of his husband was enough to make him happy. It probably was.

Persinette couldn't imagine how much harder it was to be separated from one's spouse. Even without that tie, it was nearly impossible to be away from Manu. She didn't even share a bedroom with him. But knowing he wasn't just down the hall from her was strange. She'd caught herself more than once heading to his room to check in on him, only to stop with her hand on the doorknob, remembering that he wasn't there. The wrongness of the knowledge sat constantly in Persinette's chest, like the swoop of her heart when she missed a step in the dark.

"Let me know if he's learned anything new." Not that she wouldn't be in contact with Manu later, but it would be good to hear it from someone who was slightly more objective. Plus, Agnes had been doing this a lot longer than any of the rest of them. If there was something to see, he'd see it.

"Aye, aye, cap'n." Sully dipped his head, tipping an invisible hat before he spun on his heel to disappear through the door, a lightness to his steps that hadn't been there all day.

"And the rest of us?" Kindle asked. She stretched her legs out in front of her, bobbing her knees up and down as if to shake out pins and needles.

"Benard, get us headed in the right direction." Pushing to her feet, Persinette ignored the way her own legs had grown a little numb from the lack of blood flow. "Owen, I want to know what weapons we have should we need them. I don't know what kind of fight Ivy will put up."

Both men stood as one, gave a quick nod, and started off the way Sully had disappeared, leaving Persinette with Penny, Roy, and Kindle. She let out a breath, her shoulders stiffening a little under the expectation in their stares. The captain, *she* was the captain, their leader. Without Agnes and Manu to give orders, it was just her. Sweat prickled at the base of her spine, and she resisted the urge to squirm.

"You all can return to your quarters. I'll have Benard sound the alarm when we reach Hugo. Till then, you should rest." That felt like the right direction to go, didn't it?

Penny and Roy followed the others, but Kindle hung back, scuffing her shoes on the floorboards. She still wasn't used to wearing them, she'd told Persinette, having spent so many years running around the library barefoot. Persinette could understand that, the strangeness of an ever-widening world. Maybe that's why Kindle had been avoiding her for so long. Because Persinette understood her a little *too* well.

"I'm going to look through the library, see if we have anything about Ivy Warner," Kindle offered like an olive branch.

"I didn't think you'd grabbed any journals from your library." Persinette scrunched her nose. She thought that all they'd grabbed were storybooks, things that would bring Kindle comfort in a world that was more dangerous and wider than she'd ever known before. Persinette could under-stand *that* too, and envied Kindle for being able to bring some of her home with her when none of the rest of them could.

"Maybe not. But Manu has his own personal library, if you wouldn't mind allowing me access to it? I'm not . . ." Kindle brushed at her nose, sniffing hard. "I'm not good at magic yet, still trying to get my own under control. And I've never been a fighter. But research? I'm good at research."

The confession sent a pang through Persinette's chest, and she had to swallow back the comforting smile she wanted to offer Kindle. That was the exact wrong reaction. Kindle wanted to feel useful, not pitied. "I'll help. Two sets of eyes are better than one."

"They are." Kindle's lips twitched at the corners, her dark eyes lighting with something that might have been gratitude, then she spun to lead the way toward Manu's personal quarters—the office that Persinette had claimed as her own since his leaving. Persinette tilted her head back and prayed to whatever gods were listening that she wasn't leading her crew into more trouble than they could handle.

HOURS LATER FOUND Persinette's eyes fuzzy from too much reading. She'd been squinting for at least the last half an hour, and a headache had started up between her eyebrows where they were creased together. But she didn't want to stop.

"You should go to bed," Kindle said from where she was sitting up straight on a pillow stolen from the couch, her back leaning against the bookcase.

"Can't yet. Still too much to read."

Kindle hummed thoughtfully and turned another page in the stillness of a too-late night on the *Duchess*.

It wouldn't be this quiet if Manu were here, and the absence of him sat cold in Persinette's chest, threatening to weigh her down almost every moment of the day. She breathed through another sharp twist at the reminder and forced herself to focus on something else, now that she had Kindle's attention.

"When everything finally– When we're–"

Kindle looked up from her book, her dark brown eyes—almost black in this lighting—fixing on Persinette like she was another problem to solve, another book to read.

"When the final battle comes," Kindle supplied for her, which was a kindness in and of itself.

"Yes." Persinette nodded, her fingers flexing around the book in her lap. "When the final battle comes, I need to know how much . . ." She frowned, thinking over her words again before finishing with, "How many *activities* you'd like to be a part of."

"You mean, do I want to be the one to kill my siblings?" One red brow lifted on Kindle's face, her lips ticking at the corners, but it was hard to tell if it was in a smile, a sneer, or a frown. She didn't give Persinette the time to confirm or deny if that was what she was asking. "Yes, I think I'd like to be the one to finally put an end to both of them." Her dark eyes flicked away from Persinette, staring off into the middle distance for a moment as her brows pinched together. "They took so much from me. It seems only fair, doesn't it?"

It did seem fair, but Persinette had never been one for vengeance, even when it was justified, even when she knew they couldn't escape blood being shed. "Is that what Chirp would want?"

A snarl curled up one side of Kindle's lips, showing off teeth sharp enough to bite through steel, and her eyes jerked back to Persinette. If they hadn't spent the last few weeks together, Persinette might have flinched and cowered away from the look. But she thought she knew something of Kindle, so instead, she waited for Kindle's answer.

"Chirp isn't here." The words sounded like they came from a vacant, hollowed-out place. Like the loss of her friend had left Kindle empty in a way she refused to admit, to show apart from this moment late, late at night, when it was just them and the books and the fire to hear about it.

"No. They aren't," Persinette agreed, and in the ensuing silence, her mind drifted to the others of their crew who weren't there. The others they'd lost along the way. It was only a few, but it was a few too many.

# SIXTEEN
## CHIRP

"I don't care if you think he's an idiot," the Ringmaster said, his eyes narrowed on Chirp in a way that meant he was seeing everything about them. Every twitch, every fidget, every over-exaggerated blink—gods, why were humanoid creatures so prone to useless motion?— as they tried to make themselves seem less nervous and jittery than they actually were.

"That's not what I said." Well, it wasn't *exactly* what they said, but it was at the heart of what they said. A loose translation. An oversimplification of the argument they'd been trying to make to the Ringmaster. One that might save the prince's life. Not that Chirp was sure why they were *bothering*. He'd proven he was no better than any other human. Maybe worse in his ignorance than the ones who had separated so many families, imprisoned them. Turned them into just another cog in the machine of a queen who cared nothing for them. "What I said was, he doesn't understand what's going on. He's not the reason this is happening. I don't see why he has to be killed when he's clearly just a boy, too naive to really understand what his mother is doing to our people."

"An idiot," the Ringmaster reiterated, and Chirp resisted the urge to roll their eyes. Gods, he could be annoying. "But still an idiot in *power*. What do you think will happen after his mother is gone and he ascends the throne? He's been told this story of our people all his life, what do you think he'll do to the Enchanted when he's given the crown?"

"He can still be reasoned with, taught differently. Maybe that's what we should be focusing on, not—"

"I didn't ask for your opinion, Chirp. We made a deal, didn't we? Your freedom for his life. Are you really willing to sacrifice your entire existence for some naive boy?" The Ringmaster leaned forward, bracing himself on the desk, his eyes gleaming as if he already knew the answer. He had to, Chirp reasoned because they were no fool. But they knew if they gave up what little chance they had at a normal life for a self-centered, spoiled prince, then they would be. When they didn't answer, the Ringmaster's smile sharpened, and he pressed himself to stand, towering over Chirp. "That's what I thought. Now, back to your quarters. You have another show in the evening, and I'll have you well rested."

"I just performed." Weren't there other performers? Other acts the royal family might want to see?

"Yes, you did, and the queen was dazzled." The Ringmaster's sharp-toothed smile stretched further up his face, cold and cutting, and Chirp resisted the urge to take a step back as a shiver raced up their spine. It would be better to be away from him, to not be under his eye anymore. They couldn't imagine an eternity of this, of the Ringmaster giving orders and leering at them while he awaited their compliance, their submission. No, the prince wasn't worth all that, whatever hope he might have of being reformed. "She requested a repeat performance."

"Fine." Chirp shifted back on their heels, taking a step toward the door behind them.

"Uh, uh, uh," the Ringmaster tsked, pulling them up short. "That's not at all how we talk to our Ringmaster, is it?"

Tightening their jaw to near creaking, Chirp dipped into a shallow bow and hissed through their teeth, "It would be my pleasure to entertain the queen this evening, Ringmaster."

"That's better. Now, off with you, I have other things to see to."

Chirp didn't wait for him to change his mind. They spun on their heel and made a hasty retreat, hoping to make it all the way back to their cell without any other conversations.

They weren't so lucky.

Just as they were striding past Felicity and Drea's room, Felicity stumbled out, a feathered boa that matched her hair around her neck, feathers sticking to the gloss on her lips. Her eyes widened when they met Chirp's, and she let out a soft chuckle, tilting her head to one side as if trying to decide something, then nodded.

"You're coming with me."

"I am?" Chirp squeaked.

"Yup!" Felicity grabbed Chirp by the wrist and dragged them into her and Drea's dressing room, which was mysteriously sans-Drea.

"Where's your, uh . . ." *Roommate* sat heavy on Chirp's tongue, but for some reason, they knew that wasn't quite right. What they had seen of Drea and Felicity in the short time they had been with the circus—soft touches, softer words—went deeper than just roommates.

"Girlfriend," Felicity supplied, disappearing behind a screen in the corner to get changed. "Drea is across the hall with the rest of our cr—" She stopped herself, clearing her throat as if she realized whatever she had been about to say was likely to get her in trouble, then poked her head over the top of the screen. "I need your opinion on something."

"My opinion? Why?"

"Don't know." Felicity shrugged and disappeared behind the screen again. "You're just the first person I saw outside of our little group in the hall, so I figured, why not ask you, right? Besides . . ." Felicity grunted, her shadow stumbling across the other side of the screen as if she'd lost her balance. "You look like you could use a friend."

"I do?" Chirp wasn't sure what *looking like they could use a friend* meant, but they weren't exactly going to argue. Felicity wasn't wrong. They *were* lonely, and it *would* be nice to have some friends in the circus in case they were unable to fulfill their mission. Not that they planned to not be able to do it, but just in case. It paid to be prepared. Maybe they would have to seek out some others in the interim. Maybe not.

"So," Felicity said, throwing the boa over the top edge of the screen, "I saw you were out with the prince last night."

Chirp frowned. For some reason, they thought that whole thing had been more discreet. If the Ringmaster was going to force them to murder someone, surely he'd hide the fact they were spending time with the intended victim, not make it so people knew what they'd done. But, they supposed, what did he care if they were caught? So long as he got what he wanted, it didn't matter.

Their stomach did a sickening swoop, threatening to bring up what little breakfast they'd eaten that morning, head spinning. They really ought to go lie down, just as he'd recommended. They wanted to ask how Felicity had seen, maybe press her for more information about what kind of gossip was going around, but they knew that would make the whole thing look more suspicious.

"What do you think?" Felicity continued, moving past her prior point, maybe to try to spare Chirp the discomfort, or maybe because she realized she wasn't going to get an answer. Either way, Chirp was grateful for the reprieve. Although, now they had to give some kind of opinion on Felicity's outfit, which was a sparkly teal monstrosity the likes of which Chirp had never seen before in their life.

"Uuuuh . . ."

"I told you it was awful," Drea said, barging in, the door smacking against the wall as she narrowed her eyes on Felicity. "Stop trying to get people on your side and go put on something that won't assault everyone's eyes within a five-mile radius."

Felicity huffed, sticking her tongue out at Drea, and disappeared behind the screen again. Chirp blinked over at Drea, who looked like she was trying not to laugh.

"Run," Drea mumbled around a snort, "run while you still can."

Chirp blinked, their eyes flicking from the shadow of Felicity to Drea, unsure what to do next. Was Drea kidding? Was she being serious? Was Felicity going to show them more gaudy outfits? Probably. Drea was right, they should definitely run. "I need to get back to my room and rest for this evening's performance. Excuse me."

They nearly tripped over themselves in their rush to escape, and only paused long enough to hear Felicity whine, "Aww, was it something I said?" before speed-walking back to their own room and disappearing beneath the covers of their bed.

*Sweat trickled down the side of their neck, making their long hair stick to their skin as the heat grew more intense. Where was it coming from? And why was it getting harder to breathe?*

*Someone scooped them up, pressing them in close to their chest, protective. "I've got you, sis," a deep voice rumbled through the bone.*

*Chirp blinked up through the blurriness of tears and smoke to try to get a look at the face of their savior but couldn't make it out.*

*Dark hair. Dark skin. Dark eyes. But no discerning features. Nothing that would let Chirp know who he was. Still, they knew— they knew without a shadow of a doubt. This was someone important to them. Someone who had loved them. Someone who had lived with them in that apartment building so long ago, before they'd run away and signed up for the circus.*

*"Put me down, I can walk for myself," a tiny voice huffed, raspy from the smoke, and Chirp only realized it was themselves because the person holding them looked down, his thick brows pressed together. "I can walk!"*

*"Are you sure?"*

*"Yes."*

*He waited, thinking over their words, his dark eyes lifting to look around the street they suddenly found themselves in.*

*When had they left the building? Chirp wasn't sure. And why did they feel so small? Chirp held firm, their gaze not drifting from his face. He nodded and bent to set them on bare feet.*

*The cement was cold and rough under their toes, the night around them dark and twisting with shadows. They stepped closer to him, hoping he'd shield them from whatever was coming for them next, after the fire, after they'd lost their home.*

*Looking around, Chirp frowned. Someone was missing. Not just someone,* someones. *Important people. People who were meant to stay with the both of them.*

*"Where's Tutu?" Chirp asked, looking back up at him, hoping for reassurance and safety but finding neither. There was only darkness, an empty street. A cold wind swept through, making the hair that had been stuck to their neck raise. In the distance, they heard circus music. The lilting tunes of an organ. Haunting and luring all at once.*

*Chirp spun, looking for him, looking for anyone they recognized, but there was no one. No one at all. And a moment later, they saw the shape of the Ringmaster in the distance, the glow of the circus behind him as he reached for them, hands claw-like and vicious.*

*He reached, his fingers seeming to stretch and stretch and stretch, the cold, leathery skin brushing their still too-hot cheek, and—*

Chirp sat up in bed, breathing ragged, sweat dripping down their back.

Someone banged on the door to their room. "Time to get up, Ringmaster wants you ready for curtain call in an hour and a half!" Whoever it was didn't wait for a response before continuing down the hall, knocking on the next door with the exact same message.

Sucking in a breath, Chirp tried to steady themselves, make sense of the dream. It didn't help. The longer they tried to focus on the face of the boy who'd saved them, and the details of the street where they'd been, the more scattered it became, eventually dissolving into nonsensical blurry shapes.

"You're all right." Amara's voice came from somewhere in the dark room, soft and soothing, but Chirp couldn't figure out where. "You'll be all right now."

"How do you know?"

"I just do."

Chirp wasn't sure they believed her. She had disappeared after they'd changed rooms, and now that she was back... Chirp was beginning to question if she existed at all. Couldn't be sure that Amara wasn't just a figment, just like the dreams, just like—

The person alerting the performers came back through, although they didn't bang on Chirp's door again. But they could hear their heavy footsteps in the hall and muttered curses on the other side of the door. And Chirp knew they were wasting time when there wasn't any. So they pushed themselves to their feet, swallowed down a cough crawling up their throat, and started getting ready for the show.

B rend didn't know what had changed Chirp's mind, why they'd agreed to go out into the city with him again, but he'd be eternally grateful for it. Still, it *was* strange, seeing as how he knew his royal status didn't impress them. In fact, it seemed to make Chirp think less of him. Which, if what Brend had learned about Chirp last time was anything to go by, was entirely fair. They had lost everything, even if they couldn't remember it, and his mother was the cause.

Lucky, he was *lucky*, he recognized. He shouldn't look a gift horse in the mouth. Shouldn't think too hard about how suspicious it was that, when he'd gone looking for Chirp down the narrow hall that connected the castle to the circus after their performance, they hadn't slammed the door in his face. Anyone else would have, surely. *He* would have after how things ended the previous night. But Chirp was a forgiving sort, it seemed, and Brend was choosing to be thankful for that instead of looking for a hidden motive where there might be none.

"Did *he* have to come with us?" Chirp asked out of the side of their mouth, their tone distinctly grumpy.

Not that Clancy's lack of friendliness helped.

Brend could understand him not trusting them—Chirp

hadn't exactly done anything to earn that trust. But he really wished Clancy would at least pretend he didn't think Chirp was going to run away with Brend and lock him in a dungeon somewhere to leverage him against his mother. Which was a very real—

*Woah, down boy.*

Brend took a breath and reminded himself that everyone wasn't against him. That his mother's paranoia did not have to color the way he saw the world around him. That was what this whole thing was about, wasn't it? Seeing the world for something other than the things she'd always told him it was. It was going . . . Well, it wasn't going very *well*. But that was all right, he supposed, it was still early yet.

"I did," Clancy called, making it clear he was listening to every little thing Chirp said. Not helpful. Not helpful at all.

Brend turned to shoot Clancy a warning look over his shoulder, swallowing around a hissed *Shhhh* that would no doubt draw more attention to them than anyone wanted. He couldn't believe how someone who could be so calm, cool, smooth had turned into an abrasively loud hanger-on. Maybe it was because he was jealous.

No. That couldn't be it. Clancy had never seemed the jealous type. And besides, there was nothing between Brend and Chirp to be jealous *of*. Not even a budding friendship, Brend was certain of that. Or he had made certain of it, rather, the night before when he made a complete ass of himself.

"I feel like I should apologize." Brend didn't take his eyes off the street in front of them. It wasn't quite night yet, and the city hummed with life.

Chirp had set their heading, not really telling him where they were going, and he was content to follow, wondering if maybe Chirp would show him something that meant a lot to them again. He was beginning to ponder if Chirp were real at all, or if they were a simple manifestation of his own guilt. Like the Ghost of Christmas Past, there to show him all the mistakes he had made but not how to rectify them. That would be useless to a fault, but also couldn't possibly be true as Clancy saw Chirp too. Unless they were a shared delusion . . .

Brend shook himself. He'd tumbled down the thought rabbit hole again; time to pull himself out by his fingernails. So he repeated, "I feel like I should apologize."

"Yes, you said that." Chirp didn't sound impressed. They also didn't sound like they were accepting his apology, which was a little rude, wasn't it? Didn't people usually just accept apologies when they were given by royalty? It always worked for his mother. In fact, it didn't seem like it really mattered what his mother had done. So long as she apologized, it was all well and good. Brend apparently didn't have that kind of power. Again. Rude. "Well?"

"Well, what?" Brend tilted his head at Chirp, the hood of his cloak almost blocking his view of their contorted face. They looked annoyed at this entire situation. Which made him wonder why they bothered to bring him out at all. If they clearly didn't like him, it'd have been easier to just leave him back at the castle. But maybe Chirp was giving him a second chance, just like he was doing for Clancy. That seemed . . . fair?

"Where is your apology?" Chirp prompted, stopping in the middle of the cobblestone road to turn to face Brend fully. Their eyes were so dark, bottomless, a hole that Brend could fall into and never reach the end of. Terrifying and mysterious all at once. What lay in those depths? Were there monsters? Would he drown?

Clancy cleared his throat, and Brend saw him reach for his pistol out of the corner of his eye. He likely thought that Chirp had cast some kind of spell on Brend. Maybe they had.

Maybe that's why he'd agreed to try this again, in spite of him knowing *what* Chirp was, knowing their stance on things, knowing what they thought of him.

"Oh, right." Brend laughed, running a hand through his hair and knocking his hood aside, only to have to scramble to get it back over his head, hiding his face. It was too bright outside still, and his red hair shone like a beacon in the early night. Not that Brend knew why it mattered—the queen wasn't ginger, so there was no way for people to connect him directly to her that way. But Clancy had made a point of it when he laid out his rules, so Brend supposed he could give him this if nothing else. "I'm very sorry for the way I acted last night." Brend dipped into a low bow, which made his joints crackle, but he ignored it. "It was closed-minded and not at all indicative of who I am as a person."

"Isn't it?" Chirp asked, their head tilted to one side, a frown pinching their brows together.

Brend scowled. He wasn't sure what Chirp meant by that, or even how to answer it. There seemed to be something more to the question than just the surface-level meaning, and Brend wasn't sure how to dig for it. Which seemed to be the whole thing with Chirp. There was more to them. Layers buried under layers. Would he ever reach the core of Chirp and really understand who they were as a person? Was there time for that?

When Brend didn't respond to the question quickly enough, Chirp sighed, scrubbing at their face, reddening their skin. Then they turned and started walking again, leading Brend wherever it was they had in mind in the first place. "Whatever. Come along."

Picking up his pace to catch up to them, Brend rubbed his thumb over the top of his cane, wondering if that meant he was forgiven. Chirp hadn't said so, and the need for verbal reassurance sat like a weight at the base of his spine, threatening to drag him down into the cobblestone street. Straightening his shoulders and lifting his chin, Brend refused to yield to the heaviness of it. There was no point in letting Chirp's disapproval drag on him that way; he didn't even know them.

Clancy pushed forward to stand at Brend's other side, his hand brushing against the edge of Brend's cloak, a reminder that he was there and a comfort all in one.

"Where are you taking me this time?" The streets had grown narrower, darker. The buildings around them shorter and shorter. It felt like they were headed toward the outskirts of the capital. Brend had never been there, but that went without saying—he hadn't been anywhere outside of the castle until about a week ago, much less the outskirts of his own city. What did that say about him? Probably nothing good.

Clancy fiddled with the safety on his pistol, and Brend could hear the *click, click, click* of it being flicked on, off, on, off. No doubt Chirp could hear it too, but they had decided to ignore it, probably for the best. If they did say anything about it, there might be a duel between the two of them, and Brend didn't think he had the wherewithal to step in. They were both terrifying in their own right.

Brend thought to ask a second time, but one glance at the hard press of Chirp's lips convinced him otherwise. There was confusion written across their face, just as there had been the night before when they led him to their home. Like they didn't actually know where they were going, they were just following their feet.

"Why don't you remember?" Brend asked instead because that seemed safer. But as Chirp's jaw clenched, he realized perhaps it wasn't. Perhaps he should just . . . stop prying into other people's business. They would tell him when they were ready.

"Nevermind," he mumbled and fell back into a silence that was cut short by a ragged gasp, the humid air dragging in his lungs, as he came face to face with—"The docks."

"The docks," Chirp echoed, but they sounded just as surprised by this as Brend was. As if they hadn't meant to bring him here at all.

"What are we doing at the docks?" Clancy growled, and Brend could see his hand tighten around the pistol grip, jerking in a way that meant he was about to pull it out.

A hum left Chirp. Their head tilted one direction, then the other, as if considering their options, an interesting thing to watch since Brend was pretty sure this whole trip was based on Chirp's instincts. Should that have worried him? Probably. But it didn't. "We're going to take a gondola ride."

"*What?*" The word came out choked with disbelief from Clancy's mouth, but it didn't seem to stop Chirp, who was walking again, their steps unhurried but purposeful. Clancy looked at Brend, his gray eyes too wide in the darkness, pupils looking as if they might swallow all the color. "What?"

"A gondola ride," Brend repeated, then rushed to follow behind Chirp, his heart *thump, thump, thumping* in his throat, making it hard to breathe. But that wasn't going to stop him, *nothing* was going to stop him. Because he was going up in a gondola!

CHIRP DISAPPEARED for a few minutes to talk to someone, and when they returned, there was a young man with them, a stocking cap smashing dark hair of some unknown color to his forehead and hiding the tips of his ears. Enchanted, Brend was sure, fear making his heart rabbit even quicker.

"This is Jerry. He's going to take us up in that gondola."

Chirp thumbed over their shoulder, pointing to a small, rickety looking little tugboat, the wood worn and splintering. It didn't exactly look air-worthy.

"Brend," Clancy said, a warning.

"Oh, come on, Clancy." Brend laughed, the sound high and a little nervous but also excited. "What's the worst that could happen?"

Clancy's pressed lips said that he was swallowing down a whole list of the worst that could happen, but when he met Brend's gaze, his own eyes softened, and he sighed. "All right, let's go up in this rickety old boat. But if we plummet to our deaths, I'm telling the queen it was your idea."

"Deal!" Brend spun back to Chirp and offered them his widest smile. What he got for his troubles was a curt nod in the direction of the little boat before Chirp turned to head toward it themselves.

## EIGHTEEN

## CHIRP

Chirp didn't understand why it seemed so difficult for the bodyguard to say "no" to the prince. All it seemed like Brend needed to do was fix Clancy with a specific smile, and he was putty. Which was kind of gross, if Chirp were being honest with themselves, but it got them what they wanted, so who were they to argue? Maybe when all this was over, they'd thank Clancy for the part he played in their freedom. Or maybe they would kill him too; that seemed like it might wind up being necessary, given he was Brend's bodyguard and all.

"Wish we didn't have to bring the stiff," Chirp muttered, although they were only mostly serious, as Brend's sharp shoulder jostled them in the arm. Clancy was on his other side, making the little gondola a much tighter fit than it had looked even from a distance. Maybe if they had planned this in advance—which they hadn't, they'd just let their feet guide them to the docks—they would have tried to find a larger boat to take up.

Clancy grunted back and jostled Brend between them, in turn jostling Chirp, making their body tip dangerously over the edge of the little boat. Gods, they really wished they had been able to leave him behind. Not because Chirp was planning to throw Brend over the side of the boat, but that was looking like an increasingly good option for *Clancy.*

"And away we go," Jerry—who Chirp was fairly sure was not actually named Jerry—said before pulling a lever on the panel in front of them. A puff of steam obscured their view of the ground, but the swoop of Chirp's belly told them that they were going up, the street falling away to give way to an open sky. They wondered for a moment what it must be like to not be tied to the ground. To know freedom like that.

*One day we'll get out of here, sis,* a voice whispered in the back of Chirp's mind. It was familiar, soft and warm, but they couldn't place where they had heard it before. A dream maybe. A distant memory that the Ringmaster had tried and failed to erase. Chirp reached for it, hoping to latch on and pull the thread of the memory so they could learn more about that person, but it slipped away like the tides.

"How did you even know this was here?" Brend shouted above the sound of the steam huffing out from the mechanism, pushing them upward. Slowly, so slowly, the city was coming back into view as they left their original cloud of steam behind. Shapes forming and rendering themselves into buildings and houses. A whole city emerging from the steam.

"I don't know." Chirp rubbed at the bridge of their nose. They wished they could stop saying that. *I don't know* just felt like such a horrible thing to say when asked such a personal question. But that was the truth of it. They had let their feet guide them, and here they were. They wished they had a better answer for Brend, but a moment later, that became unnecessary as they had cleared the tops of the nearest buildings and the city sprawled out before them like an ink drawing.

Brend gasped, stumbling back as if he'd been shoved. Clancy reached for him but was quickly brushed aside as Brend reeled himself in and leaned forward again, bent double over the low rail of the little boat. Chirp thought they saw Clancy take ahold of the back of Brend's shirt under his cloak, in case he suddenly lost his balance, but no one said anything, and Chirp turned their attention back to the landscape.

It *was* breathtaking in its own uniquely terrible way. A hodge-podge amalgamation of human society before the war. Buildings from every era were shoved together like mismatched puzzle pieces. The history of one society, one culture, slowly erasing and eating another—and itself. It made a shiver roll up Chirp's spine. They tugged their sleeves down farther over their wrists, curling their arms around their middle to try to conserve what little warmth there was.

"You've never seen your kingdom like this before, have you?" Chirp asked, turning to look at the awe plastered across Brend's face. They wondered if he felt the same horror they did. If he knew what had been lost for this to exist. Chirp did. Not because they remembered, nor because they had been there or because someone told them stories of it growing up—although they might have, once upon a time. They knew because they'd researched it. They'd delved into what memory stores they had left and came up with the horrific history of Daiwynn, the truth of it. The kingdom that was slowly devouring itself as if to prove a point that it could.

"I've never seen my kingdom at all," Brend whispered. The wind almost carried his voice away from them, but Chirp caught it. They wondered if that was intentional, or if maybe the words had been a slip of the tongue. A sad truth not meant to be spoken aloud at all. He seemed to do that quite a lot, mutter, murmur, state loudly in a tone that sounded like certainty but rang with insecurity. Things that Chirp knew he had not properly thought out beforehand. Was that a human thing or just a Brend one?

Either way, that answered so many questions about him, including how he knew so little of the world around him. He hadn't *seen* it. He had been locked away in that stuffy castle, only able to know his own kingdom through whatever filter his mother set in place for him. What a sad, sad way to experience the world.

"We'll have to rectify that," Chirp said with an air of finality. A gift, before they took his life: the ability to know his people and his home before he lost both. Was that a cruelty or a kindness? Chirp wasn't sure. They also weren't sure if it would make them feel better or worse about what they had to do. But it was a thing they would do, a decision they'd made, and they were nothing if not decisive. They thought.

"We will?" Brend turned shining eyes on them, the light of stars and a hundred streetlamps reflected there.

*Worse*, Chirp realized. It was going to make them feel worse. Make their job that much harder. Didn't mean they wouldn't do it, but at least now they knew what it would cost them. That was fine. They didn't deserve their freedom free and clear, not if it came at the price of another's life. They should have to suffer too.

Chirp hummed in response, ignoring a huffed snort from Clancy. They'd have to find a way to ditch him next time, and not just because he would get in the way when it came time to ending Brend but also because he was just annoying in the worst way possible.

The gondola drifted over the tops of buildings, heading in a circuit around the outskirts of the city. Chirp hadn't given not-Jerry any instructions on where to take them, but he seemed to have decided on his own to give Brend a tour of the capital from above, and that was fine. Let him see it all. Let him know what his mother, and by extension what *he* was doing to their people.

"We should turn around," Clancy said, his eyes squinting

into the distance. Chirp copied the gesture, trying to figure out what he had taken issue with, but their eyes were not nearly as useful as their visual circuits had been, and in the dark and the drear, it was hard to tell what was out there.

"Why? What is it?" Brend leaned forward more, his shirt straining where Clancy still had ahold of it, knuckles turning pale as he gripped the edge of the rail to keep himself aloft. Whatever Clancy said, Not-Jerry didn't seem like he was listening. The boat continued lazily in the direction Clancy didn't want it to go, and Chirp felt their own stomach drop as the darkness shifted and twisted like a monster on the horizon.

"Didn't you hear me? I said, turn this bloody boat around!" Clancy roared, letting go of Brend's shirt so he could swat at Not-Jerry behind the controls. Brend wobbled, his balance made precarious by the force Clancy had been applying to keep him in the boat. The boat hit a bit of turbulence, knocking them all off balance, and Brend teetered forward. Chirp didn't think, they just reacted, lunging and grabbing Brend by the waist. The motion made them both overcorrect, and they fell onto their backsides on the boat's deck, jarring something in Chirp's spine that they were fairly certain should not be jarred and flopping Brend into their lap.

"Ouch," Chirp grumbled, lifting their back from the deck to rub at the base of their spine, where a sharp ache had settled. Then they looked at Brend, who was staring out into the darkness, his eyes wide, his mouth gaping. "Are you hurt?"

Brend shook his head as if to clear it, but it didn't make the stricken look leave his face. At this rate, Chirp was starting to worry it may never leave. He scrambled off of their lap but didn't go far. And Chirp leaned forward on their hands to get a better look at what was out in the gloom—

they might need glasses when all of this was over—but they couldn't make out the shapes . . . until the moment they *could*. Until the moment it all made sense.

"What . . . What is *that*?" Brend asked, his voice a broken shard of what it was before.

"Nothing," Clancy said in what he seemed to hope was a tone that would cover for the barbed wire fences and dilapidated buildings spewing smoke in the distance. It didn't. If anything, it drew more attention to them. Made Brend more curious as he crawled over to the rail of the boat to get a better look.

"That," Not-Jerry said over the sound of the engine as he steered them closer to the buildings, "is Labor Camp 5J."

With more and more of the capital's lights falling behind them, the buildings of the labor camp were easier to make out: squat, white-washed things with layers of coal dust clinging to them that made them look gray in the moonlight. Of course those words meant nothing to someone who hadn't seen one of these places up close and personal, who hadn't been threatened with them or at least seen photographs. Chirp hadn't ever been to one, but they knew enough to know that the very sight of it should terrify them more than all of the Ringmaster's pointed teeth combined. It didn't. They felt oddly detached from it, and what emotions there were felt like a pull to their gut, a line tied around their middle, tugging them in that direction.

"It's closed down now," Not-Jerry went on, "but it used to be the biggest producer of coal this side of Daiwynn."

"What's it for?" Brend asked as if in a trance.

*He really doesn't know?* Chirp would almost pity him if it weren't for the fact that he would never have to know the fear of such a place.

Clancy opened his mouth to speak, probably to lie, but

Chirp cut him off. "It's where they take the Enchanted after MOTHER abducts them."

Brend mouthed the word *abduct* like he'd never heard it before.

"MOTHER takes them there, and there they stay."

"Until?" Brend turned a hopeful, wide-eyed look on Chirp that made them pity him all the more. Chirp shook their head, sadness crawling into their bones as his face fell, his eyes going shimmery. "Until?"

"No 'until,'" Not-Jerry said, brutal and efficient in his flaying of what little hope Brend had left. "They stay there for the rest of their days."

"They can't—That's not—" Brend's back hunched, his chin resting on the rail, curling in on himself. Chirp couldn't see his face, but they imagined if they could, it'd have been washed pale as the moon in some emotion, whether outrage, disgust, or despair they might never know. His fingers gripped the rail so tightly, the knuckles turned white. And then the shaking started. The hitched breaths that might have been sobs.

An uncomfortable itch started in Chirp's muscles, a longing the likes of which they'd never known before and couldn't accurately describe. All they knew was that it was urging them to reach out for Brend. To pull him into their lap again and soothe what ached. To make this better. Which made absolutely no sense. They didn't know Brend. They had no particular attachment to him. And besides all of that, Chirp had been hired to kill him. It was his life or theirs, they couldn't start getting ... *feelings* now.

"We should get you home," Chirp said, taking more pity on him than they had ever shown themselves and giving in to the itch just a little with a step forward to give his shoulder a firm squeeze.

Clancy watched the whole exchange, his jaw clenched and eyes furious.

That was going to be a problem. But it was a problem for later. Right now, Chirp just wanted to get Brend back to a safe place where he could process what he'd just learned, think it through. "Could you drop us closer to the castle, Jerry?"

"Of course," Jerry murmured, his tone suddenly subdued.

"Thank you for showing me this," Brend whispered into Chirp's ear as they bent to help him stand. His hands clutched theirs so hard that Chirp could feel the knuckles rubbing together. "I needed to see this."

Chirp didn't say anything. They just nodded and pulled away before Clancy could get it into his head to shoot them for getting too cozy with his prince.

# NINETEEN
## PERSINETTE
## & CREW

"**H**e's got one of his people buddying up to the prince," Felicity hissed, her face mostly obscured by the darkness of the wardrobe in her and Drea's room. They'd had Rose do a quick sweep of their room when they joined the circus, and she found multiple listening spells and devices, making Persinette that much gladder that she chose Rose to go along with them. She was clever, and she'd keep them all out of trouble. And honestly, the more people there to look after Manu the better. Especially when Persinette wasn't there to do it herself.

"Who?" Persinette's fingers drummed on the desk where she'd propped the hand mirror against a stack of books. The captain's quarters were quiet around her, the *Duchess* and her crew asleep as they readied for the mission ahead. But Persinette hadn't been able to sleep, a problem that only seemed to snowball the longer Manu was away. Benard had offered to make her something for it—he wasn't as adept at potions as Felicity, but he had plenty of practice with sleeping draughts from the early years after Manu first came to them. Or so he said. Persinette tried not to think of what that meant, it just made her ache all over.

"An acrobat." There was a creak as Felicity shifted about in the old wardrobe, the wood moving to try to accommodate a body where it usually only had to deal with clothes and shoes. Persinette hoped Drea hadn't fallen asleep where Felicity had left her keeping lookout, but she wasn't going to ask. She trusted the pair of them. She trusted all of her people, honestly. They were all fighting the same fight, hoping for the same outcome. That made it almost easy to trust even the newest additions to her team. "I haven't gotten their name."

"What about Rose? Has she been able to access their records? He has to keep something on all of you. I know she said that she was going to look for them. We need it so we know which of the circus members we can trust and which of them are working for Eddi." Not that it would matter, Persinette reminded herself, scrubbing at the ache between her eyebrows. She couldn't remember when it had settled there—it felt like it had always been there at this point. Like she'd had it since the tower, but she knew that wasn't right. It was this infernal war.

Felicity shook her head, the gesture almost invisible apart from her nose and the glimmer of her eyes where the light of the mirror from Persinette's side reflected against her face. The ache increased. Persinette should really get some sleep, there was a long day ahead of her. But she needed as much information as she could get from their people in the circus so she could gauge how much time they had. The answer was, of course, not much. Eddi wouldn't wait long to make their move. Every single heartbeat counted.

"What about the Ringmaster? Whose side is he on?" There had been some hope that he was neutral. Evil, yes, but still neutral. That he wouldn't take either the queen or the Uprising's side.

"It looks like he can be bought." Those words should have made Persinette feel better, but they didn't, and it was clear Felicity knew that by her tone. For all they would have inspired hope in someone else, those words left Persinette with only dread. *He can be bought.* His loyalty would go to the highest bidder. And that would not be her or her people. Damn it.

"All right, that's enough for now," Persinette said, sighing tiredly. She didn't have to be able to see Felicity to know that she, too, was exhausted; they all were. And on top of information gathering, those who had gone with the circus needed to perform, otherwise the Ringmaster might get suspicious. "How is everyone else holding up? Manu, is he—"

"He's himself, which is to say loving the drama of being a part of the circus." Felicity let out a soft laugh that actually sounded like she might be having a little bit of fun there. It was a nice sound. The kind that warmed Persinette's heart. Her people were all right, for the time being. She could— Well, maybe not relax. But she could definitely worry a little less about them. "Hasn't he told you?"

"Yes, but you know he lies."

"He just doesn't want you to worry." A truth that sat hollow in Persinette's stomach. Manu never wanted her to worry about him. He wanted to seem untouchable. But as Ivy Warner had proven, that wasn't the case.

"I know." Persinette scrubbed at her face again, fingers rough and calloused from months of being on the *Duchess*, agitating the soft skin under her eyes where bags no doubt resided. "I know," she said again, leaning back farther in her chair.

"You should get some rest, captain. We can't have you passing out from exhaustion on us. Manu would never forgive us." Felicity was teasing, but only mostly, and Persinette could hear the concern lining her tone now. They were all worried about each other. All waiting for the other shoe to drop and all of this to fall apart. Wondering who they would lose next now that Tobias and Chirp were gone.

Persinette sagged, the pain throbbing through her skull again. "Good night, Felicity."

"Good night, captain."

Then the call ended, leaving Persinette to the silence of a sleeping ship.

PERSINETTE HAD NEVER BEEN to Hugo, but she imagined this was not what it had looked like when Manu and the others had last visited. A thought only confirmed by the look of abject horror that crossed Benard and Owen's faces when they docked. It was hard to see the little city through the haze of smoke and steam, but what Persinette could make out she didn't like.

"I didn't think the war had begun yet," Kindle said from where she stood next to Persinette, her long red hair whipping around them in a torrent as they landed. Most of the crew was distracted, which might be for the better. Persinette didn't know where many of them hailed from, but she imagined seeing any of the cities of Daiwynn like this . . . Well, it wasn't good for her either. It'd be better if they didn't see it from above.

Benard snorted, leaning forward on the rail of the ship as if trying to get a better look at the city below. Not that he needed to; the destruction the fighting siblings had caused was clear as day. "The war started the day Eddi left MOTHER."

"It's been a hundred years." The wind almost sucked Kindle's voice away, but even if it had, Persinette knew she would have heard it because that truth sat heavy across all of their shoulders. Had touched all their lives—as war was wont to do—and shaped each of them into who they were. It was also not technically true; it hadn't been a hundred years, it had been *at minimum* a hundred years, and Kindle knew that. She knew the exact date the war began—she'd told Persinette so one night while they researched, whispered it into the dark like a dangerous secret. Persinette supposed that it was, in a way. Knowing something like that, something that was the truth, could get them both killed. But so could planning to overthrow the ruling system, and that wasn't going to stop Persinette from doing it.

"Aye, it is." Benard's words left him on a sigh that sounded distinctly sad, resigned. Persinette looked over at him and saw his shoulders sagging forward with exhaustion. How long had he been fighting this war? And for how long on the wrong side? It must've eaten at him to know that, for a time, he'd aided in the continued destruction of their world. That he even brought Manu and Owen along for the ride. Persinette couldn't fault him for it; none of them could. They had all been fooled by Eddi's "revolution." Taken in by the way they said they wanted a better world for their kind.

"This isn't a better world," Persinette murmured to herself, watching green smoke rise from one of the destroyed homes on the outskirts of Hugo. A magical weapon, the likes of which MOTHER and their people didn't usually use. An Uprising attack. And even if not for that, Persinette knew that at least half of the destruction on Hugo had been caused by a group she had once considered *her* people, and she hated that more than anything else. The truth of how she'd helped Eddi, made this possible, sat bile and acrid at the back of her throat, threatening to have her breakfast making a second appearance at any moment.

Swallowing thickly, Persinette lifted her chin, sucked in a breath of sulfur and destruction, and moved on, because what else was there to do?

Someone grunted their agreement to the statement,

maybe Benard, maybe Kindle, maybe both, it didn't matter. What mattered was Persinette had finally found her side, her people. She'd gotten lucky that way. Far luckier than she thought she'd get months ago, when Gothel first told her she'd be going out into the field.

The *Defiant Duchess* touched down at what was left of the docks of Hugo, the jolt making Persinette stumble a little. She didn't think she'd ever really get used to the movement of the airship. But once she'd righted herself again, it was time to get moving. They didn't have time to waste, not if what Felicity told her was true.

"Sully, do you have an address for us?" Quick strides took Persinette to the place where Sully and Owen were going over a map, their shoulders pressed together as they leaned over the rig meant to adjust the balloon.

Sully looked at her over his shoulder, his smile sharp, the dark-eyed kelpie peeking through the edges of his humanoid appearance. Persinette thought she might've heard water dripping on the deck, but she knew if she checked, there would be none. "Aye, captain."

THE LITTLE HUT didn't look like much—more hovel than home, with a back door that had been blown completely off its hinges at some point and now lay beside the darkened doorway, leaving the house exposed to the elements. Or so it seemed, anyway.

"Are you sure this is the place?" Owen asked, his hand twitching on the little dagger Persinette had allowed him to bring, which was tucked beneath his shirt. She hoped that if they showed up seemingly unarmed, Ivy might be more willing to speak to them, but there really was no way to tell.

And it wasn't like it mattered—if they didn't have physical weapons, they had Persinette, and that would be enough, even if she was inexperienced compared to someone like Ivy. She was definitely more motivated.

"This is the place," Persinette answered for Sully, even as he checked the map. "There's too much magic in the air for it not to be." Her teeth practically ached with it, the power vibrating in her gums. It was amazing the others couldn't feel it, but she supposed they drew on a different type of magic and that made a difference.

They crept toward the doorway, and the hum became almost unbearable, making it feel like Persinette's teeth might fall out. *That's one way to keep other witches from invading one's territory.* Sucking in a deep breath, she gave one final order before diving into the darkness of the doorway: "Stick together."

Then they plunged into the darkness, the magic across the threshold like cobwebs raking over Persinette's face, and came out on the other side in a shadowed hallway that seemed to stretch on forever. There were no doors off of the main hall, at least not that she could see, but someone was watching them, their gaze sitting on the back of Persinette's neck and lifting the baby-fine hairs there.

"Which way?" Owen whispered. Persinette glanced at him and Sully on either side of her. The two largest men on the *Duchess,* and they were both standing hunch-shouldered while flanking her, as if trying to make themselves the smallest targets possible. It was patently ridiculous, but then, Persinette couldn't really judge them for it, especially if they were feeling the same chill of magic crawling over their skin as she was.

Reaching for the pouch at her waist, Persinette retrieved a tiny vial of powder and lifted it to the light. There wasn't much—there hadn't been time for Benard to make a lot—but it should suit what she needed. Tipping the vial to spill it into her hand, she took a deep breath, then blew the powder out in front of them, where it glittered in the air.

For a heart-*thud*ding second, nothing happened, and Persinette wondered if maybe Benard made it incorrectly. Then the powder settled onto the floor, gathering in the footsteps left behind by whatever magic user had come before them. There was no way to be sure it was Ivy. All they could do was hope that luck was on their side.

## TWENTY

## BREND

Brend didn't understand it, couldn't make sense of it. Everything he'd seen the night before, it had been . . . eye opening. Alarming. But he still hadn't been able to fit the pieces into the puzzle of his world. Hadn't been able to whittle out the truth from the lies. Hadn't been able to separate the– That was one too many analogies, wasn't it?

Either way, there was a lot to think about, a lot to consider, and while the library had information on Enchanted arrests by MOTHER, and even on MOTHER's labor camps, Brend still wasn't sure who to believe when it came to this. The texts provided made it very clear that the Enchanted arrested and housed there were degenerates, criminals, dangerous. That they had done something to deserve it. But that's not what Chirp made it sound like the night before, and Brend just didn't know who was lying to him.

"What do you think of this?" Brend asked Clancy. He tapped on the page, turning it so Clancy could read the words more easily when he leaned over Brend's shoulder, his chest pressed to Brend's back, spreading warmth down Brend's spine. Normally, he would have leaned into that warmth like a flower toward the sun. Soaked it up and let it leave him loose-limbed and languid. But not now. Not when everything was so jumbled in his mind.

"What do I think of what?" Clancy's hand tangled in Brend's hair, thumb brushing over the back of his neck in a gesture that might be a little too intimate if someone were to see. But no one would bother them there in the library, no one ever did, and Clancy and Brend had become comfortable with that. Probably a little too comfortable, but Brend wasn't really in the mood to think about that, not right now.

"These people," Brend clarified. There was a black-and-white photo of a group of Enchanted in front of one of the older camps with a list of their names below it, but he could find no record of their crimes. Nothing to tell him what they'd done to deserve their fate, and he found *that* far more unsettling than anything else he'd seen in the few hours since beginning his research.

"They're criminals." Clancy shrugged, retracting his warmth from Brend's back long enough to move into a chair beside him, scooting it closer so he could press his thigh to Brend's under the table. "Whatever they got you thinking last night, the people who go to those camps are criminals. They deserve to be there."

"But who decides that?" There was no record of *that* either, of who made those decisions. Of the trial and the judge's ruling. Of the evidence presented. Just the photo of the Enchanted who were taken there, all of them lined up, with flat faces and gazes that looked lost and hopeless. Brend supposed someone else might look at that photo and see something else. See a group of people who were cold, hard, deadly to the human race. But he couldn't. Not after everything he'd seen since meeting Chirp. He couldn't dismiss them that way, and honestly, he just wanted to understand. He didn't think that MOTHER was wrong, not necessarily.

He just wanted to understand why things were done the way that they were.

"MOTHER." The book made a soft scraping sound as Clancy pulled it over to himself, flipping through the pages so quickly, Brend had to wonder if it was more to see what he had been reading than to read it for himself.

Maybe he meant to tell Brend's mother about it.

No. He wouldn't betray Brend a second time.

"So the humans who arrest them make that decision?" Acid roiled in Brend's stomach, burning at the lining as if to put a hole straight through him and spill itself at his feet. "That doesn't seem terribly fair."

"Neither is them having magic when we don't." Clancy shut the book with a hard clap, finality in the gesture that Brend didn't approve of. This wasn't his choice, it never would be. Clancy didn't get to end the discussion just because he didn't want to talk about it anymore. Brend reached for the book, glared when Clancy pushed it across the table, then rose to retrieve it. "Why do you care, anyway?"

"Because they're my people too." Brend held the book to his chest tightly enough that he could feel the spine digging into his ribs.

Clancy clicked his tongue, his fingers twitching against the table, very much like he wanted to snatch it away, but he wouldn't. Because that would be a direct attack on the prince, and he knew better. "Come on, it's time for lunch."

Holding the book tighter to his chest, afraid that if he put it down, it might disappear, Brend nodded and followed behind Clancy.

HE WAS STILL HOLDING the book tightly to his chest when Charlie appeared for his fitting later that afternoon. She took one look at him, clicked her tongue, and shot a glare at the other servants in the room. Every one paled a little, afraid to stir the tailor's ire any further, and made themselves scarce.

Once the room was cleared, Charlie looked Brend directly in his eyes and tilted her chin back in question. From there, it was easy to spill everything—or almost everything, anyway. His research. His new friend. His confusion. It warbled out of him in a constant stream as Charlie tucked pins into a new set of trousers, humming in all the right places.

When he was through, Charlie simply looked up at him and, with all the wisdom of a woman who had likely seen too much in her long life, she said, "I think you ought to tell Clancy to stuff it."

"Excuse me?" Brend choked on a manic laugh.

"You heard me." She dipped her head back to her work, muttering around a mouth full of pins, "Your body might be failing you, but your hearing works just fine."

And he was stunned to silence for the rest of his fitting because . . . because maybe Charlie was right. Maybe he should just forget about trying to make Clancy see how important this was to him and go off and do it by himself. What exactly he was going to do, he hadn't figured out yet.

Not exactly what she'd said, but he thought that was the gist of it.

BREND KNEW Clancy wouldn't allow him to get to the bottom of this. What with his tendency to toe the party line and regurgitate exactly what Brend's mother had always said to him. And how he always pushed Brend to take his medicine and stay inside. Always pushed him to not say hello to the staff, especially when they were Enchanted. Always reminded Brend that magic was dangerous, that it would *hurt* him. But Brend was starting to wonder if . . . maybe that wasn't necessarily true.

So that evening, Brend faked sick. It wasn't terribly uncommon for him to be ill. In fact, he spent more time ill than well at this rate, whatever illness he had—the doctors had never been able to give it a name—wearing down his body slowly but surely over time. One day, he may not even be able to walk, they said. He had to be careful. He had to reserve his strength. He had to do his exercises and eat right. No sugar. No junk food. And no overexertion. He had to be bored out of his bloody skull because that was the only way to ensure that he didn't die before he reached thirty. It was delightful.

It was also not the point. The point was that his illness made it terribly easy for him to lie and say that he didn't feel up to tonight's circus performance. Clancy might have insisted, even offering to pull the wheelchair out of the supply closet, but Brend brushed him off. He was too tired, worn too thin. There had been too much excitement as of late. Clancy should just go without him. That was what sealed it: the desperation in Brend's voice when he said that he didn't want Clancy to miss out on the chance to see the fire eater. The begging for Clancy to tell Brend all about it and whether it was worth a second showing.

Clancy had offered his best smile and sworn he would, leaving Brend alone in his bedroom, the lights dimmed to allow him to rest.

Brend waited, starting the count in his head to a thousand as he squinted, straining his ears to listen to the sounds of the corridor on the other side of his door. When it had been a good count of five hundred without a peep, he threw the covers back and rolled from his bed. He'd left his best cane—best because it was the one most comfortable for speed and uneven terrain, not because it was the prettiest—leaning against one of the posts of his bed, which no one had thought anything of, and it was grabbed quickly before he scurried across the cold floors, grabbed his boots from the door, and slunk out into the hallway.

He waited until he was at least five passages away from his own quarters to stop at one of the windows with a deep ledge to put on his boots. It was easy enough, having done this so many times with Clancy already, to stick to the shadows and the lesser-traveled corridors of the castle. To slip undetected through his home. Brend supposed that was one good thing about not having ever really been able to leave: it left him with a deep knowledge of his own castle and all the best hiding spots therein.

There was only one time where he feared he'd been found out, when a servant and a young guard nearly stumbled upon him in their own bid for privacy. But they ducked into an empty linen closet before they could discover him in the neighboring alcove, and Brend pressed on.

When he reached the quarters of the circus—a corridor that had been added on to the castle when the circus's ship had docked right alongside it, with a strange mechanism like a tunnel attaching the two structures—he found the dressing rooms a flurry of activity. Which made sense because they were trying to put on a show. Brend pressed himself against one side of the hall to get out of the way of a performer who was throwing on their costume on the way to the ballroom.

"Oh, it's you," a girl with bright blue hair said from farther down the hall where she was hopping on one foot, trying to pull on her stockings.

"It's me," Brend echoed, although he wasn't really sure

what he was confirming at this point. He supposed it didn't really matter; he'd been seen. If they wanted to hand him over to this mother, now would be the time. But the girl didn't look like she was going to turn him in. She was just watching him, one leg still lifted, her stocking halfway up her calf, head tilted to one side.

"I'm, uh . . . I'm looking for–"

"They're three doors down that way." The girl gestured over her shoulder with her thumb, a knowing little grin ticking up the corner of her mouth. "On the right."

"Yes, thank you." Brend offered a smile and a little dip of his head in return, side stepping her and skirting around several other performers getting ready on his way to Chirp's door. He raised his hand to knock, but the door was flung open, and Chirp's wide, dark eyes appeared before his knuckles could connect with the wood. Like they had been expecting him. Maybe they had. Maybe that meant they were a danger to him. Brend didn't care.

"Where's your bodyguard?" Chirp asked, their dark eyes flicking over his shoulder, then they leaned forward, bracing themselves on the doorframe to look in either direction down the corridor. When they pulled back, there was a little twitch of one brow that might have been conspiratorial glee if they let the expression bloom fully, which they didn't seem to want to. "Slipped your leash?"

"It appears so." Brend couldn't quite swallow down his own grin, even if he'd tried, which he didn't.

They straightened up, tugging the long trench coat they were wearing up by the collar as they gave Brend another once-over, like they were checking to make sure he wasn't hiding Clancy in his pocket. "Have you eaten?"

"I, uh . . ." Licking his lips, Brend wondered how Chirp could jump from topic to topic like that. Like their brain was always ten steps ahead of the average person's. "No. I haven't."

"I've got just the place." Chirp leaped forward, grabbed his wrist, and spun him around to tug him back the way he'd come without any other prompting.

Hours before Chirp *knew just the place*, they didn't know anything at all about where they were going. Because, in spite of the lingering knowingness of this city, they couldn't remember any of it. Even as they pushed and prodded at their memories, they remained elusive, strands of silk so fine, Chirp couldn't wrap their fingers around them.

The dreams had gotten worse, though. Fire and longing. The ragged hole in Chirp's chest throbbing. Because someone was missing from their life. Multiple someones, and Chirp couldn't help but feel that at least some of them were dead. Probably most of them. Maybe all of them. Even if they weren't, with the way things were, there was little hope of finding them. Little hope of returning to the life they had before. Because that life was gone, lit aflame, no doubt by MOTHER and their machinations.

Still, that didn't mean Chirp was wholly without allies.

*Allies.* What a strange way to think of vague acquaintances.

"I could help, you know," Amara's voice murmured from the back corner of Chirp's room. It seemed she'd given up trying to pretend she was real. Which was a relief to them both.

"No, you can't, you only know as much as I do." Chirp shook themselves, tugging their corset down a little farther. They didn't understand the need for such things—they were uncomfortable and they rode up whenever Chirp walked. But they had seen enough people wearing them, and there were a few in their wardrobe, which made them feel like if they wanted to be presentable, they ought to wear one. And they *did* want to be presentable. They wanted Felicity and Drea to be impressed by them enough to offer their help. Not that they seemed the kind of people who wouldn't help when it was asked of them, but still. "Why am I even talking to you?"

They wanted to add *It's not like you're real* but were also afraid of offending Amara on the off chance that she was, in fact, real.

There was a soft noise like Amara shrugging, and Chirp snorted, leaving their room and the voice behind.

Rapping lightly on Felicity and Drea's door, Chirp brushed their fingers through their long, dark hair, trying to get it into something resembling order. They hadn't been able to find their comb, and now it felt like a wild tangle, more nest than hair. But hopefully the two women wouldn't judge them for that. Chirp had done their best, after all.

There was some scuffling on the other side of the door, a muffled grunt of annoyance, then Drea appeared in the doorframe, leaning heavily against it as if it were the only thing holding her up. Her short black hair was a snarl of cowlicks and matted knots from having tossed and turned in her sleep, and she was clad in a flannel pajama set, complete with a little wolf embroidered on the breast pocket. Strange, but cozy.

"Do you know what time it is?" Drea asked, her voice groggy with sleep.

Chirp didn't, as it turned out, know what time it was.

They hadn't been sleeping well at all, and when their last nightmare ripped them from what little sleep they'd been able to get, they found themselves unable to settle down again. They spent a good ten minutes pacing their room, trying to decide what to do next, before they'd gotten dressed and headed down the corridor to Drea and Felicity's room. And now here they were.

"Who'sit?" Felicity muttered from somewhere farther in the dark room, the door mostly blocking Chirp's view of anything but Drea's perpetually grumpy expression.

Drea looked over her shoulder, biting at the corner of her lip as if debating something, then shrugged. "It's your new friend."

"What new friend?" Felicity mumbled, and there was some rustling that likely meant she was rolling out of bed, followed by a soft *thud* that was either her feet or her backside hitting the floor, it was hard to tell. After some more shuffling, Felicity took the door from Drea's hand, pulling it open the rest of the way so she could peer up at Chirp through crusted eyes. "Oh, it's you."

"It's me," Chirp said with a nod. They didn't really know what the significance of it being them was, but they were given to understand that it was rude not to respond when someone was speaking to them. Especially when they had just woken that someone up. "I'm Chirp." It was probably a little late for introductions, as Chirp had already been subject to a very awkward fashion show with Felicity, but names were important to people, and Felicity and Drea were most certainly people.

Felicity blinked for a moment, her nose wrinkling as if trying to place the name, like it reminded her of something or someone else. Strange, because Chirp didn't think their name was terribly common amongst people of the humanoid persuasion. But maybe Felicity had met another android at some point named Chirp. That seemed more likely. "Well, you may as well come in."

"They may as well come in?" Drea repeated, her face twisting into a scowl. "Why's that?"

"Because I said so. Stop being a grouch, Drea." Felicity gave her partner a light shove, then turned on her heel to head deeper into the room, her bare feet scuffing against the floor. There was some shuffling of papers or books or something, then a light turned on and illuminated the mess that was Drea and Felicity's dwelling.

Drea didn't move. She stayed standing in the doorway, keeping herself suspiciously in the way of Chirp entering the room, like an armed guard. Chirp didn't move either. They had no wish to enter unwanted, even though Felicity *had* invited them in. Chirp tilted their head in question, their dark brows lifting, but Drea just squared her shoulders.

"Drea," Felicity called, a warning, and Drea huffed, stepping out of the doorway to let Chirp inside.

"Thank you," Chirp mumbled as they shuffled past, unsure what they were really thanking the two women for. But it seemed important to be polite, seeing as how they were doing . . . whatever it was they were doing.

"What can we help you with?" Felicity asked. She'd moved to the vanity in the corner and was pushing around some papers, tucking others into drawers alongside tubes of makeup and discarded hairpins. Her hands moved quickly, like she was trying to hide something, but Chirp wasn't going to pry. It wasn't their business what Felicity and Drea were doing in the circus. The Ringmaster tasked them with one thing and one thing only: assassinating the prince. Any goings-on that seemed suspicious were outside of their purview, and Chirp would wisely choose to keep out of it.

"I need somewhere to take the prince tonight." Chirp looked around for a seat, and when none seemed readily available, they settled onto a steamer trunk with a pair of stockings hanging out of the side. Felicity had dropped down onto the bed, pulling her robe tighter around herself to ward off the slight chill, while Drea leaned against the wall beside the door, her arms crossed over her chest, a sentinel waiting for the order to escort Chirp out. "Last night we took a gondola—"

"Ooooh, romantic," Felicity cooed. "Why don't you ever take me on gondola rides, Drea?"

"Because." Drea scoffed.

Felicity huffed, poking out her bottom lip in a pout, but didn't say anymore on the subject, just lifted a hand and flapped it for Chirp to continue. Or at least Chirp thought that was what that gesture meant, hoped it was, as they continued on. "We took the gondola out over the city. He's never seen the capital from above, and we wound up near the labor camp on the outskirts."

"Less romantic," Felicity mumbled, but Chirp decided that was not an interruption and ignored the commentary.

"I have been–" Chirp paused, trying to think of how best to explain their goal in this. They couldn't tell Felicity and Drea that they planned to kill the prince and that this was one last hoorah before they did because Chirp didn't know what side they were on. For all Chirp knew, they worked for the Ringmaster very closely and had been brought on board to spy on people like Chirp. Maybe that's why they had been trying so hard to befriend Chirp. Bile churned in Chirp's fleshy stomach, a reaction to stress that they had decided days ago they very much did not like. Humanoid bodies were gross.

Licking their lips, they tried again. "I have been trying to show him something of the world, expose him to the Enchanted community."

Felicity's eyes narrowed, and there was a sharp light in

them now. Like this bit of information was something that she could use, something she'd been desperately hoping for. Like she was working out a plan that Chirp had just given her the missing piece to. Chirp didn't think they cared much for playing right into someone else's hands, not with how the Ringmaster controlled their life, but there didn't seem to be much choice in this matter. They needed help. And Felicity and Drea knew a little something of the world outside of the circus.

Shifting under that calculating gaze, Chirp cleared their throat, trying to move the burning bundle of bile and nerves either up or down. It didn't go anywhere, remaining lodged in Chirp's esophagus, threatening to burn its way through their throat. "Anyway, I was wondering if you two knew of any place where I could take him this evening?"

With a delighted squeal, Felicity lurched forward to brace herself on her knees, putting her face far too close to Chirp's before she said, "I think that's a delightful idea."

"You do?" Chirp blinked.

"You do?" Drea grumbled.

"I do!" Felicity nodded eagerly, leaning back again to kick her legs out in front of herself as if unable to contain her joy. "If he's going to be king, he ought to know his people, right?"

"Right," Chirp agreed, even though they got the distinct feeling that they didn't know *what* they were really agreeing to. That they might be signing a contract with some new kind of devil, or enlisting themselves in a war they didn't even know was happening. Ignoring that, Chirp forced a smile. "So, do you have any ideas?"

"I do." The springs of the bed creaked as Felicity pressed to her feet again, taking two quick strides across the room to reach the vanity, where she then pulled a sheaf of paper from one drawer and grabbed a pen from another. "But you'll want to slip his bodyguard if you can."

"We might be able to help with that," Drea volunteered from where she was still standing guard at the door. Chirp wasn't sure if she meant to keep them inside or to keep others out, but they decided that wasn't really important. What was important was that these two were going to help them. Thus, any other lingering doubts were ignored.

"How?" Chirp turned keen eyes on Drea, their dark brows raised in surprise.

"Leave that to me." Drea shrugged, looking unbothered by the clear suspicion that laced Chirp's tone, a smile lined with fangs curling over her lip. Chirp was suddenly very glad they were not the prince's bodyguard and wouldn't have to experience whatever Drea had planned for him personally.

"There's this pub," Felicity said, her train of thought still chugging right along as if Drea and Chirp hadn't been speaking into the quiet of her pen scratching against paper. "Well, it's not really a pub. It's more of a library. The Enchanted have them all over the place, little hubs that store knowledge and protect it from MOTHER," she explained, holding out a truly terribly drawn map. "This is one of those. If he wants knowledge on our history, our *real* history, this would be the place to look."

Chirp took the paper, turning it round and round in between their fingers to get a better idea of where in the name of the gods this place was located but coming up empty. They'd have to reference some other maps. Thankfully, the Ringmaster had provided them with such things for their mission.

"Password's on the back." Felicity snatched the paper away again and flipped it over so Chirp could see a word written in an uneven hand. "Should get you into the back room if you're polite about it."

"I see." Chirp's eyes traced the loopy letters, taking a moment to decipher the words *Open Sesame*. They lit something like recognition in the back of Chirp's mind, but they couldn't place them, not yet. Maybe later, after they'd had some time to think. Not that it was important where they'd heard the words before. "Thank you for this."

"No need to thank us." Felicity tilted her head to one side, her smile tugging up the opposite side of her face. "That's what friends are for."

"Good, now, you've gotten your information." Drea stomped forward, making shooing motions that encouraged Chirp to rise from their seat, tucking the paper away in a pocket. "Let us get back to sleep."

Chirp jerked their head in two quick nods and scurried from the room, not even minding as the door shut behind them with the definitive click of a lock, because now they knew just the place to take Brend when next he appeared at their door. They headed back to their own room, endeavoring to get a better understanding of where this pub was.

# TWENTY-TWO
## PERSINETTE
## & CREW

Luck, it would seem, was on their side. Persinette wasn't sure how, but it was, because when they followed the trail of magic, they came face to face with Ivy Warner, her garishly bright red hair falling into her face, sweat gathering at her temples, jaw clenched. She was standing in the middle of a well-furnished room, her body half-hidden by a chair. Plush area rugs piled one on top of the other so that no bit of the floor was visible, and Persinette's feet sank into the fibers where she walked.

Leather chairs were grouped together around a small table that looked to have a chessboard on it. And the paneled walls were painted in a deep forest green. It was kind of room Persinette would have loved to curl up in with a book. Cozy. Atmospheric.

"How did you get in here?" Ivy hissed, her eyes narrowing and sparking with a power that felt very similar to the magic Persinette had been trying to ignore their entire journey to this point. It prickled at her senses, raising gooseflesh all along her arms, like standing too close to a lightning strike. Ivy gripped the back of the chair; the leather creaked under her hold.

"We walked?" Persinette said, tilting her head to the side in confusion. Ivy hadn't lashed out at them yet, but it would happen any moment now, Persinette could tell. The buzz of magic in the air rose to a crescendo, making her eardrums itch. Her own lavender-colored magic sparked and danced at her fingertips, readying itself to protect them from whatever attack Ivy was gearing up for. She would not have another one of her family cursed by this woman.

"You—You *walked*?!" Incredulity layered every word, and Persinette almost felt bad for Ivy. Clearly she'd thought that whatever magic she wound outside of her home would keep people out. Wards—that was probably what Persinette had felt when she entered, something meant to keep other magic users at bay. Persinette wondered what they were supposed to have done? Maybe throw them all from the property? But they hadn't. They had just been uncomfortable.

"Yes. We walked," Persinette confirmed apologetically. She knew what it was to have something fall apart in front of one's eyes. To do everything one could to make sure one was safe and sound, only to find out they were anything but. She had been there enough times to know that swell of terror.

"That old goat, her magic must be affecting my wards," Ivy muttered to herself, scrubbing at her face. The magic Ivy had been drawing on to defend herself released in a rush at her inattention, flaring out over them and making Persinette's shoulders relax a little.

But Persinette didn't let her own attention waver, despite the rush of endorphins from the flow of magic. Narrowing her eyes, Persinette drew that same power to herself, just in case. Built it up into a shield that would protect herself and her people should they need it.

Now that Ivy felt like an animal backed into a corner, she would be more likely to lash out, and Persinette needed to be ready for that. She saw Owen and Sully shift off to either side of her, skirting around the furniture, bracing for an attack. None of them could predict when or how fierce it would be.

"Ah well," Ivy said after some more muttering, her head lifting to look at them, eyes too wide in her face and fear lining every movement, "that is what happens when you take someone else's stronghold for yourself."

Persinette didn't know what that meant as she'd never taken over another witch's home, and she was fairly sure she didn't want to find out. Whatever Ivy had done to the witch who created this place was probably worse than a blue jay throwing another bird from its nest, and the very thought sent a shiver up Persinette's spine that she didn't have time to deal with. Now that there was an opening in Ivy's defenses, she had to take it. "We are here to propose a truce."

"A truce?" Ivy snorted, her gaze finally seeming to focus on Persinette, like she was seeing her for the first time. Where before there had been not a trace of recognition, now Ivy seemed to know exactly who Persinette was. "You're Manu's little witch, aren't you?"

"I'm Persinette," Persinette said, lifting her chin with no small amount of pride, "co-captain of the *Defiant Duchess*."

"Co-captain?" A laugh left Ivy, her eyebrows rising up into her hairline. A smile, dark and cruel, curled up one corner of her mouth as she said, "Well, I suppose he needed one of those, didn't he? After what I did to him."

Biting down on the tip of her tongue, Persinette held her words there. The ones that would tell this woman that wasn't why Manu had done it. That there was more to them than Manu simply needing her because he'd been rendered blind by Ivy's magic. Ivy was baiting her, and she knew it. She wouldn't rise to that challenge. But whatever her face did must have been answer enough for Ivy because that wicked grin crawled further across her face.

"That curse was meant for you, you know? Eddi wanted it

to hit you, not him."

Yes, Persinette did know that. Had lived with that knowledge for months upon months. Grappled with the guilt and the questions that came with it. Because she wanted to know *why*. Why had Eddi told Ivy to do that? Why did Manu get in the way? Why did it feel like destiny that it all happened how it had? Why couldn't she *save* Manu? Why the curse was *irreversible*? Just . . . *why*.

The guilt, the confusion, the betrayal sank into her muscles like glue and tar, making them heavy. Sticky. Slow.

"Persi," someone said from very far away, their voice more growl than words, a snarl in her ears, but she didn't recognize who they were.

How could she through the sinking deep, deep, deep into the depths of her own mind. Of her own regrets. Because this was her fault, all of it. Manu's blindness. The world crumbling around them. The loss of Tobias. Chirp's disappearance. The war. The carnage. The *death*. They were all her fault. If only she hadn't been born. If only she had simply never existed. This all would have been different. This all would have been—

"Persinette!" someone roared, grabbing her by the shoulders and shaking her hard enough that her teeth clacked against each other. "Snap out of it!"

Persinette blinked hard once, twice. Squeezing her eyes together with enough pressure that she saw stars and opening them again to see an irate expression on Owen's face. There was a smear of blood dripping from a cut above his eyebrow, a smudge of something that looked like ash across his cheek.

"What happened?" A headache had settled behind Persinette's eyes, heavy and throbbing. Like someone had taken a mallet to her head and pounded away at it until she'd lost consciousness.

"Looks like we tripped Warner's wards," Owen said on a breath that sounded like relief. His eyes were bloodshot, a little glassy. When he opened his mouth to say something else, an explosion cut him off, drawing both their gazes to the scene over his shoulder.

The room they were in was entirely different from the one that Persinette would've sworn she'd been standing in, but maybe that had been part of the magic of Ivy's wards. There were mountains upon mountains of just . . . *stuff*—old magazines, crushed cans, broken glass bottles—that went up so high, Persinette couldn't see where they ended. They teetered precariously, only magic keeping them upright. And at the center of several of these piles stood Sully and Ivy Warner, locked in what looked like some kind of grapple.

"What's he doing?" Persinette was still dazed from whatever spell Ivy used on her, mind foggy as she tried to process everything around her. None of it made sense. None if it lined up with the well-furnished, well-lit room she'd thought she was in just a moment ago.

"Keeping her from putting you under again." The words rushed out of him as Owen grabbed her by the wrist and jerked her behind what looked to be a broken refrigerator to hide from a stray spell. "We need you to stun her before she brings this whole place down."

Persinette didn't understand what he meant by "putting you under again," and there wasn't really time to ask because the second half of what he'd said was a far more immediate threat. Peeking out around the edge of the yellowed refrigerator, she tried to get a better look at the scuffle going on between Ivy and Sully.

Sully seemed to have the upper hand. He had more strength and height on Ivy, but that didn't really matter when magic was involved. And Ivy was drawing power for something, the tops of the piles around them turning toward her like sunflowers following the sun. Owen was right: if they left her to her own devices, they'd all be crushed to death by the trash that surrounded them.

"I'm afraid I'll hit Sully," Persinette whispered, the magic tickling at her fingers as she thought of the spell, words forming on her tongue even as she held them back. They *wanted* to be released. They *wanted* to weave themselves into the air and do their work. Because that's all magic ever wanted, to be allowed out into the world, to exist. It burned on her tongue, making it feel like sandpaper. "If they'd just stop moving so much."

"You let me worry about Sully." Owen shifted beside her, crab-walking around the edge of the fridge to find cover behind another appliance that wasn't really big enough to cover his large frame. "Just be ready with that spell."

Persinette swallowed hard, the magic scalding the back of her throat, and nodded. The spell would be ready all right. She inhaled through her nose, hoping to cool it as it made the insides of her cheeks blister, or *feel* like they were blister-ing, anyway. The magic itself wouldn't do any actual damage to her, but it would make it feel like it was until she let it loose. Offensive magic was like that. Hot and angry and so alive, it could hurt the wielder as much as the person they were aiming at if they weren't careful. That's why she hated it so much, why she'd rather use defensive magic. But there wasn't time for her to back down now, and she hadn't brought any weapons with her. This would have to do.

Narrowing her gaze to peer through the dim lighting of the room, Persinette waited, watching as Owen crept closer and closer. She didn't know what his plan was, but she trusted him and Sully enough to give her an opening to land the stunner spell.

A sharp whistle cut the air, drawing everyone's attention. Except Persinette, who had been expecting some kind of distraction. Sully and Ivy's heads whipped in that direction, and whatever Sully saw made him tilt his head down in a subtle nod and twist Ivy around, baring her back to where Persinette was hidden.

The spell came alive again, burning her lips as she let it roll off her tongue and out into the air, not even needing a pointed finger for direction with how her eyes were locked onto the bright red hair of Ivy Warner.

Ivy yelped when it hit her, her body tensing and head tipping back to cry out at the ceiling, then she went limp in Sully's hold. He scooped her up, throwing her over his shoulder like a sack of potatoes, and shot Persinette a proud grin as she stepped out from her hiding spot.

There was a loud creak. They all looked up to see the towers of stuff teetering more dangerously.

"Time to go!" Sully shouted, and the three of them took off back toward the exit, Persinette lagging behind a little, her hands twisting and turning around one another as she worked up a shield spell to protect them from any falling debris. It sprang to life just in time to keep a glass bottle from shattering over their heads and a bundle of rolled up newspapers from braining them just before the rest of it started to fall like rain.

Owen ripped the door open, and the three of them, along with their prisoner, stumbled out into the hallway where they had started, chests heaving. It was silent in the hall apart from the noise of their breathing, no signs of the avalanche that almost crushed them on the other side of the door. Which was only a small relief.

"We should get back to the ship," Persinette said, her hands shaking as she pushed her short hair back from her sweaty face.

"Aye, cap'n." Owen chuckled softly, almost disbelieving at their near escape, and led the way to the door.

"Just the place" turned out to be a pub. There was a sign swinging over the door from a little metal arm, hanging by a single eroded chain. It was so worn with age that the only letter Brend could make out on it was an R. Through the dust-covered, cracked front window, light filtered out onto the street, warm and inviting. It looked like the kind of place Brend had read about in a novel once upon a time. Where quests started and men had secret dealings to keep villains from finding out about their plots. Where magic was tucked into every corner.

"What is this?" Brend asked, leaning back on his heels, trying to get a better look at the whole of it. But no matter how far back he leaned, he couldn't seem to get it all into focus at once. He could only look at it in parts. Tragic, really. If he had a camera, he might try to take a picture so that he could remember this forever, return to the image of it again and again. Maybe write his own story about it. But there he stood, camera-less. Another great tragedy. He'd just have to commit it all to memory.

"It's a pub," Chirp said, voice flat as if mocking him for his silliness. Fair. Rude, but fair. They let him soak it in for another moment before pushing past him, their shoulder brushing his, and grabbing the door. A bell over top of it jingled merrily to let everyone in the place know that new customers had arrived.

"It's a pub—I can see it's a pub, Chirp!" Brend laughed, following behind them, letting the warm air and the smell of stale ale sink into his skin. It would probably have been gross to anyone else, but to Brend, it smelt like adventure, the opening of a door to a world he may never get another glimpse of.

"You can?" It sounded like they were teasing him, and Brend supposed that was definitely warranted it. It had been a stupid question. But he couldn't seem to help himself. Couldn't seem to not make an absolute fool of himself in front of Chirp. Especially when they were taking him places he'd only ever dreamed of, showing him things he'd never imagined before. Chirp cut him a sideways glance and muttered, "It's not *that* exciting."

But they were wrong. Because it *was* that exciting. Every moment outside of the castle in Chirp's presence was a new and terrible adventure. And even for all that Brend was beginning to question things he didn't think he wanted to question, he wouldn't trade these stolen moments for all the safety in the world. "It is."

Chirp looked back, their eyes raking over him for a moment, then they let out a murmured sound of approval before making their way over to the bar. Brend thought perhaps they meant to order a round of drinks—probably not the best idea, as he had no idea how alcohol would interact with his medication, he'd drink it anyway—but all they did was lean over the bar and whisper something to the woman cleaning glasses behind it. The woman's too-bright green eyes flicked from Chirp's face to Brend, who stood behind them, and she lifted a brow.

"He's with me." Chirp gave a little shrug, not even bothering to let their gaze flicker back to Brend. There was enough trust in that gesture that Brend had to forcefully keep his lips from ticking up in a smile. It was a struggle, *such a struggle.* The bartender seemed to realize this, because her eyes narrowed in suspicion. Noting the expression, Chirp tilted their head to block the bartender's view of Brend and repeated, "He's with me."

"All right." The bartender set down the glass she'd been cleaning the entire time—probably getting it perfectly spotless and then some—and made her way over to the little door that allowed her to step out from behind the bar. Flopping the rag onto her shoulder with a wet slap, she looked once over her shoulder to make sure Chirp and Brend were following, then headed deeper into the pub.

The air seemed to thicken the farther they went. Brend's eyes widened. The pub hadn't been that large, had it? It hadn't *looked* that way from the window. From the view outside, it seemed like there was just the main room, large enough for twenty or so people but definitely smaller than the ballroom in the castle.

"Cozy" was the word Brend would've used to describe it. But there were more tables. The room seemed to expand almost endlessly until the bartender took a right and ducked behind a booth along one wall.

Chirp and Brend were brought to a stop by the bartender's steps halting in front of a peeling wooden panel. No one else in the pub seemed at all interested in what they were doing. In fact, as Brend took a look around, it was like no one even noticed they were there. Every patron along their path continued talking or staring into their drinks as if nothing at all had changed.

The bartender, for her part, lifted one hand to press her palm against the panel, applying just enough pressure for something to click. There was a faint sucking sound, then the panel popped open, and glittering golden light filtered out like sunshine. Brend looked around again, checking to see if anyone noticed the sudden change in the pub's wall, and still, no one looked up from their drinks. So either this was completely normal for this particular pub, or there was some kind of magic going on that Brend couldn't sense. Both options were equally likely.

"First door on your right," the bartender said, pulling the door open farther to allow Chirp and Brend into a long hallway lit by sconces that glowed strange colors: blues and greens and even purples. *More magic.*

Chirp nodded, grabbed Brend's wrist, and tugged him gently through the opening without first checking if he wanted to follow them into this great beyond. He did want to, but a check-in would have been nice. The door shut behind them, cutting off the sounds of the bar, making it feel like it was a world away. Maybe it was; Brend didn't know how magic worked.

"First door on the right," Brend repeated, narrowing his eyes at the hallway that stretched on forever and ever. He didn't see any doors. "Where is it?"

"I suppose it's a bit of a hike." Chirp shrugged and started walking again.

Brend followed along silently, his head swiveling this way and that, trying to take in everything around him as they went, but there wasn't really much to see. Just the walls, which were covered in wallpaper that had a watercolor painting of a forest on it.

Only, the longer he looked at it, the more he was sure he saw something moving in between the trees. Something magical and massive. Something that would probably eat him alive if given half the chance. He found himself stilling, trying to get a better look as it twisted and turned in the shadows of the trees. The world tipped. Or maybe it was him, tipping forward to get a closer look, and the thing loomed closer, its mouth an opening like a pit, dark and bottomless.

"Keep up," Chirp said, giving his wrist a gentle tug, and Brend jerked away from the creature, shaking himself.

When he looked back at the wallpaper, there was just the watercolor forest, nothing in the shadows of the trees, no yawning mouth.

"So, what's with you and that bodyguard of yours?" Chirp asked, drawing Brend's attention away from the wallpaper again, and he turned to follow behind them. When Brend didn't answer right away, they added, "Why isn't he with us?"

Pursing his lips, Brend chewed on the words, wondering how best to explain the complicated relationship that he had with Clancy. All the years that bound them together but were also threatening to tear them apart at any moment. It was, he realized, perhaps belatedly, all a bit dramatic. And probably completely trivial when compared to everything else going on in his kingdom.

"You two have a fight?" Chirp pressed.

Brend wondered if it was because they just didn't know when to quit or if they got the sense that he actually wanted to talk about this. He found he *did*, actually, want to talk about it. He'd never had anyone to talk to about Clancy and all that went on between them—aside from Charlie, of course, but she was a servant. It was different, having a friend, someone to listen and maybe not give advice but to empathize with the difficult position he found himself in.

"Sort of." Brend huffed, hoping his stuttered step didn't give him away, but he wasn't stupid enough to think it didn't. Chirp seemed to be able to read him easily, and he wondered why that was. Whether he was just an open book or if they were just good at that sort of thing. He hoped it was the latter. "We had a discussion about the labor camps, and he wasn't really open to a differing opinion."

"But," Chirp prompted, seeming to sense that wasn't all there was to the complicatedness that was Brend and Clancy. And they were right, it wasn't. There was so much more beyond that. Even without the intimacy between them, so, *so* much more.

"But . . ." Brend swallowed around an ache in his throat. Betrayal. He recognized it now. He wasn't sure if it was associated with the fact that it felt like betraying Clancy to have this discussion with Chirp, to lay Clancy bare before someone who clearly didn't like him, or if it was because Brend had been betrayed. It didn't matter, he decided. Either way, he was going to tell Chirp what happened. "Well. After the first couple of times we went out, he told my mother where I'd been. I've never left the castle before, and I knew she wouldn't approve. I was right, of course, and she tried to bind me to the walls using some kind of spell. I wasn't able to get out for several days . . . until you showed up."

With their dark eyes facing forward, Chirp didn't even spare him a glance at this confession, but Brend thought he saw a tightening of their jaw. Like there were words on their tongue that they weren't letting off. An opinion that was perhaps a little truer and a little meaner than he was ready for. But now he had to know. He didn't know why, but he'd begun to trust Chirp and their opinion. Likely because, on that first outing, they'd shared something with him he didn't think he'd ever have the bravery to share with anyone else. It really wasn't fair to weaponize one's vulnerability like that, but it didn't matter.

"I believe," Chirp said, their voice soft, as if they were afraid of Brend's reaction but that wasn't going to stop them from saying what was on their mind, "that when someone tells you who they are, you should believe them."

Brend wrinkled his nose, his eyes flicking over Chirp's face to better understand what they were trying to tell him.

After a moment, he nodded. The words didn't make sense, but he thought he may understand the sentiment. "I think maybe you're right."

A door appeared to their right, pulling them both to a stop and ending the conversation, which might have been for the better. Chirp had given Brend plenty to think on.

"Are you ready, Your Highness?" A smile titled the edges of Chirp's voice, their eyes bright with excitement.

"Ready for what?"

But they didn't answer. Instead, they grabbed the knob, pushed through, and Brend was brought face to face with a room full of more books than he thought he'd ever seen in his life. He choked on a breath, coughing around where it lodged in his throat, his head already spinning from trying to look everywhere all at once. Tomes upon tomes lined the walls, stuffing the shelves to the brim. They overflowed onto the floor in stacks that towered above even Chirp's substantial height, and Brend wondered, dazed, how someone would get to the books at the bottom without toppling the entire stack.

"What is this place?" He only knew he'd said the words because they rasped harsh and dry in his throat. A tentative step forward brought him into the heart of the room, but the smell of old paper hit him hard enough to send him stumbling back into Chirp.

Chirp caught him by the shoulders—hands gentle and warm even through the fabric of his tunic—and laughed softly. "A collection of books that has not been censored by the queen."

"Where did they come from?" The leather cover of a book brushed roughly across his fingertips, sending a shiver all the way up Brend's spine. Here was knowledge he would not otherwise have, truth he might not otherwise know.

"All over, I think." Chirp scrubbed at the tip of their nose thoughtfully. "I don't really know. Felicity and Drea just told me this was someplace you needed to see." They stepped forward, shutting the door behind them and picking up the volume Brend had just been running his fingers over. "Shall we?"

Brend looked up, his brows lifted in question, asking permission. At the subtle nod from Chirp, he leaped forward to grasp the book from their hand with a startled laugh. "We shall."

Awe. Everything Chirp showed Brend seemed to inspire it. An emotion Chirp thought they'd probably never felt before. An emotion they never thought they'd be *able* to feel again. But somehow watching it flicker across Brend's face was almost enough to have them feeling it too. Not nearly as good, but Chirp would take all they could get at this point. They would bask in the warmth and the light that was Brend and his open admiration. That's what they were good at after all, wasn't it? Taking. In the end, they'd take Brend's life, just like they were feeding off his awe. Because they were a leech. Selfish.

"I'm not—" they started to say, and Brend looked up from where he sat cross-legged in an old wingback chair that was sagging on one side. His eyes were too wide for his face, like a child or a kewpie doll. Alien in the amount of emotion they showed, even when he didn't seem to be feeling much of anything, like even his base emotional state was something . . . *more* than Chirp thought they'd ever experienced in their life. What must it be like to feel things that way? "I'm not a good person, Brend."

"What?" Brend asked, confusion pinching his red brows together.

"When I told you earlier," Chirp continued, hoping to

explain themselves and the sudden outburst, though they didn't really know if it was possible at this time, "that you should believe people when they tell you who they are . . . I'm telling you who I am. I'm not a good person. I'm selfish."

Brend looked at them for a moment, his tongue between his teeth, nose scrunched just the slightest as if he were working out a particularly difficult equation. Chirp shifted beneath that stare, wishing he would look anywhere else, but then he hummed and shook his head. "I don't believe you."

"What?" Chirp squeaked, their voice a rusting hinge in need of oil even in this humanoid body.

"I said I don't believe you."

"But—"

"I think," he said as if he was trying out the words, like no one had ever allowed him to say what he thought out loud before, "that when you said that, you meant to believe their actions. That those would speak more loudly than words."

"I did, bu—"

"And so far, what I've seen of *your* actions goes against everything you've just said." Brend was staring at them steadily now, a challenge set in his jaw, as if he was daring Chirp to contradict him. What he didn't know was that he *was* daring them to tell the truth, and Chirp wasn't so certain they could avoid it now. He had to know what was really going on.

"What if I'm only doing these things to get close to you? What if my motives are nefarious, and in the end, I mean to hurt you?" The words sat sticky like goop in the back of Chirp's throat, but they pushed them out anyway. Because he had to know. Because it seemed a pity, a shame for him to *not know* the truth of it, of *them*. For this not to be an even playing field. Chirp wanted to play fair.

"Are you?" Brend countered, unbothered by the turn of this conversation when he really ought to be. He ought to be *so* bothered by it. Especially when not but two days ago, it seemed like he believed all Enchanted were evil. Wasn't Chirp proving his mother—and Clancy—right in admitting this?

"I am." Because what else could they say at this point? It was the truth, and the only way they could warn him away from them was to be honest. Maybe this would save him, although Chirp wasn't sure when they'd decided that was a thing that they wanted. Maybe the moment they'd seen his reaction to the library. There was something beautiful and strangely wonderful about the way Brend looked at the library, like it was a chest full of treasure instead of a room full of dust and dead trees. It wasn't logical, but Chirp thought they might finally understand Brend, or at least some of what he valued.

Brend hummed, his head tilted to one side so a strand of long red hair fell across his jaw, considering Chirp with those eyes that seemed to see all and yet not enough at the same time. How could someone be wise beyond their years and yet also so naive to the world? Brend was a study in contradictions that Chirp thought they might like to better understand one day. If only they had the time to inspect every facet of him. To push him into situations he wasn't comfortable in. To experiment.

"I don't think I believe that either." Brend shrugged, then ducked his head back to the book he'd been inspecting as if that was the end of the conversation. Which was just . . . Well, kind of frustrating if Chirp were being honest. Chirp was trying to warn him away, to save him, and he was being willfully ignorant of the information they were providing. Was this a royalty thing? Where they didn't believe it when people told them something that was for their own good? What a strange way to live.

"Why not?" The words sprouted from Chirp's tongue

without any approval from the rest of them. They probably didn't want to know the answer—it wouldn't be conducive to what had to come next. Only, they *did* want to know. Burned with the need to better understand this young man.

"Because there are better—easier—ways to earn my trust." Brend lifted his head and flashed Chirp a close-lipped smile, crinkling his eyes, like it was some kind of secret just between the two of them. And suddenly, Chirp's tongue felt too big for their mouth. "Don't you think?"

More shifting under that knowing look. Chirp wasn't sure what to do with themselves when Brend was looking at them like that. Where did their hands go? Should they look him in the eye or just over his shoulder? Was it rude to look directly in people's eyes? Was it rude not to? Chirp didn't understand any of these vague human idiosyncrasies.

"Maybe." They didn't know. Maybe there *were* easier ways —there probably were, but they hadn't thought too much about this one. Because it wasn't *really* about making him trust them. It wasn't *really* about getting close enough to do what they needed to. It was about showing Brend a little of the world before he went. In that, Chirp supposed he was right. There would have been more expedient ways to get this done.

"If you need some pointers, I'd be more than happy to help," Brend teased, a wicked smile curling up the side of his face, showing off his teeth and making his eyes squint. Something in Chirp's chest gave a sickening lurch. Their heart, maybe, but they were fairly sure hearts weren't supposed to do that. And they'd only ever heard of that happening in romance novels . . .

*Oh.* Oh, they were in trouble, weren't they?

CHIRP HAD NEVER GIVEN pacing a thought before, even if they'd done it themselves recently. It seemed a strange behavior that humanoid beings did which was entirely unproductive. It burned too many calories, and didn't seem to help them think at all, or quell their anxiety like they thought it would. What they hadn't realized was that it was also wholly *involuntary*.

A fact Chirp was becoming intimately familiar with as their muscles burned with a jittery need to move. The nerve endings of their entire body were on high alert, feeling every brush of the trousers they'd tugged on, every fold of the blouse they'd tucked into the waistband. How did non-android beings deal with this much sensation on a daily basis? It was enough to make Chirp go mad.

If the Ringmaster didn't do them in for the decision they'd made, then the anxiety burning through every pore of their body very well might. Maybe it would be better to go back to being an android. To not feeling. Then they could do what they had to and move on with things. They wouldn't have a heart to lurch or break at the realization that the first being in their memories who looked at them like an actual person was someone they would have to kill. That they would be the one to snuff that light out. To deny the world the paradox that was Brend.

"Ah, you're early," the Ringmaster said, a grin crawling up the edges of his mouth, more wound than expression of joy really, as indulgence settled into his eyes. Like he knew what Chirp was about and he didn't care. He was going to *make* them do this whether they liked it or not.

Chirp swallowed around a fluttering in their throat, butterflies trying to fly up their esophagus and escape through their mouth. They were going to be sick. They were *definitely* going to be sick, they realized, as the thickness of their spit slid down too hot and too slick. Sucking in a breath through their nose, they filled their lungs, focusing on the feeling of them expanding against their ribs before they said, "I can't do this."

"Can't do *what*, Chirp? You're going to have to be more specific." The Ringmaster settled into the chair behind his desk, his hands folding on the surface in front of him, and Chirp knew, they knew without a shadow of a doubt, that he was toying with them. Delighting in the way Chirp's weight shifted from foot to foot. In the fidgeting of their fingers. He had clocked every sign of discomfort, and he found pleasure in it. The sadist.

"I can't kill him," Chirp said, not even bothering to beat around the bush, because what point was there? The Ringmaster knew exactly what they were there to say, and he was going to make them say it. Just so he could refute it and give them no other option, Chirp gulped around the sudden realization. That was it, wasn't it? The Ringmaster already had a plan to make it so they couldn't back out. Even armed with that knowledge, they had to play this conversation through till the end, or they'd never sleep again.

"I'm afraid you don't have much choice. You signed a contract, remember?" He tapped his fingers once on the desk, and the piece of paper that Chirp had signed what felt like eons ago appeared. He tapped again, and it was gone. A brief flash. A threat. "If you don't, you're mine. For the rest of eternity."

"Eternity?" They hadn't– They hadn't *realized* that's what they were signing. But it would make sense. Without a mortal body, the Ringmaster didn't need magic to keep Chirp alive for forever if he so chose. He could have them dancing on his strings until the end of time. It wasn't just a lifetime they'd bargained away, it was their very soul. What had— What had they *done*?

"So I suppose you need to think," the Ringmaster

continued as if they hadn't spoken at all, his tone condescending and cruel, a pistol ready to deliver the killing blow. "What's worse? Living the rest of your life as a murderer? Or spending an indeterminate amount of time under my care?"

He had his answer before he'd even said the words, and they both knew it. Because what kind of choice was that? Who *wouldn't* choose themselves if given those two options? Chirp had tried to tell Brend that they were selfish; he didn't believe them. They wished he had.

"How would you like it done?"

The Ringmaster tapped on his desk again, and a little vial of a glowing blue liquid appeared. It blinked once, twice, then turned clear. "A couple of drops of this in his drink, and that should do it."

"Will it– Will it hurt?" They needed to know. They didn't want him to suffer. It was the least they could do for him. "I don't want him to be in any pain."

"You don't need to worry about that. He'll just go to sleep." There was something the Ringmaster wasn't telling them. Something he was hiding behind that smug twitch of his lips. But it likely wouldn't change anything if Chirp knew it. Any way they went about this, Brend would have to die, and Chirp may as well earn their freedom for doing it.

They lunged forward, snatching up the bottle before they could change their mind, then spun on their heel to leave before the Ringmaster could say anything else. They were back to their own room before they realized that the vial was slipping through their sweating hands and their heart was leaping up their throat. Tucking the vial away, Chirp scurried to the bathroom to dispel the contents of their stomach.

A soft noise of disapproval from Amara followed.

# TWENTY-FIVE
## MANU & CREW

"He has to be working for the Uprising," Agnes grumbled, his voice muffled and echo-y enough that Manu could tell he hadn't even bothered to set down his mug of tea to do it. Which was just so typically Agnes that Manu had to choke back a scoff.

"There's no evidence of that," Rose pointed out, the voice of reason as ever. Manu missed the rest of his crew. He missed Benard and Owen. But above all others, he missed Persi. The missing her sat like an ache in his bones, making every movement feel like he was pushing through water. She would have found a positive spin to this. She'd look at this situation and bring something good to the discussion. How he'd wound up with only the pessimists on this mission he didn't know, but it was a little depressing.

"Other than that Felicity thinks he's trying to kill the prince." Drea shifted wherever she was sitting, her clothes rustling softly in the darkness of Manu's vision. Seeing all of their expressions would've been helpful—it would tell him how much hope they still harbored—but unfortunately, that was out of the question. He'd just have to make due with what he could hear from their tones and movements. No easy task, but he was getting better at it every day, or at least he thought he was. Maybe one day, he wouldn't even miss his sight. Well, that probably wasn't true. He would always miss his sight. But it wouldn't be so bad once he got a better feel for how to read people without it.

"But that could be just rumors. Workplace gossip," Rose said, her patience stretched thin if the tightness of her voice was anything to go by.

Gods he hoped this didn't dissolve into shouting as it had so many times recently. He already had a headache starting behind his eyes just thinking of it. Without Persinette and Sully—the two calmest voices in the group—things frequently *did* end in shouting. It seemed every bullheaded person on the *Duchess* had been sent along with him. Maybe to keep them out of the way. Maybe it had been Benard's idea, payback for all the trouble Manu caused him over the years. Or maybe it was just because they were the ones most likely to cause trouble if the *Duchess* ran afoul of Eddi and their Uprising. Manu didn't know, but if he'd known this was how the teams were going to work, he'd probably have suggested something else. Yet here they were, "Team Manu" as he'd taken to calling them in his head—because if he said it out loud, he was sure more than one of them would throw something *at* his head.

"Or they could be true." Felicity had been quiet for the majority of the conversation, just soaking everything in, but there was a certainty to her voice now. Something that said she might know more than the rest of them. She probably did. She was the most friendly of the lot of them and thus the most likely to get people to talk to her.

If they *all* had that ability, they would have halved the time it took to find things out. But Manu supposed the others had other useful skills. Agnes was a superb planner, able to figure things out down to the most minute detail and have multiple backup plans in case things went to pot. Rose was clever beyond reason and probably could take over the Ringmaster's ship without him having noticed she'd done it until they were flying away. Drea was . . . All right, so Drea's skill set was mostly brute force, but that had its place too.

"Why?" Rose's chair creaked under her, likely because she had leaned forward to press her face in close to Felicity's, hoping to get a straight answer. "What have you heard?"

"It's not about what I've heard, it's about what I've *noticed.*" Anyone else might have been annoyed by having to explain themselves or justify what they said, but not Felicity. She was just young enough to realize she had a lot to prove, and just old enough to actually be able to prove it. They were lucky to have her. *Really* lucky. "And I've noticed that one acrobat, the one who does the act with the ribbons?"

Manu nodded, and he assumed everyone else did as well, confirming that they knew who Felicity meant.

"They've been going out with the prince the last few nights."

"She's right. They came to us yesterday looking for some-place to take him that might impress him." Drea's voice was a soft rumble, pride lining her tone, likely at the fact that Felicity had managed to get just what they needed before any of the others who were more than twice their age. "We sent them by the Dogeared Inn."

"That doesn't mean anything." Agnes scoffed, and Manu could imagine him rolling his eyes, although it was hard sometimes to remember what Agnes even looked like. He'd met the man exactly once, in the heat of battle, before he'd lost his sight. He was mostly a blank face with long rainbow hair at this point. "Maybe the acrobat just likes the prince."

"I mean . . . That's not *un*true," Drea murmured, then let out a soft *oof* when Felicity presumably elbowed her.

"That's not all there is to this," Felicity said, her voice stronger than Manu thought he'd ever heard it before, confidence lining every syllable. "The Ringmaster is up to something with that one. *Making* them do things."

"How can you be so sure?" Agnes still sounded skeptical, but like maybe he was willing to take Felicity's word on this. He just needed a little more proof, a little more time to think things over. Manu was glad they were taking Felicity seriously, not dismissing her out of hand because she was young. Persinette would be happy about that too, as she had begun treating Felicity as her second in command almost immediately.

"There is only one way to know for certain, really." Manu rubbed at his eyes with the heels of his hands. He didn't know that they could get tired even when they didn't work—what a strange concept—but they *were* tired. The lids were heavy, and the feeling of fuzz filled them, like when he'd been reading for too long. Manu lifted his head, the prickle of all the gazes in the room running across his skin. He was still their captain, even for all he'd basically ceded his place as leader to Persinette. He was still the one in charge, especially when she wasn't there. "We need to get into his office."

"And how would you suggest we do that?" Rose huffed, disbelieving. Hiccup whistled his disapproval, and Manu wasn't sure if it was for him or for Rose, but he got his answer a second later when Rose muttered a quick, "Sorry."

"I've got some ideas," Agnes volunteered, his tone going up a little, like he was smiling or sneering, the words coming out through his teeth. It didn't matter which it was. The point was, Agnes had a plan—multiple plans, very likely—and Manu wasn't going to look a gift unicorn in the mouth.

THE FIRST OF Agnes's plans was a complete and utter disaster. Which was both unusual and unsettling by turns. Manu hadn't known Agnes long, but in the time that he *had* known the unicorn, he hadn't seen a single of Agnes's plans go so entirely wrong from the start as this one did.

"You're just going to sneak in," Agnes had said, a verbal shrug in his voice that Manu kind of felt like he needed to shake away. "You and Hiccup, you're the least conspicuous."

"How are we the *least* conspicuous?" Manu muttered now.

Hiccup gave a soft twitter of confusion from where they were both ducked down under the well of the Ringmaster's desk waiting for the man to leave.

It had been nothing short of a miracle that Hiccup heard the Ringmaster coming and warned Manu in time for Hiccup to hide them away before he opened the door. And while Manu appreciated that Agnes wasn't treating him like he was incapable just because of his curse, it still seemed terribly unwise for the blind man and the robot to be the ones to search the Ringmaster's office.

Or maybe that had been *intentional.* Maybe Agnes *meant* for him to get caught, to lull the Ringmaster into a false sense of security, let him thwart their—

"Who's there?" the Ringmaster asked, his voice hard. He had been humming since the moment he came into the room but stopped at some noise that Manu hadn't heard over the pounding of his heart in his ears. Boots stomped against the floor, a clear warning of the Ringmaster getting closer and closer to Manu and Hiccup's hiding spot. Hiccup's sharp little pincers dug into Manu's skin, which would leave behind welts, no doubt, but that was the least of their worries.

They didn't know what kind of power the Ringmaster had, and although they hadn't given him any of their true names, that didn't mean he couldn't wield his magic against them in other ways. Especially if he were to actually catch them snooping around his office.

Yes, this had *definitely* been a part of Agnes's plan, Manu decided. In a game of chess, he was the knight Agnes was sacrificing to protect the queen. All Manu could hope was that the queen was their mission and not Agnes himself. He thought maybe he knew the answer to that worry, but he couldn't be certain, and it was that uncertainty that sat like lead in his stomach as he listened to the Ringmaster slowly make his way toward the desk.

"Eeny. Meany. Miney. Moe. Catch a tiger by his—" the Ringmaster sang, his voice soft and warm and impossibly beautiful. It wasn't really fair that a man who had likely done so many horrible things—if the reports were correct, and there was no reason to assume that they weren't—should be so charming and handsome. Manu didn't have to see him to know that he was handsome—the Ringmaster oozed it in every smooth word he said. The unearned confidence of a man who had never once in his life had to ask twice for something. Manu would know because he'd been much the same before Persinette, before leaving the Uprising, before the war. The last word left the Ringmaster as a hushed breath against Manu's cheek: "Toe!"

Hiccup squealed so loudly, he sounded like a baby fox just learning to scream. He also must have tried to stand to escape the Ringmaster because there was a loud bang on the underside of the desk, jolting the heavy piece of furniture around them both.

Manu, for his part, aimed to look unfazed. It wouldn't help any of them if he were to get ruffled in this situation. Besides, maybe he could play this off. Say they were playing hide-and-go-seek with some of the littles amongst the circus or that he'd just gotten lost.

"Captain Manu Kelii, as I live and breathe," the Ring-master said with a chuckle.

Maybe not.

"I'm not—I'm not—" He was supposed to be glamoured. He hadn't taken off the pendant that Agnes magiced days ago to hide his true identity. But then he remembered: Agnes had borrowed the pendant under the pretense of recharging the spell, something like a lie in his voice. At the time, Manu thought nothing of it. Agnes frequently sounded like he was lying—mainly because he was always lying to himself to some degree—and besides, what was there to lie about with the pendant? It wouldn't serve any of them to be recognized on the Ringmaster's ship except . . .

"How did you get in here?"

Manu bit the inside of his cheek, his jaw clenching as he lifted his chin just the slightest. "Wouldn't you like to know?"

"Yes, I would, that's why I asked." The Ringmaster sighed, and it sounded like he was standing up, the floorboards creaking under him before he settled his weight into his chair. "I don't suppose you came with a team, did you?"

"Of course not." Manu scoffed, leaning heavily into the man he had been before leaving the Uprising. Overconfident. Fool-ish. Brash. That was who the world still knew him as, and if it would protect his people, his mission, he'd be that man again. He only hoped Persinette would be able to forgive Agnes for using him this way. *He* certainly wouldn't. He also hoped that the Ringmaster would brush Hiccup off as just another H1-CCUP droid. He pushed to his feet, letting the little droid help him up so he didn't bump his own head on the bottom of the desk. "Who needs a team when you're Captain Kelii?"

"Of course not," the Ringmaster repeated, amusement still lining his tone. But it didn't sound like he thought Manu was lying, which was good. If this was all he could do to aid the mission right now, then so be it. But then the Ringmaster said something that left Manu's head spinning. "Honestly, you Kelii siblings are such a hassle."

"Wait . . ." *Siblings? Is my sister here?* "What?"

But he never got an answer because a moment later, the Ringmaster murmured a quick spell and snapped his fingers to knock Manu out.

## TWENTY-SIX

## CHIRP

*'m not a good person. I'm selfish.*

The words echoed in Chirp's mind, playing over and over again. They told Brend what they were. They were honest with him. They tried to *save* him.

*I don't believe you.*

How could a person be so naive? How could he have seen all that Chirp showed him, read the books in the library at the back of the pub, learned the history of Chirp's people, and still not have believed them when they said they meant to harm him? They had every reason to *want* to harm him. He was the son of the queen who'd made a scapegoat out of their people. The son of the woman who had arrested, enslaved, killed entire races simply because they had magic humming in their veins. And the longer Chirp stayed in this humanoid body, the more they realized that they, too, had magic humming in their veins. They were one of the Enchanted that Brend had seemed so afraid of on that first night.

He didn't seem afraid now.

"That's because he's a fool," Chirp said, trying to convince themselves of the fact. But it didn't really work. Nothing they tried worked.

Sleep wouldn't come. Their mind raced. The vial of clear

liquid—*poison, it's poison, Chirp*—sat on the window sill, catching the light of the moon like a prism, casting a ghostly glow on the floor that Chirp couldn't tear their eyes away from for long.

They wished it were true. Wished that they could shrug all of this off as Brend just being the biggest idiot known to Daiwynn. Attribute it to the fact that they'd just done that well in convincing him to trust them. But that wasn't the truth. The truth was that Brend seemed to see Chirp for all that they were, the good and the bad. He seemed to understand what was happening and the danger they posed him. He likewise seemed to realize that they didn't really *want* to hurt him.

The only fault in his logic? Chirp didn't have much of a choice in the matter. No way out. At least, not one that they could see. The Ringmaster made sure of that.

"Who's the real fool here?" Amara asked, her voice taunting from where it echoed around the inside of Chirp's mind. "The fool who believes someone is good when they are not? Or the fool who believes themselves bad when they are not?"

"Shut up," Chirp hissed, running a hand through their already terribly mussed hair. They let out a long huff that made their shoulders hunch forward. No way out. No way around. No way through. They were trapped. They didn't think they liked being trapped. Although they didn't know many people who did.

If only they hadn't signed that contract, then—

The contract. They lifted their head from where it had fallen to rest against their knees, their heart hammering against their chest in something that might have been hope.

They were bound by the contract and the contract only, as far as they could tell. Chirp and the Ringmaster hadn't shaken hands. He hadn't asked for a sampling of their blood.

Yes, the old contract might have had all of those precautions, and the Ringmaster might be able to hold Chirp to *that* bargain, but not this one. Not if they destroyed the contract.

And if they were able to destroy it, then maybe they could get a look at the old one, see what the conditions were in it. Maybe find a way to wiggle out of that one as well. Freedom could be within Chirp's grasp without ever having to give a single drop of that poison to Brend. Chirp could save them *both*.

But they would need help. A *lot* of help.

"I could help you," Amara argued, and Chirp knew for certain they hadn't said that last bit out loud.

"You can't."

"Why not?"

"Because you aren't real!" Chirp's chest heaved, their mind buzzing with frustration and too many thoughts, too many options. But their outburst made Amara fall silent, leaving Chirp the room they needed to think. Thus far, there was only one person they trusted to help . . . Felicity.

The thought sprang to Chirp's mind as if it had been planted there, roots digging into all the hidden corners of themselves. Was that what having a friend was like? Someone who they could count on? Chirp didn't know—they'd never *had* a friend before. At least, not that they could remember. And Chirp didn't really spare the sensation much thought as they exited their room and strode down the corridor to where Felicity and Drea were staying.

The couple would be asleep, no doubt about that. It was very late, or very early, depending on who you were talking to, and Chirp knew for a fact that Drea, at least, would be grumpy at her rest being interrupted. A thought that didn't actually bring Chirp pause. It probably should have—there were probably rules about this sort of thing, but whatever they were, Chirp didn't know them. So they lifted their hand

and knocked loudly enough to wake the occupants, then stepped back to wait for an answer.

There was some grumpy-sounding shuffling on the other side of the door. A muffled, "You answer it." Then the door creaked open to reveal a blurry-eyed Felicity. She blinked lazily at Chirp, heavy-lidded and tired.

"Chirp?" Felicity croaked, scrubbing at her face with her free hand as if trying to better understand the sight in front of her.

Which was entirely fair, Chirp supposed, as they must look a sight. They didn't have to see themselves to know that their hair was sticking up all over the place, and there must be bags under their eyes. Not sleeping more than a few hours and hardly eating would do that to a person. Gods, Chirp missed their android body more and more. At least the maintenance required to keep it looking presentable was minimal.

"What's wrong?"

There was no simple answer to that question, so Chirp just said, "May I come in?"

With a glance over her shoulder, Felicity let out a soft hum, then stepped back from the door, opening it farther to invite Chirp in wordlessly. The door shut softly behind then, and in the soft glow of the bedside light, Chirp could see Drea sitting up, her back to the wall beside their bed, knees drawn up to her chest. She didn't look happy, but that, too, was fair, as Chirp had just woken them up in the middle of the night.

"You look like you should sit down," Felicity offered, not unkindly, clearing off the stool from beneath her vanity so that Chirp would have a place to sit that wasn't the bed. Chirp was grateful.

"Thank you," Chirp murmured, settling into the seat and waiting until Felicity moved to the edge of the bed, leaning forward on her knees so that she could meet Chirp's eyes.

Tired but no less determined to help. *That's nice.* Having someone who they could go to, who would look at them like that, like they cared, was nice. They wondered idly if they'd ever had that before. If they deserved it. Probably not.

"So, what's going on?" Felicity pressed, her voice still a little scratchy from sleep, but there was a warmth in it that curled around Chirp's shoulders like a blanket.

Sucking in a breath, Chirp focused on the expansion of their lungs, on the press of them against their ribs, to try to ground themselves, but by the time the breath released, the dam had broken. Maybe it was the kindness in Felicity's eyes. Or the late hour. Or maybe it was just that Chirp was so very tired, that the last handful of days had been so very long. Whatever it was, they told Felicity and Drea everything, talking well into the morning as the sun broke over the horizon and filtered glaring light in through the window.

All about waking up on that table not even a month ago, and how the Ringmaster had come to them with a deal. The kind of deal they couldn't pass up even if they'd wanted to. Which they did, as it turned out; they *did* want to.

Sunshine gleamed bright against Felicity's eyes, making her squint in a way that looked more like determination than discomfort, but it wasn't she who spoke first once Chirp was through.

It was *Drea* who lifted her head from where Chirp had kind of thought she'd fallen back asleep against her knees and said, "Looks like we're going to be breaking into the Ringmaster's office again, doesn't it?"

"It does," Felicity agreed, her lips twitching up at the corners. "We're going to need more than just the three of us."

"I'll go get the others." Drea scooted herself forward off the bed, pressing to her feet and stretching her hands above her head. "The Ringmaster should still be asleep, at least for another hour. That will give us plenty of time to decide on a plan."

"Be careful waking Rose, you know how she can get." The grin spread, warm and real, across Felicity's face, setting her alight in a way that Chirp felt maybe they shouldn't be seeing. That light wasn't for them. It was for Drea. It was for Felicity's little family unit.

"Yes, ma'am," Drea teased warmly, dipping down to press a kiss to Felicity's cheek before shuffling for the door to find the others.

THE PLAN, which had actually been concocted by someone named Agnes, who looked very unimpressed with the fact that he was being pulled out of his bed to help plot such a thing, was simple. But just because it was simple, Chirp was realizing, didn't mean something couldn't go wrong.

For one, the Ringmaster was supposed to have been back-stage, directing the acts for that evening. Orchestrating, shouting orders, and making sure everyone was where they were supposed to be. Everyone except Chirp and Felicity, who had somehow managed to get out of performing that night by saying they needed extra rest before the big finale. Only, he wasn't. He was walking down the long corridor toward his office, his head ducked over some piece of paper that he seemed to be reading as he went. Correspondence, maybe.

For two, Brend was not supposed to be there. He was *also* supposed to be at the performance, enjoying the show as Chirp made sure he stayed alive long enough to see his next birthday at the very *least*. Only, he also wasn't.

"Chirp!" Brend called, pulling everyone in the hall to a

standstill, including the Ringmaster, who turned to look over his shoulder at where Chirp and Felicity had been tucked around a corner.

"Brend," Chirp laughed, too high, too false. They knew the moment Brend wrinkled his nose that it didn't sound like them at all. Gods, they were in so much trouble. *So* much trouble. "I thought you'd be at the performance?"

"Decided to skip it." Brend shrugged, seeming to be trying for nonchalance, but there was a nervous twitch to his jaw. Like that wasn't all there was to it. "When I heard you weren't performing."

*Ah, there it was,* Chirp thought as Felicity elbowed them in the ribs. Chirp could still feel the Ringmaster's attention on them. He might not have turned all the way around, he might not be in sight, but he was listening. Obviously hoping to catch something that might be useful, or maybe confirm that Chirp was about to complete their mission. *Blast.*

"I went by your dressing room, but . . ." Brend shifted on the leg he frequently favored as if it were bothering him. Chirp had never asked why he used the cane, but they noticed the way he seemed to favor that one side. The way he would stumble sometimes if the ground was too uneven. He would tell them when he wanted to. When he was ready. If he were still alive to do so, anyway. "You weren't there."

"Oh. No. I wasn't." Chirp fumbled for a lie, *any* lie, that would alleviate the crawling feeling of the Ringmaster watching and the pressure of Brend's too-wide, too-trusting gaze on their face. Gods, would everyone just stop looking at them for a second and let them think!

"We were just looking for the Ringmaster," Felicity said, springing into action. At least one of them could think on their feet. "We came to tell him that one of the dancers is hurt. It's Petunia," she continued, loudly enough for the Ringmaster to hear from where he was skulking around the corner. "We think she's twisted her ankle."

"Oh." Brend sounded disappointed, but Chirp didn't understand why. It wasn't like he was going to the performance anyway, so why should he care if one of the dancers was injured and the act would have to be swapped out for another? They were taking the gamble that it would be Agnes', but there was really no way to know with the Ringmaster. "I should– You should do that then."

"No worries, I can handle it." Felicity flapped her wrist, swatting his words away like flies. "You should go on, Chirp."

"I should?" But weren't they supposed to help Felicity search the Ringmaster's office? If they weren't with her, who would play lookout? Who would have her back?

"You should. I've got this covered." Felicity tilted her head forward to give Chirp a meaningful look and said, like it was a promise, "Really, it'll be okay."

"Okay," Chirp all but squeaked, then stumbled forward at a gentle shove from Felicity toward Brend. "Come on, then, before someone notices you're missing."

Brend nodded, his face lighting in a sunny smile that made Chirp's heart stutter in their chest again. This was such a bad idea. The worst idea. But Chirp couldn't tell Felicity that without exposing their whole plan. So, off they went.

# TWENTY-SEVEN
## BREND

Chirp said to believe people when they told him who they were. Then they told Brend exactly who *they* thought they were. *Selfish. Not a good person.* And maybe Brend should have believed them. They did admit to only trying to become friends with him so they could hurt him. But everything he had seen of Chirp since they'd become friends told him a different story.

Someone who was selfish wouldn't take the time to educate Brend the way Chirp had. They wouldn't take steps to expand his worldview. And they certainly wouldn't have pulled Brend from the circus ship and out into the cool night air in spite of the clear risk it posed to their own safety.

No, if Chirp wanted to hurt Brend, they'd had plenty of chances so far and hadn't taken any of them. In Brend's mind, actions spoke louder than words, and Chirp's actions were too good for them to be anything but.

So, he'd slipped his guard again and snuck away to the halls of the circus to hunt down his new friend. Then he wasted not a single moment when Chirp muttered, "This way," and started leading him through the streets of the capital. Off on another adventure the likes of which he'd only ever read about.

It was thrilling. Which might have been clouding his

judgment about this whole thing—he was sure that Clancy would say that it was—but he didn't care. When would he ever get the chance again? Never, probably.

"Where are we going tonight?" Brend asked, keeping pace with some effort. They seemed to be in a rush tonight, nerves making their grip on his wrist clammy. He had stumbled upon something back in the corridor of the circus. Something with Chirp and that blue-haired girl, but he didn't know what. That probably should have worried him too, but it didn't. Maybe he *was* just as naive and foolish as his mother always admonished him for being after all.

"You'll see," Chirp said. There was a bright, almost shy smile stretched across their face, their dark eyes glittering with something that Brend hadn't seen before. Like they'd discovered something in the hours that Brend had spent apart from them. And it all made his breath catch in his chest in a way he didn't rightly understand.

He hoped they'd share it with him, whatever it was. Because so far, everything Chirp had shared with him was equal parts terrifying and illuminating. Not because he wanted to know more about Chirp and where they came from. Not that at *all*.

The streets wound smaller and smaller, twisting through depths of the capital city that Brend hadn't even known existed. He'd seen plenty of maps of his city and never once noticed these alleys before, but Chirp seemed to know them like the back of their hand, stepping lightly over uneven cobbles and never hesitating at a fork. When they finally stopped, it was in front of a solid cement wall, the dingy gray of it almost disappearing in the darkness of the evening light.

"Did we take a wrong turn?" Brend asked, leaning to one side so that he could look around Chirp standing just in front of him, almost blocking his view entirely. From what he could see, it looked like a dead end. Which was strange since Chirp had known where they were going, hadn't they? They'd seemed so sure of themselves. But maybe in their speed, they'd gone right when they should have gone left. Easy mistake to make, really. Brend had done it more than once in his own castle, and he'd grown up there.

"No." Chirp sounded like they were swallowing back a laugh, their hand tightening almost reflexively around his wrist as they inhaled deeply. "Just catching my breath."

Brend nodded absently, tugging his hand a little so he could pull his wrist from Chirp's and link their fingers together, pressing Chirp's damp palm to his own. He thought he could maybe feel Chirp's pulse pick up, beating harder in their veins. But maybe that was his own. His breath did stutter a little in his throat at the intimacy of their fingers threaded together. Clancy never held his hand like this. It was always fingers closed, wrapped tight around his smaller palm, as if it were a struggle for dominance and Clancy was winning. This was better, Brend decided immediately, so much better.

"All I've shown you so far . . ." Chirp licked their lips, their thumb brushing over Brend's knuckles, a soothing gesture, perhaps for themselves as much as it was for Brend. "It's been a little sad."

"It has, but it's been true," Brend agreed with a soft hum. He couldn't deny that it had hurt his heart to see the labor camp, to read about them and all the people who lost their lives under his mother's rule. But it was necessary that he saw those things. It had been good that he learned what his mother was doing wrong so he could do things differently when it was his turn. Chirp was doing him a favor by showing him those things, even for as sad as they were.

"Yes, it has been." Chirp's thumb was still brushing over his knuckles. Perhaps the action was involuntary. Brend didn't know, but he wasn't going to draw attention to it at the risk that they might stop. Their skin was calloused, perhaps from the ribbons they used during their act, but the gesture itself was so soft it almost tickled, sending a pleasant shiver up his arm, lifting the hair in its wake. "But you haven't been able to truly appreciate the beauty of my people."

The way they said "my people" sounded like they were unsure of it, like it was perhaps the first time they had said it out loud. Brend could only wonder what that meant, as a moment later, Chirp pulled him forward, walking straight for the wall. Brend braced for impact, his eyes squeezing shut, but instead of hard stone slamming into him, something wet and cold slapped against his face. Like walking through a curtain of water. There one moment, soaking him through to the bone, and gone the next, leaving him dry as a bone on the other side.

"Open your eyes," Chirp whispered close enough to his ear that he could feel their breath against his skin, warm and shiver-inducing.

Brend didn't wait for further prompting. He gave his eyes one final squeeze, then forced his eyelids upward to take in what was on the other side of that cement wall. Everything rushed in all at once: the sounds, the smells, and the sights.

Stuffed into a narrow alley were rows upon rows of shabby but colorful stalls, all lit by softly pulsing floating lights. The market wasn't as crowded as the one Clancy had taken him to a handful of days ago, but it seemed somehow more *alive*. People chattered softly with the vendors. There were food stalls every couple of feet, wafting smells about the space the likes of which Brend had never experienced before. And everywhere he looked, he found a new Enchanted feature. Pointed ears. Neon green hair. Glowing eyes. Wings! There were so many of them, all meandering through the tight space as if they did this every day.

Chirp let him soak it all in, a smile tilting the corner of their mouth as they stared at him, their attention heavy. When he was finally able to draw himself away from trying to take it all in all at once, Chirp raised their brows at him. "What do you think, Your Highness?"

"It's amazing," Brend breathed, his own mouth stretching to match Chirp's grin, as if their happiness was infectious. Maybe it was; he wouldn't doubt it. It was hard not to smile back at someone when their smile looked like Chirp's. A dimple settled into one corner of their mouth, their nose wrinkled slightly like they were just on the verge of laughing, and their eyes were alight with the kind of joy Brend didn't think he'd ever know again.

"You think that's amazing?" Chirp whispered, leaning toward him as if to tell him a secret. "Wait till you see some of the goods. But first—"

They took ahold of his chin, rough fingers brushing against his stubble in a touch that made his heart stutter, and tilted his head back so his eyes were on the sky above them. Well, not sky. Roof? Ceiling? He couldn't tell what it was, but he could tell it was *beautiful.* It swirled with colors and slowly blinking lights littered amongst the smokey clouds like stars in a rainbow sky.

"What is it?" Brend stuck his tongue between his teeth, his eyes narrowing, trying to get a better look at it even for all that it was so far away.

"Magic." Chirp chuckled.

"Well, obviously. But what's its purpose?" Brend tilted his chin back down so he could eye Chirp curiously.

Their brows scrunched together. They shook their head and released a soft laugh. "There is no purpose. It was created, it is maintained, because it's beautiful."

"Oh," Brend breathed. He thought he might understand that, although he'd never really known anyone to do it before. In his world, things were done with a purpose. Everything had an endgame. Even Clancy's affection for him had likely been because of some perceived benefit to Clancy. Brend wondered what it would be like to have someone do something for him just because they wanted to. Just because it would make him happy. Just because it would bring a little beauty to the world. Maybe he'd never know.

Chirp must have seen the melancholy roll across his face because they gave his hand a little tug and said, "Let's go see what everyone's got for sale, yeah?" Then didn't wait for a reply before they pulled him out of the little alley they'd entered the market through and into the slow push and pull of shoppers.

In spite of it being eerily similar, it was also not the same at all as when Clancy took Brend to the human market. When the wil-o-wisp had . . . No. There were better things to think of. More exciting things. And besides, perhaps the wil-o-wisp hadn't been trying to hurt him at all. What he'd seen of Chirp's people since meeting them seemed to indicate a sincere lack of bloodlust.

Chirp held his hand the entire time, the rough pad of their thumb brushing over his knuckles whenever it seemed like the people around them might be too much for him. And when Brend asked a question, Chirp was happy to answer, or to find the answers if they didn't know, delighting in their shared wonder at discovering something new.

And the people . . . The people were as alike to the people in the human market as night was to day, yet so very much the same. Because the more he saw of the Enchanted, the more Brend realized that they were just people. Just mothers, fathers, sisters, brothers, aunts, uncles, daughters, sons, and everything in between, trying to make a home for themselves in Daiwynn. And there was wonder to be found in something as simple as that.

Brend felt safe with Chirp. So safe, in fact, that he forgot what they were and what they'd tried to tell him only the night before.

*What if my motives are nefarious, and in the end, I mean to hurt you?*

It happened as they were returning to the door they'd used to enter the city, their bellies so full that Brend was amazed he was still walking at all. Chirp turned their back to press the key into the keyhole. Then there was a crack in the quiet of the night, loud enough to make his ears ring, followed by a burning sensation. Sharp. Ripping through Brend so quickly, his knees buckled.

Someone shouted—Brend couldn't make out the words through the wobble of his heart pounding against his ribs— the voice vibrating through him from where he was suddenly lying on the ground.

Brend opened his eyes—he didn't know when he'd closed them, but he opened them just in time to see Chirp being shoved to the side and Clancy's face hovering over him. Clancy didn't look surprised, Brend noted, to see him lying there in a puddle of something warm and slick. Nor did he look angry.

In between one slow, heavy blink and the next, several more people were standing over him.

*Guards. Castle guards.*

There was a *thud,* and he looked over to see Chirp being forced to the ground, their ashen face stained red by something they hadn't even bothered trying to wipe off, a uniformed knee pressed into their back. Their brown eyes were wide, scared, red-rimmed, and they were the last thing Brend saw before he lost the battle with blood loss.

**P**ersinette's gaze swept across the assembled group in the mirror. It was hard to tell if they were all there in such a small space, but—"Where are Manu and Hiccup?"

Felicity shifted uncomfortably, her eyes looking over the top of the mirror on their side as if she were afraid to meet Persinette's gaze. The others weren't doing much better; they all looked guilty to some degree. Even Agnes. Although he perhaps looked the *least* guilty of the lot.

"We had to sacrifice them to keep the Ringmaster off our trail," Agnes said without a trace of remorse.

Persinette's heart lodged in her throat, her vision swam, and she choked around the words, "You *what*?!"

With an unrepentant shrug, Agnes met Persinette's hard stare. "He was getting suspicious, Persinette. I had to do something. And Manu had already drawn his attention. You're not here to make these decisions, you left them to me."

"No, I left them to the *group* as a *whole*, and that *included* Manu and Hiccup." The words slid through clenched teeth as Persinette bit back every nasty French curse word Benard had taught her.

Agnes sighed, and Persinette couldn't tell if it was because he was annoyed, tired, sad, or some combination thereof. She hoped he was sad. He *deserved* to be sad. Then he said, so soft that she almost thought it was Sully speaking, "They're fine, Persi."

"How do you know that?" So much had changed already, she'd lost so much, Persinette didn't know that she could handle any more. Not when it came to the family she'd built for herself. She'd protect each and every one of them with her life, with the last of her strength. Agnes seemed to know this—maybe because he was the same way, Sully always said he was a sap—and fixed her with an expression that was equal parts sympathy and kindness. It looked strange on a face she'd spent most of her life watching sneer and scowl at people as if they were lesser.

"Because I checked on them myself," he said, and for all it was meant to be a reassurance, it sounded like a confession. Agnes would never admit willingly that he'd started to see the crew of the *Duchess* as anything more than allies in a war he didn't want to lose, pawns he could move around at will. But he had wanted to get married in front of all of them. He had wanted Rose to stand by his side when he did it, and Persinette to officiate. This might be as close as he ever got to actually calling them family, and Persinette was going to cherish it. Well, she wanted to, anyway, until Agnes said, "Hiccup has been powered down and put in storage. And they've imprisoned Manu in the queen's dungeons. They're torturing him, but—"

And then she wanted to come through the mirror and shake Agnes until his teeth rattled again. "*Torturing* him?"

"It's nothing he can't handle, Persinette." Agnes tilted his chin back, inviting her to contradict him. "I asked him myself if he was all right. Do you not trust me to take care of our people?"

The wording was a challenge, but the tone was anything but. Agnes was trying to reassure her in the only way he knew how. *Our people.* Sully would've been delighted to hear Agnes say those words. Too bad Sully was busy interrogating Ivy.

"I do trust you." A strange truth, considering where Persinette and Agnes had started not more than a few months ago. The victim and her bully. But war changed people. Made some more sympathetic and others tougher around the edges. The same boiling water that softened the potato hardened the egg, after all, or so Persinette had once read in one of her books.

Surprise filtered across his face, Agnes's dark brows raising up high enough to almost touch the short pastel-rainbow hair that tickled his forehead. Then he nodded. "Good."

A smile pulled up one side of Persinette's mouth, warmth flooding her system at the strange camaraderie she'd built. It felt nice to be on the same side as Agnes the unicorn—strange, but nice.

"Tell me what you've found," Persinette said, clearing her throat so they could get back to business. Because Manu was being tortured. A war was on the horizon. And they were only a couple of steps closer to finding Eddi and their hide-out, which wasn't close enough.

"The Ringmaster is working for Eddi," Felicity said, taking a little step forward and shooting Agnes a look to check if it was all right for her to report. Agnes nodded, and Felicity continued, "He cornered one of his performers into getting close to the prince in the hopes that they'll be able to kill him when the time comes."

"And the time is coming quickly," Persinette muttered mostly to herself, but at the hum of confirmation, she lifted her gaze to meet Agnes's again. "We haven't gotten anything from Ivy yet on where the main Uprising base is, but Roy and Penny told me that they're on the move."

"Three days is our guess." Rose rubbed at the bridge of her nose where her spectacles had cut into it.

"Three days?" That wasn't much time at all. Not nearly enough for them to get to the Uprising base, take out Eddi, and be back in time to wage war on the queen. Even if they split their forces, it wouldn't do. Not if they didn't get answers from Ivy *today*. Persinette needed to contact Alys and Stella and get them moving, but she needed a direction to send them in first. Gods, everything was falling apart.

"The plan is to have a ball to celebrate the prince's engagement." Felicity's nose wrinkled, distaste coating her words. In any other circumstance, that expression would have made Persinette chuckle and ask Felicity why she was so disgusted by the idea of the prince getting married. But now wasn't the time for that.

"If I know anything about Eddi"—Agnes's mouth twisted into a sneer that once upon a time would have sent Persinette cowering—"they'll want to be there for that."

"Why?" Drea blinked, her head tilted to one side.

"Aside from the fact that it's their only nephew's engagement party?" A scoff left Agnes. "All the important people in Daiwynn's upper crust will be in the same place at the same time. It's the perfect place for Eddi to take out their sibling and force all the others to kneel before them."

"So you're saying all of our enemies will be in the same place at the same time?" Brushing hair back from her face, Persinette leaned in closer to the mirror to get a better look at everyone. The words tasted suspiciously like victory. "That seems terribly convenient."

"It does," Agnes agreed. Even though they both knew it would make their lives easier, he didn't look relieved by this fact. Maybe he, too, understood that this wasn't the solution they had all been hoping for; it was more likely to be another problem. "That doesn't mean we won't have to have our people take over the base. Just because we cut off the head of the snake doesn't mean it's going to stop wriggling."

"Ivy will give us what she has." Persinette would make sure of that. Even if she had to barter away her own magic to get it. "Sully's with her now."

Pride darted up Agnes's muscles, settling in his mouth to form a grin the likes of which only Sully could pull from Agnes. Love did strange things to people, and even Agnes wasn't immune.

"Right, we'll see what else we can find about Eddi's plan and what it has to do with the circus," Agnes said, then didn't wait for a goodbye before closing the connection between their mirrors.

Manu

PAIN MADE everything hazy and heavy. His own muscles worked against him as Manu tried to lift his head to meet the eyes of his torturers, more out of habit than anything else. He knew it wouldn't have the same effect as it had all those other times he'd stared down the blade of a knife and unsettled the person holding it. But old habits died hard.

"Tell us who else is working for the Uprising," the guard said, cracking his knuckles, which had just put a no doubt impressive bruise on Manu's jaw. Honestly, did they have to go for the face? He was vain about his good looks, and they were spoiling them. When Persinette showed up, she'd take one look at him and– Well, to be perfectly honest, she'd probably take one look at him and go scorched-earth on every guard in the vicinity. His little *hala kahiki* was a spitfire if he'd ever met one, and she would not take lightly the queen's men hurting someone she loved. Good. Manu's only regret was that he wouldn't get to *see* Persinette in all her vengeful glory.

Manu hummed, turning his head to spit blood onto the floor before saying, "No," with a laugh.

He wasn't sure why the guards thought he worked for the Uprising. Well, aside from the fact that his face was plastered all over Daiwynn. But there had to be more to it than that. Maybe Agnes wasn't the only one who had decided to use him as a pawn, sacrificing him in the name of getting the heat off of himself. That did fit with what they knew of the Ringmaster and his relationship with Eddi. The man would do anything for a bit of coin and power, and once Eddi had their way, they would have as much of both as Daiwynn had to offer. Manu didn't have to wonder what they'd promised the Ringmaster to see how this all fit together.

All he could hope was that Agnes was able to get what they needed now that the Ringmaster's attention was diverted to Manu. Enough to fit all the pieces together like a mismatched puzzle.

With that thought in mind, all there was left to do, really, was wait this out. Deal with the torture and try not to die in the time it took for the others to come and rescue him. Because they *would* come, of that he had no doubt.

"Get him up and take him back to the cells. He's not going to give us anything useful," the guard said through clenched teeth, frustrated. Good. At least Manu wasn't the only one, then. They dragged him to his feet, and Manu almost blacked out from the rush of blood to his head but managed to stave it off with a deep, wet gasp of breath and a clenched jaw. Then they practically dragged him back to the cell they'd pulled him out of what felt like forever ago.

"Is he all right?" someone asked from the cell next to Manu's. He didn't think they were asking about him, but that didn't seem to matter much because . . .

Because he *knew* that voice. Or at least he used to know someone with a voice like that. Only it wasn't *just* like that. It had been higher in pitch, the words more unsure, a child trying to sort out their thoughts as their mind moved faster than their tongue. On second thought, maybe it wasn't that someone's voice at all. But the way they spoke was the same, the measured-ness of their words. And Manu would swear he'd know that voice anywhere, even so many years later.

Maybe it was just wishful thinking, though. A hallucination brought on by the torture. The longing for something familiar in a situation that was terrifying without his sight. Torture. Imprisonment. They weren't new to him. But being able to see had made this all so much less scary. He could tell what guards he would be able to push and which ones would be the worst on him. He could see them coming. Without all of that . . .

Manu shook himself. He needed to stop hoping for someone who was long gone. Someone who had probably died decades ago.

Still, as he drifted out of consciousness, he couldn't help but murmur the name "Amara" to himself.

# TWENTY-NINE
## CHIRP

In all honesty, Chirp really should have seen this coming. The writing had been on the wall since the moment the Ringmaster first pressed that key into their hand. It was always going to end this way—Brend hurt, possibly dying, and Chirp locked up—whether Chirp was the one to pull the trigger or not.

"You can't fight fate," Chirp reminded themselves, leaning their head back against the cold, damp wall of their cell. It was almost amusing, *almost*, to think that when they first woke up on Rowan's ship, they'd thought of that little room as a cell, a prison. Even though they were free to move about the ship if they so chose. But *this* was a cell, complete with dripping stone walls, a hard stone floor, not more than a blanket for a bed, and bars. This truly was a prison. And soon, they would no doubt be executed for a crime they didn't commit.

There was still blood under their fingernails, probably still clinging to their face where it had splattered when Brend was shot. Shot. *Shot.* By his own *guard* of all people! As if Chirp had ever even held a pistol before. They hadn't. At least . . . they didn't think so. That was no doubt why the Ringmaster handed them poison instead of something a little more bloody to handle the job.

But that didn't seem to matter. Their protests, the truth, had gone unheard as the castle guards surrounded them and the slowly bleeding-out Brend. *Clancy* hovered over them, looking pleased with himself, like he wanted a pat on the back for a job well done. Chirp had thought to ask *why* he would do this to the man he seemed to care for. Why he would frame *Chirp* for it.

To the last one of those, the answer seemed patently obvious. Chirp was an Enchanted, an outsider; it was easy to pin something like this on them. But even with that in mind, Chirp couldn't help but wonder, *Why me? Why was I chosen as the sacrificial lamb in whatever Clancy is planning?*

It didn't matter, Chirp supposed, why it had been them, why Clancy had done it. The point was, it was done now, and Chirp was being blamed.

What did matter was—

"Is he all right?" Chirp asked the first guard that had come to visit them since they'd been locked in the cell however long ago. Hours? Days? They didn't know. There were no windows at all to gauge time by, and anything they might have had—a pocket watch, their bootlaces, the stays from their corset—had been taken off them.

"Is who all right?" The guard's mouth twisted up into a disgusted snarl, like they didn't want to speak to someone so lowly as Chirp, but they'd done it out of habit.

"Bre—" Chirp bit down hard on their tongue when the disgusted look morphed into something furious, then course corrected. "His Highness, the prince. Is the prince all right?"

"Why do you care? You *shot* him!" The last statement was spat into Chirp's face, spittle peppering their cheeks to join the blood and the grime from the city streets.

A cry choked them, strangled and desperate to tell the guard what happened, to have him believe them. An explanation, the truth, it all rushed up their throat like bile, threatening to spill itself onto the cold stone floor, but by the time they managed a stuttering, "I didn't- I wouldn't- Shoot him- " the guard was clicking his tongue and moving on to complete whatever task he'd come into the dungeons to do.

Chirp was alone with the truth of what happened again, and they couldn't erase the memory of Brend lying there, his blood turning the cobbles a red so deep, it almost looked black in the darkness of the alley.

"It'll be okay," Chirp had lied to Brend, ripping off the shawl wrapped around their shoulders to try to staunch the bleeding. The gray-brown fabric turned red so fast, *too* fast. He was going to die. He was going to die, and Chirp didn't know how to make it stop, how to fix it.

"This is your fault," Clancy said, letting the pistol clatter to the ground beside where Chirp was kneeling and removing the gloves he'd been wearing to stuff them into his pockets. He was devoid of blood, not a single drop had hit his perfect waistcoat. He didn't even bother to bend down and check on Brend, just stood leaning over him, watching him gurgle as blood coated his teeth. "Yours and his. It didn't have to be this way. If he'd just stayed inside, taken his potions, done as he was *told.* None of this had to happen. He could have died peacefully, and I would have had my title, just like she promised."

"I don't care whose fault it is!" The words came out on a gasp, Chirp's heart hammering against their ribs so hard, it was encroaching on their lung space. "Just help him! *Please.*" A choked sob accompanied the *please,* but Chirp didn't do anything to stop it. They were beyond caring what Clancy thought of them.

Clancy hummed, still not moving to help, and said, "Just keep applying pressure, the guards will be here soon."

And Chirp had little choice but to do as he instructed, leaving them no chance to escape—not that they'd tried.

When the guards found them, Brend had been unconscious for a long while, his blood had soaked into Chirp's trousers, and their tears were cooling on their face. They'd taken one look at the scene and hadn't even needed the tale that Clancy spun them about coming upon the two of them just in time to catch Chirp shooting their prince.

Never mind that Clancy was still hovering over them, not doing anything to try to staunch the bleeding. Never mind that, for all the blood Brend had lost, it couldn't have happened just before the guards arrived. Never mind what Chirp said to try to convince them that it had been *Clancy* who'd shot Brend. They took one look at Chirp's slightly pointed ears and shoved them onto the ground to shackle them in iron.

Chirp was pulled from their memories by the screech of a door and the sound of something heavy being dragged across the rough floors. They didn't bother to stand to see what it was. Whatever was coming their way—another prisoner or someone to execute Chirp—they wouldn't be able to fight it. Louder and louder the sound grew, until the guards passed Chirp's cell, dragging a man between them, his dark hair hanging in his face, obscuring most of it. What Chirp *could* see of his face looked battered, like they had taken several swings at his jaw and cheeks.

"Is he all right? What have you done to him?" Although Chirp wasn't sure why they cared. They didn't know this man. But something about him called to them.

He groaned when they dumped him in the cell next door to Chirp's, the bars slamming shut to keep him from escaping. Chirp didn't think he was going anywhere, even if they hadn't locked him in. They supposed he could be faking it, but it didn't seem like he was.

"What of the prince? Is he all right?"

Chirp was met with brusque silence as the guards strode

past them like Chirp didn't even exist. Their jaw shut with an audible click, and they retreated to their blanket, curling under it as if perhaps they could disappear or simply stop existing by hiding every part of themselves from anyone watching them.

It didn't work.

"THE KELII SIBLINGS, always causing me so much trouble." The Ringmaster clicked his tongue, rocking back to lean against the wall opposite Chirp's cell. Their new neighbor hadn't woken up yet, if his soft snoring was anything to go by, and the hours had slipped by in a haze of *drip drip dripp*ing and cold. Neither of which did anything to keep Chirp's mind from racing, wondering if Brend was alive, if he was receiving care, if Clancy had done permanent damage.

"What?" Chirp asked, poking their head out from under the blanket to glare at the Ringmaster. They didn't have the energy to deal with his cryptic nonsense right now. They may never have the energy for it again, if the queen executed them soon. Which she very well might. Shooting the prince had to be a hanging offense at the very least.

"Nothing. Nothing." The Ringmaster's smile had gone sharp and mocking. He tugged his jacket down into place, rubbing his fingers over imaginary wrinkles as he straightened from the wall. Five even steps brought him to the bars of Chirp's cell, ringed fingers clacking as they wrapped around the metal so he could sneer down into the dark at Chirp. "They're going to execute you, you know?"

"I'd assumed." It was really just a matter of time in Chirp's mind. They weren't fool enough to think that they'd get away with what happened. Especially as Clancy would want to shut them up as quickly as possible. No one would believe the truth, but it still wasn't ideal to have someone running around accusing him of shooting the prince. People might start asking questions. Chirp wasn't stupid. "Is that why you've come? To let me know that you're releasing me from your service since I'll be dead soon anyway?"

The Ringmaster scoffed, rolling his eyes. "Oh no, dear child, I came with another deal for you."

Another deal. Because the Ringmaster always had one more deal up his sleeve. One more way to get Chirp to do what he wanted. They supposed they shouldn't be surprised. He was the puppet master, after all, wasn't he? Tugging on Chirp's strings at every turn. Would those strings ever be cut? Would Chirp ever be truly free? Not until they were dead.

"What sort of deal?" Chirp pulled the blanket down from where it had been wrapped around their neck, muffling their words softly with the thin fabric.

"I can get you out of here," the Ringmaster vowed, dangling the possibility of it like a string in front of a cat. "Set you free *entirely*, just like I promised."

"Why and how would you do that?" Chewing on the inside of their cheek, Chirp narrowed their eyes on the Ringmaster. He always had an ulterior motive. Was always up to something. But with the noose tightening around their neck, what choice did they really have? And besides, maybe it would give them the chance to check on Brend before they went, to make sure that he was all right.

"I'll just tell the guards it couldn't have been you, you were with me the whole time, and that I had a couple of shapeshifters amongst my crew for a while, but they've since disappeared. Oh my, you don't think one of them may have shot the prince, do you?" The Ringmaster's eyes went comically wide, one many-ringed hand lifting to his lips as if he were shocked. "They'll believe me," he said with a shrug. "I have the records to prove it, and I've built a rapport with some of them."

Chirp's eyes narrowed further, not quite believing what he was offering them. There would be a cost, something he wanted in return. There always was with him. "And what do I have to do to get you to vouch for me like that?"

The innocent expression fell away from the Ringmaster's face and was replaced with something darker, more sly. "Just do what you've agreed to: kill the prince. He's already so weak from being shot, and with his declining health, it'd be easy. Slip the potion into his drink on the night his engagement is announced and this will all be over. You can return to your life, your family, completely free of my influence."

Blinking hard, Chirp wasn't sure which part of what the Ringmaster had just said confused them more. Brend was getting *engaged*. Their *family* was still out there, somewhere. They weren't all gone. Chirp wasn't alone in the world. And if they just did what he asked of them, then they could remember them, find them, reunite with them. Chirp wouldn't ever have to be alone again.

"Think about it," the Ringmaster said, patting his hand against the bars with another soft *ting-ting* of his rings. "You've got a couple of days to decide. At least until the ball." Then he turned on his heel and strode away before Chirp could rip any more questions from their spinning brain.

# THIRTY
## BREND

Everything hurt.

But by some miracle, he wasn't dying. Not yet, anyway. Things had been touch and go for a minute there he remembered. The doctors sounding panicked and harried, his mother shouting at them to fix it! Keep her son alive! She'd execute them and every member of their families if they didn't! Which might have been nice, a reassurance that she loved him, if she weren't doing it from across the room. If he hadn't woken up many a time since then and found no one at his bedside worrying over him. No chair pulled close so someone could sit beside him while he slept and make sure he didn't die between doctors' visits.

Not even Clancy. God. Of course not Clancy. Because Clancy had shot him.

Or at least, Brend was reasonably sure it had been Clancy. His back had been turned, and there was no way to really tell for certain. But Clancy had been there when he shouldn't have, and he knew Chirp hadn't shot him because he'd been facing them as they fiddled with the key in the lock one handed, trying to get it to fit while also unwilling to release the hold they had on him.

So, by process of elimination, it had to be Clancy.

Oh God.

Clancy had *shot* him.

Right there in the *street*.

Why? Why had he done it? Why, when—

It wasn't important. They *why* wasn't important. And he didn't have the energy to ponder the question for too long. His focus drifted between the way he could see the molding of the ceiling through the canopy of his bed, how different it was than the magiced sky of the market, and the pain that periodically radiated from his shoulder.

It could have been worse, he supposed. Clancy was an apt shot, and at the distance he'd stood from Brend, he probably could have shot Brend right in the back of the head without even trying. Brend liked to think maybe that was due to some lingering sentimentality. Or maybe he'd wanted it to be slow. Had wanted Brend to *suffer*. Or maybe it was an issue of identification of the–

Brend shook himself.

So, all things considered, it could have been worse. He could have been dead.

He wasn't dead. Nor dying. Both of which he was definitely grateful for. But he might be a little more grateful if someone would bring him some pain medication for the pounding behind his eyes.

Everything around Brend was too loud, too bright, like waking up after a midday nap and finding he'd developed a migraine in the interim. The world was a study in sharp edges, threatening to cut Brend into ribbons. And whoever was yelling outside of his door seriously needed to be *quiet*.

No. Not whoever. It was his mother. Her voice sharp and cold, like Brend had only ever heard it a handful of times in the past. Turning his head, Brend was able to peer through the crack between the doors to his bedroom at where his mother was talking to someone. A doctor, maybe, if the words "He's not in any shape for a ball, Your Highness" were anything to go by.

"He will be in a couple of days' time," his mother said, certainty lining every word. Brend didn't know how she knew that he'd be fine—she wasn't a doctor after all—but he did already feel much better than he likely should have given the circumstances. It had only been . . . two days? Maybe three? Since he'd been shot, and already he felt he had the strength to sit up. He hadn't tried it yet, of course, but he felt like he could if he wanted to. He didn't want to. He didn't want to go dancing either, but he supposed he'd get little choice in either of those things. What queen Eloise wanted, she generally got.

"Your Highness, I really don't–"

"I don't pay you to think," she snapped, then took a step closer to the doctor, looming over him like only a queen could. The lights dimmed a little as if to give the queen the mood lighting she wanted, the smell of petrichor thickening the air.

The doctor opened his mouth, and Brend could imagine him saying that the queen didn't pay him at all, but he seemed to think better of it and shut it again with a loud click of teeth.

"I pay you to do as you're told." One reddish-brown brow rose on her pale face, challenging and knowing all at once.

"Yes, Your Highness." The doctor's graying head dipped forward, his gaze fixing on his shoes as if afraid to meet the queen's eyes.

Brend knew that feeling well: the anxiety of trying to look his mother in the eye and tell her something she didn't like. He knew how it could crawl under a person's skin. Leave them itchy with the need to put distance between themselves and her disapproval. In any other circumstance, Brend might've been pleased to learn that he was not the only one who suffered from this feeling when faced with his mother. But as he strained to hear their conversation, his temples throbbing, he couldn't find it within himself to be amused. All he felt was pity that this poor man was being forced into something he didn't agree with.

"Good. Then you'll have him up and ready for a ball in three days." His mother's tone shifted from threatening to brusque. Like listing off items on a to-do list for the servants to carry out. Which was, Brend realized, exactly what she was doing, exactly what *he* was. Just another item on the ever-lengthening to-do list of the queen's life. Was that how it had always been? Had he ever been more than just a chore to her? To Clancy? He . . . he didn't know. "We need him presentable when we announce his engagement."

*Engagement?!* Brend jerked, and pain ripped through his shoulder, lighting every nerve on fire from there to his toes and drawing a whimper from him that was completely unintentional. It brought both people outside his door to stillness. Damn it.

"You'd better go and check on him," the queen murmured, annoyed.

"Yes, Your Highness." The doctor bowed so deeply, Brend wondered if he'd even be able to leverage himself back up again once Queen Eloise left.

The queen turned her back on the doctor and Brend's door, dismissing both in one motion. Then she stopped, humming to herself for a moment before she added, "Remember what I said, doctor. You have three days to get him up and about. If you can't manage it . . . Well, you know what will happen, don't you?"

"Yes, Your Highness."

"Good."

He waited until the queen had gone, her clipped footsteps retreating off into the distance until they were nothing, then the doctor turned for the door and entered Brend's room. He seemed unsurprised to see Brend watching him, or maybe he was just so stressed about the queen's threats that he couldn't feel anything else. Still, as he approached the bed he asked, "Are you in pain, Your Highness?" with a kindness the likes of which Brend had never known from another, except for maybe Chirp, and Charlie.

"A little," Brend admitted, hating the weakness in his voice.

The blankets were pulled off of him so the doctor could peel back the bandage on Brend's shoulder and examine the wound. "You are healing much more quickly than I expected."

"I feel strange." Swallowing against a throat lined in sandpaper and cotton, Brend frowned. He hadn't noticed it a moment ago, but he *did* feel strange. Very strange. Not so much in pain, aside from the headache, but rather like his veins were humming, his muscles jumping a little with the vibration in his blood.

"Yes, well, you *were* shot."

He was, but Brend didn't think that was it. There was something . . . *else* happening here.

The doctor leaned over to grab a fresh bandage from the nightstand, his fingers making quick work of covering the wound again. "You were listening, weren't you?"

With a sigh, Brend nodded. There was no point in hiding it. "Why is she selling me off?"

"I don't know." But the doctor looked upset by it, his gray brows pulled together as if he were trying to understand it himself.

It was sudden. There had never been discussion of an engagement before he'd been shot. Brend didn't even like anyone enough to marry them. Maybe before all of this, Clancy would have been an option, if that were allowed. But now . . . Brend shook himself.

"It's likely to try to cover the attack by that Enchanted."

"What?" Did they really believe that Chirp had been the one to do this? That was impossible. Clancy had been holding the gun! Hadn't he? Maybe not. Either way, it hadn't been Chirp, Brend knew that for certain.

"Yes, something to make the kingdom happy again. We're on the brink of war, you know. With the Uprising." The doctor wrapped Brend's robe tightly around his shoulders, then piled his blankets back on top of him, and the warmth threatened to drag him back down into sleep. But he fought the pull in order to pay attention. War. With the Uprising.

"We are?" A stupid question. But he was having a hard time getting his brain to process all of this. The engagement. His mother's tone. Clancy shooting him. A war! There was too much going on. How had he missed all of this happening right under his nose? Easily. He'd been too wrapped up in Clancy and the limited affections he would give Brend. Clancy had been the perfect distraction from the reality of his situation, feeding Brend just enough crumbs to keep him coming back for more.

"That's why they shot you," the doctor said, his voice quiet and gentle, like he was talking to a small child, explaining a very complex math problem. "To draw your mother into the war. They wanted to force her hand so she'd fire the first shot and be blamed when people were upset about the conflict."

"That's—" That didn't make sense, Brend wanted to say, but a yawn cut him off, making his jaw crackle.

Tsking softly, the doctor pulled the blankets up to his chin, patting his arm gently. "You don't worry about it. The point is, your mother is doing everything she can to protect you, as well as the rest of us." He pulled a syringe from the bedside table and added something to Brend's IV. "You should get your rest."

Brend wanted to argue; he did. He wanted to tell the doctor that he didn't need to rest, that he needed to see Chirp and make sure they were all right. But he didn't get the chance because already sleep was tugging him down, down, under the heaviness of whatever drugs the doctor had given him.

WHEN NEXT BREND WOKE, it was to a bright light in his eyes and something poking his back. He shifted in his still half-awake state, trying to get comfortable again, but nothing he did helped. Grumbling, he sat up in bed. Even as he leaned forward, whatever it was still poked him in the back. Sharply. With another grunt, he turned to look over his shoulder, then choked on a yelp at the sight of two crimson wings attached to his back.

They were small, not even stretching past his shoulder blades. But they were still *wings*.

Impossible. Magical. Not supposed to be there. *Wings!*

"Your Highness," a maid said from the door, knocking gently against the wood. "I've brought your breakfast. May I come in?"

He couldn't tell her no, could he? It would look suspicious! He'd never been the sort to deny a servant entrance when they were willingly bringing him food in bed. Piling the pillows behind him, Brend leaned back against them, tucking the wings into the softness of their down.

"Please do," he said, hoping his voice didn't sound stressed. Maybe the maid would just think it was because of his injury. The door creaked open, and in she came with a breakfast tray, which was left across his lap before she exited again without a word, leaving Brend alone with his *wings*.

He'd have to . . . He'd have to find a way to hide them, somehow.

T he man in the cell next door was muttering something over and over again in his sleep. It sounded like a name or a place. The word just quiet enough that Chirp had to strain to hear it, and when they did, they still couldn't be sure if they were hearing it correctly.

*Amara.*

It also sounded . . . familiar.

Not just because of their imaginary friend, but also because of the way he said it. The way it sat familiar on his tongue, like someone close and loved.

The familiarity was why the name had invaded their dreams, sinking into their very marrow like it belonged there. The reason they could smell ash and tar on the air when they woke up, choking on the taste of it. That was the only reason. Not because there was any connection between Chirp and the man on the other side of the stone wall. Not because he meant anything to them. But because they were trapped there, and he repeated the name over and over again like a mantra, like a prayer, until there was no escaping it.

The dreams had become more and more distinct. The haziness of them clearing away like fog after sunrise, leaving behind so much more than impressions as they had once before. Now there were faces, names in their wake. A mother. A father. A grandmother. And a brother with dark eyes, a strong jaw, and flopping black hair. A family. Chirp had had a family once upon a time. Before the Ringmaster sank his claws into their very soul. And if he was to be believed, some of them were still out there somewhere. Maybe not Chirp's grandmother, but their parents? Their brother? They could still find them, still be with them, if they did what the Ringmaster asked.

But would they take Chirp back after finding out what they'd done? Would Chirp be able to live with themselves after taking the life of someone else in trade for their own? Not just someone else—a friend, someone they cared for. No . . . maybe not.

And what if the Ringmaster was wrong? What if their family *wasn't* still out there? Was there anything else to live for if they weren't? Any other reason to survive this if they were just going to be alone?

No. Probably not.

They had been on their own this entire time, and it made them realize something about being alone.

It was lonely. And they hated it.

"Well?" the Ringmaster asked from where he was leaning against the outside of their cell, his shoulder pressed into the bars like one might lean on a lamp post out on the street. All he was missing was a cigarette and he'd be the villain of one of those movies the humans made long ago.

"Well, what?" Chirp curled their knees in close to their chest, trying to make themselves as small a target as possible. It wouldn't do much if he decided to shoot them through the bars because they had outlived their usefulness, but it was better than nothing.

The man in the cell next door had ceased his muttering shortly before the Ringmaster's footsteps approached, and

Chirp didn't know if that was because he'd fallen into a restful sleep or because he was listening. If it was the latter, it was a delight to know that someone else would witness their shame and destruction. Someone else would know what they were giving up and that they didn't have the strength to do what needed doing, to save themselves, maybe even save their people. Pitiful.

"You've had a few hours now. Have you made a decision?" The Ringmaster pressed his face in through the bars until his cheeks became squished.

Maybe if they played stupid for a little longer, they could get him to sweeten the pot further. But also, maybe not. "I'm not going to help you kill Brend."

*Brend.* Saying his name like that out loud just cemented it further. He was Chirp's friend, the first one they'd made since waking up on that table. They couldn't betray that trust. Not even if it would cost them their life to keep it.

"This won't save him," the Ringmaster warned, his eyes narrowing into something cutting and cold, hands gripping the bars harder until his knuckles turned white. "And why are you working so hard to save a prince who doesn't care about you, anyway?"

That was a question Chirp didn't really have an answer to. It was true, Brend probably didn't care about them. If he did, then he'd have made some attempt to save them from the dungeons, from whatever fate was coming their way. But no one except for the Ringmaster had been down to visit them in their cell since they'd been brought here, and that was answer enough.

Chirp lifted their chin, meeting the Ringmaster's eyes in challenge. He was right, of course, they knew that. No matter what Chirp did or didn't do, they wouldn't be able to save Brend. Even if they agreed to the Ringmaster's terms and left the cell with that intent, they would likely fail. Someone else would do the job assigned to them. Or maybe Brend would die without any outside help. It seemed like any way the dice were thrown, fate had made a decision about the prince's life and when it was to end: sooner rather than later. What little food Chirp had eaten soured in their stomach, and they swallowed thickly around the rise of bile in their throat.

"He and his mother mean to erase our people. Do you know that?" the Ringmaster hissed, his eyes gone cold and flat. Lifeless. "Exterminate every last Enchanted that's out there."

"Brend isn't like that!" Chirp snarled, their lips peeling back over teeth that had lengthened. They didn't know when that happened. They'd have to inspect it later, they realized, as a dribble of blood slid down their chin. "He's a good man."

"Sure he is." The Ringmaster scoffed, pulling away from the bars and standing up straighter so he could look down on Chirp as if he pitied them, every line of his face knitted in condescension. He held Chirp's gaze for one beat, two, before letting out a soft, annoyed laugh. "I see I've wasted both your time and mine with this."

"You have." The hairs on the back of Chirp's neck rose in annoyance, their sense of smell sharpening in a way that they hadn't noticed before. The Ringmaster stank of fear. Not irritation. Not derision. *Fear.* He was afraid of whatever was coming next, and maybe even a little afraid of Chirp and their sharpened nails, which were now tearing holes into the thin blanket covering their lap. Good. Chirp *wanted* him afraid of them. They wanted him to never come back to this place. To take his ship and run as far and as fast as he could. Then he would no longer be a danger to Brend or any of them. If the beating of his heart—which Chirp could strangely hear now—was anything to go by, that might be his intent the moment he left the dungeons.

"Then I bid you farewell," he said, bending at the waist to

flourish a bow. When he lifted his head again, the Ring-master had a smile on his lips that said that he knew something Chirp didn't. That he was about to say something that would completely derail whatever momentum they had built up. "But as a parting gift . . ." He licked his lips, savoring the moment of Chirp narrowing their eyes in suspicion. "I'll give you this. Your name. Your real name. Amara Kelii."

The statement knocked the breath from Chirp's lungs, making them double over, wheezing loudly trying to regain it. By the time they got control of themselves again, the Ring-master was gone, the corridor outside their was cell empty, and Chirp could hear the man in the cell next door shuffling closer to the wall.

"Amara?" the man repeated, hope in his voice that Chirp didn't think belonged there, that they were going to have to dash.

"That's not my name," Chirp bit out, the lie coating their tongue and throat in acid. It *was* their name. They could feel it in every fiber of their being. It had always been their name. Even now, after so long not having heard it, it fit like a second skin.

A grunt came from the cell, and Chirp could see the man stretching his hand out toward them. "Come here. Let me get a look at you."

"I don't want to." Poking at one sharpened canine with their tongue, Chirp eyed the hand. They didn't trust this man. Not that they had any reason to *not* trust him, but they didn't have any reason *to* trust him either. For all Chirp knew, he was a criminal. He'd been arrested and detained by the queen's men, tortured for information. Maybe he was some kind of serial killer.

"Why? What's it going to hurt?" He wiggled his light brown fingers, a little taunt to his tone. "You're not scared, are you?"

"No." Yes. Maybe a little. The last time they'd held someone's hand, he'd been shot shortly after. It seemed like tempting fate to try it again so soon. "What's going to happen if I do?"

"If I'm wrong, nothing." His hand moved like he'd shrugged, lifting up and falling back down in the space where it hovered outside Chirp's bars. "If you are who I think you are, then touching my hand will tell me."

"Who do you think I am?" Chirp only realized they were creeping across their cell toward the hand right then, and they stopped, blinking at how much larger the hand seemed to have gotten in the last couple of seconds. Up close, Chirp could see callouses along the palm and several scars on the knuckles, no doubt where the man had gotten into a fistfight or two.

"I think you're my little sister," the man said, his voice soft, leading, a siren calling Chirp in ever closer till all they had to do was reach out and link their fingers together.

"Not sister." Chirp shook their head. That word didn't fit how they felt anymore. Maybe once upon a time it would have, but now, they didn't feel like a sister. They didn't feel like a *she* at all. "I don't think of myself as a woman."

"Little brother?" the man tried again, his fingers flexing in uncertainty.

"No."

He clenched his hand, the nails lengthening a little in his agitation, leaving red marks on his palm, before he flexed again, shaking his fingers out, the claws disappearing. "Little sibling, then."

The acceptance in his tone hit Chirp square in the chest, stealing their breath, leaving them wheezing and gasping again, and stumbling forward to hold on to the bars with white-knuckled fingers.

"If it helps," the man sing-songed softly, dragging out his

words like they could draw Chirp in closer—and they could, they almost had. Chirp's very muscles burned with the desire to reach out and take his hand. "My crew will be coming to get me out soon. We can take you with us. Maybe even save your prince."

And that sealed it, because the chance to save Brend was worth the fear associated with possibly finding their family, with the fact that this man, if he *was* their brother, could either accept them or reject them for everything they were and everything they'd done. "You promise?"

"I promise."

Maybe Chirp shouldn't believe him. They didn't know this man from anyone else. He'd given them no reason to trust him outside of respecting their choice in identification. But . . . they *wanted* to trust someone. And he was the closest. Physically, at least.

A stupid reason, really, wholly emotional, irrational, human. Chirp registered this as they reached for his hand. They also registered that it wasn't going to stop them just before their fingers threaded through his, and they lost all sense of the world around them, diving deep into a pool of memories that they felt would no doubt drown them.

I vy Warner wasn't afraid of Persinette, and Persinette supposed that she'd never really given *anyone* a reason to be afraid of her before. She didn't like to hurt people, to see them in pain. Maybe no one really *liked* that, not even Agnes, but some were certainly better suited for it than she was. Hardened to it, in a way. That's why this job had been handed to Sully. He had far more experience with getting people to talk than Persinette likely ever would. And he'd offered. Which, again, came as something of a relief to Persinette. A kindness she hadn't really thought she deserved —and apparently wasn't going to actually be gifted she realized not long after her talk with Agnes.

The soft knock at the door drew Persinette out of the fear spiral threatening to take her down. Reminding her that even if Manu was locked up and Hiccup was powered down, she wasn't alone. She'd never have to be alone again, even if she were to lose them both. That didn't dull the terror associated with losing the people she loved, but it did help it feel manageable.

"Come in." Persinette ran a hand through her short lavender hair, trying to keep the strands out of her face where they threatened to hang shaggily in her eyes.

The door creaked open, and Sully peeked around the

edge of it like a child seeking permission to enter. Which would have been a little funny if Persinette hadn't just learned that the man she loved was being held prisoner by their enemy. He raised his brows in question, and Persinette waved him in, hoping he didn't see the strain on her face. A foolish hope if the little frown that wrinkled his brow was anything to go by.

"What is it?" Good news, she hoped, though the crease in Sully's brow said otherwise. Whatever he was coming to tell her wasn't something she was going to like.

"She wants to see you." Sully looked apologetic, and that was nice. It didn't change the circumstances of what Persinette was sure was going to be an unpleasant talk, but it was nice that at least someone knew how much she hated confrontation. There was no blood staining his hands or clothes. *Yet.*

"Why?"

"You're the captain." Sully's hands flexed around the edge of the door. He didn't come inside, Persinette noted. It couldn't have been that he was afraid of her reaction to the news. Persinette was a pacifist—for the most part. And besides that, she loved her crew, her family, she'd never do anything to hurt them. Especially Sully. Even when he brought her bad news.

She didn't have time for this. Scrubbing at her face, Persinette rose. "Suppose she thinks I'll be able to give her something you haven't already offered."

"Very likely." Sully fell into step beside her as Persinette entered the hall, his stride carefully shortened so he didn't outpace her. "I told you we should have just tortured her instead of starting with bartering."

Slanting him a mildly annoyed look out of the corner of her eye, Persinette said, "And I told you that torture won't get us the truth. Bargaining will. Torture is our last resort."

"It might have, if you'd let me do it the way I wanted to." Sully huffed, petulant.

"No, it wouldn't have. She was one of Eddi's elite, just like you. Ivy Warner can take whatever pain you planned to give her. What we need to play to is her greed." Easier said than done, Persinette was sure.

"She wants to be on the winning side." His boots scuffed against the wood beside her, uncertainty and exhaustion making his movements clumsy. They would all sleep better once this was over and their people were back on board the *Duchess*. Once they no longer had to worry about what the queen or Eddi would do to them if they were caught. But that was still a ways to go, and in the meantime, there was work to be done.

"I can't make that promise." She wished that she could. Not just for Ivy Warner but for all of them. As their leader, Persinette wished she could tell all of them that they would win, that when the smoke cleared and the battle was over, it would be *their* people standing victorious. That they would all make it out of this okay. But she couldn't promise any of those things, and that made this all impossibly worse. Because not knowing the end was slowly wearing away at all of them. Not being sure if they would even achieve what they were setting out to do . . .

"She knows that." Sully clicked his tongue in annoyance that was almost palpable. Persinette understood that. She hadn't known Ivy Warner before all of this happened, when they were both on the same side, but what she had seen of the other woman so far hadn't impressed her.

When they reached the hold, Ivy was sitting in the middle of her cell in a simple wooden chair looking entirely relaxed. Like she had come willingly instead of being captured. The only indication that she was suffering any discomfort was the reddening of her skin where the iron cuff sat against one pale wrist, dampening her magic and keeping her from escaping. It was that, more than the bars, keeping her in place.

"Captain," Ivy said, a smile curling up her too-red mouth, showing off teeth that looked a little too pointed to be those of a witch.

Cold sweat trickled down the back of Persinette's neck as the memory of the fight came back to her. The realization that everything bad that happened to Manu had been *her* fault. His blindness. His imprisonment. Persinette shook herself, her hands clenching at her sides. "Warner."

Ivy splayed her hands out to either side, palms up, as if to say "Here I am," then gave a little bow. "At your service, Captain Persinette."

"You have information we need." There was no use in beating around the bush. Ivy knew why Persinette was there, and they both knew what Persinette needed from her. They also both knew that Persinette would be willing to pay a pretty penny for it, if she could, putting all the balls in Ivy's court so to speak.

"I do," Ivy agreed readily, seeming to delight in the fact that she had the entire crew over a barrel.

"What do you want for it?" Better to get the conversation over with. Either Ivy would give them what they needed and Persinette could relay the information to Alys and the others, or she wouldn't and they would just have to find another way to take control of the Uprising.

Ivy's smile turned sharper, cutting into her cheeks like a jagged wound, and Persinette saw Sully twitch beside her. A low growl started up in his chest, the *drip-drip-drip* of kelpie magic rolling off of him to puddle onto the floor as his rage began to overwhelm him. Persinette held up a hand, staying his movement and drying up the murky waters that threat-ened to drown them all. The low chuckle that left Ivy at the action raised the hairs on the back of Persinette's neck, but she didn't move, didn't say anything. Let Ivy Warner dig her own grave.

"I'd say I want a place on the ship, but we both know it would be in name only." Ivy brushed long red hair back from her pale face. It was scraggly, unkempt, but she didn't seem to care. She just sat up straighter, like she was the most beautiful thing in the room and the rest of them should bow down and give her her due. Persinette gritted her teeth around the jealous rage that ripped through her. Not because Ivy was objectively beautiful—although she was—but because Ivy had a confidence Persinette would never be able to boast no matter what she did. It made something nasty and green curl up in her chest that took every ounce of strength to swallow down. "We both know you'll never be able to trust me again. Not after what I did to Kelii."

Persinette breathed around a well of emotion in her throat and said through clenched teeth, "No, I wouldn't."

It was the truth. Whatever trust Ivy might have been able to barter with once upon a time had gone out the window the moment she'd hurled that spell at Manu. Persinette would never be able to sleep knowing Ivy was on board, free and unhindered.

"Right. Didn't think so." Ivy nodded, pleased with herself. Which didn't fit at all with the conversation they were having. "So, what's your best offer?"

The answer was, Persinette didn't have one. Eddi and the queen would be able to offer Ivy much more for the information. Jewels. Money. Mansions. They would be able to give the woman anything and everything she'd ever desired.

"I'll give you your life," Persinette said after a long moment of letting the question hang heavy in the air between them.

A disbelieving snort left Ivy, her red brows lifting high

enough that they disappeared into the sweep of her bangs. "My life? Is that all you have?"

"It's more than anyone else would offer you." Persinette shrugged easily.

The truth was digging out a place for itself in Ivy, Persinette could see it in the way the smile was slowly, *ever so slowly*, falling. Inch by inch.

"Eddi would give me power," Ivy argued. "The queen would give me a title, enough riches to clothe myself in gold every day of my life and still never wear the same thing twice. And you'd give me my *life*?" Ivy scoffed.

"Think about it, Ivy." Persinette licked her lips, playing into the hand she'd been dealt. It was a gamble, and Manu had said she was a terrible poker player because her face always showed her cards. But the thing she was bidding with wasn't a lie, it wasn't a bluff, it was the truth. She could only hope that Ivy would see the situation for what it was and understand the choices in front of her. "Would they let you *keep* those things?"

"What?" The word came out half choked by a startled chuckle.

"You betrayed Eddi for MOTHER. And the queen, well, she'd hardly let an Enchanted live, much less continue to hold a title and wealth in her land." Persinette paused, letting those words sink their claws into Ivy. The smile had almost entirely disappeared from her face. "They'd give you those things, sure. But once they got what they wanted?" Shaking her head, Persinette clicked her tongue in honest sympathy. "They'd never let you live long enough to enjoy them."

"And you'll—*What?*" The words left Ivy on a breath, like everything Persinette said had knocked the wind out of her. Maybe it had. It was hard to hear that the people one thought they could trust would sell them out in a second.

"I'll make sure you live through this whole thing."

Persinette leaned on the bars of Ivy's cell, casual, calm. "No matter which side wins, I'll make sure Ivy Warner is still standing when the smoke clears."

"How?"

"I have friends in The Wilds, ready and willing to give sanctuary to anyone we send their way." Alys wouldn't be happy having someone like Ivy amongst her people, sure, but she'd deal with it for as long as she had to to keep Persinette's promise. It wasn't a perfect solution, but it was a better one than Ivy was going to get from anyone else. "Or I can leave you here with Sully . . ."

"And how do I know you won't do as they would? Turn around and kill me once you have what you want?" Ivy's eyes narrowed. She had every right to be suspicious. Persinette had absolutely no reason not to go back on her promise, not after everything Ivy had done to her and hers. Other than the simple fact that—

"I *always* keep my promises, Warner." Persinette pushed off from the bars, standing up straight again so she could meet Ivy's gaze more fully, letting her see that there wasn't a trace of a lie on her face or in her body language. "You've got exactly ten seconds to take this deal." Persinette held up two hands, all ten fingers lifted, then carefully lowered one. Two. Three. Four. She said, "Or we're dropping you at the next port and leaving you to fend for yourself when everything hits the fan."

"Fine. Fine." Ivy flapped her hand as if it were her that was doing Persinette the favor. "Bring me a map."

# THIRTY-THREE
## BREND

"Your Highness," Charlie said in a voice rough with age.

Today her sharp, amber-colored eyes were looking at Brend with something a little more worried than the usual sympathy he usually saw there. Her wrinkled brow pinched together in the middle.

"Charlie," Brend breathed, the sound rough and broken. Less word, more sigh. So relieved to see a familiar face, he could hardly keep his knees from buckling under the weight of her watery stare. With a flick of his wrist and a murmured, "Leave us," he cleared the room.

Charlie waited only as long as it took for the door to click shut before she was hustling forward, her quick hands gently guiding Brend down into a chair, tutting over him like a mother hen. "My boy. My boy. What has she done to you this time?"

"Ironically," Brend laughed humorlessly, "it wasn't mother this time."

Her hands perched on her hips, Charlie fixed him with a disbelieving look, unimpressed by what little bravado he'd mustered to hide the pain he was feeling from both gunshot wound and realization.

The betrayal.

Chirp tried to warn him before. They'd told him to believe Clancy when he told Brend who he was. To believe him when his actions said that he could be bought. But Brend hadn't, and this is where it had gotten him. He should have had Clancy dismissed after the first betrayal.

But no.

"This was Clancy." Saying it out loud didn't make it hurt any less like Brend hoped it might.

"Ah, so that's why that bastard asked to be reassigned." Charlie shook her head, a lock of faded brown hair falling into her face, her strong hands flexing on Brend's shoulders in sympathy.

Brend relaxed under the familiar touch, grateful to have someone on his side, at least for now. He'd soak it all up, affection-starved, selfish, lonely thing that he was.

"I always said that boy was no good. Didn't I tell you?"

"Yes, you did." Brend tilted his head back so he could smile up at her. She'd told him—numerous times. Especially after Brend and Clancy became more intimate. Charlie hadn't hidden her view that Clancy was just using Brend for his title, his wealth, his power, and she'd been right, in the end. Although, neither of them could have suspected that Clancy would *shoot* him.

But those memories brought with them another realization. That here stood Brend's only and truest confidant. The one person, outside of Clancy, who Brend told everything to —always had, since he'd been a child. Charlie knew about how Brend liked both men and women. She knew how Clancy had drawn him in with his charming smile and gentle affections, the likes of which Brend had never known before.

Charlie knew every scar, every wound, every time Brend cried. She may not have been there for all of them—she couldn't be without drawing too much attention to herself—

but she knew. And she always accepted him, always loved him in her way. No matter what.

So what was one more secret between them? Besides, she'd see them anyway when she went to take his measurements.

"Charlie," he said, all the heaviness of a confession laying thick on his tongue, "I have something I have to show you."

She opened her mouth to say something, but whatever it was, the expression on Brend's face cut it off short. Snapping her jaw shut with a hard click of teeth on teeth, Charlie nodded.

"Help me get out of my shirt." Brend leaned forward, his fingers already working over the buttons, and Charlie, bless her, didn't wait for further instruction. By the time they peeled the shirt away, Brend felt sweat trickling down his spine from the pain the movement caused, but he didn't let it slow him.

He knew the moment Charlie saw them because she gasped loudly, her entire body stilling. The wings fluttered self-consciously behind him. They'd gotten bigger in the day or so since he'd first noticed them, now spanning almost to the outsides of his arms. Soon they'd be impossible to hide without help. That's why he needed Charlie. But . . .

She still hadn't moved.

"Oh, child," Charlie said after a silence that stretched on too long, making the breath in Brend's chest stutter. His heart shuddered, trying to regain its normal rhythm as if it had stopped entirely while waiting for Charlie to say something. Her next words, though, sent it galloping along at double time: "They're back."

"What?" Brend asked, trying not to choke on his own panic. He didn't quite manage it and wound up coughing anyway. "What do you mean *they're back?*"

"You don't remember?" Curiously, Charlie tilted her head,

then frowned as if she'd just realized something. "Of course you don't remember. That old bat had your memories wiped. Selfish, self-centered, power-hungry old—"

"Charlie . . . tell me what this means." Brend pleaded, cutting off the train of insults Charlie was hurling at whoever. Maybe his mother, but Brend had no way to be sure.

With a long exhale, Charlie deflated like a balloon, settling into a seat on the coffee table that sat in front of the chair she'd pushed Brend into. She leaned forward, bracing herself on her knees, and took his hands, a gesture so kind, so motherly, it made his eyes burn with tears. Then, rubbing slow circles with her calloused thumbs over the backs of his hands, she said, "Your mother and you are dragons, Brend. When—"

Brend opened his mouth to ask a question, his head spinning with that single statement, but Charlie clicked her tongue.

"No. Let me finish this. Before someone comes to check on our progress, all right?" She waited for Brend to nod once, quick and sharp, then pressed on with her story. "You're actually more like half-dragon. Dragon mother. Human father. I think your mother hoped that meant you'd be human too, but . . ."

She shook her head, sadness pinching her mouth and making her eyes droop a little. "So, when you were born with wings, your mother had your father executed. Shame, too, he was a sweet man. Wholly devoted to her. Then she bound your magic to hers so she could feed off it for the foreseeable future. It's why you've always been so weak."

"*Why?*" The question was choked, involuntary. And Charlie looked sorry for the pain her words caused him. For the fact that hot tears trailed down his face. His mother . . . How could she have done that to her own son?

"Who can tell with that one." Charlie scowled, her hands tightening around Brend's for a moment before she softened her grip again.

"Why didn't someone tell me? Why didn't *you* tell me?" Accusation made the words come out harder than he meant for them to. But this felt like another betrayal. First Clancy. Then his mother. And now Charlie. Was every person in Brend's life keeping something from him? Using him? Lying to him? Maybe Chirp had been right before when they'd tried to tell him that they were a bad person there to hurt him. Maybe he should have believed them.

Charlie gave his hands a careful tug, drawing his attention back to her face. "I couldn't. Your mother sealed the knowledge with magic. No one who knew could tell anyone who didn't." Her thumb pressed into his knuckles as if willing him to believe her, to understand her. "But now that you know, the binding is broken. And I can tell you—"

She stopped, turning to look at the door over her shoulder. It had remained closed through their entire conversation thus far, but Brend didn't know how long they had been talking. Soon, someone might come to check on the progress of his suit. No one could see them like this. No one could overhear what they were saying. If anyone else saw his wings, he was sure that he wouldn't live to make it to his engagement party.

Charlie waited a long moment, her fingers working over his hands unconsciously. When no sound came, and the door wasn't flung open on its hinges by guards coming to take them both away, she said, "We don't have much time."

"Much time for what?" His eyes flicked from the still closed door to the harried expression on Charlie's face. Her lips pursed for a moment as if considering her options, maybe trying to decide if she ought to tell him the next bit, then she made up her mind.

"For me to work my magic." She winked and pushed from the table with surprising swiftness for a woman as old as she looked. Brushing a lock of hair back from her face to reveal one sharply pointed ear, Charlie turned to dig around in her sewing kit. "I'll have to wing it a little, no pun intended. If the suit gives off too much latent magic, someone will know what's going on."

"What?" Brend blinked, watching as Charlie dug out threads and swatches and a book of needles that glittered in the light.

Charlie paid him no mind and kept right on rattling things off to herself as she moved to the cart of fabric she'd left by the door. "And my protection magic isn't what it used to be. I'll have to ask Harry to give the fabric a poke while I've got it in my workroom."

"Protection magic?" Brend stood to follow her, trying to catch every word of the too-quick diatribe. "Harry? You mean Harriet the gardener?"

Barking a laugh, Charlie whirled to hold a bolt of green fabric up to his chest, her tongue between her teeth as she considered it. "Yes, Harriet the gardener. My wife."

"Harriet the gardener is your—Harriet the gardener is your *wife*?" Honestly, he was starting to feel a little faint with all these revelations. He was a *dragon*. His *mother* was a dragon. Charlie was *Enchanted*. Harriet *the gardener* was Enchanted. Harriet and Charlie were *married*?! He wasn't sure why that last one was the most shocking—maybe because he'd always assumed the two women hated each other with how they bickered. In fact, he didn't think he'd ever seen them in a room together where they weren't yelling, or at the very least fuming in each other's direction.

"Oh yes." Charlie stopped for a moment, her eyes bright with affection and pride. "And she's *fantastic* at warding magic. Who do you think did that little diddy when your mother thought she was going to lock you in your room?"

"But it didn't work," he said, confused, still trying to get his brain to catch up with everything Charlie had said in the last ten minutes.

"Didn't it?" The grin on her face stretched and sharpened, mischief lining her face.

"I escaped," Brend huffed flatly.

"Exactly." Charlie winked again, and grabbed another bolt of fabric, deep blue velvet to hold up to his chest. She hemmed and hawed for a moment before going back to the green. "Yes, this will do nicely, I think. Brings out your eyes."

She took him by the wrist and dragged him over to the little podium, helping him onto it, her hands gentle and guiding as Brend continued trying to make sense of everything she'd said, everything he'd learned. His mind was spinning, spinning, *spinning,* and didn't stop until a few minutes later when he had a bit of fabric draped over his shoulder.

Brend grabbed at Charlie's hands to stop her fiddling and draw her attention back to him. "Charlie," he said, licking his lips, only half certain he wanted the answer to what he was about to ask. "Why do I need protective magics in my suit for the engagement party?"

"Oh, honey." Charlie looked up at him, soft and sad, then said something that made the bottom drop out of Brend's carefully constructed world. "Because your mother plans to have you killed."

The memories rushed back like a tidal wave, an avalanche, pulling Chirp under and sucking the air from their lungs.

They had been small once upon a time—*so* small—small enough to cram themselves under the big bed they shared with their brother and parents. Right in between the suitcases that always stayed packed, just in case the family had to leave without warning again. They didn't remember the previous times it happened, but their brother told them about it. Told them that, before the apartment building— packed with too many Enchanted—they'd lived in a tiny cottage out on the outskirts of a tiny village. They'd lived there with their grandmother, he said, but Chirp didn't believe him. Because they didn't remember having a grandmother.

"One. Two . . ." Manu counted, his voice loud enough that Chirp could hear him even from the other room. Chirp wriggled, pressing themselves deeper into the darkness under the bed, their legs curling up against the wall as they ducked all but their eyes behind a suitcase. He wouldn't find them this time, they were sure of it. Not like the last time when they hid in the linen closet with nothing to tuck themselves behind.

"Ready or not, here I come!" Manu called, his footsteps loud on the old floorboards as he made his way from the front room to the narrow hall. There was the creak of a door hinge, either the bathroom or the linen closet, as Manu checked there first since those were places they had hidden before.

Swallowing down a giggle, Chirp lifted their little hands to cover their mouth just as Manu's bare feet came into view in the open door of the bedroom.

"Now where could you be . . ." he murmured to himself, pulling the door closed a little so he could check behind it. "Not here." He crouched down beside the empty bedside table, his face coming into view in the dim light as he peered beneath it. "Not here either."

A squeak left Chirp, giving them away, and Manu's face split into a wide, arrogant smile before his head turned slowly to peer at Chirp under the bed. "Gotcha!"

The memory shifted just as Manu reached for them.

The view was the same, but different. It was darker, all the lights in the apartment turned off, no sign of the sun coming through the windows, and the face peering at Chirp from the floor wasn't Manu's. It was a woman's, their mother's maybe. It was a little blurry, a little indistinct, like even now Chirp's mind couldn't fill in for all the time that had passed.

"You have to stay under there, stay hidden," their mother whispered, fear in her eyes. Her hands were shaking where they clutched at the handle of one of the suitcases, preparing to slide it in front of Chirp to hide them completely.

Something banged in the front room, either dropped or thrown, and their mother jerked, her eyes widening further. Her breath hitched, and they both lay there on their bellies, listening, waiting, but no other noises came.

"Your brother will be back from the market shortly. When he gets here—"

"I wanna go with you," Chirp pled, their voice small and frightened. They didn't know how they knew it, but they knew that this would be the last time they saw their mother. They knew that their mother and father were going away for forever. That every day thereafter, it would just be them and their brother, their family irreparably broken. "Please don't leave me alone."

"I have to." Their mother's voice had gone firm. She would not have any more of Chirp's whining or crying; this was for their own good. And Chirp knew that set-jawed look from all the times their mother made them eat broccoli and go to bed before they felt like it. "You stay here until Manu gets back, and don't make a peep. Am I clear?"

"Yes, mama," Chirp whispered, jerking at another bang from the other room. There was muffled shouting, then their mother slid the suitcase in the way of Chirp seeing anything else and rose to her feet.

After that, it was dark for a small eternity, the silence only broken by the occasional sniffle from Chirp, who didn't remember when they'd started crying nor how to stop.

They must have fallen asleep there, because the next thing Chirp remembered was opening their eyes to a room hazed in smoke, the smell of it choking them. There was no fire, not that they could see, but they couldn't stay there. Could they? No. Their mother said to stay put until Manu came, and that was what they'd do. They had to be good for their mother.

It was getting so unbearably hot, Chirp's shirt sticking to their back, sweat trickling down their neck. But they stayed because they were going to be good. They hadn't been good for their mother for much of their life, and now seemed the perfect time to start.

The door burst open, smacking loudly enough against the wall beside it to make Chirp's ears ring, and they wriggled farther under the bed, almost plastering themselves to the wall on the other side to hide from the intruder. But then the person's boots came into view, and relief washed through Chirp.

"Where are you?" Manu coughed into the handkerchief he'd tied over his nose, bending down to look under the bed for his sibling.

"I'm here!" Chirp pushed off from the wall and crawled toward him, letting him grab onto their wrists and pull them out before hauling them into his arms.

"We've got to get out of here. The whole building is about to go up." His footsteps were hurried, clumsy on the uneven floorboards, but he carried Chirp like they weighed nothing.

They coughed, ragged and wet, into their sleeve. "Where are mama and papa?"

Manu didn't answer, he just held Chirp closer to his chest, shouldering his way out into the streets of the capital. The air was cold, burning Chirp's lungs as they gulped down mouthfuls of it to stave off the looming suffocation of all that smoke. Looking over Manu's shoulder, Chirp saw the top floors of their building crumbling into a roaring fire, the first home they ever remembered going up in smoke.

"We left him behind." Chirp gasped at the realization, the sharp inhale of breath making them cough some more, their eyes burning.

"Left who behind?" But Manu didn't stop to go back, wouldn't, if Chirp knew anything about him. He had likely been given instructions for if this happened, just as Chirp had to stay put. And just as Chirp had felt the need to be good for their mother, Manu would feel that need too. The necessity of two orphans fulfilling their parents' last wish, although Chirp hadn't realized that was what that desire was at the time. It all made sense now.

"Chirp," they said, their mind flashing to the little crocheted robot they'd always had. They didn't know where it had come from, but it had been their constant companion. Hiding under the bed beside them. Sitting on the counter while they took a bath. Always there. Always watching out for them. Without it, they felt empty.

"We aren't going back." Manu set his jaw and kept trudging forward, even as his shoulders started to sag. He was tired.

The finality of his words crawled like bugs along Chirp's skin. "Manu," they whispered, only half-hoping he'd hear and answer their next question, "where are mama and papa?"

"They're gone."

Time raced past Chirp again, like a movie in fast-forward, every memory blurring together until they and Manu were standing on the docks of one of the cities, both of them a little older. There was screaming in the distance, a warning of what was to come. Manu looked back over Chirp's shoulder, his fingers tightening around theirs, fear making his gaze go too wide for his face. Then he was dragging them into a run, their steps harried and clumsy as they zig-zagged through the crowds of people packed onto the docks.

A crack split the air, cutting through the muttering and murmuring of the people around them, then everyone was running. Pushing and shoving and trying to get onto a ship as quickly as possible. Manu's fingers grew slick with sweat, but he did his best to hold on, keeping them connected until Chirp tripped, stumbling, and he was carried off by the crush of people.

What happened next was a blur, likely because they'd hit their head so hard on the cobbles.

The next thing they knew, they were scooped up by a

slightly younger Ringmaster, his face split in a kind smile Chirp didn't think they'd ever seen before, and maybe never would again after that moment.

"Where is your family?" he'd asked, warmth in his voice that drew Chirp in like a moth to a flame. They were still a child then. Still too young to know any better. And they were all alone in the world. His next words sealed their fate almost entirely. "I'll be your family now."

Months passed, and every day, the Ringmaster's smile morphed a little bit at a time, until one day, Chirp looked up and it was not kindness they saw there but the twisted blade of greed. A knife so sharp that not long after, he used it to rip Chirp's soul from their body, forcing them into a clockwork marionette whose strings only he could pull.

Either the pain of the transformation or something the Ringmaster had done in the process erased everything Chirp had known before—their memories, the faces of the people they loved, their own name, leaving behind only the android. And for a time, they were easy to manipulate via their strings. But some kernel of themselves must have lingered, and it fueled their desire to escape.

Left them burning with it until one day, all that was left were the scorching flames on their sensitive circuits, and they had to go. They just *had* to.

The tricky part, they soon realized, wasn't in escaping, it was in *staying* escaped.

Thirteen tries.

It took thirteen tries for Chirp to escape and stay out of the Ringmaster's clutches for any substantial amount of time, and that was just because they got lucky. Stumbled upon the library when it and the circus happened to be in the same place.

What followed was years upon years of friendship with the grumpy dragon that lived there. Kindle had never been particularly kind, not in the way the Ringmaster had pretended to be at the beginning, but Chirp could tell she cared about them in her own way. And that was enough. It would have to be enough.

Because what else was there for an old android?

"There's me," Manu said, his voice breaking through the memories and answering Chirp's question. He hadn't released their hand, and Chirp wondered how much of that he'd seen, or if he'd kept himself out of it to give them privacy. No, remembering their older brother, he wouldn't do that. But he might not bring any of it up right away, if only to give the illusion that he had. *Jerk.* "There's your brother and a family that will welcome you with open arms."

"Why?" Chirp wanted to tug their hand away, to put space between them again. Whatever connection tied them together and returned their memories still zinged under their skin like static.

"Because that's what family does." The hand in Chirp's grip gave a little tug, as if Manu had lifted the shoulder attached to it in a shrug. "They're coming for us," he said, tapping his thumb against Chirp's knuckles. "And when they get here, we need to be ready."

Chirp let out a long breath and gave their brother's hand a little squeeze. They would escape again, but would they stay escaped this time?

# BREND

The clothes wouldn't be enough.

Charlie and Harry's magic wouldn't be enough.

Knowing what was coming wouldn't be enough.

*None* of it was going to protect Brend from the inevitability of his fate. If his mother planned to have him assassinated tonight, he would die, and that would be it. Unless he found some way to fight against it, some way to save himself. But given his lack of resources . . .

His mother would get her war, and what residual magic lingered in his veins would go to her to fuel this petty feud with her sibling.

It was almost worse to know that his death—his power— would be the cause of so much destruction. His own people would suffer for his mother's greed, and she would use Brend as a catalyst to do it.

Yes, that was much worse than knowing he was going to die.

"You could run away," Charlie said through the pins in her teeth. She had been trying to soothe him out of the state of disassociation he'd found himself in for the last hour. It wasn't really helping. It was kind of her to try, but he didn't think there was anything she could say that *would* help.

The ball was hours away, and he still hadn't thought of a

way out of this. *Hours*. He was going to die in less than a handful of hours. He had less than a handful of hours to live. Someone else would be blamed for it. And his kingdom, the place he hadn't even gotten to see much of in his short life, would descend into war. The labor camps would go, yes, but so too would the underground market with the magic sky and the square where he and Clancy danced. It would all burn, leaving nothing left. No one left.

"Did you hear me?" Charlie poked his side with one boney finger, her words a little less distorted. Maybe she'd taken the pins out of her mouth.

"What did you say?" Brend scrubbed at his face, trying to get his mind to focus. It didn't work. Everything was distant, like he was watching his life slip away from him through a window. "I'm sorry."

"I said you could run away." The fabric across his shoulders tugged a little, a pin carefully inserted where Charlie needed to alter the jacket. She clicked her tongue in disapproval. "You've lost weight again. Keep it up and you'll waste away to nothing."

Brend opted to ignore the comment about his weight because Charlie knew damn well *why*. The stress of this situation may very well kill him before his mother's men could do their work. "What would running away solve?"

"You wouldn't be dead, for one." Another little tug, another pin. Charlie was right, he really had lost far too much weight in the last couple of days. His mother hadn't said anything about it yet, where she might have usually, probably because it played into her narrative. He was sick. He was already dying. The gunshot had been the fatal blow. Brend could see where all of this was playing right into her plan. He should really eat something, if for no other reason than to save his strength for what was coming. But every time he tried to choke down food, he was hit with the realization that he was going to be dying soon anyway, so why bother?

"She'd just tell everyone the Enchanted kidnapped me and start her war anyway." *And I'd probably still die,* he didn't add. But it was the truth. Even if Brend were to escape, he didn't see any way that he could live outside of the castle. Constantly on the run? His wings getting bigger by the hour? The enemy of not just the humans but the Enchanted as well? Who would take him in? Who would offer him protection? No one.

Charlie tilted her head so she could look up at him from where she stood below the podium. "Is that all you're worried about?"

"Aren't you?" He frowned, his nose scrunching up a little. It seemed a very real concern to Brend. If he died and the war started, all of this went away. Not just Charlie's job as the prince's royal tailor but her home, Harry's job, her life. It might be nihilistic to think that of course a war would ruin everything, destroy everything, but Brend was intimately aware of how his mother was. If her sibling was even close to the same, there would be nothing left once the fighting started because neither of them would give up until Daiwynn was in ruins.

"You're too good, Brend." Charlie sighed, patting his shoulder lightly. He didn't really see how that was the truth, but he'd take the compliment and the affection like the selfish man that he was. It might be the last he ever got, after all.

SWEAT COATED HIS PALMS, making the skin sticky and slick in turns where Brend held onto his cane. The suit Charlie made for him was beautiful, dashing, made him look every inch the prince he was supposed to be, and it was suffocating him. The fabric, was soft on the outside—enough so to encourage beautiful young ladies to run their fingers across his forearm, his shoulders—but it didn't breathe.

"You should have left extra space for the wings," Brend rumbled toward where Charlie was adjusting the trousers with nimble fingers. His wings were harnessed down against his back to keep them hidden for the most part. His mother couldn't know they were there—*no one* could know they were there—the tips of them poking into the skin below his shoulder blades. They seemed to be growing every second now, inching bigger and bigger until one day they might support his weight like the dragon he was.

"You're supposed to be able to tuck them away. Hide them," Charlie shot back.

"I haven't quite figured that out yet." He hadn't quite figured *anything* out yet. How to hide his wings. How to regulate his body temperature that now seemed to run too hot almost constantly—seriously, he was sweating through his shirt. How to harness any of the powers he'd apparently been gifted by his dragon lineage. It wasn't like he had someone he could ask about this. The only other dragon he knew was his mother, and she could never know that he knew what he was. And, finally—most importantly, maybe— how to save himself and prevent the impending war.

This was exhausting.

The tone of defeat softened Charlie, and she let out a soft breath, her shoulders lowering. In a gentle voice she said, "You need to relax or you're going to burn a hole in your suit."

"I'm not going to—"

Charlie lifted one sweating hand by the wrist to reveal fingertips so hot, they had turned pink. Which proved nothing other than the fact that he was hot. From her pocket, Charlie produced a little pad she used to jot down measurements and pressed the edge of it to his fingertip. The paper caught in a blink, burning away to smolders as Charlie dropped it to the floor to snuff it out with her boot.

"That's– Well, that's just– What *is* that?" Confusion and terror strangled his words. His mother was going to realize what was going on with him before he'd ever set foot in the ballroom. Blood rushed to his ears, making them throb with the pounding of his heart. He was going to faint. He was *definitely* going to faint. Brend swallowed with a click, swaying a little on his feet.

"Whoa there. Let's sit down before we fall down." Charlie coaxed him into a chair and grabbed a fan from one of the tables to try to cool his overheated face.

He wasn't sure how yet, but his mother realizing what was going on with him would change things. Maybe she'd say that he was an imposter, a changeling put in place by the Enchanted to lower her defenses until he could kill her. Maybe she'd have him publicly executed instead of just making it happen in private. Would that be better or worse? Probably worse. She'd want it to be painful, to make an example of him, if she did it publicly. In private, it would probably be poison, something quick and painless. He'd just go to sleep.

Blast, this was making him panic more.

"Brend. Brend. Brend!" Charlie smacked him across the face with a force that he didn't think was necessary, but the sting of it cut through everything else.

Blinking up at her through eyes burning with tears, he pinched his brows together. "Did you just slap me?"

"Yes, sorry about that." Charlie smiled, sheepish, shaking out her stinging hand.

"No, it's all right. Had to be done." He shook himself. "So, you were saying?"

"Right. Yes." Charlie's throat bobbed with a harsh swallow, her eyes still too wide for her face. She looked almost as shaken as he felt, which probably wasn't for the best. "As I was saying, this is a good thing." She reached for his hands, then seemed to think better of it and gripped his knees instead. "You could use this as a means to protect yourself against whoever your mother is sending to kill you."

Hope fluttered in his chest. Then his eyes caught on the mound of charred notebook and his heart shuddered to a stop. No. This wasn't a solution. This wasn't going to save him. Nothing could. Nothing would. And in the end, the only people who would care would be Charlie, Harry, and maybe Chirp.

Chirp . . . He wondered where they were.

"Just think about it." Charlie patted his knees again, seeming to see the moment he realized it was hopeless. It was sweet of her to think there was a way out of this but—

"The ball is in an hour. I don't have any kind of *time* to figure this out, Charlie." He gave voice to his hopelessness, taking a deep breath to cool the heat of his skin. It worked, if just for a moment, his fingers turning from pink to pale again, long enough for him to reach forward and take Charlie's hands in his own. "I'll be all right. You needn't worry about me. Just . . ." Swallowing, Brend licked his lips. "Just make sure you and Harry are safe. Get out of the castle as soon as we're finished here. Yeah?"

"Is that an order?" Charlie raised one graying brow and rose from where she knelt before him with a little groan.

"It is. From your prince," he teased, but there was seriousness behind it. He needed to know that at least someone he loved was safe.

Charlie shook off the sentiment and held out her hand to

help him from the chair. "Let's just get you ready for this ridiculous dog and pony show, shall we?"

"Yes, if I'm going to the executioner's block, I may as well look dashing doing it, aye?"

"That's the spirit!" Charlie gave him a friendly shove, and then they got back to work getting him ready for the farce that would end his life.

They weren't there yet. Manu said his people were coming. His crew would never leave him behind, and when they broke into the castle to rescue him, of course they would take his sibling along. Chirp was family in more ways than one. And honestly, with their memories returned, Chirp was excited to see all of them again. To renew their friendship with Kindle and Rose, to learn more about Manu's Persinette, to get to know the crew.

But they weren't there yet, and Chirp was pacing their cell, counting down the minutes until Brend was sold off to some socialite for his mother's benefit. Currently, they had just under an hour, fifty-six minutes to be precise, and the crew of the *Duchess* wasn't *there* yet.

"Where are they?" Chirp asked on their next round as they reached Manu's cell. Manu, for his part, seemed perfectly at ease with waiting. His faith in his crew ran so deep, there was never a doubt they'd reach them with time enough to do everything that needed to be done. But then . . . they didn't know Chirp was intent on saving the prince too. How could they? "We're running out of *time.*"

"Relax," Manu called back, his tone easy and light. Chirp couldn't see him through the wall that separated them, but they were sure he was lounging back on his thin blanket, perfectly relaxed. Did he ever take anything seriously? Well, sometimes, Chirp knew from experience. And although many years spanned between the time Chirp had known their brother and now, he didn't seem as if he'd changed much at all. Not that there was any way to really tell with a wall between them and the tension of a knifepoint pressed threateningly against Chirp's chest. The composure could be an act for all Chirp knew. Chirp couldn't tell which they were hoping was the truth—that it *was* an act, or that Manu really was just that calm about this whole thing.

"How can I relax? We've got fifty minutes until the ball starts." The words left them as a hiss through Chirp's teeth as they clenched their jaw.

"How do you know that's how long is left?" There was a smile in his voice, like he was teasing Chirp, just like he used to when they were children. It was strange how easily they were falling back into the roles of older and younger sibling, how natural it all felt. Chirp thought maybe it shouldn't. They thought maybe, after so many years, their relationship should be different, but Manu had never been the type to linger on things. He had always been the type to jump in headfirst and deal with the consequences later. This must just be another one of those times.

"I just know." They weren't going to confess to him that they'd done the math in their head. That they'd been counting down the minutes since they had been put in that cell. Belatedly, they admitted, "It's an approximation."

Manu made a noise at the back of his throat like he'd known anyway and had decided not to comment on it. "They'll get here after the ball starts."

Chirp stopped their pacing, their hands midway through raking their hair, and blinked at the wall that connected their cells. "What? Why?"

"Because," Manu said, sighing like he was explaining

something very obvious to someone who hadn't been paying attention at all, which was just rude. When had their brother become so rude? He continued after some shuffling, "That's when the security on the outside will be at the laxest. They'll be so focused on securing the room and making sure that everyone inside is doing what they're supposed to, they won't be looking at the entrances from outside the castle."

"That seems . . . terribly unsafe." But logical to some extent. Except—Chirp moved to the bars, leaning forward until their face was pressed hard enough against them that they could feel the bones grinding against metal. "Why is the queen expecting an attack from the inside?"

"Why, indeed." Manu's tone was knowing, teasing, like when they'd been children and he'd taunted Chirp with a secret. Dangling the information over their head and just out of reach until his amusement faded and he inevitably told them.

"Manu," Chirp said, their tone a warning.

A soft laugh rumbled through the cell wall, settling warmly and contently in Chirp's chest, an old friend they hadn't heard in far too long. They hadn't even known they missed that sound, it having been erased by the Ringmaster and his magic. But now the reminder sat as an ache in their chest. Their brother was back, and Chirp didn't have to ever give him up again, not if they didn't want to. Which, they were realizing more and more by the minute, they didn't. Chirp waited for an answer that never came. Manu seemed happy enough to hang the information above their head for an indefinite amount of time, maybe wondering if they'd figure it out themselves. And Chirp wasn't going to even try, but then a thought struck them—

"The queen invited the people most likely to attack to the ball."

"Mhm," Manu murmured like a proud parent, their child the smartest in the room.

"But why would she *do* that?" It was nonsensical. One didn't just send party invites to their enemies. That was a sure-fire way to get oneself killed.

"Because," Manu said again, ever the patient teacher, "it's poor manners not to invite your siblings to your son's engagement party. Isn't it?"

Everything clicked into place then. Chirp had forgotten, with the flood of memories, all of the information they'd learned while they had been searching the library with their best friend. About Kindle and her siblings. How this entire war between MOTHER and the Uprising was just a way to keep people under control, to keep them scared. Just a fight between two siblings vying for power when really it shouldn't have fallen to either of them. It should have fallen to their youngest sister.

Kindle.

"Where is Kindle?"

"Oh, she should be getting here any minute now," Manu said, all sharp teeth and bite. "I'm sure she'll be very excited to see her siblings again, and to meet her nephew."

"Forty-four minutes," Chirp breathed.

"Approximately." It sounded like he was laughing again, teasing, and it eased the tension that had settled between Chirp's shoulders, making them slump a little.

"Approximately."

They were silent for a while after that. Chirp still counted down the minutes until they would be free to save Brend from whatever horrible fate his mother had planned for him, and Manu thought about whatever he was thinking about. Maybe seeing Persinette again. Chirp didn't exactly know what his life was like anymore. But they wanted to. They wanted to so badly, it made their chest ache.

When there were only fifteen minutes left to wait, Chirp heard Manu shuffle to the wall between them, his steps a quiet scuff on the floor. "So," he started, sidling up close enough that Chirp thought he might be pressing his shoulder to the stones, "tell me about this prince of yours."

"He's not mine." Heat crawled up the back of Chirp's neck at the insinuation.

"He's not yours, but you're willing to risk everything you've just gained to save him," Manu said with a certainty that Chirp didn't like. But it was true, wasn't it? Brend wasn't theirs. But the moment they escaped from that cell, Chirp would be running back to him, to protect him like some dashing hero saving their damsel in distress. It didn't matter if Brend hated them, if he thought Chirp shot him. None of it mattered because he was in danger and Chirp was going to do everything in their power to give him the chance he wouldn't get otherwise. It was the least they could do, wasn't it?

After a silence that must have stretched on for too long— Chirp losing count of the minutes that ticked by somehow— Manu said, "That's what I thought."

"I know it doesn't make sense." Chirp sighed, scrubbing at their face.

"It doesn't have to," Manu said simply, like it was a truth that Chirp had somehow missed in their analysis of the situation. Maybe it was.

"He probably thinks I shot him. He probably hates me."

"Nonsense." Manu scoffed. "No one can hate a Kelii. Our charm is irresistible."

"So you'll help me?" It seemed too much to hope for. Too close to something good after so many bad things happening. Chirp didn't *deserve* this, they knew that, but they weren't about to look a gift tiger in the mouth. *Selfish.*

"Chirp," Manu rumbled softly with a little chuckle, "that's what big brothers are for."

Movement flickered out of the corner of Chirp's eye, and when they looked at the space outside their bars, they saw Manu's hand, fingers waving, and they couldn't help but laugh. Hope burbled up in their throat, threatening to choke off their breath and bring tears to their eyes, but—

Shouting broke the moment Chirp and Manu shared.

Manu ripped his hand back through the bars so he could press his face in close, his breath stuttering as he listened. There was more yelling, followed by a bang, and the door to the dungeons clattered open, nearly ripped off its hinges it sounded like.

"Ah yes, my co-captain is here," Manu said through a smile.

Chirp couldn't help pressing their face in closer to the bars to get a better look at the petite lavender-haired woman who strode down the hall past them. Her face was littered with freckles, and Chirp didn't remember her looking quite so young the last time they'd seen her. But in spite of that, or maybe because of it, Persinette held her chin up high. Magic sparked around her fingertips like static, purple and threatening. But the moment her green eyes landed on Manu, it all fell away like a mask.

"Manu!" Persinette cried and rushed to his cell, her small hands lifting to pass through the bars. Chirp couldn't see what Persinette was doing, but they got the distinct impression that they were intruding on something private. "Oh, what have they done to you?"

"Pers," Manu murmured back through what sounded like the biggest smile he'd maybe ever worn. "Beautiful as ever, my darling co-captain."

"Oh, stop that. Now is not the time." She huffed and pulled away from him so she could glare at the lock on the bars, but her ears were distinctly pink, like she was pleased by the attention.

"If not now, then when?" Manu rumbled, undeterred by the gentle admonishment.

Persinette merely rolled her eyes and didn't let Manu draw her attention away from the lock. Her magic began to flow from her fingers into the hole meant for a key. The stream of it grew brighter and heavier, then eased off, as if she were trying to pick the lock instead of force it open with her power. Her pale brows drew together in concentration, freckled nose wrinkling.

"How's it coming?" someone called from the door, their voice too loud in the silence of the dungeon.

"It would be going a lot better if Benard had let me practice this on the locks in the hold!" Persinette fired back, a little trickle of sweat sliding down her neck as Chirp watched her, fascinated. "You could try to find the keys!"

"Now what would be the fun in that?"

"Helpful as always, Sully." Persinette grumbled, but a moment later, her face lit in a smile as the lock released with a click and she yanked the door open. "There it is."

Manu stumbled out, trying to make it look like a flourish and failing miserably.

Persinette caught him in her arms, shaking her head.

"Have I introduced you to my younger sibling?" Manu asked, his hand flapping in the vague direction of Chirp's cell, and Chirp saw it for the tactic that it was. "Pers, this is Chirp. Chirp, this is Pers."

"Chirp? Like the—"

"Long story. But yes. Now, if you'd be a dear and get them out? They have a prince to save."

Persinette turned her gaze from Manu to fix wide green eyes on Chirp. Her mouth ticked up at one corner in amusement. "A prince to save, huh?"

"If you wouldn't mind?" Chirp couldn't help but ask.

"Persi, I hate to break up this touching family moment," Sully called again, his voice harried, "but we should be hurrying!"

"Right." Persinette pressed a kiss to Manu's cheek as she helped him brace himself against the wall. Then she looked back to Chirp, her smile near feral when she said, "Let's get your sibling out so we can go slay some dragons."

THE CREW of the *Duchess* had cleared a path from their point of entry at the circus to the dungeons, but that still left plenty of guards standing in between Chirp and Brend. Guards who, Chirp was finding, were ill-prepared for their claws and jaws of a Cindaku.

"This is where we leave you," Persinette said, her hand tightening on a pistol. They were just outside the doors to the ballroom, where at least eight guards stood at attention. "You sure you can handle them on your own?"

Chirp groaned through the transformation from tiger to humanoid again, the bones and sinew of their body rearranging and reshaping themselves in a way that would have been unbearable if they didn't have such a high pain threshold. Maybe the Cindaku were built that way on purpose? Built to withstand the change. Chirp didn't know; they'd have to do some research on the subject when all of this was over, to better understand their dual nature. But until then, there were at least eight guards standing in their way. Maybe more—it was difficult to tell from this angle without being seen.

"I'll be all right," Chirp said, their tone thick with a bravado they hadn't ever felt before. But it had come along with the memories of their life. A confidence that was born of watching Manu smile his way through almost everything. If their big brother could do it, so could they.

"Have you ever used one of these before?" Kindle asked, pressing a pistol into each of Chirp's hands. She hadn't said much to Chirp since joining the group as they made their way through the castle—this was no time for reunions—but there was a concern in Kindle's expression that Chirp had never seen from her before. Like she was worried about losing a friend.

Chirp smiled, running their tongue along one pointed canine and tasting blood. "Trust me, I've got it under control."

"Gods, you really are Kelii's sibling, aren't you?" Kindle huffed, but said no more on the subject, and she and the others left Chirp tucked around the corner from the entrance to the ballroom. It wasn't the only entrance, of course, just the main one. The one that would have the most dramatic effect should Chirp enter through it.

Checking the pistol in their hand to make sure the safety was off and that it was loaded, calling on knowledge from when they were a child and needed to know such things, Chirp took a step around the corner, making themselves completely visible to the men standing between them and Brend, and opened fire.

# THIRTY-SEVEN
## BREND

T he room was stifling. Too many people packed in too close with the music blaring much too loudly. Or maybe that was just Brend, his sanity slowly trickling away as the cravat around his neck tightened inch by inch, making it harder and harder to breathe. Sweat dripped down the back of his collar, trailing the valley between his wings and making the holster that held them in place chafe.

Death was imminent now. No longer a foregone conclusion that might be prolonged with sly words and smiles. No. It was at his door, knocking and waiting to be let in. Brend had an hour, maybe an hour and a half left to live, depending on how long he could drag out this ball.

His mother might humor him if he begged for just one more dance with his betrothed. If he said the right words. But Brend was tired, so *very* tired, of all of this. Of the farce of it and the truth of it. Every part of his body ached with being forced to stand and bow and prance around like a show pony for all to see.

The servants had provided him with little to drink. He could hardly eat when a tray did happen to pass him, and he had yet to find the time to take a seat or any kind of rest. His mother knew she was pushing the limits of Brend's body, especially after such a grievous injury. Calculated. Cruel. He saw it for what it was. She wanted him to fall, faint in front of everyone so she could chalk it up to his illness. Tell everyone how unwell he'd been since he'd been shot by that terrible Enchanted. Play it up like it wasn't *her* —his own mother—sucking away his magic and making him sick.

No. It wouldn't be long now. She'd get what she wanted soon enough, for all that Brend was railing against it. For all that he was gritting his teeth to keep his balance and ignore the swaying of his vision. For all that he was leaning more heavily on his cane than he ever had. He couldn't keep this up, Brend knew that, but he'd be damned if he went down without a fight.

So, he forced himself through one more dance, two, all the while his head spinning faster than his feet. The woman in his arms was lovely, with a smile that was bright, eyes the color of ground coco, and hair the color of cornsilk. He hadn't quite caught her name when she'd given it, but he was given to understand that she was his betrothed.

If this weren't all some elaborate con planned out by his mother, Brend thought he might have been able to be quite content with what's-her-name. Not happy. She wasn't sharp as a knife's edge like Clancy, ready to slice Brend to ribbons with his wit and his cruelty by turns. Nor was she clever and curious like Chirp, eyes sparkling with a hidden mischief that only ever came out when they were alone. No. This girl's eyes, for all their beauty, were dull, with little behind them. No wit. No curiosity. Nothing except the warm brown.

The music ended, and a round of applause rent the air. Brend stumbled a little on his now numb knee as he stepped away from his dancing partner. If she noticed, she didn't say anything, didn't check to see if he was all right as Chirp might have, didn't reach for him as Clancy might have. Just dipped into a low curtsey and fixed him with that same vacant smile.

In an instant, Brend could see his life with this woman laid out before him, if he were allowed to live it. They would live in the castle, forever under his mother's thumb. And his new wife would never question this, never wonder what life was like outside of the same walls Brend had known growing up. She would not ask for adventure or knowledge. She would be content, and she would pressure Brend to be content as well. Cow him into silence and complacency where Chirp might have challenged him out of it. Brend's heart gave a traitorous lurch at the thought, threatening to crawl up his throat and spill onto the floor with what little food he'd managed to choke down earlier that day.

Well. On the bright side, at least he was probably going to die before that happened. *Yay.*

The music started again, and the young woman in front of him dipped into another curtsy, her head tilted to stare down at his shoes. "May I have this dance, Your Highness?"

God, he was going to die on this dance floor, wasn't he? Forget dying of poisoning, the exhaustion alone would do Brend in.

He opened his mouth to make up some excuse, to maybe run away with his tail between his legs while he still could, but was cut off by the tinkling sound of silverware on crystal. Brend looked up to find his mother standing in the mezzanine, a glass held high.

"A toast," she said, her voice carrying across the space, making everyone in the ballroom stop what they were doing to look up at her, "to my darling son."

A glaring spotlight broke off from the one pointed at his mother and slid across the floor until it found Brend in the crowd. It prickled too hot on the skin on the top of his head, and everyone stepped back to leave room for him and his betrothed, forming a circle around them that did nothing to stop Brend from suffocating on the feeling of too many bodies. Because now they weren't just pressing in on him, they were watching him too. Their gazes heavy, expectant. A weight he'd never be able to crawl out from under.

"To my darling son," the queen repeated, her glass still held aloft. She'd tilted her head just so, almost like she was looking at Brend, but she didn't meet his eyes. He'd like to think it was because she felt guilty, but he knew better. "On the day of his engagement."

They hadn't formally announced it yet, but as the queen said the words, the woman Brend had been dancing with stepped closer, as if she expected him to . . . what? Loop an arm around her waist and pull her in close? Take her hand and give it a squeeze of excitement and affection? They'd known each other for all of an hour, and he hadn't even caught her name.

"I am so pleased to welcome you to the family, Lady Lily." His mother brushed at her face, pretending to wipe a tear from dry eyes. "Please take care of my little boy."

"Of course, Your Highness," Lily—apparently—called back, reaching for Brend's hand and forcefully unclenching his fingers so she could thread her own in between them. Her palm was too dry, too small, the fingers too thin, every part unfamiliar, making the ache that had started in Brend's chest spread out from that single point to the tips of his own fingers, to his toes, every inch of him a throbbing bruise that ached for someone he may never see again. Someone who probably hated him after everything that happened, after they were blamed for something *Clancy* had done.

"To the happy couple." The queen lifted her glass higher, an instruction more than anything else, and Brend saw every person out of the corner of his eye follow suit until he was surrounded on all sides by people toasting his happiness with a woman he hardly knew. God, he was going to be sick, right there on Lily's pretty pink dancing slippers.

The doors to the ballroom banged open, slapping hard against the walls and startling several people enough that they spilled their drinks.

"Yes, yes, yes. To the happy couple," a familiar voice said, and Brend looked over to see Chirp over the heads of some of the people nearest him as the crowd began to part. They took a glass off someone near the door, not even bothering to hide the way their trousers were stained in something rust-colored, and blood dribbled from a cut above their eye. In the hand opposite the glass, a pistol hung almost limply, carelessly, from Chirp's fingers, as if they'd held one a thousand times. Chirp raised their glass, their eyes gleaming as they locked eyes with Brend. "And to the queen who plans to kill them both."

Several people gasped, and at least one person screamed, the sound shrill, glass shattering a second later, but Brend didn't look to see who it was, it didn't matter. Because Chirp was there, dashing as ever, their long dark hair falling into their eyes, their lips curled back from teeth that looked unnaturally sharp. Wild. Beautiful. God, how had Brend missed how breathtakingly gorgeous Chirp was? Maybe because, up until that point, they always seemed unsure. Always seemed like maybe they didn't really know who they were. But this Chirp . . . this Chirp was different. They strode through the crowd with a swagger that Brend had never expected to see from them.

"What is the meaning of this?!" the queen shouted, and Brend could only just make out the words over his heart pounding against his ribcage, threatening to leap out of his chest and right into Chirp's still mostly-full glass of champagne.

"The meaning of this, Your Majesty"—Chirp swept into

an exaggerated bow, then stood to knock back the entire glass of champagne in one gulp before passing it off to someone in the crowd, who just took it, looking dazed—"is that I've come for a dance with the prince. That's what happens at balls, isn't it? People dance? I wouldn't know, I've never been invited to one."

Chirp's loping steps ate up the space between them and Brend, and as the space shrank, the pounding of Brend's heart grew louder. His world narrowed down to a point, till it was just him and Chirp.

"Seize them!" the queen shouted, but Chirp had already made it close enough to Brend to be a real threat, within arm's reach now. Brend could reach out and pull them close if he wanted to. He *did* want to.

"Ah, ah, ah." Chirp clicked their tongue, lifted the pistol with all the steadiness of a trained marksperson, and pointed it directly at Brend's forehead.

Brend blinked, confused, a frown tugging at his lips, and a seed of doubt took root in his belly. But then Chirp tilted their head and winked, and it dissolved to nothing. "One move and I kill your *little boy*."

Brend wanted to tell Chirp that that was what his mother wanted. That she'd hired Clancy to shoot him. That all of this was an extravagant execution. But he couldn't get his tongue to move; it sat heavy and useless in his mouth. And they knew anyhow, didn't they? They'd said as much. Still, his eyes must have shown some of his panic, because Chirp tilted forward a little more, their hair curtaining around their face so only he could see it when they mouthed the words "Trust me."

They didn't wait for Brend to respond before they pushed their hair from their face with a free hand and tilted their head again so they could meet the gaze of the queen pistol still pressed cold to Brend's skin. "And my people will fire into the crowd."

Just then, at least half a dozen armed Enchanted melted from the shadows of the room, like they'd been there this whole time, watching and waiting for the summons to make themselves known. The guests cowered, slinking away from their aim, but they couldn't go far as Chirp's small army approached from all sides. Two people with pistols pointed right at his mother appeared on the mezzanine. One of them had long red hair and wings much like his own. A dragon. Maybe a relative?

"So, what do you say, Your Highness?" Chirp asked, ignoring the queen's sputtering and pulling Brend from his thoughts. "You have one more dance in you for a lowly Enchanted?"

Lily was squeezing his hand in a death grip, making his knuckles grind together. He shook her off and lifted that hand to Chirp, palm up. "I think I just might."

Chirp's lips spread into a victorious smile, and they dipped into another low bow, this one more sincere some-how, before straightening up again and taking his hand. They tugged him in close, looking down from their slightly taller height, and started moving even before one of their people kicked the band into playing again.

# THIRTY-EIGHT
## PERSINETTE & CREW

Chirp was spectacular. Persinette didn't think Manu could have done a better job himself. Not that she'd say that out loud—his pride was already wounded by the fact that he'd been forced back to the ship with their other injured. A fact she hated just as much as he did. It was strange to not have him at her side during this last battle; it settled wrong and ill-fitting over her shoulders. But he was so sick from dehydration, malnutrition, and blood loss, she couldn't expect him to fight alongside them. Not in good conscience. Even if he claimed he was fine, Persinette felt much better knowing he was safe back on the *Duchess*.

Still, if he could have seen Chirp . . . He'd have been so proud.

"Any word on where the Uprising forces are?" Persinette asked from where she stood in the shadow of the mezzanine, her voice a whisper.

Kindle's wing twitched, but she didn't take her eyes off her target, and her aim had never been steadier. There was fury in her gaze, a snarl on her lips. Persinette didn't think she'd ever seen so much hate on someone's face, but there it was plastered across Kindle's.

"You remember me, big sister?" Kindle had snarled when they made themselves known. Eloise hadn't made a move to respond other than lifting her chin and curling her nose at Kindle as if she were refuse stuck to her shoe.

"Not yet," Kindle murmured back now, jabbing the pistol's barrel into Eloise's arm hard enough to leave a bruise. "What do you think, big sister? Do you know where our other sibling is?"

"Weren't you supposed to be locked away, little sister?" Eloise snarled back under her breath, never once taking her attention off the people below. Persinette couldn't see her eyes to know where she was looking, but she could guess. Brend and Chirp made quite the pair, twirling about the dance floor as they were. Brend in all his finery, and Chirp looking like they'd just crawled off the battlefield. Manu would've definitely approved.

"I got out." Kindle snorted.

"Obviously." Eloise clicked her tongue in annoyance, probably rolling her eyes.

"You had to have someplace where you were going to meet Eddi," Agnes said, his tone flat, almost bored. He was probably put out by the fact that he hadn't been allowed to be the one to cause the spectacle down below. Honestly, how had Persinette ended up surrounded by people who loved dramatics? At least they'd make her life interesting from here on out, she supposed.

"They were going to find me." Eloise lifted one shoulder, unbothered by the weight of two pistols trained on her. Persinette wondered what it took to get her ruffled, of it would have to be something even more dramatic. But then the queen's lip peeled back in a snarl, and Persinette looked down to find Chirp dipping Brend, and she knew. Still, when Persinette looked back to Eloise, it wasn't the protective instinct of a mother that she saw written there. It was possessiveness. Brend was nothing more than an object to her, just another thing to be owned and used up. Persinette's stomach twisted with the knowledge.

"Chirp will take better care of my nephew than you ever could," Kindle said, vicious and spiteful. "You can be damn sure of that."

Eloise's jaw tightened, but she still didn't look away from the scene down below.

"In a bind, Elly?" someone said from the mezzanine beside them, poking their head around the curtains to reveal eyes turned too big and too wide behind goggles, and a wrinkled face that split into a cruel smile. Eddi. They tsked, their eyes bright with condescension. "I told you those labor camps would come back to bite you."

"Those were *your* idea," Eloise said through a clenched jaw.

"Yes." Eddi grinned wider, showing off too many teeth, like they could unhinge their jaw and swallow everyone. Persinette felt frozen on the spot, the pistol at her side heavy in her hand but immobile. "But I told you it was going to bite *you*. Didn't I?"

"Why you little—!" Eloise grabbed the pistol from Agnes's grip, wrestling him for it. A shot went off. The bullet embedded itself in the ceiling of the mezzanine. Dust rained down on them, bits of plaster coating them all in a fine layer of debris.

"Get after Eddi!" Agnes snarled, fighting with Eloise for his pistol, and Persinette looked back to realize that in the struggle, Eddi had used the confusion to escape.

Persinette hesitated, her gaze flicking to Kindle, who'd joined the struggle, her taloned fingers reaching for Eloise's wrists to help wrestle the gun from her. With a grunt at an elbow to her stomach, Kindle looked up at Persinette. "One sibling is enough vengeance for me, you grab the other one."

"Right." Persinette nodded firmly and ducked out of the

booth just in time to see Eddi rounding a corner at the end of the corridor. Boots thumping loudly against the marble floors, Persinette chased after them. Running down halls, skidding around corners, ducking through doorways. Persinette's chest heaved with labored pants, and she wondered how much of Kindle's magic Eddi was using to stay one step ahead of her. It didn't seem possible otherwise. No wonder Kindle was so tired all the time!

Every guard they passed on their way had fallen. Blood pooled around them on the white marble floor. Had Eddi done that? Or had they brought their own forces? Persinette couldn't tell. And there wasn't time to ponder it because a moment later, she managed to catch up to Eddi. Her lungs burned, each expansion feeling like it might pop one of them as she gulped down air. The pistol at her side weighed a ton, but she lifted it, her hand shaking, to take aim.

"Come now, Persinette, you don't want to do that, do you?" Eddi asked, their hands raised up next to their head as if in surrender. "You were never the killing type."

"You *used* me," Persinette said, taking a step forward, and Eddi took a step back toward the doors that overlooked a courtyard several stories down.

"I use everybody." Eddi laughed, their hands waving a little by their head. They hadn't let their wings press out from their back, Persinette noticed, nor had they thrown up any magical defense. Maybe they couldn't? No. That couldn't be right. They had been siphoning magic off Kindle for centuries now, there was no reason that they wouldn't be able to. Unless they'd used it all to get into the castle . . . "Look at my own family."

"It's not funny!" Why were her eyes burning with tears? Why was a lump forming in her throat? There was nothing to cry about. Nothing at all.

Except, there was *everything* to cry about. Eddi had done

awful things to her, to her family, to her people. Eddi had turned on their own kind in order to win a fight with their sister, and for what? For *what*?! In the end, it had come to naught.

"You used me!" Another step. "Then you threw me away!" Another. "Used Manu, blinded him, threw *him* away!"

Eddi's back was pressed to the double doors now, their wrinkled face looking distinctly nervous.

"Used Agnes and Sully and Kindle and Rose, and so many others! *So many!*"

"Like I said, it's what I do." Eddi shrugged, nonchalant, but their eyes were flicking from the shaking pistol in Persinette's hand to the space behind her, then to the view over their own shoulder, looking for a way out. There was no way out, Persinette realized. This was the end. It had been many long months since Persinette left her tower in MOTHER HQ, and this was the end.

"You don't even feel *guilty*, do you?" The realization hit Persinette hard, leaving her chest aching. Eddi didn't even care that they'd ruined so many lives, that they had so much blood on their hands. They were worse than MOTHER, worse than the Gothels, worse than almost any other villain Persinette had faced because at least those people truly believed what they said. They truly saw Enchanted as lesser, as dangerous. But not Eddi. Eddi knew better and they did it anyway. Eddi knew better and they weren't *sorry* for it.

"What do you want me to say?" Eddi took a step toward Persinette, closing the distance they had carefully cultivated. "Do you want me to apologize?"

"No, I—" Persinette frowned, confusion filtering in, her mind going fuzzy now that the adrenaline was wearing off. "Yes. Yes, I want you to apologize."

"Well," Eddi said, their voice gentle, almost kind, until the very end when they lunged for the pistol. "I'm *not* going to!"

Persinette didn't think, she just reacted, just as she'd done with Gothel all those months ago. Her hand flew up, throwing out a spell that was more instinct than anything else, and sent Eddi hurtling away from her.

Through the doors, shattering their glass, and over the rail of the balcony. Either Eddi didn't have enough time to use their wings or the blood on what was left on the doors meant they were dead before they ever hit the ground. Either way, Persinette held her breath, hoping to hear the swoop of wings and instead hearing the hard *thud* of a body hitting the courtyard below.

Hesitant steps brought Persinette to the railing. The cold wind bit at her cheeks, and when she looked down, she saw Eddi lying on the cobbles, broken. Spinning quickly, Persinette was violently sick in a potted plant in the corner of the balcony, her entire body shaking.

"Are you all right?" Rose asked. She'd appeared as if by magic to lean almost lazily against the doorjamb, her face a bruised patchwork from where she'd been fighting with the guards.

Persinette didn't know how much she'd seen, but it must have been enough, and the guilt of having killed Eddi turned Persinette's stomach again, making her vomit bile into the plant.

Rose sighed, moving to Persinette's side to rub her back while making awkward tutting noises.

"I killed them. I killed Eddi," Persinette said through choked-off tears. "I'm so sorry."

Rose gave Persinette an awkward pat. "It's all right. You did what you had to do."

That didn't make Persinette feel any better. Didn't make the guilt stop churning in her stomach. It was worse than when she'd accidentally killed Gothel, she realized, because now that it was all almost over, she would have plenty of time to dwell on it. To live with it.

"Come on, we've got work still to do." Rose offered a hand to help Persinette up from where she hadn't realized she'd knelt beside the plant. Taking it, Persinette rose to her unsteady feet and gifted Rose a shaky smile. Then she let Rose lead her back to the fray. There would be time for her guilt. Later.

# THIRTY-NINE
## CHIRP

"You're different," was the first thing Brend said to them once they were as alone as one could get in the middle of a crowded room. He'd pressed his face in close to Chirp's ear, his words a brush of breath that sent a thrill down their spine. Chirp hadn't realized how much they'd truly missed Brend until that very moment. How close they had gotten in such a short time. They were friends, yes, but there was something more than that simmering low and warm under the surface. Something Chirp hoped they weren't the only one feeling. That was impossible, wasn't it? For them to be the only one feeling it?

"We're both different," Chirp breathed against his hairline, taking in the smell of him. Expensive hair products and cologne, smells that would no doubt go away after this. Because Brend would no longer be a prince. He would just be a man, a man on a pirate ship. Well . . . he'd be a pirate, Chirp supposed. They thought they might like that, seeing Brend all swashbuckling and flushed from adventure. He'd love every minute of it, no doubt.

Brend pulled back a little so he could look up at Chirp, his red brows creased at the center. "Are we?"

"Aren't we?" Chirp couldn't help but smile. They *were* different, so very different, and yet very much the same people they'd been not more than a handful of days ago when someone shot Brend and Chirp was blamed for it. "The man I knew at the beginning of this," Chirp said, swallowing against the cotton at the back of their throat, "he would be shaking in his boots right now."

"He would not!" Brend hissed back, frowning at Chirp, but there was no real heat or offense behind it. Nothing but a teasing glint to his eye. Chirp thought maybe they could get used to being this close to Brend. To being able to read his eyes like some people read books.

"Do you know how many weapons are trained on us right now?" Chirp continued the game, leaning in closer so they could whisper their next words directly into his ear, a secret and a taunt all in one. "He would too."

Brend was smiling again, mischief crinkling the corners of his eyes into something beautiful and golden, like the first rays of the spring sun after a long, cold winter.

"But they're not trained on me, *are they?*" He kept his voice low, just for the two of them. If anyone outside of their little bubble noticed that the prince being held hostage didn't look particularly frightened, Chirp hadn't heard them say anything yet. Maybe the queen had noticed, but she had other problems to deal with. Then Brend said the thing that would be the nail in Chirp's coffin: "I'm safe with you."

Heat crawled up Chirp's neck, burning the tips of their pointed ears, and they wanted nothing more than to shy away from Brend's knowing look. To tuck their face into his neck and hide there until the rest of the world disappeared around them. But that wouldn't work, would it? Because they were in the middle of a war here, and Chirp couldn't hide, not if they wanted to make sure everyone they loved came out on the other side of it. Brend was on that list, whether Chirp was willing to acknowledge it or not. "Yes. I suppose you are."

The smile that lit his face after that was so bright, Chirp had to look away because if they didn't, then they may very well do something intolerably stupid. Like tell Brend their life story. Or kiss him. Or ask him to marry them. All foolish behaviors that they didn't have time for with the queen watching them and Eddi lurking somewhere around the periphery. All they could be thankful for—and Chirp would be grateful to Agnes and Rose until the day they died for it— was that the Ringmaster had been taken care of before the crew even showed up to retrieve Chirp and Manu. Shot down just as he was trying to escape the castle. Apparently it had been necessary, so they could use his ship as a landing port. And besides, he was as guilty as the rest of them. There was no great loss in that, Chirp told themselves, their chin lifting just a touch.

"What happened to you after—" Brend stopped himself, chewing on the inside of his cheek like he was chewing on the words. His brows drew even closer together, creating a wrinkle between them Chirp wanted to smooth away, but they denied the urge.

"*After* I was blamed for your shooting?" Chirp prompted, ignoring the gnawing in their gut that made their fingers itch with the desire to tuck Brend away into a corner where they could inspect his injuries, see how he was healing. But that would defeat the purpose of the whole spectacle.

"Yes," Brend said, the word seemingly forced past something lodged in his throat as he swallowed once, twice in quick succession before adding, "That."

"I uh—" Their hand flexed behind Brend's back as they worked through their thoughts. It was such a very long story. And honestly, Chirp didn't know where to start. "I—" A gunshot rang out, cutting Chirp off, and they both paused their dancing to look up at the mezzanine, where Kindle, Agnes, and the queen were wrestling for one pistol. Chirp's next words came out rushed as they pushed Brend behind them. "It's a long story, and we don't really have time for it right now."

The crowd was moving again, muttering in terror. Someone was crying. And if they weren't careful, Chirp was sure that they and Brend would be squashed in the ensuing stampede should the crowd become any more frightened.

"I hate to cut this short," Chirp apologized, pressing a kiss to Brend's lips—too short, too chaste for the heat swirling in their veins—before spinning to look for Sully in the crowd. "Sully!" Chirp called over the heads of those closest to them, making eye contact with the kelpie standing nearest the band, which had stopped playing. He stepped through the crowd to get within hissing distance, and Chirp hoped that everyone around them had largely stopped paying attention to them, but they knew the chance of that was slim. "Start getting some of these people out of here."

"But some of them might be Uprising Agents," Sully argued, his dark eyes flicking from one face to the next as the crowd began to ebb and flow toward the exits. Panic was spreading like a plague, a flame they wouldn't be able to put out no matter what they tried. They were losing the advantage. And if they weren't careful, all of these people would turn on them, just as they were likely to turn on the queen once she was dethroned. Besides, if these people grew any more frightened, it wouldn't matter how many weapons their people had—the crowd would kill them.

"We'll worry about that later! We can't have anyone getting hurt."

Sully looked from Chirp to the mezzanine, where Persinette had been posted to keep a look out for the Uprising leader. Chirp hadn't seen her since she'd gone up there, and they took that as a sign that Persinette was either still looking or she'd found them. Either way, there was little choice left.

Snapping their fingers in front of Sully's face to get his attention again, Chirp said, "We're different than they are, aren't we?"

His jaw set, Sully nodded and turned back to the others to start firing off instructions. With the exits blocked, Chirp watched as the crew of the *Duchess* got everyone into an orderly line and started checking them on the way out the door. It wasn't much. Someone still might sneak past them, but it was something. Likely more than the queen or the Uprising would have done for their enemies. And that's what these people were to the crew of the *Duchess*, at least until someone new was put on the throne: enemies.

Chirp brought up the rear with Brend, murmuring assurances to a dazed Lily and her mother as they shuffled to the exit around broken champagne glasses and overturned tables.

*We're different than they are, aren't we?*

It was those words that left Brend awestruck. He didn't know much of Chirp or their past. He didn't know anything at all about the crew they'd come with or where they came from. But he saw the close-shaved heads. He recognized the gaunt look. And he'd be willing to bet that if he asked any of them to pull up their sleeves, he would find the tattooed number of a labor camp upon their arm. A labor camp that all *these* people profited from. A labor camp that probably not a single one of them had given a second thought to. And yet, here was a group of Enchanted willing to take the time and the added risk to get them out safely because they were bystanders. Not *innocent* bystanders, but bystanders.

He knew there was more to it than that; there always was with Chirp. This risk was calculated, just like every other one they'd ever taken. But that didn't change the fact that Chirp and their people didn't have to do this. They didn't have to bother. They could have just gunned down everyone in the room and started fresh come morning. But they hadn't. Because they didn't think of life as expendable like Brend's mother seemed to. And that was the long and short of it, wasn't it? Chirp and their crew were different than the queen and MOTHER and the Uprising. They didn't want people to get hurt in a war they hadn't signed on for.

They were *different*. They were *honorable*.

And Brend wanted to be like that too. He smiled, only half-realizing the expression had split his face in two, as he watched Chirp help Lily's mother over an overturned platter of finger foods. Once upon a time, Charlie had called him good, but she had been wrong. *Chirp* was good. So good.

Another gunshot rang out, making Brend's ears ring, and he had just enough time to turn and see the bullet graze Chirp's arm. They cried out, blood splattering on the floor in front of them. Their hand flew to their arm to staunch the bleeding. But the damage was done.

Panic ensued.

Suddenly everyone was pushing and screaming to escape, and all Chirp's people could do was get out of the way. Brend tripped over to Chirp, his arms already outstretched to help them to the floor, to get a good look at the wound. To wrap it in something, anything, to keep Chirp from bleeding more than necessary.

Then a second shot rang out, this one landing just beside Chirp's foot. Brend whipped around and found his mother bracing herself on the balcony of the mezzanine, broad blue wings spread out behind her. But that wasn't what terrified him. No. It was the pistol in her shaking hands as she lined up another shot. He didn't know what had happened to the two people who were supposed to be holding her. Maybe she'd disposed of them. Or maybe they'd run off to help their crew do something else. Either way, he wasn't letting his mother shoot Chirp *again*.

Enough was enough.

He put himself in the way, his back hunched as he grabbed at Chirp's elbows where they threatened to shrink to the floor. Helping them gently down, Brend remained bent over them, blocking his mother's shot.

"Damn it, Brend, get out of the way!" his mother shouted, sending another shot just wide of him and Chirp.

"No," Brend whispered. His wings flexed hard against the harness at his back, the leather creaking as if it might give at any moment.

He took a breath to control the rage that burned through him, but then a fourth shot pinged against the marble floor, sending bits of rubble and debris up at Chirp's face. Blood dripped from a fresh cut, and Brend was *done* with *all* of this. With his mother trying to take everything that meant anything to him. With the people in his kingdom suffering, whether they be Enchanted or human. With being trapped in his own home. With his power being siphoned off, used in a never-ending war with a relative he'd never met.

Done with all of it.

"What was that? I can't hear you, *boy*!" his mother jeered, and he could hear her clothes rustle as she took aim again just before the wings broke free from the harness at his back. They spread wide behind him, protecting Chirp with their width, and left his shirt and jacket in tatters.

Chirp blinked up at him once, twice, their mouth hanging open, and he wanted so badly to lean forward and capture that awe on his tongue. To keep it with him forever. But he wasn't going to let this go on any longer.

"Enough, Mother," Brend snarled, turning toward her and letting his wings flex behind him. They were so large now, he didn't doubt he'd be able to soar with a little practice. Maybe he'd learn eventually. If he survived this.

"Oooh, you've finally got your wings, so you think you can talk back to mother now?" Eloise asked, her hand tightening on the pistol. Brend didn't know how many bullets were left in it. He didn't care either. Let her take her last few shots at him, then let this be over with. If nothing else, this would provide the distraction they needed to get the last few people out, for someone from the crew to come and help Chirp to safety. It wouldn't be much, but it would be enough. It was what he could do.

She took another shot. The pain of it burned through the thin membrane of Brend's right wing but did not come out the other side, and Brend's lips peeled back from his teeth, victorious. Before his mother could recover from her shock, Brend launched into the air, the sound of wingbeats loud in his ears, and flapped hard until he was standing in front of her on the railing of the mezzanine.

"I said *enough*, Mother," he repeated, then ripped the pistol from her hands.

She recovered, a roar leaving her as she grabbed onto him, her hands fisting in what was left of his shirt. A dagger had appeared from somewhere—maybe her boot, he didn't know, he didn't care. All that mattered was how it sliced into the thin skin of his chest, leaving behind trails of blood.

"You were an accident," she hissed, slashing at him, and he grabbed for her wrists, trying to wrest the knife from her. But even if he had wings and magic now, he was outmatched. Queen Eloise was older by far, and more powerful after the last twenty-some years of siphoning magic from her son. Brend was no match for her. But he had to try. He *had* to, he reminded himself as he grabbed for the knife and the blade cut deep into his palm. "You were never supposed to be born!"

"What a hateful thing to say to my nephew," a voice groaned from their right, and both mother and son stopped to look at the red-winged dragon laying off to the side, blinking back to consciousness. She sat up, shook herself.

It was all the distraction Brend needed to snag the knife and turn it. His mother grabbed for it again, to yank it away from him, not realizing the point was now pressed to her belly, and buried it in her stomach with a grunt. The blood came quick and slick, the color draining from his mother's face as she started coughing, the sound distinctly wet and gurgling.

"Mo– Mother!" Brend reached for her, pulling the knife out without thinking and making it worse, so much *worse*. He pulled her to him, reaching within himself for the magic that had lain dormant, but it sputtered, useless, ineffectual. He turned to plead with the dragon beside them. "You have to help her. You have to help my mother!"

His mother reached up for him, her fingers ashen and shaking as they brushed his jaw. Then she scraped nails turned talons down his cheek, ripping through the skin. "I hate you!" she screeched, reaching up to claw at him again, only to be stopped by the firm hand of the red-haired woman. "You were never supposed to be born!" She coughed, blood splattering against Brend's neck and chin, warm and thick. "Your father was weak! You are weak!"

But for all of her howling, snarling, and clawing, Brend never took his pleading gaze away from the woman, who might have been a relative of some kind. He should hate his mother. He *wanted* to hate her. After everything she had done to him, to their people, she deserved his hate maybe more than anyone else in all of Daiwynn. But she was still his mother. She was still the woman who had birthed him, cared for him in her own warped way. And even as her words twisted in his gut, a knife in their own right, he loved her. Might love her for the rest of his life.

"Please. You have to save her."

"I can't," the woman said, shaking her head, her voice a hoarse, choked sound just barely distinguishable over his mother's continued ranting. "We came here to kill her."

His mother's slaps grew weaker and weaker, her coughing more wet, more persistent.

"Why? Why would you come here for that?" The question left him automatically, trite. But even as he asked it, Brend *knew*. He knew all of the things his mother and her sibling had done to the people of Daiwynn. All of the discord they had sown in their own people. All of the hurt and the hate and the death. And for *what*? What had it achieved? Nothing.

His mother went limp in his arms, her breaths a rattle as her eyes fought to stay open. But she wasn't fighting the inevitable anymore, and neither was he.

"Will you kill me too?" he asked, brushing his mother's hair away from her face. If he looked at her just so, she might've been sleeping. Maybe he could pretend that for a while. Maybe not. Which would be worse? Which would be more painful? He didn't know.

"No. We won't." The woman shook her head, frowning.

"Why not?" Brend looked up from his mother's still face to fix his gaze on the woman.

The woman tilted her head, bright red hair falling into her face, her brow wrinkled a little. "Because you have someone in your corner." She hooked her thumb over her shoulder, and when Brend looked where she was pointing, he saw Chirp being helped to their feet by Sully. Their legs were wobbly and weak beneath them, but they stood mostly on their own power just the same. "Manu's little sibling wasn't about to let us off the last of my bloodline who seemed to have any decency in them."

"Your bloodline?" Brend's eyes flicked back to her, brows creased.

"Yeah, I guess I'm your aunt." She laughed, holding out her hand and not minding one bit when Brend shook it with his own bloody palm. "Kindle."

"Enough chatting," another man groaned from where he'd

been slouched against the wall. "We've got a lot of cleanup to do, and we could use your help since we're two down."

"Two down?" Brend frowned.

"Our co-captain, Manu, and his seeing-eye-robot, Hiccup." Kindle shrugged, pressing to her feet. Brend looked down at his mother. His fingers shook as he closed her eyes. He didn't know how long it had been since she'd stopped breathing, but she was starting to go cold. "We'll hold a service for your mother when all of this is over."

"You will?'

"Yeah, kid. We'll show her and all the others who lost their lives on the wrong side of this respect."

Brend thought to ask why, but then he remembered what Chirp had said.

*We're different than they are, aren't we?*

This was what being different looked like, and Brend liked it. Couldn't wait to be a part of it. So he stood, taking the man's offered jacket to cover his mother, and followed the others down the stairs into the main ballroom, where an exhausted looking Chirp waited.

They looked up from where someone was tying a bit of fabric around their wound to stem the bleeding and smiled at him, all teeth, eyes wild, and Brend was lost to it. Utterly lost to it. He took one step, two, before he was running across the ballroom and scooping Chirp up into his arms. They grunted at the tightness around their middle, but when he tried to pull back, they wrapped their arms just as tightly around him and didn't seem as if they'd ever let go.

He waited, feeling Chirp's heartbeat against his chest for a small eternity before the rushed, chaste kiss returned to his mind, and then he was pulling back, but not far, never far again, and kissing them with everything he had in him. He hardly noticed when they both sank to the floor, didn't feel the hard bite of marble against his sore knees until someone cleared their throat loudly behind them, and Chirp pulled back.

"Sorry, but uh . . ." Sully smiled at them, his tone apologetic. "We should probably get started on the cleanup. Sooner it's done, the better."

"Where do you need me?" Brend asked as he stood.

*Brend*

As it turned out, where they needed him was *everywhere*. To help clean up. To calm the guests. To bring order to a world left in chaos by the absence of his mother and her sibling. To dismantle everything they'd built and fill the void left behind by MOTHER and Uprising alike.

Brend spent the better part of the next few years just trying to detangle the political knot that his mother left Daiwynn in. And when the dust finally cleared, what was left was no longer a queen or a king but a council of seven—the odd number was necessary, Chirp said, to make sure there was never a stalemate when they voted on things.

There was Brend, in spite of his best efforts to be left out of it. He'd been assured—again, by Chirp—that remaining a part of the ruling council would ease the minds of those who had been loyal to his mother. It did, to some extent. There were people who fought back, some rebellion, but those voices were small, easy to drown out.

Roy and Penny joined as well. Roy said it was necessary to always have a human representative, and when he passed, there were talks of allowing the people to vote for the next in line.

Kindle, who hated absolutely every minute of it, joined too. She would much rather have been cloistered away in the library or in Rose's lab, but two red-winged dragons were better than one, and Brend appreciated the support from his aunt. He also appreciated how close they grew over the years, how easy it was to fall into something like friendship. It made the adjustment from human to dragon much easier.

Of course, there was Chirp, who didn't leave Brend's side through all of it. Who was his rock and his shelter when he needed it more than he could put into words. He was so grateful to them, for their help and for everything else they offered him. Love the likes of which he'd once fooled himself into thinking he had with Clancy. But this was better. This was realer.

And finally, Alys and Stella rounded them out to seven. Even years later, Brend still wasn't sure how he felt about them and their partner, Hatter, but he supposed it didn't matter. What *did* matter was that they brought the voices of the people who had escaped to the Waste to the table. What *did* matter was that the council was able to provide those people with the aid they desperately needed, and even bring some of them home if they wanted to return.

The others didn't join, but Brend heard from them regularly enough to know how they were doing. It was strange how a family could form under such extreme pressure, like diamonds.

And sometimes, he thought of his mother and Clancy and all that he had allowed himself to accept from them. Sometimes, when he was alone late at night in his office, Chirp having already gone to bed—although not for long, because they'd be back for him soon enough, he knew that—he'd compare the family he had now to the family he'd had then.

See the differences. And he began to understand that maybe Clancy and his mother hadn't been family at all. To think of just how lucky he'd been that everything had fallen into place the way it had.

"Fate" was the word Persi liked to use for it. But Brend didn't think he agreed with that. Saying it was fate awarded the gratitude Brend felt every day to some unknown, unseen entity for what essentially had simply been the goodness and kindness of the people he loved—the people who loved him—coming together to make a brighter future for themselves and those who came after them.

So, not fate at all. Just good people.

*Persinette*

"If you don't hurry up, we're going to be late!" Persinette called to Manu through the door to his closet. It had been years, and he still insisted on getting ready *inside* of his closet and then doing a grand reveal to her like he was some kind of magician. Some might've found it annoying, but Persinette got a little thrill every time the door opened and Hiccup gave that small trumpeting sound of triumph to say that he had dressed her co-captain immaculately again.

"Oh, pish posh," Manu called back, a little laugh in his voice. "We can't be late to our own ceremony."

"It's not *our* ceremony." Persinette huffed a laugh, brushing her fingers over the neat braid she'd tied her hair into. It felt good to have it again, hanging against the center of her back, thumping against her spine when she ran. "We're just officiating."

"Who knew captains could officiate civil unions as well as weddings?" Manu muttered mostly to himself. "No, Hiccup, I don't think that we should wear chartreuse to Alys, Stella, and Hatter's ceremony."

Hiccup chirped in response.

"Oh, fine, maybe a little bit."

"Besides, we've still got to pick up Sully, Agnes, and the baby." The baby was less a baby and more a little girl these days. A fairy child that they'd found at one of the camps, orphaned when her parents died in the queen's mines. She didn't talk much at first, but after a few weeks with Sully and Agnes, she'd bloomed into a bright little thing. Himari had even adopted Agnes's superior taste in cravats.

"All right, what do you think?" Manu asked as the door opened with a flourish, his blank eyes falling where he expected Persinette to be waiting for him.

She scooted over a little to accommodate him and gave him a quick once-over. "Charming as ever, my dear co-captain."

Running his hands down over the rich paisley fabric, Manu preened. "You think?"

"I do."

"Good, now, where's my hat?"

Hiccup whistled his disapproval, and Persinette saw him kick the offending hat back into the corner of the closet where it very well might be carted off by bilge rats just as the last one had.

"What do you mean I can't wear that atrocity? It's a very charming hat! Persinette said so herself when I—"

"Manu. Hiccup. If you keep it up, we won't be able to have tea with Himari before we have to get on our way, and you know how cranky she gets when she doesn't get to have tea with her favorite captain," Persinette chided softly, her hands lifting to straighten Manu's waistcoat a little.

A smile crawled across Manu's face. "Well, when you're right, you're right, my dear," he murmured, leaning forward to press a kiss to her lips before pulling back to thread their fingers together and give her hand a gentle tug. "And you're right. Let's go."

And off they went, on to their next adventure.

**The End**

# Acknowledgments

First off, thank you—the reader—for joining me on this final adventure in Daiwynn. This cast of characters has been with me for a few years now, and I've grown quite attached to them, so I hope you love them as much as I do.

Although the Clockwork Chronicles is over, and all my darlings found their happy endings, there are so many more worlds in my head to explore, and characters to get to know. I hope you'll join me on another big adventure soon.

Next, I'd like to thank my family who has listened to me ramble on about my characters and worlds, and who has supported me in this little dream of mine. I know they'll probably never read this, but everyone needs to know they're great.

I'd also like the thank my small hoard of beta-readers. You guys gave some excellent insight, and I really appreciate all of your hard work!

And last but certainly not least, are my writing support group. From the friends I've had for decades who have helped me to grow into the writer I am today (Elle, Tiss, and Jasmine) to the new ones I've acquired through MTP like Nancy, Brindi, Hannah, Adina, Nicole, and Steph. And of course my beautiful, supportive editor, Meg. Writing a book takes a village, and you guys are my village.

# About the Author

Born and raised in a small town near the Chesapeake Bay, Lou Wilham grew up on a steady diet of fiction, arts and crafts, and Old Bay. After years of absorbing everything, there was to absorb of fiction, fantasy, and sci-fi she's left with a serious writing/drawing habit that just won't quit. These days, she spends much of her time writing, drawing, and chasing a very short Basset Hound named Sherlock.

When not, daydreaming up new characters to write and draw she can be found crocheting, making cute bookmarks, and binge-watching whatever happens to catch her eye.

Learn more about Lou and her future projects on her website: http://louinprogress.com/ or join her mailing list at: http://subscribepage.com/mailermailer

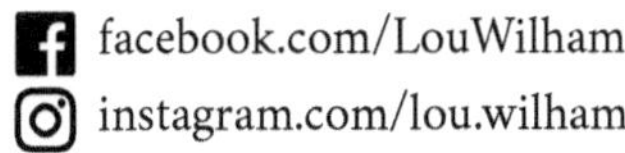

facebook.com/LouWilham

instagram.com/lou.wilham

ALSO BY LOU WILHAM

The Curse Collection
    The Curse of The Black Cat
    The Curse of Ash and Blood
    The Curse of Flour and Feeling

The Clockwork Chronicles
    The Girl in the Clockwork Tower
    The Unicorn and the Clockwork Quest
    The Rose in the Clockwork Library
    The Marionette in the Clockwork Circus

The Heir To Moondust
    The Prince of Starlight
    The Prince of Daybreak
    The Crown of Night

The Witches of Moondale
    The Hex Next Door
    The Ghost of Hexes Past

Overkill

Sanctuary of the Lost
    Of Loyalties and Wreckage
    Of Love and Ruin

**Completed Series**
    The Tales of the Sea Trilogy
    Villainous Heroics

**Sneak Peek!**

continue reading for a sneak peek of Lou's

# Hex Next Door

PREVIEW

"What the fuck," Rus muttered, her gaze fixed on the Moondale town sign. She'd said she'd never come back to this place. But that was the thing about where you grew up: it had the power to drag you back like the fucking Bermuda Triangle. And Rus would know—she'd been to the Bermuda Triangle four or five times in the years since she'd left Moondale behind. The particulars weren't important. What was important was that Rus was sure she'd wind up there four or five more times before she died.

"Rus?" Nesta tilted their head, a piece of floppy black hair falling into their eyes. They looked just how Rus remembered them, and she still wasn't sure how to feel about that. But she'd likely beg for Nesta's skin care regime before the day was done.

"Nothing. Let's just get this over with." Rus shook herself and jerked her gaze back to the view through the windshield.

Moondale looked different and yet the same. It had sprawled out past the little dot on the coast where its founders had originally settled, up into the mountain beyond to include a ski lodge and even a few big-name hotels. Of that Rus was grateful; she didn't think she could stay in one of the inns in town with the kids. Not if she wanted to keep the Board of Magic off her ass for more than a week.

Nesta was still glancing at her from the driver's seat. Rus could feel those cunning eyes looking for . . . something. Maybe some sign of what Rus was thinking. They wouldn't find anything. More than a decade spanned between them, and Rus had learned long ago to keep her thoughts tucked away where they couldn't be used against her.

"I just can't believe you became a realtor." Rus tilted her head, letting a teasing smile tug up the corners of her mouth. It would hopefully be enough to keep Nesta from asking inconvenient questions.

Nesta shrugged, turning down one of the side roads off Main Street. They were headed toward the older part of town, the buildings around them changing from relatively modern retail to small suburban homes to Gothic-style houses that would make the Addams family jealous.

"How did your parents take it?" Rus pressed. Anything to ignore the way her stomach was writhing with nerves. She hoped she wouldn't see anyone else she knew, not before she was settled. But in a town that hardly had more than a few thousand residents to boast, that was likely impossible. At least *she'd* be at work, so Rus could avoid that particular awkward encounter. "I mean . . . a cupid not becoming a matchmaker for the board? That's—"

"I told them I didn't think the board would be using matchmakers much longer," Nesta said, and they sounded smug about it. Like they'd realized a new hairstyle would be trending long before anyone else could.

"And?" Rus had to know, because she could just imagine old man Holyore absolutely losing his shit at his child chucking tradition out the proverbial window. He might quiver right out of his beard.

"And they didn't agree . . ." Nesta's mouth twisted up into a knowing smirk, their eyes still firmly on the road. "At first."

Well. That sounded like a story and a half. One they probably didn't have time for, and it would likely require wine. Lots of wine. Rus snorted, rolling her eyes. "Okay, but a realtor though?"

"Why not? The same principles apply. It's all about listening to harmonizing energies. And this house?" Nesta put the car in park outside of yet another Gothic-style house perched on the far end of one of Moondale's more ancient-looking cemeteries. "It wants you, Rus."

"Ew. Don't make it sound creepy." Rus huffed, her hand twitching to give Nesta a fond shove, but she resisted the urge. They weren't friends like that, not anymore. So instead, she turned her attention to the house.

Rus blinked up at it. It looked like something out of Hansel and Gretel, with a small porch, three walk-out balconies off the rooms upstairs, and a legit tower. Or . . . maybe *tower* wasn't the word for whatever that was, but Rus imagined the room on the first floor would be the perfect place to put a reading and playroom for the girls, and the second an ideal shrine for their parents' tablets. The only thing was—

"Nesta, you are aware that this house is . . . *pink*, right?" Rus cocked her head. It wasn't unbearably pink. It didn't reek of Barbie Dreamhouse. But it was most definitely a shade of pastel that Rus was sure she'd never worn in her entire life.

"Lilac, actually. And what's that saying about not judging a house by its siding color?"

"I'm pretty sure that's not a thing."

"You ready to see inside, or what?" Nesta asked, already reaching for the door to climb out.

Rus nodded dumbly, scrambling from the car to follow them through the little wrought iron gate and up the walk. The door opened onto a small foyer bedecked in black walls, and a little gray bench off to the side with hooks hanging above it for coats.

Nesta was saying something about the history of the house, and the remodeling, and something about all the furnishings coming with the place if that's what she wanted, but Rus had largely stopped listening. Because the house— 157 Mourning Moore—was exactly what Rus had always imagined when she'd thought of a home for herself. The walls were all black, but there was enough natural lighting about the place that it didn't feel dark and gloomy. And there were pops of color here and there: A throw pillow on the bench in the foyer. Silver birch tree wallpaper in the study. A collection of velvet pillows in the strange round room of the tower that Rus had decided would make a great study and playroom. It was—

"Who's watching the kids?"

"Huh?" Rus shook herself, tearing her eyes away from the frankly spectacular nursery. Aihuan was a little old for a crib, but that was an easy enough fix. She'd love the brightly painted forest critters on the black wallpaper. "Oh. Their Uncle Fernando. But I can't leave them with him long, or by the time I get back they'll have given him a makeover. Buzzcut included. Meiling is a menace."

"Fernando?"

"Yeah. He's one of the witches I met online. Good kid. Little awkward, but who isn't these days? He'll be moving in with us for a bit until we're settled in and we can find him his own place." Rus paced to the window. The view from the nursery was of Moondale, and not the cemetery. She'd have to check to make sure Meiling's window didn't overlook it either. Neither of her girls needed to see the spirits that were standing on the edge of the property looking up at the house. Even now, Rus could feel their gaze on her, making the hair on the back of her neck stand on end. Really, she'd thought the board had Rules about letting spirits languish without rest like that. But then . . . maybe they hadn't had another medium in town since she'd left. And if those spirits weren't doing anything other than just floating around, no one would notice them outside of a medium.

"Is he your . . . ?" Nesta drifted off, their perfectly plucked brows turning down to wrinkle in the middle.

Rus laughed. "Goddess no. We're just friends. He's good with the girls, though."

"I see. Well. There's still the attic." Nesta gestured to the narrow stairs that led up to the last room in the house.

"Lead the way." Rus gestured for Nesta to go first and followed them when they turned on their heel to head upstairs. She'd have to set wards to make sure the girls didn't leave the house without her knowing if she wasn't on the same floor as them. But what was magic for if not to keep her girls safe?

The little door at the top of the steps opened to a large bedroom with stripe charcoal on black wallpapered walls, an awkwardly cut ceiling, and a heavy-looking fourposter bed. In the one little nook in front of a window that overlooked the cemetery was a small desk, which would be perfect for Rus's more . . . unsavory experiments. And opposite that was a small bathroom with a clawfoot tub, two tiny stand sinks, a toilet, and a plant in front of a window that would definitely not live to see the end of the week if Rus had anything to say about it.

"Okay. You're right." Rus laughed a little to herself as she turned to tip an imaginary hat to Nesta. "Me and this house are soulmates."

"I hate to say I told you so—"

"No, you don't."

"I'll go grab the paperwork out of the car. Meet me on the back porch. And feel free to look around the yard."

"Is it screened in?"

"Would I show you a house with a porch that wasn't?" Nesta winked, and then disappeared down the steps.

Rus went back into the bedroom and turned on her heel, looking around. It would need some personalization, but she could see herself being quite happy there. "Well," she said to the house because places, like people, liked to be acknowledged. "I hope you'll take good care of me and my girls."

The house didn't respond. They never did. But when Rus made her way past the nursery again, the crib had been swapped out for a little gray loft bed with a slide and a toy chest underneath. And, she supposed, that was enough of an answer.

The yard abutted two sides of the old cemetery, which seemed to have been built around the house instead of vice versa. Rus exhaled loudly, her breath pushing strands of chin-length bright pink hair out of her face.

"I'm going to have to do something about you, aren't I?" she said more to herself than to the spirits toeing the line between the yard and the cemetery. There was no fence to distinguish one from the other, but it was clear where her yard ended and the graveyard began because the spirits wouldn't cross the property line. "The worst part is, the board probably won't even give me credit for it. They'll attribute the lowered negative energy to like . . . their attempts to promote unity through more frequent clan and coven meetings or some shit." Rus snorted, rolling her eyes.

"It's warded." Nesta slapped a manila folder down onto the back porch table.

"Hm?"

"The whole property is warded against malignant energies. That's one of the selling points."

"Who did the wards?" Rus sat in one of the wrought iron chairs and started flipping through the contract, pretending to read it. They both knew that was bullshit; Rus had never read paperwork a day in her life. But she liked to pretend she was an adult who considered big commitments like a house carefully.

"Crimson Tide Coven."

"Of fucking course it was them." Rus huffed. "You think Greer will be super pissed if I take them all down and put up my own?"

"Probably. But when was the last time you cared what Evander Greer thought? Plus, if you sign here"—Nesta tapped the paper with one neatly rounded fingernail—"it'll be your property and there's nothing anyone can say about it, not even the sheriff."

"Doesn't mean the board won't try," Rus grumbled, grabbing the pen to start signing her life away. "Wait." She stopped halfway through the fourth page. "Did you just say *sheriff?*"

"Yeah. Sheriff Evander Greer." Nesta tilted their head, but their mouth was twitching up at the corners.

Rus groaned, dropping forward to smack her head on the table. It hurt. But likely not as much as a run-in with *Sheriff Greer* would. "Remind me to stay out of his way for the next like . . . hundred years or so."

"Oh, don't be silly. I'm sure he's not still holding a grudge because of the time you—"

Rus lifted her head just enough to raise one brow at Nesta.

"Well, maybe he is. But either way, you'll be fine. I mean, you've got your girls, and the house, and the business. There won't be time for you to stir up trouble."

Rus continued to stare at them with the same brow lifted.

"I won't tell him you're back in town, and maybe he'll never find out?" Nesta sagged.

"That's all you had to say." Rus sat up and went back to signing the papers. "Maybe I shouldn't have come back, though. We could have gone . . . somewhere else."

"Why *did* you come back?" Nesta pulled out a chair to sit across from her, their face suddenly open with curiosity.

"Moondale's got a good school system for witches." The lie slipped easily off her tongue. It wasn't even really a lie—Moondale did have an excellent magical school system. But she was sure she could have found someplace equally as good in Europe if she'd wanted to. Or even taught the girls herself. But there was safety in a place as steeped in magic as Moondale was. The very earth the place was built on would give off enough ambient energy to hide Rus and her children. Or so she hoped.

"Fine. Keep your secrets." Nesta leaned over to watch Rus scrawl her untidy signature across page after page of legalese.

Rus lifted the pen to shake out her hand where it had started to cramp when she finally got to the last page.

"So, are you going to see Azure?"

Rus's hand jerked, the pen skittering and leaving a nasty mark across the page that she was sure Nesta would need to reprint. "What?"

"Azure Elwood. Are you going to go see her? Does she even know you're moving back?"

"I'm pretty sure Az hates me," Rus said, instead of telling Nesta that *no, Az did not know she was moving back to Moondale.* She finished the final signature with a flourish then pushed the folder over to Nesta for them to sign.

"*Hate* isn't the word I'd use." Nesta closed the folder with a snap.

"What?" Rus frowned.

"What?" Nesta tilted their head, their nose crinkling up in an expression of innocence that no one who knew anything about Nesta Holyore would ever believe. "You can start moving in tomorrow. You're keeping the furniture, right?"

"Yeah. I mean, I don't have any of my own, so." Rus stood, stretching out her neck from side to side where it had grown stiff from being hunched over the papers.

"All right then. I'll have my crew come by and help out if you need it?"

"That'd be great. I have to finish opening up the shop tomorrow, and Fernando needs to be there to help wrangle the kids while we work."

"You know, I never asked." Nesta headed back through the house toward their car. "How old are your kids?"

"Aihuan will be four in October. And Meiling just turned thirteen. I've already got her signed up over at Moondale High."

"Ah, so they're . . ." Nesta drifted off, looking like they expected Rus to fill in the blank of what they were trying to say. But Rus had spent the last six months filling in the blank for people, and she wasn't about to do that. Not here. Not anymore.

"They're amazing," Rus said. It didn't matter if they weren't hers biologically—they were hers in every way that counted.

"Right. Well, you can stay the night here if you want." Nesta pulled a key from their pocket to hold out to Rus. "I'm sure the bedding is clean. The house generally takes care of all that."

"Before you go, can you tell me what happened to the previous owners? I mean . . . it's so well-behaved, I can't imagine a magical family just up and leaving it."

"Well," Nesta said, a little smile crinkling their eyes as

they looked back to the house. "It's got a bit of a sassy streak. I guess the previous owners didn't find that amusing. But I'm sure you'll get along with it just fine."

"A sassy streak?"

"You'll see." Nesta winked, and then they climbed into their car and pulled away from the curb without another word.

Rus crossed her arms over her chest and turned back to the house. The little cherry blossom out front was swaying gently, its orange and red leaves falling to the ground in a hush.

"You're not going to give me any trouble, are you?" she asked the house.

The house didn't respond.

"Didn't think so." She pulled her phone from her pocket and dialed Fernando. "Hey. You can bring the kids to the house. I'll send over the address."

"Do we need to bring the truck?" Fernando's voice was soft on the other side of the line, but Rus could hear Aihuan squealing at something and Meiling talking probably too loud for the small hotel room.

"No. Nesta said they'll send by movers to help us. We'll deal with all that tomorrow. For tonight I'll just order us a pizza, and we can rest. Do you need me to come help get them in the car?" A crow cawed, its black body swooping low over the cemetery to better assess the threat levels before Darcy came to rest on Rus's shoulder, his talons digging into her thick hoodie. "Cause if not, I've got some cleaning up I need to do around here."

"I don't think so." Fernando was smiling into the phone; Rus could hear it. "I think I've finally figured out Aihuan's car seat."

"If you need help, just ask Meiling. She knows what to do. I'll have dinner waiting for you guys when you get here."

"Is that Aunt Rus?" Meiling asked in the background.

"Yes." Fernando pulled his face away from the phone, and Rus could imagine him turning the full softness of his smile onto Meiling.

"Did she get us a house?"

"Yes! I got you a house!" Rus shouted into the phone, her excitement unseating Darcy, who cast her an annoyed glance that she shrugged off. "The perfect house! You're going to love it, A-Ling!"

"YEEEEEEEEES!" Meiling cheered. "Huaner! We have a house!"

"We have a house! We have a house! We have a house!" Aihuan shouted, feeding off her big sister's excitement. It sounded like Fernando had put Rus on speaker.

"But that means you two need to help Uncle Nando get packed up and get over here so you can see your rooms." Rus felt her cheeks aching from the smile that split her own face.

"Okay!" Meiling called, and then Rus could hear some commotion on the other end as she presumably got to work picking up all of Aihuan's toys or maybe just shoving stuff into the oversized duffle Rus had left on the floor by the door.

"You sure you don't need me to come help herd the cats?" Rus asked with a little laugh.

"No. I've got it covered." Fernando's shirt rustled against the phone as he too began to help packing. "I think you managed to get all the really important stuff into the car before you left."

"Toys are important!" Aihuan shouted.

"Right, sorry, of course, Huaner. Anyway, we'll see you there." Then he hung up, and Rus was left standing on the porch of her new house, listening to the silence of it. Darcy settled on her shoulder again, giving his witch an affectionate nip to her ear. A gentle reminder.

Movement out of the corner of her eye made her turn her head, and she saw the restless spirits on the edge of the graveyard again, turned milky in the fading light of early evening. "Right. Got to deal with them real quick before the girls get here."

She tucked her phone into her back pocket and strode across the yard.

If you loved the first chapter of *The Hex Next Door*, you can grab your copy at https://books2read.com/u/3Ln7z7

**Alter by H.R. Truelove**

## WHO DO YOU TRUST WHEN YOU CAN'T TRUST YOURSELF?

*Lennox, Erris, Wisdom...*
*There are many voices in Laura's mind but no one,*
*not even her family will believe her.*

Laura's life is far from normal. After spending years in a medical center for seeing visions no one else can, Laura is transferred to the Tomlinson Institute of Research. There, she's promised, lies the truth she's been after her entire life.

But as her eighteenth birthday looms closer, Laura's already complicated life takes a sudden turn. When she discovers what hides behind her unusual abilities, Laura's reality is blown to pieces, and she must learn to make sense of her supernatural gifts. With a little help from the voices in her head, Laura needs to fight to save herself, the world she lives in-and every other world in the multiverse.

*Alter* is a gripping and intricate tale of conspiracy, mad scientists, and broken lives. A multiverse of blurry lines, lies, and deceit where we come face to face with the best of humankind... and its very worst.

386

*Available Now*

**The Last Daughter by Alexis L. Menard**

She's cursed with a dead witch's power over fate, he's a heartless demigod born for revenge and redemption. Once her enemy, now a conflict of interest. The fate of the Nine Realms dangles on a dangerously thin thread.

Fate was cruel enough by dealing Ailsa with a fatal illness. But when her father and sisters are killed at war, she becomes the Last Daughter in a long line of shieldmages. This power comes with a price, however, coincidentally getting her kidnapped by an elfin she's only heard of through legends.

Vali's realm is dying, inflicted by the black magic, sedir, and the only way to heal his land is by delivering the Tether to Odin, king of the gods. When he finds this power bound inside a mortal woman, he is forced to bring her and her shapeshifting wolven back to his home in Alfheim.

But their journey across the Tree of Life is perilous, and betrayal is imminent. Vali and Ailsa must depend on each other for survival, a mutual dependency that turns into a passionate love affair. With Odin waiting on this promised power, a kindred spirit found in her enemy, and a dark threat neither Ailsa nor Vali intended to find in the bright lands of Alfheim, what started as a simple quest has turned into a fight to save all gods, mortals, and fae alike. Vikings meets magic in this fresh retelling of Norse Mythology.

*Available Now*

Secrets of a Rose by Adina Chiles

**A kingdom built with secrets is bound to unravel.**

During the month of Amira, the silver moon emerges, and the kingdom of Zyra comes alive with anticipation for its annual ball. Mellana Goodwick, finally at the rightful age of sixteen, receives her first invitation, but when unexpected events take place, immediate regret sets in. Mellana finds herself caught in a strange storm—casting down green lightning and filling the sky with ear-splitting thunder. To make matters worse, the kingdom comes under attack by Prince Lorian, a man removed from the line of succession for murdering his sister, the future queen, and her newborn child.

After escaping the attack with her best friends, Mellana stumbles upon a box left by a woman named Rose. With the power to see glimpses of the future, Rose warns Mellana of hidden powers the kingdom has covered up and Lorian's desire to unleash them all. Rose instructs Mellana to gather the sacred article from each of the seven kingdoms before Lorian and his deadly group can gain access to them. Together, the items unlock a barrier that is meant to stay shut.

In Secrets of a Rose, Mellana will discover remarkable abilities that stir around her and some that even rise within. In order to keep what she loves, she must embark on a race against the person who dares to threaten it all.

*Available Now*

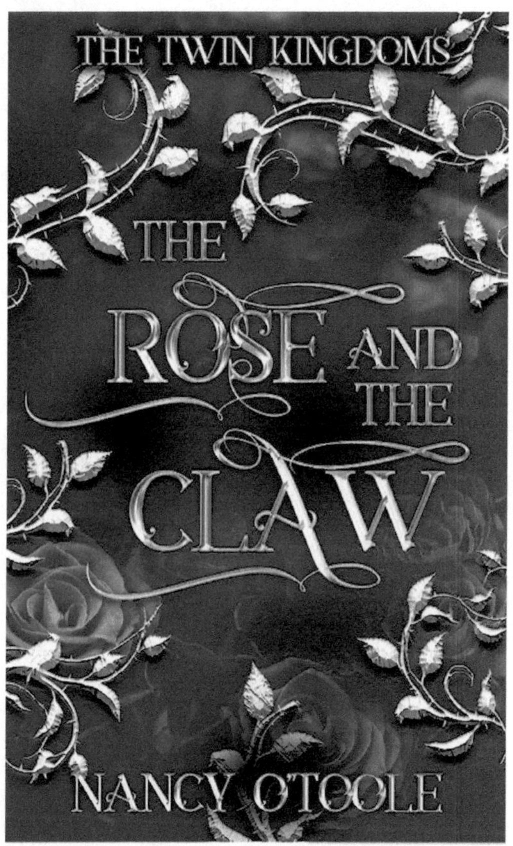


The Rose and the Claw by Nancy O'Toole

A woman on a mission...

Rose Gardner never thought she'd leave the small town of West Ridge. But when her husband dies at war, she must return his arms to his place of birth to set his spirit to rest. After traveling into enemy territory, Rose falls into a trap. Held captive in an enchanted manor, she finds herself face to face with a beast who is equally horrifying and kind. Will she manage to complete her quest or be pulled in by the secrets of the manor?

A man haunted by his past...

Trapped within his own home and in the body of a hideous beast, Kris never wanted to share his prison with another. As much as Rose may draw him in with her beauty and stubborn strength, he knows she must escape before the next full moon. After all, he remembers all too well what happened to the previous caretaker.

The dead won't let him forget the blood on his hands.

*Available Now*

**Fires of the Forsaken by** *Stephanie E. Donohue*

*Addie wanted a gosh-darn pizza.*

*Lass wanted to avoid being cooked over a spit.*

*Neither figured they'd end up with a one-way ticket to the end of days.*

Addie did not have "getting plucked from the 21st century and thrown into a rudimentary fantasy world" on her "fun things to do at 30" checklist. Yet here she is, struggling to survive in the hellscape known as Sakar, a place where Wraiths flame-broil humans and Celestial armies wage war with each other over a centuries-old spat. Thankfully, Cheriour, the hunky commander of the human army, takes her under his wing—although he's allergic to giving straight answers. And talking.

As Addie reluctantly starts to care for him, and the rest of the Sakarians, she also learns why she was sent to this world. And it's a doozy...

The violent society of Sakar is the only home Lass has ever known, and it's been a wretched one. She has spent her life being tormented and twisted into an inhuman hybrid by the Celestials and hunted by the humans who fear her. But she finds solace with a cocky, blue-eyed boy who comforts her, even after she accidentally slaughters innocents.

As Lass struggles to control her volatile powers, she slowly transforms into the monster the humans believe her to be. And even the boy she loves is in peril…

At the end of time, there is only fire. And neither Addie nor Lass will escape unscathed.

*Available Now*